The

Table of Contents

Preface

I enlisted in the Army at the age of 22 and served only 4 years, from May 2002 until June or July of 2006. At the time of my enlistment, I was married and already had one child. I had been working in small time construction while attending Pensacola Junior College, where I had been spinning my wheels as a very mediocre student, with no clue of what degree to pursue.

I had always wanted to join the military, but my parents always tried to dissuade that decision – to them it was unwise and presented too many potential complications or issues, of one sort or another. As a young husband and father, the decision was easier to make with the benefits that are afforded to servicemember's families. However, enlisting wasn't as easy for me as it was for most.

I was not the best high school student, but I wasn't bad. I didn't party, didn't drink, and after my athletic season ended I got a job without my parents having to make me, or even to suggest it. However, while in high school I had been arrested and charged with "making and possessing a destructive device," which was a felony. I was arrested two weeks prior to my 18th birthday, which saved me a few extra hassles since I was still a minor. This arrest connects with my enlistment in at least two ways:

1) The felony charge made me ineligible for certain military jobs.

2) The "making and possessing a destructive device" charge was a Florida Department of Justice euphemism for "making a bomb."

One of the things that I had to do in order to get a waiver to enlist in the Army was to sit down with a full bird colonel, so that the officer could interview me and give his personal assessment of me. I cannot recall his name now, but if I had to guess his age at the time, I'd guess that he was somewhere around his early fifties, give or take. He had a full head of gray hair that had been combed and parted neatly. He wore nondescript eyeglasses and sported a regulation military mustache. The man appeared to be fit, with no visible gut or muffin top; no double chin or rounded cheeks. I do not recall anything specific about his uniform except that it looked the part and that he had a yellow Ranger Tab.

I relayed to him what had happened, that late one evening my friend and I threw a coke bottle bomb from my friend's speeding car before it crashed, sliding for a surprising distance sideways down the street, and that my friend was not speeding to make a get away, but was speeding to get to the target house before the bomb blew up in the car. For what we were trying to accomplish, we were successful.

It was the car crash that brought all of the neighbors out, and it was the following bomb blast that turned their faces of concern into looks of skepticism and loathing. I should point out that the "bomb" was really just a harmless noisemaker made from a plastic coke bottle, tinfoil and a chemical to create pressure. When the police arrived, Scott and I learned what "making and possessing a destructive device" was, as well as what the backseat of a police cruiser and the inside of a jail cell looked like.

The colonel nodded his head with a smile. No problem, I could join the Army.

However, having written an apology letter as part of my pre-trial intervention, the US Army viewed that as a confession of guilt. And I *was* guilty, so I could hardly complain.

As a consequence, instead of barring me from service, the United States Army felt that it was wise to take certain Army jobs off of the table for me. I looked down the long list of military occupational specialties and pointed to 12B (Twelve Bravo) and asked if I was allowed to have this job. They said "of course" and wrote out a contract.

12B is a Combat Engineer. Combat Engineers are also known as Sappers and run right along with infantrymen and tankers, carrying rifles and lots of explosives: C-4, TNT, dynamite, land mines, det cord and what have you. One of my brothers from D-10E, Chris Marshall, described Combat Engineers as "battlefield engineers; need an obstacle to be put in place, a 12B would do it; need an obstacle removed, a 12B blew it up."

Each explosive had its own properties and detonation velocities; TNT might be preferred for certain scenarios while C4 was preferred for others, like cutting the steel of bridge structural members, for example. It had occurred to me that there must be intricate mathematical formulas or engineering tables that would determine, not only which explosive was best, but also what quantities were ideal for a given task; but the only formula I remember using was "P for plenty." It was a blast.

My time in the Army was a tremendous experience. A few of the men in my company were injured, but nothing serious; none of my close friends were killed or maimed. We were fortunate, and had that been different, my overall outlook on my service might have also been different. I count the men I served with as family, and I learned more during my time in the Army than I could ever share. I witnessed great acts of courage, loyalty, comradery, hospitality, leadership, villainy and even cowardice – you know who you are.

It was surreal invading Iraq, being at the tip of the spear, making our way through several cities and areas of resistance on our way to Baghdad. Once in Baghdad I had the unique privilege of being placed on an Engineer Recon Team, which pulled four of us away from our company to stay at the Battalion HQ at Sadam's Baghdad palace, while the rest of our company settled into the Baghdad zoo, just across from the famous crossed sabers of Sadam's parade field.

Our mission on that Engineer Recon Team had us going out among the population every day and required us to speak with the locals and drive all over the city (by now I've forgotten most of the Arabic I learned). We eventually received a local interpreter, and since we were a special team, no one questioned when we'd come or go. We did our job, fulfilled our mission, but we also got to enjoy meeting countless regular Iraqi citizens and ate at the local markets. Our interpreter hosted us at his modest home many times, where we ate several delicious meals with his family. I have never experienced such hospitality in my life. We were offered hot tea each day, welcomed into people's homes as honored guests and got to meet and befriend a number of others. It was one of the best experiences of my life.

I should mention and thank all of my brothers in Delta Company, 10th Engineers and Echo Company, 1/64 Armor – each of these men are family to me, and while many soldiers contemplate applying for Rangers or Special Forces, I would not have traded my time with D Co. / E Co. for anything.

I was fortunate to have good leadership. LT Niles and SFC Gipson, to me, set the highest standard for an officer/enlisted leadership pair. It is a detriment to the Army that they're no longer serving together. I regret that I do not have the space to speak of all the guys in more detail – you're all family to me.

It was during my time in Iraq that I first had the idea about an old man who'd been through decades of war, but that had never received a scratch from combat. I was fascinated as to what one could read into that, or by what could be inferred by way of destiny or some grander purpose. Then I also imagined an emergence of an American feudal system, where private military contracting firms became the norm, allowing several companies to grow so large that their employees began to have more loyalty to their employers than to their own nation. But also, I started to grow tired of beautiful, former teen-model, twenty-somethings on the WB who were always the heroes or protagonists – I wanted someone older, grittier and maybe a little less attractive...

These three ideas were the sparks that provoked me to write *The Blacksmith*.

Chapter 1

The Champ

Everyone in the tavern went silent and fixed their eyes upon the dirty and bloody figure that staggered through the doors. Dust erupted around him as if he had been carried in on the wind. As the door slammed open against the wall, Alex the guitar player stopped playing so abruptly that he broke a string. The only noise, beside some patron coughing, was Tyler Johnson breathing heavily as he tried to hold himself up against the door frame he had just blown through.

No one knew Tyler well. They had first seen him the night before when he and his two companions arrived in town and strolled into the tavern, displaying their old military carbines with pride; cowboy hats cocked to a side. All three were loud, and Tyler must have been proud that he had tweaked his trigger mechanism, because he told everyone in the tavern (several times) that it could kill 250 people a minute. Tyler also wore an obnoxiously large belt buckle that read, "Champ." Tyler didn't have scars.

Tyler's belt buckle wasn't shiny anymore. There was no sign of his rifle. His clothes were torn, dirty, and bloody, much like the rest of him, and his cowboy hat was nowhere to be seen.

"Champ?" Alex asked, squinting as if it would help him see through the layers of dirt and blood. "Champ, looks like you been drug through the dirt."

Tyler, with his back against the wall and arms spread straight out to his sides trying to keep from falling to the floor, only shifted his eyes to Alex in response.

"Where's yur friends, Jed 'n Tim?" Alex asked. Everyone in the tavern was waiting for his answer.

Tyler looked at Alex again. His friends were Jim and Ted, not Tim and Jed, but Tyler didn't have the energy to correct him. At hearing his friends mentioned, Tyler peeled himself off the wall and just made it to a chair where he slumped down as dust rose off of his body like smoke.

"They're dead," Tyler let out in a whisper as someone poured him a drink. "He killed 'em."

Everyone's attention was now secured.

"Was it Jeremiah Pratt?" the old tavern owner, Jerry, asked through his well-kept, but bushy mustache, "the blacksmith?" Jerry was balding, but let the hair on the sides of his head grow out, trying to disguise the fact that he was missing an ear, much like he pretended the mustache covered the scar on his lip and face.

Tyler looked up at him and whispered a quiet, "yeah." His mouth was suddenly dry even though he had just had a drink. Everyone was quiet now, watching him.

"That old man?" Alex belted out. "Last I heard, he was up north; an' besides, he's like seventy or somethin'."

"Sixty-two!" Tyler said in defense, almost rising out of his chair. "He's a blacksmith," he said softly, slumping back down in his seat, realizing how pitiful he had just sounded. His friends had been killed and he had been dragged for what seemed like miles by his horse. What had happened?

"What happened?" Jerry asked. "Surprised he didn't kill you… you're just loftin' irons."

"They all said Pratt's been up north," Alex said, even though no one cared.

"I don't know." Tyler said a little too quickly, ignoring the slight. It was true, and his mind was grave from the recent events. He was glad to be alive.

Tyler remembered some things. He remembered why he had come to these parts and why he had come to find Jeremiah Pratt. He remembered coming to the tavern and impressing everyone here. He could recall heading out to finally meet the "Great Jeremiah Pratt," but nothing else.

"He got us by surprise." Tyler finished his last thought in a whisper hoping everyone believed him. *The bartender was right*, Tyler admitted to himself. He and his buddies weren't experienced – they were too young to be. They were wanna-bes, "just loftin' irons." Pratt was dangerous; living by his guns, his "irons." He was expertly qualified – a blacksmith, THE Blacksmith.

Tyler was already weak and in pain, and in his own mind he began to recall the recent events that had taken the lives of his friends. His heart began to pick up pace, and he could suddenly feel it beating in his neck. His head was starting to spin. "I don't feel good," he said as he gripped the arms of his chair tightly, drawing Jerry's attention.

"Don't get sick in here, Champ." Jerry was looking worried.

"I feel sick," Tyler said sheepishly, turning pale.

"He's gonna get sick," Alex echoed, looking intently at Tyler.

The tavern's customers watched as Jerry and Alex quickly escorted Tyler through the doors, recklessly releasing him as soon as they passed the threshold. Tyler stumbled down the steps onto the dirt road at the tavern's entrance. Lying weak and defeated on the ground, Tyler was engulfed by the darkness of unconsciousness as he succumbed to pain and fatigue. Jerry andAlex had already gone back inside.

***

It had not been too many hours prior that Tyler, Ted, and Jim rode their horses toward the old oak on Watchman's Hill just north of town where they found an old man hunkered beside a fire, warming himself in the morning cool. Tyler and his friends had their military carbines slung to the front of their bodies as they approached. Each man had his cowboy hat down low and his shooting hand on the pistol grip of his weapon, with the other hand guiding his horse's reins, as they rode casually in the saddle. Ted and Jim were on Tyler's right as they came to a halt right in front of the old man sitting against the oak tree.

"Lookin' fur Jeremiah Pratt, old man," Jim said and spit out a long string of tobacco.

The old man appeared to be annoyed as he turned to face them. Tyler wasn't sure if it was the interruption to his breakfast, or just the unexpected company that annoyed Pratt, but whichever it was, it gave Tyler a sense of power. The old man stood slowly, laying his modest meal on a log. The old man's hair was carelessly long, and his face carried an unkempt beard that would easily convey a lack of concern or maybe even madness. As he stood, he swiped the wood smoke from his eyes with his forearm, not bothering to answer Jim. From the old posters and illustrations, they had not expected the long hair or gray beard, but still, they all knew who he was. Everyone did.

Tyler noticed that he did not look as old standing as he did sitting. Jeremiah looked as strong as the oak he was shaded beneath and as dangerous as the old US service handgun holstered to his thigh. Tyler noticed the pistol, thinking that it looked like it had seen more action than Pratt, having noticeable scars and pockmarks on the hand grips.

But another observation led the Champ to feel confident, despite Pratt's appearance. *No rifle*, Tyler thought smugly as he placed his finger on the trigger of his own.

"Enjoyin' yourself a last meal?" Jim asked rhetorically, glancing coolly at his friends; obviously impressed with his own cleverness.

The old gray-haired man just stood staring at them, not saying a word, as a good breeze shushed at them through the oak leaves. The old man had the eyes of a hawk, and Tyler couldn't help but be intimidated by them, though he tried denying that fact to himself. Their horses were uneasy, and Tyler's was especially so.

Tyler was not as confident now, seeing the man in person. He suddenly felt foolish for coming. He, like Ted and Jim, had grown up hearing the stories of the Great Jeremiah Pratt. Tyler wondered if his friends felt the same, and looked over to them for verification but saw nothing. He had to follow through now after coming so far and telling so many people that he would kill the old man. "I'm like Johnny Appleseed, baby; they're gonna' write songs about me," he would say. Jeremiah Pratt was past due after all. All of his peers had been killed or maimed long ago. As far as Tyler was concerned, it was Tyler Johnson's time, and it was for that reason that Tyler and his comrades followed after Pratt since he had been seen passing through, near their post-wars community in the neighboring territory. *I've come too far...* Tyler thought to himself, even though he had only followed Pratt from the previous town, just across the territorial border.

"Is that a blacksmith?" Ted mocked with a confident sneer.

"I didn't see any scars – looks more like the bottom of a grave," he added as his sneer gelled into a grin.

Tyler's weapon was ready to fire, as he seldom kept it on "safe." He knew that it was time and was about to say, "Jeremiah Pratt, I've come here to kill you. Your time has passed and so you will with it." It was a little speech that he had practiced with the hopes that his friends would spread the account to others in order to immortalize the name "Tyler Johnson" as "Jeremiah Pratt" had been.

Tyler was about to speak, but as he opened his mouth, Jeremiah Pratt suddenly took a quick sidestep and reached to his thigh for that sidearm. Jeremiah had moved so quickly and so abruptly that it completely took Ted, Jim, and Tyler off guard. Ted let out a noise of surprise as all three jumped and shut their eyes with their faces in that contorted, flinching-child look. Tyler was so startled and off-guard that he jumped wildly, falling from his saddle, squeezing his carbine's trigger all the way to the ground, firing an array of lead wildly before Old Man Pratt could bring his weapon to eye level. Tyler's foot caught in the stirrup like a snare, causing him to be violently dragged behind his animal nearly the entire way back to town in a trail of dust and pain as his horse fled in fear.

Tyler's foot finally broke free, and he rolled to a stop on the dirt road. He opened his eyes and could just see his horse still running in the distance. Tyler's body burned and ached all over, and he realized that he must have dropped his carbine somewhere between the fall and the drag. The smell of cordite and gun smoke was still in his nose. He managed to get to his feet, though his body ached and hurt over every inch, and slowly made his way into town, trying not to pass out.

Jeremiah had been equally surprised by their reaction. He

knew why they had come. They all came for the same reason. Jeremiah had moved for his forty-five, hoping they would have been distracted just enough by the fire, but they were scared far worse than Jeremiah had anticipated. Because Jeremiah had taken them so off guard, he never had to fire a shot. The one on Jeremiah's right, the one with the huge belt buckle, had sprayed his automatic rifle right into his buddies and their horses, rendering them a distorted, bloody mess. They didn't have a chance.

Jeremiah stood perplexed as he watched that poor idiot being dragged like a tin can behind a boy's bicycle back down the same road they had come in on. The two lifeless and contorted men and horses that lay in a smoldering pile in front of him was also an oddity, he thought. Jeremiah Pratt had never been called out by a young man that mowed down his own partners and rode off before firing the first shot at him. Their inexperience should not have been surprising; *those who wish for war the most have mostly never been*, he thought.

Jeremiah's time was short now. Even though gunfire was all too common these days, he knew it would still draw attention – and probably the very attention he was trying to part with. He holstered his sidearm, slung Ted's carbine over his shoulder (it had the least amount of blood on it), and quickly gathered what magazines he could. He then grabbed one of his assailants' bags that he would search later for food or supplies, crammed the rest of his breakfast in his mouth, and headed off of Watchman's Hill, annoyed with himself.

"Getting old and slow," he said out loud to himself. He had not noticed the men coming until they were there. He made it through alright, like always, but he couldn't afford to be so careless again. He left his fire burning and headed off into the wilderness.

Chapter 2

Jeremiah's Youth (Flashback)

It was later than the scene would imply and Jeremiah was tired. He and the others were in an abandoned downtown area of some forgotten place. Ravaged cars and buses dotted the streets and alleyways while damaged and smoldering military vehicles acted as both barricades and cover. Dust and soot rolled through these war-torn streets and the sound of gunfire and explosions were heard both near and far, as each army's soldiers ran amuck, firing indiscriminately. It was as if the only goal was to reap as many souls as possible; a phrase Jeremiah's team shortened into RAMSAP.

Jeremiah was not in uniform, nor was he wearing outdoor or hunting gear. Instead, he was wearing a plain black suit with a plain black tie and white button-up shirt. Most of those engaged in battle were in a more standard military uniform, but not all. Each combatant, on either side, had their headgear with comms and a heads-up display that helped identify friendly from foe. The objective in this case was pretty straightforward, no matter what wardrobe was brought to the arena.

Despite his business suit, Jeremiah was armed with an old military model carbine, the M-4A4; basically a short barrel M-16 with a collapsible buttstock and rail system along the barrel for added goodies, like lights, lasers, handles or grenade launchers. Jeremiah's had the M203 grenade launcher attached under his carbine's rail system. The M203 fired 40mm grenades, and Jeremiah only had a few. His M4 had the red dot reflexive fire optics, making transitions from target to target easier and more efficient than the more basic iron sights.

Jeremiah also carried an old 1911 service pistol with a seven round magazine of forty-five caliber, as well as two flashbang grenades. He had plenty of spare mags for his rifle and pistol – running out of ammo was not a concern in this fight.

Neither Jeremiah nor those on his team bothered with any squad formations or movements. Instead, each man relied on their comms and heads-up displays to keep their attacks choreographed, even if they looked chaotic and disorganized.

Despite his weapons, technology and experienced team, Jeremiah felt out of his element. It wasn't just the suit – he wanted to wear that (maybe the first time he'd ever wanted to wear a suit) – instead he felt out of place because he wasn't as adept as the others, not as experienced. He might say that he didn't want to let his team down, but it was probably more that he didn't want to be embarrassed in front of his team if and when he failed.

He knew his weapons and could handle the trigger, so no matter what degree of anxiety he felt, he told himself that he was prepared for war and was there to reap.

At the start of their raid, his team separated, each taking a different route into the derelict town. Almost immediately the gunfire started in thunderous fury. Certain that the reference would delight his comrades, one of Jeremiah's teammates shouted, "There was a *FIREFIGHT*," over his comms, as they each contributed to the volley.

Jeremiah skirted along the perimeter in a sprint, bringing his rifle up to his shoulder, and placing the red dot of his optics onto the enemy combatant that appeared in front of him, dropping him mid-stride with a well placed controlled pair. Jeremiah didn't pause, no time for self-reflection or a change in course; he hoped that stealth and speed would be dependable tactics. Jeremiah hurriedly moved onward. He had only fired two rounds, but he felt the compulsion to change out magazines in a tactical reload, which he did on the run. Locked and loaded with a full mag, he rounded the corner and was surprised by an operator decked out in full kit right there in arms reach. The operator swung a knife, which Jeremiah barely dodged, firing several rushed rounds, but none hit their mark. Jeremiah and the operator swung around one another, each striving to survive the encounter and kill the other.

The encounter took only seconds, but feeling disoriented, Jeremiah fired wildly, hoping something would land into his target. Despite the frantic firehose-spraying shooting method, Jeremiah hit nothing and was shot by a second enemy operator, the bullets landing in dull thuds. Jeremiah's vision slowed and faded as he fell helplessly to the ground, until his entire view was gone. He was no longer looking though his own perspective, he was now watching the scene from above, in a third-person perspective as an operator with the gamer tag "SlickSallysDaddy33" repeatedly squatted up and down over Jeremiah's dead avatar.

"I'm out, fellas," Jeremiah said to his team over his headset, as he slumped back in his chair in frustration.

"You suck, Pratt," someone replied over the line.

Jeremiah nodded with a frown, took his headset off, tossing it carelessly to the side, and powered his machine down.

***

The next morning Jeremiah's alarm woke him. He had to wake up earlier than this over the summer for two-a-day football conditioning, so the 7:00AM wakeup wasn't a difficulty, and the alarm switched off when Jeremiah lifted his phone and made his way to the bathroom. The lights automatically came on when he entered the room, and the shower started itself according to Jeremiah's preset preferences.

Showered and clothed, Jeremiah headed downstairs for breakfast without bothering to shave. A few day's growth was all it was, and he wasn't looking homeless or cultish yet.

"Good morning, honey," Jeremiah's mom said, turning away from her morning news program as he entered the kitchen. "Ready for your…"

"Rachael, turn that up," Jeremiah's father interrupted as he entered the room, still tucking in his shirt. "They're talking about those security firms," he finished, motioning with a nod toward the news broadcast.

"James!" Jeremiah's mother interrupted back with vitriol. Jeremiah's father looked sheepishly to the floor, clearly overruled. "I'm talking to Jeremiah about something important!" Leaving the scolding tone she used with her husband, she casually turned back to her son. With a sweet and loving tone she asked, "Ready for your first day of senior year, sweetie?"

Jeremiah shrugged and only said, "Good morning," as he rummaged through the pantry for breakfast. He didn't bother answering, and his mother wasn't really expecting a response, already plugged back into the morning news.

Jeremiah felt ready to be done with high school and onto the next thing; he didn't even really understand the question. What was there to be ready, or not ready for? As simple and as rhetorical as the question sounded, and as much as Jeremiah appeared to dismiss it without a thought, he actually pondered it as he ate breakfast, as he brushed his teeth, as he packed his gym bag for football practice, and as he rode his motorcycle to school.

Much like in his first person shooter game, Jeremiah felt somewhat out of place. He was not a standout student. And while he was a decent high school athlete, he was not the stereotypical jock. Jeremiah looked like an athlete. The casual observer may have assumed he was high-school-popular with lots of friends, but the truth was that he had lots of acquaintances. He never quite felt like he fit in perfectly with anyone.

Jeremiah parked his bike in a motorcycle spot at the school and made his way toward the school's entrance. Contemplating the implications of a final year, he walked circumspectly and as if he were a conscientious observer instead of an active participant in this formal gathering of youths. He watched acquaintances trapped in their phones. He watched them sporting the most up-to-date fads and styles portrayed and modeled by celebrity social media influencers. He passed through the locker-lined corridors, watching other acquaintances walk awkwardly, while others strutted with unmistakable and sometimes irrational confidence, as everyone made their way to their classes. Jeremiah almost felt contempt until he realized he had also succumbed to the inescapable forces of the blackhole that technology, excess, and luxury had become. He bought and wore clothes that he liked. He liked his older model gas engine motorcycle, as opposed to the mainstream electric machines. He would get lost in his phone like everyone else, though they had become such a necessity in everyday life it was hard to imagine living any other way. The level of encryption had advanced enough to allow these personal devices to be used for essential functions such as identification and banking, completely replacing plastic cards or paper documents.

"Dude, you suck so bad," John Benjamin chided, breaking Jeremiah out of his introspection.

Trevor laughed, as he and John joined Jeremiah in their walk to class.

Jeremiah looked up quizzically in response. John had a broad, stocky frame that made him seem shorter than he really was. He had the face of a football player and a cauliflower ear which spoke to his other sport. Trevor was tall and vain, but nice enough. Trevor usually had a large winning smile and even better charisma.

"I can see why you left mid-game," John continued with innocent ribbing, "I would hate to lose so bad too."

"Then you'll hate practice tonight," Jeremiah quipped, getting another laugh out of Trevor.

***

Mr. Terrell started the first day of history class with a lecture on the Great War. Mr. Terrell was easy to pay attention to, but mostly because his shirt was untucked and his soft, rounded belly protruded under it. His hair was messy, maybe not even clean, and he wore large glasses that were stylish in the "anti-stylish" way.

"Is his shirt too small," a voice whispered to Jeremiah from the side, "or his belly too big?"

Jeremiah looked over to Lilly with a grin. They had essentially grown up together – as acquaintances. She was attractive, but he'd never thought too much more about it. In fact, their parents knew each other, and Jeremiah's mother would sometimes try to play matchmaker and encourage Jeremiah to take Lilly on a date, which actually made Jeremiah want to do the opposite. "She's a sweet girl," his mom would say.

"Or," Lilly continued, "is it that his wrinkled child-sized shirt makes his hairy beer gut look bigger than it is?"

She wasn't that sweet. Turning toward her with an acknowledging smile, Jeremiah found himself eye to eye with Lilly, closer than he had realized or expected.

She was pretty. He grinned wider, caught in her eyes until his face felt warm. Suddenly feeling self-conscious during their unscripted staring contest, he turned his attention back to Mr. Terrell who was passionately explaining how World War One was fought on horseback.

Jeremiah was hardly interested in antiquated warfare that the world would never see again, nor was he concerned with Mr. Terrell's unseemly and unkempt appearance; instead, he was fighting the temptation to look over at Lilly again.

She was attractive, but it wasn't just her physical appearance. He wouldn't have been able to articulate what exactly had flipped the switch; it wasn't just because of her sense of humor, her witty remarks, her independent nature, the way she thought about things, and the fact that she was unafraid to walk at her own pace – there was something else. Jeremiah wouldn't have put any thought into whether it was a combination of the recent summer break, the unexpected close proximity, or even the secret, shared jokes about their teacher; whatever the causes, he felt a pull – he just told himself that he didn't.

He wouldn't give her another thought.

***

"Dude, you smoked John," Trevor said, laughing after Jeremiah knocked John Benjamin's helmet off in a tackle at practice. Trevor was an athlete as well, though a little bigger than Jeremiah. Trevor may have been stronger, but he wasn't as fast, or as fit, nor did he look it. Trevor had that charisma, that winning smile, and was very personable. Jeremiah counted him as a friend, but "acquaintance" was of course the more appropriate term.

The stocky John Benjamin was a red headed bruiser of a guy. Quick and powerful. He was friendly enough, but thought he was better than he really was. He was one of those guys who talked about playing in the pros as if it was merely a matter of when, not if. Now, he was wondering where his helmet had gone.

Jeremiah hustled back to his huddle, never saying a word, content with the thought that SlickSallysDaddy33 would have been impressed.

***

Despite football, school work, and video games, Jeremiah had noticed Lilly and suddenly couldn't stop noticing her. He couldn't *not* give her another thought. He'd find reasons to speak to her at school and sometimes would catch her looking back at him from the across a room.

One morning as Jeremiah was approaching the school, he saw Lilly sitting on a bench at the entrance. "What's up, tough guy?" Lilly said, greeting Jeremiah as he approached.

Although Lilly's tone was fairly nondescript, Jeremiah felt like she was flirting with him. He couldn't hide his smile and stopped for a word. "Just another day," he said, trying to be as cool as he could be. He wanted to talk to her but didn't want to look like he wanted to talk to her.

Jeremiah stood there casually, resting his hands on top of his head with interlocked fingers as he and Lilly engaged in small talk about whatever, while she remained seated on her bench just outside the school's glass storefront entrance. As they talked, he could see Lilly staring at his muscular arms as they were exposed from the sleeves of his t-shirt in their current position. After noticing Lilly stare, he glanced beyond her at his own reflection in the large tinted glass storefront.

"I see you looking at yourself," Lilly said, diming Jeremiah out for vanity.

Jeremiah only smiled wider as he replied, "I just wanted to see what you were staring at," which embarrassed Lilly, causing her to blush and look away. Jeremiah was both surprised and delighted at her reaction – there are only so many reasons to react in such a way.

***

Jeremiah quit playing video games, which was something he never did that much anyway. And while he always went through his football conditioning workouts with intensity and played on the field with brutality, his mindset changed now; instead of merely lifting to get strong or playing to just inflict pain in the guy in front of him, he did those things hoping Lilly would take notice. If she wasn't at a game, he was let down. If she were present, he was performing for her.

Other people noticed the two's flirting as well. "Maybe you won't feel the need to make cheap shots since you got a girlfriend," John ribbed at him.

"Dude, you're the only cheap thing here," Trevor chimed in, wide smile and all. "Besides," Trevor said as his smile turned into a sly grin, "Lilly's not his girl – she's still way into me." John was laughing and smacking Jeremiah on the shoulders. Trevor smoothly swaggered on, always happy to be on top.

Jeremiah just smiled. He was happy after all, and Trevor and John both would be lining up against him later at practice – they would pay for their insolence.

Lilly and Jeremiah's relationship continued on as flirtation mingled with sarcastic jabs at one another. Jeremiah could tell that she was attracted to him, and Lilly had to have known that Jeremiah was into her. After one of his games, Lilly was waiting among other family members and friends for the players to come out of the locker room. It was the first time she'd ever waited for anyone after a game. Jeremiah saw her when he walked outside, and he immediately felt reenergized at the surprise. She seemed giddy and nervously excited to see him as well.

"Jeremiah," she called out to him playfully. Jeremiah could almost predict what was happening. He had never heard her call his name in such a way. "I'm waiting for my kiss goodnight," she finished with a playful smile.

Jeremiah smiled back. He should have walked over toward her, should have gently placed his hands gently around her and kissed her; but he didn't. He paused in a step toward his motorcycle and, as cool as he could, said, "I'm kind of tired right now, but I tell you what… Leave your door unlocked and I'll be over after I've cleaned up." Lilly was smiling, and so was Jeremiah.

He thought about her as he rode home under the streetlights. While he showered, he wondered if he would really go over to her house. And as he drove there, he wondered if she would still be interested.

When he arrived, the door was open and she stood up from the couch where she had been waiting for him just inside the entry. Jeremiah felt his blood rise to the surface as the two of them stood silently at the threshold of the dark room, lit only by the faint, flickering light of a movie playing; the sound muffled by the intensity of teenage infatuation. Despite all the thought Jeremiah had put into this moment, he was speechless. Lilly appeared vulnerable and meek as she stood dressed in a loose fitting t-shirt, waiting for him.

They were young and nervous, and Jeremiah was suddenly unsure of himself.

"You coming in?" Lilly asked in a whisper, her eyes beckoning him inside.

Jeremiah smiled and opened his mouth to speak, but nothing audible left his lips as he felt the accelerated beating of his own heart in his neck. He mouthed the word, "yeah," with a nod, taking her hand.

The pair just sat on the couch, neither of them were watching the movie playing in front of them. They sat awkwardly, side by side; shoulder on shoulder; leg against leg; hands accidentally touching on purpose, until Lilly leaned over on Jeremiah's shoulder and said, "I'm not trying to hit on you, I'm just tired and need to rest my head." Jeremiah felt his pulse increase and the dark room couldn't hide his smile – she was making a move. He took a breath and turned his head, giving the girl a soft and gentle kiss. They didn't watch the rest of the movie. He had kissed other girls before, but this was the first time he had kissed Lilly. And it moved him.

Over the next few weeks, Jeremiah and Lilly spent as much time together as possible. Jeremiah was smitten and, had

SlickSallysDaddy33 cared, he would have mocked him for it. Jeremiah and Lilly were nothing serious, not anything official, but Jeremiah wanted to be.

At school one day, Jeremiah had to run an errand to the school's machine shop class. While waiting on the instructor to formulate a response, he happened to see a small spacer on a shop table, amongst other parts and pieces of miscellaneous junk. This spacer was a dark metal, but had a subtle yet unique swirl in its coloring. He picked it up out of curiosity and grinned with delight. That afternoon when he saw Lilly again he handed it to her, "for you," he grinned wide, "sorry, it's the best I could do on a tight budget."

Lilly smiled and laughed as she placed it on her finger like a ring. They kissed and all was right with the world.

Less than a month after Jeremiah's last football game, less than a month into Jeremiah's welcome evolution with Lilly, it changed. They were at Lilly's house, watching a movie together and sitting close. Jeremiah wanted things to be official – official in the sense that people knew that they were an item, that they were a couple. Before he could steer the conversation that way, she broke his heart.

"I'm not sure this is working out," she said regretfully, scooting away from him a bit. Jeremiah was taken aback. He was confused and didn't know what to say. "I just don't feel like we're boyfriend and girlfriend," she said to him, looking at the ground.

"That's because we're not," Jeremiah answered back. "We haven't really been acting like it because we haven't been around anyone. We haven't told anyone," Jeremiah said trying to sound calm and confident, but inside he was confused and unhappy about the evening's turn. "Let's just give it shot," he hoped he didn't sound like he was pleading. *What happened, where did this come from?* Jeremiah couldn't make sense of it. "I want to give it a shot," he said, desperately afraid of sounding as pathetic as he felt.

Lilly didn't want to. It was over faster than it began. Just a few weeks. Jeremiah tried to recover from this sucker punch, but he felt powerless and lost, confused. He wanted to leave and hide, but didn't want her to see him retreat. He tried to act as if he wasn't hurt so badly. Constantly on guard, ever the watchman, Jeremiah tried telling himself that he didn't really care, and that it was no big deal.

He left shortly after their silence became awkward.

***

Jeremiah's workouts intensified. He started waking up at 5AM for sit-ups and a run before school. He pushed it harder in the weightroom. Jeremiah played angry at practice and possessed in games. He wanted to hurt those across from him. He wanted to feel the numb, crunching impacts of each collision. He wanted to see his opponent's eyes widen with realization that they were about to be hurt, and he relished the feeling of them crumpling under him.

"WOOOOO!!!" John screamed under the stadium lights of the game field as Jeremiah decimated a punter in the endzone. "Pratt killed the KICKER!!" John exclaimed in violent ecstasy, to which the coach responded with a harsh, "SHUT! UP!" from the sidelines. John quit jumping around and jogged circumspectly back to his huddle with a drooping head, embarrassed for the chastisement.

At John's shouts of excited jubilation, Jeremiah turned back around to see the kicker lying motionless on the field. He wasn't dead, and even without the awkwardly comical dead-like position of the slender punter, it brought a smile to Jeremiah's face. The smile looked less than kind under his helmet and on his sweaty, dirty and unshaven teenage face. The cheers were only static in his ears; all he saw was red. He didn't even know if the punter had gotten the kick off or not; he just wanted to hurt everyone on the field.

At school, Jeremiah would watch Lilly from across the room, but she seemed oblivious of him. He tried to get past her. He dated several girls, but nothing stuck. Lilly didn't seem particularly interested in anyone, although she dated as well. Jeremiah felt like the guys she dated were too goofy for her, but he was jealous of everyone. He knew that none of the girls he dated were as good as Lilly. It seemed to him that Lilly wasn't looking for anything serious. She was going away to school, excited about her scholarship and new life away from their home.

Jeremiah wasn't interested in accumulating wealth or status. He wasn't interested in degrees or accreditations. Jeremiah felt like leaving, but he also wanted something different. Sitting in another classroom for a degree that would get him another seat behind another desk or in a seat at some cubicle. That just sounded depressing. He decided to join the Army.

Jeremiah tried seeing if any of his buddies would join with him, but none would. Trevor and a few others expressed interest in applying for placement within one of the few security firms, which were considered very prestigious. Some of the guys were just talking, and Jeremiah knew that Trevor wouldn't actually do it, at least not right away – Trevor wanted the "college experience" and the status that came with a degree from a major university.

"You're just not smart enough, Pratt," Trevor goaded with a smile, playfully mocking his friend for having no collegiate ambition. "Hey," he continued, "While you're off playing soldier I'll keep Lilly company." Trevor feigned innocent ribbing with a smile so big you could see every tooth.

Jeremiah cocked his head back in feigned amusement and silently smiled it off. His smile wasn't as big as Trevor's.

The Security contractors were said to get better training, better pay, and better equipment. For instance, only select teams of the US military's special operations units were given the M-500 Armored Individual Mobility Enhancement Exoskeletal Suits (AIMEES). These were exo-suits whose technology accented the wearer's movements and enhanced their strength and speed. On the other hand, the security firms outfitted each of their infantry units with them, unless stealth was a priority, as the AIMEES had a recognizable, albeit faint, mechanical whine. Even so, Jeremiah wasn't interested. His family had a history in the Army, and he wanted to follow in those deep footsteps. Jeremiah couldn't see himself doing anything else.

A few of his other friends went off to college as well. John intended to walk on at a four year, division one school; completely convinced that the high school coaches did him wrong by not sending out his highlight videos. "Jeremiah, you should go with me. We were the best two players in the state," John pleaded. They weren't the best two players in the state; Jeremiah knew that, and he didn't care about football anyway.

Jeremiah only had a handful of close friends, and none were going with him. They may have just been acquaintances anyway. He felt alone, but at that time, he sort of preferred it that way.

For some reason, the promise of imminent danger and

adventure was the only path forward. And as the disheveled Mr. Terrell would say, "For Plato, athletes were perfectly suited for being soldiers."

Chapter 3

The Preachers

In the early morning, Uriah and Josiah Morris left their
congregation and headed south with Josiah's cousin, Jonas.
Uriah didn't like his nephew, but even though he thought that
Jonas was an idiot, he would never voice that to anyone. He
reluctantly agreed to bring him along, trying to go the extra mile
for his brother. Uriah's brother had pleaded with him to take
Jonas, saying that "it would be so good for him to see his other
brethren." Uriah suspected that his brother really just wanted
time without such a nuisance.

Josiah tried to like Jonas and made a real effort to tolerate
him. Jonas was 17, a year older than Josiah, but much more
immature. He talked – a lot; usually saying the wrong thing at the
wrong time. Jonas was the type who thought toilet humor was
the cleverest of musings and seemed to delight in the misfortune
of others; yet somehow managed a level of self-righteousness
that just kept getting worse with age. But he was family, both by
blood and by spirit – whether they liked it or not. Neither Uriah
nor Josiah thought that Jonas tried to be obnoxious; they just
thought that he didn't try to be any better either. Jesus' Sermon
on the Mount was much more than just a guide on how to deal
with people when it was easy – it was gospel and was meant to
be pondered and adhered to when things were most difficult.
Jonas was most difficult, and Uriah and Josiah most wanted to be
faithful Christians.

Josiah was having a harder time than usual ignoring his

obnoxious cousin. Josiah had not slept well the night before. He had dreamed that he was older and was having a conversation with a man that he used to know. Josiah awoke from his sleep, startled as the prior acquaintance of the dream had brutally killed someone by crushing their head in before turning to him and shooting him in the forehead. Josiah woke up as the bullet struck his skull. After the nightmare, he never went back to sleep. Despite his fatigue now, he knew he would have to try harder to remain of character when dealing with Jonas on this journey.

But Josiah hadn't slept well in a while. His mother had died when he was young, which would be difficult for any child, but he'd also recently lost a pet. His dog had been trampled by a bull and didn't survive the injuries, dying two days later. Josiah had taken it hard. He had a special rapport with the animal, the two being constant companions. His father Uriah would comment to others that, "they know what each other are thinkin'," so Uriah had hoped this trip would be a needed distraction.

Usually, the congregations had nothing to do with the cities and towns of the world, other than the occasional evangelism, and they were completely self-sustaining. For the past twenty-five to twenty-eight years (no one could remember for sure anymore), the congregations had lived away from the "moral pollutions of society" and raised their own crops, managed their own livestock, and made most of their own clothes.

The people of the congregations felt that the immoral state of the world was the cause of the wars and disasters that had befallen the earth in the last forty or so years. They wanted to totally separate themselves from society's worldliness and focus on service to God. They renamed themselves and named their children after biblical characters to remind them always of the scriptures. They were devoutly strict in their worship and service to their Lord.

Most burned or discarded any book other than the Bible. They also would not use electricity (even if it had been available) – and not because they thought that electricity was an instrument of the devil, but rather they believed such luxuries distracted from their total service to the savior, as they believed the past had proven. Other stories than those found in the pages of the Bible were told, but not many or often. And such stories were certainly not read. The other-than-biblical stories were not believed to be evil or sinful necessarily, but their reasoning was: "why, when all that we need is in the Holy Scriptures?" They also, very much, wanted to purge the worldliness from the world.

These religious zealots were not focused in one region but were scattered and dispersed among the world's population by the end of the wars. Many sought redemption and salvation in those bleak times. They did not practice violence and were typically known as meek, patient, hardworking, and quiet; although, there were those like Jonas. These religious zealots were called "Preachers" by the general population. It was meant as a derogatory term, but it stuck and practically became synonymous with "Christian." The Preachers would never refer to themselves by anything other than "disciple" or "Christian," although they would answer to "Preacher."

Uriah, Josiah, and Jonas left for another congregation south of their own. The congregations would customarily do this on an annual basis to keep in contact with other brethren. It was not a matter of "biblical mandate," but courtesy and relations with their "spiritual family." There were not many phone lines left functional, but even so, the Preachers preferred to communicate face-to-face or by letter, in keeping with the only biblical examples of communication. They typically did not use horses or carts and simply walked from place to place with only what they carried with them. So they headed south toward the town of Engine's Rest. They would never purposely avoid a town, because the gospel must be spread.

Engine's Rest, a border town in the L&M territory, was a unique town in that it was one of the few prewar towns left standing. Most towns and cities were bombed or demolished along with water ports, air strips and major roadways during the long and intense wars. The reason Engine's Rest still stood, and those like it, was because it had lost its significance long before the wars. It had been a ghost town. It had been named something prior to the wars, but no one remembered what that was anymore. As people started setting up towns and livings again after the wars they decided to name it Engine's Rest because of the train engine graveyard on the west side of town.

The old buildings of Engine's Rest that were in good shape had been made of brick, and the old wooden ones had been rebuilt or fixed up. It was easier to move into a town than to build one from scratch.

Many of the old rail cars in the train graveyard had been converted into housing and places of business. The town boasted a hospital that was really a doctor's office with two nurses, a grocery, gun shop, blacksmith (also gunsmith), a few miscellaneous shops, and a "Jerry's Tavern – With Lodging." The mayor and sheriff shared an office on the northern part of Engine's Rest. To the south and east were mostly houses with two schools and a few small general stores.

The sun had begun to sink, and it made the Preachers' shadows grow long toward the east. They had heard several shots ring out in the direction of their travel, but thought little of it. Gun fire was common even in this post-war era. Military arms had been mass produced and widely distributed. When the wars had ended, there were still plenty of people who wanted their weapons, and fortunately for them, there was an abundance to go around.

They were tired from their long walk and looked forward to a warm bed and some food if it were to be found in the upcoming town. As they neared the northern border of Engine's Rest they noticed a group of buzzards and a hint of smoke at the top of some hill in the distance that had a single oak at its summit. Josiah wondered at what had them so enthralled, but his father, Uriah, did not seem to notice; and Jonas was too busy pouting because Uriah wouldn't stop to eat or rest until they got into town.

Josiah was sixteen years old and had lived all his life in the congregation. He was quiet, but so were most of the zealots in this time. It was one of their virtues. His father had been a founder of their particular congregation twenty-six years before, at the age of twenty-four. Uriah was a big man with a cluster of scars on his left upper arm that disappeared under his shirt sleeve. If Josiah ever asked about the scars, as a curious son would, Uriah would only respond, "A reminder of a life before redemption."

Josiah wondered what life must have been like before the wars. Most did, he supposed. He was thankful that the Lord had not destroyed the world as he had before, but showed restraint and had only crippled it. Josiah was apprehensive about venturing into a town for the first time. He had never left the congregation and was wary of the wickedness he was sure to witness. He had prayed that they would be safe and started feeling guilty of it now. Was it selfish to pray for that? He decided that he should have prayed that the godless in the upcoming town might heed the eternal words of God, instead of safety for himself. He prayed that his father would be safe, that the townspeople might repent, and for forgiveness for any selfishness that may be in his heart – he immediately felt better.

The two Preachers each had a bible that they carried with them in the right outer pocket of their old satchels, which they wore slung across their bodies like holy bandoliers. They were sure that Jonas had one as well, but neither would wager that it had been used much. They also carried a little jerky and bread and a change of socks. For water, they had homemade water-skins slung around their shoulders. That was all they carried, believing that any other necessity would be provided.

When the three entered town, they found a man who evidently had been beaten and robbed, left in the road. Uriah rushed to the man and rolled him onto his back. The man looked half dead, covered in bruises, blood, and dust. His clothes were torn and filthy, and he had a huge metal belt buckle. Uriah had already taken off his water skin and was moistening the lips of the pitiful man when Josiah rushed to his father's side and helped him. Jonas just meandered behind them dragging his feet, still sulking and even more aggravated because he knew they had stumbled onto another meal delay.

Chapter 4

Basic (Flashback)

Jeremiah's bus pulled up to the Army's Reception Building around 1AM. The early morning was still and heavy with humidity. The air in the dark sky was warm and stale. The smell could have been the vinyl bus seat upholstery, but Jeremiah wasn't really paying attention. He was watching the people with the round-brimmed and brown hats exit out of a side door of the building and head toward the bus. There were giggles and vulgar jokes being told on the bus; scared boys trying to act brave and unimpressed. If any of the recruits were hiding their fear, it seemed to be revealed when the brown, round hat and the large man wearing it boarded the bus and began yelling and singling out the fearful, like a shark torpedoing toward a flailing, wounded seal.

Jeremiah didn't understand people. The military wasn't a new institution. Everyone had seen movies or heard stories from veterans about basic training, yet there were really people stupid enough to talk back to a drill sergeant, or who truthfully seemed surprised that they were being yelled at for apparently no reason. The drill sergeants seemed to live for that type of person and were visibly bored with the recruits smart enough to play by the rules; the ones who could stand still, stay quiet, and answer every question loudly with "yes drill sergeant!" or with "Hooah!" the Army's everything word. Nothing was ever easier.

The rest of that night was filled with yelling, purposely induced confusion, sleep deprivation, administrative paperwork, and standing in lines. The recruits were allowed 30 minutes of sleep, and then head shaving, shots, and uniform and gear issue. The uniforms issued to the new recruits were plain olive drab fatigues with the front billed patrol cap. "You're not soldiers yet!" the reception cadre would yell, "only soldiers get camo!" It had been this way for years; everyone knew the "earn your camo" custom. It was the Army's way of making sure that the recruits knew their place – which was at the very bottom.

Though there didn't appear to be any females in Jeremiah's particular training class, the Army had been using females in combat arms units for quite some time. The United States military had been using the formal terms of "female" and "male" for women and men for more than a century. The intention was that these robotic terms would induce more scientific train of thought, subconsciously conveying asexual perspectives and identities… in reality, men and women are men and women; *a rose by any other name would smell as sweet.*

The physical standards for the combat arms jobs in the military were not lowered for females, as in the administrative military jobs. In the past the bulk of the military forces balked at allowing women in combat roles, and would often use those lower standards as a reason to preclude them from direct combat, saying, "A bullet won't hit a woman with less force, and a hundred pound rucksack won't weigh less on woman's back, and a twenty mile ruck march won't suddenly be ten miles..." Now, however, women were allowed in combat roles and jobs as long as they met the universal physical standards required for both men and women. Sports and workout/training programs had evolved enough that they routinely produced high performing female athletes. Plus, there were plenty of nutritional supplements that many of the infantry women took to aid in their performance; of course, many of the males did as well.

Initially, the integration had been difficult for many to accept, despite the fact they were required to meet the male standards. It wasn't until several years after they first started allowing females in combat roles that the females really started being viewed as equals. The Army's elite infantry unit, the Rangers, have a yearly competition called the Best Ranger Competition. It's a long and grueling multi-day event that is tough to complete, much less win. When the infantry was opened up to women, so was the competition.

At first, the competition went from having a one team victor, to recognizing the top male and top female teams. This created resentment among many of the male competitors. It was supposed to be a fair opportunity without lowering standards... and even though this was only a competition, there were those who viewed this as watering down an event and treading on a hard-earned reputation and tradition. Three years into the integration, the top female team refused to be recognized because they had not finished as the top team overall. The event coordinators then offered the prize to the second female team, who also then refused recognition.

That particular year, the top female team had only beaten one of the male teams. How could they accept a first place award, when they were far from it? In their minds, combat wouldn't have male battles and female battles – just battles. They would not accept segregation – even if it was supposed to be in their favor.

The females of that Best Ranger Competition wanted so badly to be treated as actual peers, to be recognized so badly as equal infantrymen, that they refused any recognition on anything that was based on a reduced scale. No female team has ever placed among the first at any following Best Ranger Competitions, but every female combat arms soldier has had equal respect of their peers since then. If they pass the standards, then they are allowed.

Even so, few women volunteered for the infantry.

While in-processing at reception, a few men were pulled out of line at different times and taken into different rooms. These soldiers had been selected for additional testing. One of them was Pratt's bunk mate, Mick Towers, who was selected for two service related exams. Later, Mick would tell Jeremiah that it was to take a language aptitude test, but never commented on the other. Apparently the military was pulling individuals out of line based upon their entrance test scores to see if they would be of use in other fields, or whether the men had the aptitude to learn other skills quickly. Language was just one of several side tests. Jeremiah never figured out what the other tests were for, nor did he really care. He would not be selected for any such additional testing.

From the Reception battalion, the men were shuffled to their training companies, once all of their gear had been issued and all the documentation was made. Each training company was to have roughly ninety recruits. All the recruits were herded into large cattle cars, now powered solely by electric engines; packed in tight, standing-room only. Each man had a rucksack on his back and a duffle bag on his front. Talking was not allowed, and there were no windows and little ventilation. Jeremiah assumed that they were supposed to feel uncomfortable and were supposed to feel disoriented, and maybe even frightened. He supposed that it had that effect on some of the guys, not that he cared, but since he felt like he understood what they were trying to do, it seemed easy. It was like playing a game to him. They make the rules, and the game is rigged to where they always win – the best he could do was wait out the game's time limit.

The cattle cars hummed to a stop and the doors were swung open into a bland courtyard surrounded by bland multi-story barracks. The yelling started again. Now there were fewer recruits and more Drill Sergeants. The recruits scurried out like a chaotic flock of birds in the wind. The Drill Sergeants were screaming all sorts of things. "OVER HERE! HURRY! HURRY!" from one. "GET OVER HERE NOW! WHAT'S WRONG WITH YOU! NOT THERE, HERE!" by another Drill Instructor. Jeremiah could have sworn that he heard one of them just shouting pure nonsense and meaningless babble.

The recruits finally made it into a semblance of military ranks, but the yelling had not stopped. The men had to empty out all of their bags, spilling out all of their gear on the ground. Some were cursed for doing it too fast, and others were cursed for doing it too slow. Drill Sergeants were tugging on shirts and pockets, knocking hats off of the recruits' heads, etc. The Drill Sergeants were really just trying to demonstrate that they were in charge and take inventory at the same time. Jeremiah stood, followed every command, and would not show frustration or any apprehension or anxiety.

Jeremiah and a few others immediately stood out from the majority of recruits. Most of the trainees were losing their composure, losing their bearing, and appeared to be losing the ability to think or stay calm. Panic was setting in; the feeling of losing all control. Jeremiah had a stoic disposition, the look of a soldier, an athlete. The Army's Poster Child.

From the courtyard, where they had been made to inventory their gear in the most chaotic manner, the recruits were taken inside one of the old multi-story buildings. The Drill Sergeants divided and shuffled the recruits into large rooms, where eight to twelve recruits were to share the space. The rooms had no doors, and were filled only with metal bunk beds and metal wall lockers, each of which sat roughly two feet off of the wall, leaving walking space behind them.

Some of the recruits were storing their gear frantically, as if something they did would keep the Drill Sergeants from harassing them again. Others were calmly putting their things away, while others still appeared to be in no hurry at all, casually milling around. The rest of the evening was filled with classes on how to make the bunks, how to fold their underwear and socks, and where it all had to go in the wall lockers.

Jeremiah lay in his top bunk that night, wondering when or if he'd fall asleep. His bunk was one of the two closest to the windows, which were open. It was quiet outside. The faint glow of a sidewalk light could be seen out the window, vaguely illuminating the grass and concrete surrounding it. Jeremiah couldn't hear anyone crying nor could he even hear people trying to subdue their sobs. He was glad for that. He had seen tears in the eyes of some of the guys during earlier encounters with the Drill Sergeants, but he would see none in the dark.

He lay there in the quiet darkness. Exhausted, his thoughts began to drift toward Lilly. The day's aggravating events hadn't really bothered him, and the Drill Sergeants' display of dominance hadn't fazed him or worried him, since he'd expected all of that; but for some reason she came to mind, and he imagined how different of an experience she must be having. The thought of her that night put a bad taste in his mouth, so he pushed her out of mind. He eventually made it to dreamless sleep.

***

The next morning they all awoke to the sound of thunder crashing down the platoon corridor. The Drill Sergeants had thrown their aluminum garbage cans down the hallways and begun screaming. Another one was saying something over a bullhorn. Jeremiah didn't know what they were saying, but it was clearly time to wake up.

Their training schedule included two weeks of "seasoning" where the recruits were supposed to be acclimated, broken down, and made fertile grounds so that the seeds of military knowledge and doctrine could germinate.

The seasoning phase included lots of running and physical exercise, room inspections, yelling, uniform procedures, military practices and courtesies, and limited sleep and chow. Jeremiah excelled in all the physical elements and stood out among the top of the class. His pal from Reception, Mick Towers, did as well. He was a little older and had been a collegiate rower. He was an athlete with college degrees in finance and philosophy (which Mick's deceased, minister father would never have approved of), and he had a dry sense of humor. Jeremiah liked him a lot and would have described him as "genuine." Plus, Jeremiah enjoyed Mick's dry and clever wit over the dimwitted toilet humor that most of the platoon seemed to have. Jeremiah laughed at some of that as well, everyone does, but Mick was a little easier to tolerate. Every little fart didn't have to turn into a joke.

Their training schedule could be broken down into two main phases: the basic phase, where basic skills and customs were addressed such as marksmanship, hand to hand fighting (which included knives and sticks), land navigation (compasses, stars, terrain features, electronic global positioning devices), etc; and the advanced infantry phase which involved longer, more grueling runs, ruck marches, and patrols, and included more detailed observation techniques, advanced hand to hand, combat marksmanship, planning and performing raids, rescues, fast roping from helos, combat first aid, simple explosives, and training in the HELIOS Warfighter System.

The HELIOS Warfighter System, or simply "HELIOS," as the soldiers called it, was a tactical aid that all ground combat forces utilized. It was a compact, rugged individual computer and communications system. A small computer pack was fastened on the soldier's forearm or belt. This computer communicated with satellites, other HELIOS systems, as well as with the command group system. Each soldier's ballistic glasses had a display screen that could be brought up for navigation and could show objectives, targets, exfiltration and rendezvous points, and satellite imagery that would highlight friendly troop locations. It could even display video feeds from other soldiers. The soldiers communicated with one another in every way with it.

In Greek mythology, HELIOS was the sun god that gave sight to the hunter; for the United States, the HELIOS system gave unparalleled sight to its war fighters. It was a huge advantage in battle.

While they were being fitted for their first exercise with HELIOS, one of Jeremiah's fellow recruits said, "You know these things have explosives in 'em." No one really paid him any attention and continued to don their systems. "These things are built with bombs in 'em," the recruit said again.

"Is that Gipson talking again?" someone shouted with contempt.

Gipson looked genuinely insulted by the comment and

resulting snickers. "Seriously!" he pleaded, holding his arms out to the side. "Yeah, it's so the command can blow us up and make suicide soldiers out of us," Gipson added with a know-it-all smirk.

"Be quiet, Gipson," Mick said. "That doesn't make any sense." He added, "they may render the device inoperable, but they won't 'blow us up.'"

There were rumors of plans the government had instituted in case a soldier wearing the system was captured, or in case the enemy could rob the HELIOS off of dead soldiers. Although there was no official literature issued to the troops, it was widely rumored that the HELIOS systems had a built-in short circuit apparatus that the command could initiate should the soldier wearing it ever become captured, or should a situation like that arise.

Gipson started to say something else, but Mick held his gaze, silencing Gipson. Jeremiah laughed and continued getting his HELIOS ready for training. No one really liked Gipson. He was weak, paranoid, and was always trying to compensate for it by talking about stuff he really didn't know about – it only made his plight worse.

All of these recruits would train through each phase together, barring some injury or ejection caused by some other unforeseen event. The Army had not always trained the infantry in such a way, but the current method was to train the infantry in a single location, or as the Army called it "OSUT" (One Station Unit Training). After the "basic" phase, which was three months, the recruits would get their camouflage fatigues and would be known as soldiers for their remaining time of advanced infantry training. Current infantry standards for the US Army had reached a level that no other time in history had experienced; in part due to the reliance on electronic devices for navigation, troop movements, communication, medical care, weapons sighting and targeting, etc. There was a new technical level to being a grunt. HELIOS was the jewel in that crown.

After the first few weeks in the actual training platoons, the Drill Sergeants eased way off as a way to reduce stress during the basic marksmanship phase. This phase offered a little more quiet time in the evenings where recruits could do additional physical training, perfect their wall lockers, or write letters home. Jeremiah thought that the military must be the only organization to use actual pens and paper anymore. He thought it made sense, though. There was a lot to go wrong with electronics in hard environments; not to mention the concussive forces and bangs from bombs, etc. Pen and paper wouldn't short out or run out of battery life.

Jeremiah wrote Lilly. He didn't know her school address, so he addressed it to her parents' home, supposing that they would pass it on for him. He didn't tell her how much he thought about her. He wouldn't say how much he missed being around her. He just told her that he was doing well, learning a lot, and briefly expounded upon some things that he thought she might find interesting and the things that would hopefully impress her. Mainly he was fishing for a response. It could be anything. He wanted to see her name, written by her own hand. He wasn't sure that he would open a letter from her, afraid of what it may say inside. Of course, he wasn't even sure that he'd get one either.

In those moments where the recruits were left to themselves, they were not only allowed to write letters or do additional exercise, but they had access to a company library and a few select games.

The books that were available were mostly around the subjects of military history, US history, literary classics, some philosophy, and a very small selection of fiction literature. The games available for the soldiers to play were those that rewarded cleverness, coordination, or strategy – games like chess, darts, dominoes, etc. The Army was trying to dominate their "free time" by steering it toward skills and attributes that would benefit the Army in some way. However, when a recruit screwed up, like leaving a wall locker unsecured or talking out of turn, the recruit was denied these privileges, and at times, the platoon could be denied the privileges based on the infractions of a single recruit. It didn't help Gipson's popularity to be the major recurring cause of these denials.

Those who have never been in the military or locked away from society may not fully appreciate the torture that can feel like; what a stress reliever those simple things can be. But when those privileges were kept back, the reason (typically Gipson) was held in much contempt.

Most of the training was physically demanding. The exercise or conditioning portion was as demanding as one made it. The field exercises are what Jeremiah liked best, which included being at certain objectives at specific times, setting ambushes, or conducting patrols and gathering basic information. By the end of the training missions, Jeremiah wasn't as winded as he was after a run, but he had a better high from it. Of course he knew it wasn't a real situation, but he could feel his adrenaline pumping all the same, and at the end, he felt a great sense of accomplishment. For the first time he really felt like he was in his element.

Other parts of training, like the obstacle courses, were easy to Jeremiah. He'd get tired during them, but finishing first, or among the frontrunners, wasn't a chore and was like recess to him. He felt a certain disdain for those that struggled or whined about having to run through them. He felt like those individuals had simply neglected to prepare themselves enough for a profession that was going to be physically demanding. Adding to Jeremiah's aggravation may have been due to the fact that he had not received any returned correspondence from Lilly. He probably wouldn't have admitted to it, and likely didn't even think about it directly, but he did feel like he'd gone out on a limb to send her a letter, and without any reply, he may have felt the slightest bit stupid.

The "basic phase" ended unceremoniously with tired recruits returning to their barracks after a weeklong field exercise. They marched back and fell into rank outside of their barracks, in the courtyard. The training company's commander actually took charge of the formation, instead of the Drill Sergeants. He addressed the formation as "soldiers," told them they had done well in completing their first baby step in the United States Army, and dismissed the company. When the recruits stumbled into their rooms, they found their new camo fatigues on each of their bunks.

The next day everything seemed the same, except the drill sergeants screamed "soldier" instead of "recruit" while the men were wearing camo. Strange that such a small change can make things feel so different. All of the new soldiers stood a little taller.

Jeremiah eventually received a letter from Lilly. He couldn't hide his surprise; he really never expected to receive anything from her. He felt like crying and took it immediately, a little astonished at how eager he was to get it. The letter was kind, filled with pleasantries and vague details of her new life and pursuits. She said that she missed him. Jeremiah assumed that was merely politeness, but liked to see it written by her, still. But she also included an actual photograph, which he thought took quite a bit of effort, as most pictures were digital and contained on digital devices. He hoped it was an indication of some deeper feelings within her, but finally assumed that was wishful thinking. He knew that he'd eventually have to put her away. She had gone a direction that Jeremiah feared he was not destined to follow. He was proving to be well suited as a soldier.

***

On one ruck march, Private Gipson couldn't continue at the prescribed pace. This particular ruck march was one that the cadets were supposedly doing out from under the watchful eye of the Drill Sergeants. Jeremiah doubted that they weren't watching, he was sure that they were, they just weren't going to lead the platoon. They wanted to see who would rise to the leadership role and who would slack off if they thought they weren't being watched. If this one recruit didn't finish with the platoon, the platoon would be penalized for leaving a man behind. If they waited for him and went at his pace, the platoon would be late and therefore penalized.

Jeremiah took Gipson's ruck and goaded him forward, determined to prevent Gipson from interfering with his free time. Jeremiah was walking up and down a winding mountain dirt road with his own ruck on his back, this other guy's ruck at his front. The platoon was moving at the right pace again and was on track to make the final destination on time. And although Gipson was walking unburdened, he continued to complain about the heat, about being thirsty, and about his feet hurting. Jeremiah kept pressing him on, although not in the friendliest of tones. Gipson tried to stop for a rest a few times, but continued on at the pressing of Mick and Jeremiah.

The platoon finally reached their correct destination near the top of the mountain within the prescribed time and were given time to rest. The day was hot, and they had proven that they could at least march along a long dirt road without cadre supervision. Jeremiah unceremoniously downed Gipson's ruck and then his own. Jeremiah's fingers were swollen, his shoulders were numb, his back ached, and he felt unnaturally light after carrying two rucksacks for several hours. His feet were sore. Before eating, Jeremiah sat and tended to the blisters that had developed on his feet. He then refilled his canteens and unsecured one of his prepackaged meals before slumping down against his rucksack.

Gipson walked up to his ruck, which Jeremiah had left next to his own, stretched and said with a grin, "that wasn't too bad," and commenced to joking around with the other guys.

Jeremiah nearly convulsed. His face went red as he gritted his teeth, reached up toward Gipson, and pulled him to the ground by his sleeve. "You get carried this whole way, and now you're gonna laugh it all off without so much as a 'thank you!'"

Gipson tried jerking away as he looked at Jeremiah, taken aback and humiliated. The fact that he seemed so confused by Jeremiah's response made Jeremiah even angrier. "What?!" Pratt said, increasing his hold onto Gipson's sleeve. "Do I need to carve it into your forehead before you get it?!"

Gipson was now conscious of the other guys who could hear Jeremiah and tried to save a little face. "Settle down, Pratt," he said trying to sound brave as he squirmed free of Jeremiah.

Everything had evidently been building up – Lilly, Gipson's

history of negligent failures, fatigue and blisters, and this moment was the boiling point. Jeremiah was getting angrier and lashed out at Gipson, rising to his feet. Seeing Gipson cower down so readily only fueled the rage more. He grabbed Gipson by the collar as he growled, "you're gonna get someone killed, and it ain't gonna be any of us!"

"Pratt," Mick interrupted with an even tone.

Jeremiah was standing over Gipson, who had slumped down with tears beginning to come down his face as he reflexively held his hands up in defense. The entire platoon was watching. They had never seen Jeremiah lose his composure in such a way, but no one (other than Mick Towers) had even said a word.

"Pratt," Mick said again, "I think you squared him away." Mick was looking at Pratt, waiting for the situation to defuse.

Jeremiah's demeanor calmed immediately. Jeremiah finally noticed that his hands were in fists and his right one was cocked back, ready to be fired. He glanced at Mick before releasing Gipson, then walked away from the group and over to a lookout point on the mountain. Jeremiah had gone too far, and he knew that. He had made his point many times over and had finally been doing nothing more than making a spectacle of Gipson in front of everyone. Jeremiah was under more stress than he wanted to admit and was embarrassed greatly because of it. He had been tempted to take out Lilly's photo and dwell on that, but kept himself from it. The fact that he still held on to her made him feel even more pathetic.

He took the picture out of his pocket, but left it in its envelope, and was about to throw it over the side when Mick spoke up behind him, "you'll never forgive yourself."

"Sorry?" Jeremiah said back, startled.

"You look at whatever's in that envelope all the time," Mick said as he came to stop, leaning on a tree next to Jeremiah without looking at him. "You were right."

"What are we talking about?" Jeremiah said, honestly confused. He turned toward Mick who was still leaning against the tree, looking out into the horizon, and snacking on the remnants of his lunch. Jeremiah placed the envelope back in his pocket as discreetly as he could.

"Gipson needed that," Mick continued, "just not all of it."

Jeremiah was quiet. He liked Mick a lot. Respect may be a better word for it, but Jeremiah hadn't settled himself enough quite yet and was beginning to get annoyed again. He wasn't sure that he needed a lecture right now.

"At some point, Pratt, you were just making a little dimwit look like a weak idiot." Mick looked over at Jeremiah, "You're better than that."

Jeremiah felt his stomach turn and forgot his anger. Mick was just a couple of years older, but this felt like disappointing his grandmother. Mick was one of those guys who was good at everything. He could have been an officer and had actually been recruited by a large security firm out of college, but he wanted to experience the Army as an enlisted man first. Mick was a natural leader. All the guys respected him and he treated everyone with nothing but respect. And Jeremiah had let him down, even if just in a small way.

"Yeah, I'm sorry," Jeremiah said regretfully and looked back out off the mountain at the countryside below. He never really was one for being long-winded.

"Hey," Mick said dismissively, "it's not a big deal. Like I said, he needed most of that, but it's sort of like the Samurai."

Jeremiah looked quizzically over at Mick. Jeremiah wondered if this was the set up for one of Mick's clever jokes.

Mick felt the uncomfortable silence and looked back toward Jeremiah in astonishment, "The children's story..." Mick waited for recognition to reach Jeremiah's face, but only saw more bewilderment. "Your parents not read to you as a child?" It was a rhetorical question. "Yeah, um... the 'Small Samurai,' or 'the Tiniest Samurai...' whatever it was called; the story about the three Japanese brothers who had to train and compete to take their father's place as the samurai who would protect the village...? Nothing?"

Jeremiah just shook his head slightly, still clearly void of any recognition.

"Well anyways," Mick continued, "one brother was big and strong, one brother was fast and deadly, and one brother was small, weak, and slow. In the end, the slower, smaller brother won the lead role because he was the wisest. Wisdom being the samurai's key weapon."

"So... you think that Gipson is smart..." Jeremiah was trying to understand what Mick was getting at, while trying not to laugh at the fact that they were seriously discussing Mick's childhood bedtime story.

"Ha, uh, no," Mick said with a chuckle. "No I don't. The story actually doesn't finish with the wise one winning. The parable concludes with the wise man understanding that everyone has value; everyone has a use. The wise brother makes his other two brothers samurai as well, because he recognizes their needed skills. Gipson may be weak, and he may be simple-minded, but I think he still has something to offer. Demoralizing a man can be like damaging a tool."

Jeremiah nodded. He got the point.

"Gipson's strength and value probably isn't the infantry," Mick continued. "It probably lies elsewhere, maybe in an area that the Army, and therefore 'we,' may still desperately need."

Jeremiah nodded.

"I think you are failing to use all of your skills, Pratt," Mick added.

"Huh?" Jeremiah was confused again and was starting to get aggravated all over.

"You're like the two stronger and faster brothers," Mick elaborated. "You're solely focused on making your body stronger and mastering the issued weapons. You've got that down, man. What you're neglecting is the most important aspect; knowledge, knowledge of how people work, how they're motivated, how they're discouraged. Knowledge in general, man."

"Is this an insult?" Jeremiah asked sarcastically.

"Not at all," Mick answered matter-of-factly. "Just making a suggestion and commenting on your potential. You're no idiot, Pratt, but focusing on everything else at the expense of your mind is a waste. Some of these dudes aren't capable," Mick said motioning to the platoon resting behind them. "You don't have an excuse."

Jeremiah was taking this to heart and felt foolish for not realizing it before.

"Do you expect to make it through life on youthful strength and luck alone?" Mick asked and finished his last bite of rations. "You're on the road to being a good soldier, Pratt. But wouldn't you rather be great?" Mick dusted his hands off and said, "Keep your envelope – we all need our security," as he walked back toward the platoon. About half way there he turned and yelled "THE LITTLEST SAMURAI."

"THANKS," was all Jeremiah knew to shout back. *That's one weird dude*, Jeremiah thought with an uncomfortable grin.

Jeremiah placed his hand in his pocket, making sure his picture was still there. Security.

Several days later, Mick approached Jeremiah during their free time and asked him to play a game of chess. "I don't know how to play," Jeremiah said dismissively, clearly uninterested in sitting still for the duration of a board game.

"Why are you wasting yourself?" Mick asked in a friendly, but disgusted tone.

"I'm building myself," Jeremiah answered back as he neared the room's indoor pull-up bars.

"You're building your body," Mick said, "but we are not this crude matter," as he poked Jeremiah's shoulder. "We are luminous beings," Mick finished, quoting an old film.

Jeremiah gripped the pull-up bar and started repping them out effortlessly and addressed Mick without looking at him, "And chess will enlighten me?"

"The body is simply a tool of the mind, Pratt," Mick said as he began to set the pieces in their proper places. "Sharpening the mind is more important than sharpening any bayonet and will pay off exponentially more than preparing the body alone."

Jeremiah released the pull-up bar. "I'm not an intellectual, Towers," Jeremiah said, making excuses, and reached back up for another set.

"But you are," Mick said flatly, as he paused from his arranging of game pieces to look at Jeremiah. "I see you thinking all the time. You are an intellectual; you've just wasted your academic opportunities." Mick looked back down at his chess board and started where he left off, placing the pieces in their squares. "Stop wasting our time. Sit down and learn the game. Think of it as exercising the mind, if you like."

Jeremiah reached for a chair and joined Mick at the table.

Mick began to go over the game's rules. He went through each piece, explaining its role and capabilities. "This is the pawn," Mick said as he held it at Jeremiah's eye level. "This is what you are. Now let's look at what you should become…"

***

At his training graduation, Jeremiah felt a real sense of pride. He had not cared at all for his high school graduation and would have skipped it had his parents allowed him to. High school was something that the vast majority of people graduated from; to Jeremiah one may as well celebrate cleaning their plate at lunch. If everyone achieves something, it's not that special.

While there are more difficult things to endure and achieve, Army basic training and infantry school signified a more profound milestone, one that most people do not even attempt. Jeremiah couldn't help but feel a sense of accomplishment and honor as he was formally graduated into this fraternity of warriors.

His friend, Mick, was the honor graduate and Jeremiah was seated next to him, receiving what was essentially a runner-up certificate. Jeremiah was aware that these certificates were just paper and would not aid him at all in his military career; regardless, he felt more pride for his second place OSUT infantry training piece of paper than he had for anything he'd received in high school academics or athletics.

Jeremiah had never been one that was overly concerned with wardrobe or name brands, but he liked his uniform for what it signified and because he felt like he had earned the right to wear it. He was happy that his parents were there and happy at the sincere pride that was radiating from their smiles and eyes. And even though it would have been impossible for her to attend, he had a momentary thought about Lilly. They'd only shared a few letters during his time in training, and Jeremiah would never have said it out loud, but he wanted her to be proud of him too. He wished that she had been there, even if he'd never have admitted it.

Jeremiah was only supposed to be on leave for a little over a week, but his leave was extended, which he hadn't thought was possible. There had been some small domestic issue that temporarily slowed the processing of the new soldiers that were en route to their permanent duty stations. Jeremiah didn't really care about the reason, he was just glad that he had two more weeks at home. Lilly was home for summer break, and Jeremiah wanted to spend time with her when he could. The only caveat of his leave extension was to check in with the local recruiting office twice daily. It was a small nuisance.

Jeremiah and Lilly had seen each other several times already since he had been home, but nothing that could be mistaken as a date – a celebratory welcome home party, gatherings with high school friends, things of that sort. So he finally asked her out to dinner. She accepted, which he took as a good sign. He had thought about wearing his dress uniform, but decided against it. It might look like he was trying too hard to impress her, and Jeremiah didn't like being conspicuous anyways. He wanted to be with her alone, and if he felt like other people were watching them, or if they stood out, that it would ruin the feeling of only being out with her.

Lilly was only nineteen by this time, but she didn't look like a teenager anymore. When he picked her up, she was wearing a red dress, and Jeremiah's eyes were filled with her. Jeremiah had dressed nice and ditched his bike for the evening and drove

Lilly to a decent restaurant in his parents' car. The conversation during the car ride and at dinner was light and easy and Jeremiah felt like they were both genuinely enjoying each other's company.

"You didn't even comment on my dress," Lilly playfully chided. "You've got to try a little harder, Mr. Pratt."

"You look fat," Jeremiah quipped immediately, with a flat, even tone. Lilly nearly gagged on her drink, spewing a little of it out of her nose, laughing so hard at the unexpected retort.

Jeremiah laughed and handed her a napkin. "I like you," he said, looking directly into her eyes with a wide smile. She was beautiful. He could tell that he caught her off guard. It wasn't so much what he said, but the manner in which he said it that articulated more than the words themselves.

Lilly wasn't smiling. She looked sort of serious and said, "I feel the same way," nodding in agreement. There was something else there, but Jeremiah couldn't tell what. Regardless, the night was going well. Jeremiah felt that the time away had done both of them good. They weren't high school kids anymore. All of the immaturity that came with trying to fit in and be cool had dropped away, and they could now just pursue a relationship like adults. Jeremiah didn't try to push his luck with a kiss or any physical contact for that matter. He was enjoying the company and didn't want to scare her off or push his luck. *No harm in taking it slow,* he thought.

The following night he was with her again. At the end of the evening, when he asked her to go out with him again, she confronted him. "Are you just trying to keep me away from Trevor?" she asked pointedly.

Confused, Jeremiah answered with a bewildered, "Um, no..." *What was going on? Last night went so well*, he thought to himself, looking at her like he was completely lost.

"Trevor thinks you only asked me out because you didn't want me to see him," she said in what Jeremiah took as a scolding tone.

A swell of pain and rage came over Jeremiah that he could barely contain. Lilly had been tattooed on his mind and now he just felt stupid. "What?!" was all Jeremiah could think to ask. It was obvious what was happening, but his head was swirling. He tried rubbing the tunnel vision out of his eyes. *Stupid*, Jeremiah thought to himself.

Lilly's face showed that she regretted bringing it up. Clearly she thought Jeremiah had known more than he did. "Trevor and I…"

Jeremiah didn't want her to finish and raised his hand, cutting her short.

"Sorry," Lilly said, clearly unsure of how to act next.

"Nope," Jeremiah answered. "I'm sorry. I didn't know you and Trevor…" Jeremiah was angry and hurt, but trying unsuccessfully to look in control. Holding back the rage and sorrow, Jeremiah said, "Look, I'll… uh, go." Jeremiah was looking at the ground as if his words could be found there. "Trevor's cool. I won't get in your way anymore," he said, sounding angry and resentful. He mounted his motorcycle and left her standing in her driveway, watching as she receded in his rearview mirror. He felt certain that his embarrassment had been obvious to her, which only wounded him further.

Don't be so stupid, Jeremiah thought to himself, *you are going to have to learn this basic fact – she doesn't like you.* He rode home, unable to ignore his wound.

The following day, he was to leave for his duty station. A welcome move at this point.

Chapter 5

Leg of LaMS

Engine's Rest sat on the western edge of the Laughton and Mills Territory which was patrolled and controlled by the remnant of L&M's army called the L&M Security Forces; most locals called them LaMS. Billy and Randy Squire were among the town's small LaMS security detachment. Billy had been an L&M infantry officer during the wars until he lost his leg in action.

Once the wars ended with the cease fire treaty and establishment of territory boundaries, Billy requested the quiet appointment of Security Rep to Engine's Rest. As an added bonus he was allowed to take his half-brother Randy as deputy, who was 15 years younger. Their small outpost couldn't be called a jail, although it did have a small cell. During this reconstruction and redefining process of peace that was so foreign now, there was little time or concern for trivial "crimes," therefore little need for jail cells.

If someone was shot or killed, the local LaMS reps would determine if there was good cause and if it were fair. If it was fair, then any reason was a good cause and overlooked. If the death was not fair, but if there was good cause determined, then the death was overlooked. If someone stole, raped, or killed without good cause, then the penalty was usually up to the discretion of the senior LaMS Rep.

Engine's Rest was like most other towns in the territory, most local action, trivial or not, was overlooked unless the LaMS had a stake in it. The President of L&M and the board, which was now the Parliament, took little concern with local disputes. If there was a fight or disruption involving significant numbers of personnel, some military action, or a security breach; the QRF, or Quick Reaction Force, would be dispatched immediately, and then the L&M governing body would be briefed on the situation.

Billy and Randy happened to be dining in Jerry's Tavern and witnessed the events with Tyler Johnson from beginning to end. Each smiled in amusement as Tyler was hurled out the door.

"Idiot," Randy muttered as he turned back to his brother.

Billy grinned and sat back in his seat. "Yeah," was all he could think to say. His leg was hurting. Not bad, but it was hurting again, and he shifted in his seat. "Didn't like him." Billy said.

"He was an idiot," Randy responded before taking another sip from his glass. He put his glass back on the table and asked, "I guess we should check it out?"

"Huh?" Billy asked. "Oh. Uh, no," he finished, rubbing his eyes. "At least not until I finish lunch, but I doubt Jeremiah Pratt is even still alive."

"Then what do you think happened to his friends, then?" Randy replied, leaning forward and motioning toward the door as he eyed his brother.

"I don't know. He probably got drunk and scared and killed 'em himself – how should I know?" Billy was irritable. He wondered to himself how his leg could ache so badly when it hadn't been there for years. Trying to ignore his leg, Billy asked, "Do you really think that that loud mouth fool could survive old man Pratt if he were really there?"

Billy was also annoyed that some people evidently thought Tyler, the "Champ," was really something impressive. Billy was irritated because some of the young ladies thought so too, and

Randy knew it. And they both knew that some idiot kids would be talking like him and dressing like him tomorrow.

"Great," Randy said sarcastically.

"What?" Billy asked, now rubbing his metal leg and staring into his drink.

"Nothin'," Randy said.

***

Eight horsemen turned their eyes toward a riderless horse that sprinted by, as they leisurely advanced into Engine's Rest from the south. Each rider carried a sidearm low on his hip, the only visible weapon, and a small bedroll on the back of his saddle. A pack mule that followed behind, without a lead or guide-rope, carried the rest of their belongings.

Two of the men dismounted at the southern entrance to town, and their studs continued behind the rest of the party. Four of the men, along with the two extra horses and the pack mule, stopped at the stables to feed and water the animals. The other two men rode on down to the northern end of town.

The stableman, a bearded, fat man in his mid-thirties, greeted the fellows who said nothing in response. The friendly smile vanished off of the stableman's face and he said, "What 'cha need?" eyeing the strangers before him. One of the strangers, a man wearing an old boonie hat, was right in front of him and three others stood back by the horses and mule, which stood quietly and in a line, side by side.

The stableman could hardly look into the man's eyes. There was something about them, like they could see through anything. It was not the color or shape, it was almost like they were seeing his own soul, the stableman thought – and even though it was indeed quite unsettling, the stableman couldn't help but grin at the silliness of the thought.

The man in the boonie hat stood, staring at the stableman for a moment with a slightly puzzled look about him. The stranger in the hat smiled, and a look of recognition enlightened his face. "The horses," he said, "need feed and water." The man's voice creaked as though it lacked the practice.

The stableman glanced back at the horses and noticed they had no bridles or reins. His eyes glided back to the man in the hat. "Feed and water," the stableman responded. "I'm Alan," he added, hoping to sound surer of himself.

The stranger grinned and said, "Stow our gear," as he left with his companions. The horses and mule moved straight to the troughs, and the stableman, Alan, stood in place and pondered. He somehow knew that two more horses were on their way, but didn't know why.

***

The two other riders dismounted their horses at the northern edge of Engine's Rest, just in time to see a ratty looking bum tossed out of the tavern. They looked up at the sign and thought, "Jerry's."

The riders' horses picked up an easy trot to the stable by themselves and the two men stepped around the roughed up man on the street and into Jerry's Tavern. The pair looked like soldiers, but wore no uniforms. It was unmistakable that they had fought in the wars; most men that age had, but most had also moved on. These two, as well as their other companions at the stable, still looked sternly dangerous. Upon entering Jerry's, one man stood by the door, surveying the room as the other never broke step and neared the balding man with the mustache.

The man by the door kept his cowboy hat on and his hands by his side, near the pistol that was undoubtedly behind his coat. His stubbled face was weathered from a life outdoors and dusty from his recent ride.

The man who approached the mustache, removed his hat in stride. "Looking for Jerry," the man said to the mustache man.

"Found 'em, I guess," Jerry said, turning to find a pair of piercingly clear blue eyes that were uncomfortable to look upon. The blue-eyed stranger was bearded with a notable scar on his cheek, which was actually more noticeable in the beard, looking as if the beard had been deliberately parted on that side. "What can I get ya?" Jerry asked.

The man with the scarred beard grinned a crooked smile as he leaned one arm on the bar and looked back at his partner. "Well, my partners and I would like some chow, and we'd be lookin' for someone, too. Maybe you could help direct us?"

***

The LaMS wore an easily identifiable uniform: red beret, dark green blouse, and cargo pants. They had a carrier vest issued that could be set up according to the user's preference to accommodate magazines, grenades, and what have you, but Billy seldom wore his. Randy did. Randy had not been in the wars; he was too young to have really participated like his brother. They both had their berets secured under a shoulder flap, and they both carried sidearms; always. Their office had a small gun safe and radio which hadn't worked in years.

Billy and Randy turned toward the door as two more strangers walked in. Randy turned back to his brother and watched his eyes. Billy watched as the first man made his way to the bar. When he cut his eyes back to the second man standing at the door, their eyes met.

Randy saw a recognition cover Billy's face that looked a lot like fear. Randy felt the hair standup on the back of his neck and couldn't bring himself to turn around. His head was rushing as he watched his brother turn pale. Randy had never seen that look on his brother's face. Randy felt like the boogie man had escaped his closet and was right behind him now – fear kept him from looking to see.

"Billy," Randy whispered. "Billy," Randy whispered again and kicked his brother's metal leg.

Billy shook off the gaze and looked at his brother, "I… I think we need to get a rider out to QRF."

The Quick Reaction Force wouldn't be quick enough.

Chapter 6

Treason (Flashback)

Surrounded by deafening ambient noise and darkness, Jeremiah sat shoulder to shoulder with the other soldiers of his new unit within the fuselage of their transport craft. Everything seemed surreal, and he was trying to make sense of what was going on – certain it was all being blown out of proportion.

Amongst people he barely knew, and given his present location and circumstance, Jeremiah found it easy to be alone in his thoughts. He looked out through the half open ramp door at the rear of their transport. The night sky was littered with a dozen or so other transports, and that was just what he could see. He watched the shrinking lights of Fort Powell disappear into the horizon. He subconsciously felt for the envelope in his pocket before tightening his hold on the pistol grip of his weapon, placing his trigger finger above the trigger port.

Awakening Jeremiah from his preoccupation with personal thoughts, a loud boom thundered nearby, and their transport abruptly changed direction, dropping in altitude very quickly. The fuselage flickered with the lights of flares spewing from the tail of the aircraft. No one said a word or made a sound, but all soldiers were suddenly placed on edge. The sound of automatic cannons erupted with a fury and were only drowned out by the ferocious roar of the aircraft's guns, the crew gunner firing bursts into targets somewhere below them as they descended.

Jeremiah marvelled at how real this all seemed. It was real, but he still couldn't believe he was in it. A whole life of battles on TV or video games made it difficult to invest in the idea that this was not a ride at an amusement park, but was quite real and very serious, with nothing to do but sit, pray, and wait.

He looked over at the crew chief who was yelling something to the soldier next to him. He looked to his side and could see the in-visor display faintly light up in the men next to him. Jeremiah had only arrived at the company the morning before, and being called up so unexpectedly and urgently, there had been no time for the programming of his HELIOS System.

Staff Sergeant Booth, knowing Jeremiah's HELIOS wasn't functioning, leaned over and yelled over the ambient noise of the aircraft, "We're taking indirect fire and have to land early. Aircrafts have been lost." Even though he yelled, his voice was barely heard. And despite the yelling and the seriousness of the situation, Jeremiah thought that SSgt Booth seemed quite calm.

Jeremiah sat shoulder to shoulder with the others. Assault pack at his feet. Rifle slung around his shoulder and resting against his chest and abdomen. Nothing to say. Nothing to be done, except sit and wait to either land or crash. Judging from the rate of descent, he wasn't sure which he was in for. He could see more flares spew from his own bird, and he could hear more booms out in the dark sky, which would light up with each thunderous crash as if by lightning, somewhere beyond his sight.

The bird landed, and the ramp door dropped in what turned out to be a parking lot, and after spilling the troops out, was back in the air, flying low and fast, back toward the direction from which it had come.

Jeremiah didn't have time to notice other transports dropping their troops off some distance away as his Platoon moved briskly into a treeline and out of the open. Everyone was receiving instantaneous mission updates through their HELIOS Systems, except Jeremiah. It was already dark out, but noticeably darker still under the trees.

He felt blind and lost, and his squad leader was treating him like unwanted baggage. "Privates are so stupid," he kept complaining yesterday, "your rucksack goes here, not there." SSgt Booth was on the lower end of average height, with a stocky build, and very short hair hugging the side of his otherwise bald head.

It was still dark out now. The platoon gathered briefly at the treeline to get a head count and then dispersed, most orders being delivered through HELIOS. The stars and moon were hidden by cloud cover in the predawn morning. Had they not been in the woods, they would have seen that the street lights and billboards and businesses were all without power.

First Squad was to stay behind, pulling rear security, until the other two squads were able to recon the woods ahead. First Squad had to stay because Private Pratt's inoperable HELIOS could create communication problems and unit maneuverability and cohesion issues, so they would be called forward once the route was cleared and the objective beyond the woods was in sight.

From what Jeremiah could gather, no one had expected the heavy anti-air weaponry, and the thick, low-lying clouds prevented satellite or drone reconnaissance. The original briefing had them being flown directly to the location of a small militia terrorist group that had abruptly attacked and taken the next city and outlying area that would be just beyond the woods his platoon just entered. The plan had to change due to the heavy guns, and their platoon was now tasked with assaulting a particular anti-air weapon position. The goal was to clear those out, so that the Army's aerial transports could land troops and supplies closer to the target area.

Now Jeremiah lay in the dirt and soggy leaves feeling lost and like an outsider. While everyone else knew what was going on, where the objective was, as well as where the recon patrol had headed, he did not. His night vision device worked at least, creating a clear and green line of sight.

There were still the sounds of anti-air artillery thundering in the distance along with the other far off sounds of gunfire, both heavy and small. *We're missing it,* Jeremiah thought to himself, feeling a loss at the prospect that they'd miss whatever little fight there was.

In the quiet darkness, an abrupt nearby roar of relentless machine guns jolted Jeremiah's squad out of their apathy as smoke gracefully rolled into view in the direction of the recon patrol. The guns sounded loud and fierce, growling and belching burst after burst of heavy lead. The flickering light of muzzle flashes danced across the smoke. Jeremiah was surprised at how loud the guns sounded at such a distance away.

SSgt Booth jumped to his feet shouting, "AMBUSH!" and took off in a dead sprint down the same trail the patrol had used, right toward the ambush and smoke and machine gun fire. He watched as the others in the platoon jumped to their feet and followed close behind their squad leader... into an ambush...

Jeremiah was taken aback at their "charge right in" reaction and tried to get their attention, but no one heard him or cared and kept sprinting ahead. Jeremiah, conflicted and confused, took two steps toward them and then stopped himself. "Booth is an idiot," he said out loud, "so are the rest of 'em," he concluded with a grimace. Jeremiah turned and scrambled another direction, which to an onlooker, would likely have looked like he was running away.

***

Roughly 24 hours earlier, Jeremiah lay in his own bed, awake, waiting on his alarm to sound. He lay still while whining in his own head about Lilly and Trevor; he could still see Trevor's wide smile, and he couldn't help himself from wondering if they had shared the same sweet moments together that he and Lilly had. The idea turned his stomach.

He lay there, angry at himself for being so stupid. He got out of bed and finished packing his rucksack and duffle bag. He tried to avoid looking at himself as he shaved. He put on his uniform and boots and stood in his room still and quiet, and then pulled the yellowing envelope from his pocket and thought about throwing it, and the picture inside it, away in the trash, before just placing it back in his pocket.

He gathered his gear and left his house early without telling his parents goodbye; something he would later regret as he'd never see them again. It was the day he had to report to his unit, and he felt like speaking to no one.

His arrival at Fort Powell, his permanent duty station and new home, went fairly uneventfully, although the predawn motorcycle ride from his house brought on a mix of memories from the home he was leaving. Riding in the cool dark air, under the glow of streetlights made him think of his ride to Lilly's house the night of their first kiss. He remembered the smell of her hair and the feel of her soft lips. He now grimaced at the thought and turned his focus to speed.

The street lights illuminated the perfectly manicured lawn and shrubs outside Fort Powell's front gate. A cluster of tall pines lined one side of the base; the trees as well as the fort's brick and wrought-iron fence that circled the base created a boundary between FT Powell and the host town. It was sterile and boring; the very place Jeremiah hoped to experience adventure and excitement.

After entering the Army post and reporting to the base's reception building, he was shown to his battalion for inprocessing. From there, he and one other soldier were told to report to Bravo Company. Private Brown had been waiting when Jeremiah arrived; a support soldier assigned to Bravo's supply room. Jeremiah's inprocessing was rapid, one station and desk after another, never allowing time to sit. He, Like Brown, waited on various things or personnel, but they waited on their feet, like privates.

Finally, at the last processing station, the clerk finished what he was doing and, without looking up, told Jeremiah and Private Brown to report to Bravo. Looking out the battalion headquarters building and seeing a row of identically dull buildings in a row, Jeremiah asked, "which one is Bravo?"

"The one with a big 'B' above the door," the soldier at the desk answered in disdain, "with the cartoon *b*ayonet drawn through it."

Jeremiah just nodded, as he walked on. Made sense.

Jeremiah and Private Brown entered the company building. The first thing that Jeremiah noticed was the lack of space. Immediately by the door was a counter to the right and an office to the left. The office door was shut and blinds closed. On the door was a sign that read, "FIRST SERGEANT YATES" and another below it that read, "TOP – BECAUSE THAT'S WHERE I BELONG."

To the right, beyond the counter was a conference table and two other offices; one for the CO (Commanding Officer), Captain Moore, and the other for the XO (Executive Officer), Lieutenant Lawrence. A blue guidon was standing in between the two offices with a white "B" over white crossed muskets, the infantry symbol.

Specialist Addison was behind the counter and the only visible person present.

Jeremiah noticed him and said, "Hi," but was abruptly cut off.

"SIT DOWN!" SPC Addison interjected, "I'll get with you in a minute," and went back to... back to nothing, or that's how it looked to Jeremiah, at least.

Taken aback, Jeremiah and Brown looked at each other and sat down in the chairs resting in front of the first sergeant's office. Jeremiah looked around. He noticed that some of the ceiling tiles had brown water stains on them, in stark contrast to the immaculate perfection of every other surface. The vinyl tile floors were as shiny as glass. The room smelled of bleach, and even the doorknobs had a highly polished sheen.

As they sat, to their left there was a hallway leading to a solid wood door, which was closed, and lining the painted cinder block walls of the corridor were pictures of the chain of command ranging from the president down to the company commander and company first sergeant. For some reason that made Private Brown smile.

Suddenly a door flung open and the vinyl and plastic of the door's window blinds crashed loudly against the door. Jeremiah and Brown were both startled from their silent thoughts, flinching in their chairs, and Brown even let out a quick yell of surprise when the first sergeant jumped out of his office.

Jeremiah regained his military bearing immediately and jumped to his feet, assuming the position of parade rest, which was the modified position of attention that enlisted soldiers were to adhere to in the presence of higher ranking noncommissioned officers, which the first sergeant was. Jeremiah stood perfectly with his hands folded behind the small of his back and his feet shoulder width apart, toes angled out at 45 degrees. "First sergeant!" Jeremiah said, gazing steadfastly ahead into nowhere.

Brown sat in his chair and was grinning at Jeremiah's reaction.

First Sergeant Yates stood there for a moment. His mustache was obnoxiously military – thin and tapering from his nostril to the corner of his mouth, ridiculously close to that of Hitler's. His hair was cut in the highest of high and tights, with the sides of his head appearing to have been freshly shaven just moments earlier. His camouflage uniform was impeccable; no wrinkles and dangerously sharp creases.

He stood there with his arms on his hips as if he were superman and donned a somewhat comical grin. Looking at Brown he said, "What's he doing?" turning his eyes to Jeremiah and exaggeratedly eyeing him up and down before looking back at Brown for an answer, still grinning.

Brown was smiling too and shrugged in response.

The expression on the first sergeant's face hadn't changed, and still with that delightful grin, he cocked his head slightly to one side and said, "Is he standing at parade rest?"

As if the first sergeant and Private Brown were sharing a private joke, Brown answered, "He is, first sergeant," with a smile.

First Sergeant Yates wrinkled his nose a bit and smiling all the while said, "And are we supposed to stand at parade rest in the presence of NCOs?"

Jeremiah was starting to doubt himself and was confused by the discussion, but stood like a statue.

Brown chuckled a little before saying, "No." He chuckled and said "No," again like a giddy little girl.

First Sergeant Yates's smile slowly left his face, exchanging it for no expression at all, as he leaned closer to Brown, reaching eye level, and screamed, "YEEESSSS!"

Brown grimaced and flinched backward as the first sergeant began spewing spit onto Brown's face while screaming, "GET UP! GET UP! GET UP!"

Brown dared not wipe the spittle from his face, which was now bright red, and rose from his chair as quickly as he could to mimic Pratt.

As quickly as First Sergeant Yates began screaming, he stopped and returned to such a professional manner that one could wonder if the previous event ever really transpired. "Private Pratt, Private Brown, welcome to Bayonet. Specialist Addison will get you signed in and dispersed to your platoons." And with that, he casually reentered his office, closing the door.

Specialist Addison led them through the door at the end of the hall after scanning their orders and placing them on the company personnel roster. Jeremiah wasn't really expecting anything in particular beyond the door and was surprised at how different this bay was from the office area behind them.

There were no architectural finishes to speak of. There was no real ceiling, just exposed ductwork, electrical and communication conduit, steel joists and roof deck. The walls were unpainted gray cinder blocks, and the floor was polished concrete.

There appeared to be only one single serving restroom to accommodate all the soldiers there, both male and female. Jeremiah knew that women served in the infantry and had known that fact for a long time, but even so it felt strange seeing them moving and going about performing what Jeremiah only assumed were routine daily duties of infantry soldiers. There were only maybe three females that Jeremiah could see. He thought they looked like boyish guys, except for one. One was pretty, he thought. She looked tough and fit, but you could tell she was female. If he had been having a conversation on the subject with someone else it might have been comical, but in his head all of these thoughts simply occurred matter of factly. It looked like her name tag read "Parks."

"Don't stare at the females. Don't you have any manners?" SPC Addison asked, as he walked them in the bay.

Sergeant Parks heard the remark and caught Jeremiah's eye. Jeremiah immediately turned his head and tried to look natural. There had not been any females in his training classes, and aside from that, he didn't know a soul and could only speculate on how his break-in time would go. He glanced back over and Parks was looking at him. He returned his attention to Addison and thought nothing more of it.

With the exception of a few buck sergeants, it appeared to be only lower enlisted doing weapons maintenance. The soldiers had been busy getting every bit of dust or carbon swiped and scraped from their rifles and machine guns, though their tempo had slowed with the appearance of the two new guys.

"Sergeant Brayboy," SPC Addison called out as he led the two new guys over to the supply cage, which was just what it sounds like; a big cage where the supplies were kept. A supply sergeant and a soldier handled the supplies for their particular company. Staff Sergeant Brayboy was a large black man who nearly always kept a sly grin on his face. Jeremiah couldn't quite read the man at first, but he felt like the guy looked like a joker; unsure as to how devious the man was or not.

"New guys," Addison continued, "Brown is yours. Brown," Addison went on, pointing toward the cage, "Sergeant Brayboy."

"Pratt," Addison said, changing directions, "this way. You're in First Platoon," SPC Addison nodded toward one of the three small offices that were made of plywood walls in the company bay area. First Platoon's office was the first one.

The door was open and five men were inside the small office. A young lieutenant was standing and sharing some information with four other seated men, who were quickly identified as the platoon sergeant and the platoon's three squad leaders, who were making manual notes in their own notebooks.

"LT," Specialist Addison said as he lightly rapped on the door frame.

Without any hint of aggravation, Lieutenant Combs turned his attention to the door with a slight tilt of the chin and raised his eyebrows. The other men turned toward the door as well. The lieutenant's rank was yellow, meaning he was brand new himself. The lieutenant was fit and young, and Jeremiah thought it looked odd that he was instructing the other men, who were all older by at least 10 years or more, Jeremiah suspected.

"Your new soldier, sir. Just got here," SPC Addison informed.

Jeremiah snapped to attention.

LT Combs looked pleased. "Ah, an athlete," he proclaimed with delight and looked over to the other men in the office. "Sergeant Booth, looks like he's yours."

"SERGEANT DEAN!" SSgt Booth yelled, looking up at the exposed ceiling. He kept his seat and looked at Jeremiah; Sergeant Dean will square you away."

Sergeant Booth had evident mileage on that stocky frame and gray hairs to highlight that notion. This guy drank the Army Kool-aid and licked the bottom.

"Hooah," SSgt Booth added.

"Hooah," Jeremiah replied, not knowing whether it was confirmation or even if Booth's was a question, but parroting the word seemed like the thing to do.

"HOOAH," the platoon sergeant added with emphasis.

Sergeant Dean, a man in his early twenties who carried a wedding band on his finger, showed Jeremiah to the barracks and chow hall and briefed him on formation times before bringing him back to the company to get a rifle issued, which Jeremiah was then to clean along with the rest of the company's soldiers.

After Jeremiah was placed with his new squad, SGT Dean, a team leader for First Platoon, offered brief introductions. It was somewhat awkward, but went well enough; your average eighteen to twenty year olds in the infantry aren't a polished bunch. Soldiers were scattered all throughout the bay, divided mostly by platoon, with chairs for some and floor space for the rest.

Jeremiah sat quietly on the floor, disassembling his rifle, and taking in his new surroundings and who would be his new family. He was there, just not *in* yet, and he knew that would take time. He watched the others interact and laughed at some of the more clever one-liners.

He saw SGT Parks again. She was attractive. She was in Second Platoon's section of the room, giving her soldiers a hard time, and engaging in effortless banter as her squad performed their weapon maintenance. *She's one of them*, Jeremiah thought, and with a grin, *just a better looking one of them...*

Jeremiah's thoughts were broken by a swift slap to the back of the head, lurching his head forward. Fire immediately boiled Jeremiah's blood and he quickly turned to see who struck him.

"What'chu gonna do, private," a barrel chested sergeant challenged, as he bowed his chest, standing over Jeremiah.

Jeremiah said nothing. The name tape on the sergeant's blouse read, "Morgan." Sergeant Morgan.

"Yeah," SGT Morgan drawled, scanning the approval of the others, "didn't think so." SGT Morgan started to sit down, but stopped himself and looked back over at Jeremiah, who had started cleaning his rifle again. "You stupid privates," he said, "when I was a private, we stood at parade rest for NCOs."

Jeremiah continued cleaning his rifle, paying him no attention.

"Hey, private," SGT Morgan said, speaking louder now. "I'm talking to you," he said, nudging Jeremiah's back with his boot. "Stand at parade rest when you talk to me."

Jeremiah slowly and carefully set the pieces of his rifle on a rag and stood, assuming the position of parade rest – feet apart, hands folded behind the small of the back – and said, "Sergeant," as innocently and as indifferently as he could.

Sergeant Morgan smiled, "Drop, 'n give me fifty."

Jeremiah got down and repped out a continuous fifty push-ups. Not allowing himself to breathe any heavier than normal, nor letting himself pause a split second before completing all fifty. Finished, he stood and resumed parade rest.

A little disappointed the new private didn't seem bothered, Sergeant Morgan smiled again and said, "Clean your weapon, private."

Jeremiah returned to his spot on the floor, picked up the pieces of his rifle and resumed cleaning. With an uneasy feeling, he looked up in time to see Sergeant Parks turn her head away from him. Jeremiah looked back down and got back to work.

Other than that, SSgt Dean and SGT Morgan rode Jeremiah like an old bicycle, which is to say hard and without apparent concern. Making him empty all his gear, criticizing him when the items weren't folded, making him do push-ups. Or when his clothes got dirty from the push-ups, they'd punish him with flutter-kicks or burpees. They smoked him on and off for several hours and only quit when it was time for the day's last formation. It was apparently some initiation they put all the new guys through, but Jeremiah didn't care for it, and it was just the first day.

Lining up in their formation, Jeremiah was sure to ask the guy next to him where the gym was, and making sure SSgt Booth and SGT Morgan could hear added, "I wanna get in a workout sometime today." Jeremiah knew that if they didn't smoke him again right away, that they'd do their best tomorrow, but it was hard for Jeremiah to give in without offering something in return. In this situation, the most he could offer back to his military superiors was the idea that whatever they did to him, they couldn't reach the level of physical punishment that he could put himself through. Whatever they could put him through wouldn't be enough.

So far he hated them and was sure round two would start at tomorrow morning's PT. But he was wrong. He was awoken very late that night by SGT Morgan and SGT Dean. At first he thought it was round two right then, but leaving his barracks room, it looked like the whole base was awake, and aerial transports were touching down in the PT field.

"There's been a terrorist attack," SGT Dean said as they made their way to the company for their gear and weapons, "Some militia; domestic terrorists."

Jeremiah started to ask for more info, but SSgt Booth cut him off. "Shut your mouth, private," Booth said. "I don't want to hear one sound coming out of your mouth. We're going to war. You better learn fast, or *I'll* shoot you."

SGT Dean shoved Jeremiah from behind. "Go," is all he said as they entered the arms room.

***

Jeremiah had picked up little bits of information here and there since then, but still was mostly in the dark as to what all was going on. He found himself running alone in the dark woods, with the overwhelming sound of barking machine guns spewing flames as they spit lead into his platoon, and he assumed his squad who'd followed in after them.

SSgt Booth had sprinted right into what looked like a killzone to Jeremiah. And Jeremiah just hadn't been able to make himself follow. Right or wrong, he did what made sense to him, which in this case was to run the other way, away from the gunfire, in an effort to flank the ambush party.

In an all out sprint, Jeremiah bound up an embankment to slightly higher ground and circled toward the noise of the guns. The sound of the fully automatic gunfire was alternating, as if the guns were taking turns in a conversation, politely exchanging their viciously rapid burps. The talking guns meant there were at least two heavy machine guns, the sound of which grew more and more awe-inspiring as Jeremiah neared with each stride.

When, through his night vision, Jeremiah first saw the faint silhouette of who had to be one of the enemy troops, hunkered down in a fox hole and feeding the raging guns, his adrenaline spiked. The muzzle flashes of the dueling machine guns faintly lit up each of the two gun teams like flashing lightning.

Jeremiah slowed from his sprint, bringing his rifle up to his cheek, acting as much from what he'd seen on TV as what he'd learned in Basic, and placing the tiny red dot of his rifle scope on one man, squeezed his trigger twice, before changing his course to a sideways sidestep, targeting the next two men, squeezing off rounds again and again. Lilly, and pretty much everything else, was absent from his thoughts.

Three men had fallen to the ground before the others took notice. Jeremiah blew out the back of one's head before the rest actually located him. All the while, Jeremiah was getting closer and closer, shooting another three at close range, as the last remaining man pulled out a sidearm and released two rounds of his own, barely missing Jeremiah in the dark woods. Jeremiah quickly transitioned, falling to a knee and bringing the muzzle of his rifle within a few inches of the man's sternum before taking his life with the pull of the trigger.

Jeremiah stood, taking deep, heavy breaths, and dispassionately emptied his magazine into the fallen machine gun team for good measure.

Jeremiah's ears rang, though the guns were quiet now. He didn't dwell on it, being compelled by the screams and groans, he leapt over the enemy's foxhole and sprinted down the bank to what was left of First Platoon. Reaching the mess down below the bank, he barely noticed Staff Sergeant Booth and two other soldiers emerging to help render aid; running into the ambush after the gunfire had erupted, they must've been able to take cover and avoid being caught in the hail of lead.

The bodies were all warm and most torn to pieces and tattered like shredded paper and pulp. The smell of spilled feces and ruptured intestines was overwhelming; Jeremiah vomited several times as he tried placing tourniquets and rendering what first aid he could. He was covered in blood and none of it was his.

This was quite real and nothing at all like the military glory of his imagination.

He barely noticed SSgt Booth screaming for MEDEVACs somewhere off to the side, as he surveyed the grisly scene in astonishment. First Platoon wasn't the only casualty of the first battle, but it was the worst.

Afterward, in the first quiet moment he had in the dark on the flight out, he placed his hand in his pocket, placing his fingers securely around an old envelope with a photograph inside.

Chapter 7

Flagstaff

Sitting there in Jerry's Tavern, rubbing his prosthetic leg and staring at the newly arrived strangers who were busy questioning Jerry, Billy couldn't remember what the exact cause of the wars was. He was probably too young; too concerned with impressing girls and downloading the latest phone application. Even though he couldn't recall the specifics he did know that the basic cause was SPARTAN – a recollection that everyone seemed to share.

SPARTAN, like L&M and Raven International, had started out as a security contracting firm that the US used to fight its wars or to police its geopolitical interests across the globe, a profitable business relationship that spanned many years. The US could boast low casualty rates and overhead in any conflict, while the security firms didn't have to post the same statistics.

Billy couldn't remember how the politicians of the old US fueled the war machine to satisfy their personal interests and to line their own pockets. He probably never paid enough attention to know that the US set the stage for its own demise; that the old nation's propensity for war and foreign intervention, coupled with a fickle war-weary population, strengthened each of these security companies by perpetual war and security contracts. These companies were hauling in money hand over fist and growing larger, stronger, and more capable with each skirmish, each year.

Billy wasn't an idiot, mind you, he was just the typical, distracted young man who couldn't see the world past his own life. He wouldn't have seen the situation for what it was: an American feudal system.

The security firms' employees/soldiers were better paid, better outfitted, and better trained within their company than they ever would have been within the US military. As a result, the firms' employees were more loyal to their employers than they were to their nation. The US had not foreseen this. The US politicians were too busy counting their own profits to notice, and they were taken completely off guard when it blew up in their faces.

The little part that Billy knew was that SPARTAN wanted to monopolize the war market. They decided that they were tired of competing over government war contracts with cost proposals and decided they could simply eliminate their competition, literally. SPARTAN engaged in a surprise attack against both of its competitors' main offices.

This may be a little simplified, but it suited Billy's purposes; SPARTAN started the wars by attacking both L&M and Raven International in order to exist in a world with no competition. The United States tried to intervene, but it was too late. SPARTAN was too big to be controlled by the thinned US military and simply decided that they could ultimately run things more efficiently than the federal government, so they declared war on the USA.

When the US failed to control SPARTAN, and after learning SPARTAN's intentions, L&M opted to fight for their own control while Raven initially had elected to side with the USA. They had both been fed up with the bureaucracy that came along with working for the government. They could see the writing on the wall, but wanted the pie for themselves. While Billy didn't know and didn't understand all the specific pieces that led to the wars, he knew that it basically boiled down to SPARTAN trying to take over, which led to a three-way power struggle, which ended many years later with the fall of the USA and the tenuously drawn territory borders that were agreed upon in the treaty that finally ended the wars.

What Billy did remember in vivid detail was a group of SPARTANs that he had encountered during the wars: Flagstaff.

After his encounter, Billy heard other rumors as well…

That Flagstaff was a product of George Myre, an executive of SPARTAN. SPARTAN stood for Security, Patrol, Armament, Reconnaissance, and Training for Army and Navy, or something close to that, but Billy didn't really care, nor was he certain his recollection was correct.

And like the other security firms before the wars, SPARTAN had used HELIOS. Once its capabilities were lost, the security firms had to resort back to the old technology of Single Channel Ground & Airborne Radio System, or SINCGARS. Eventually, even the SINCGARS would be useless without the ability to dependably charge the batteries. The US and the security firms were forced to use communication methods that didn't require electronic power, such as letters, personal dispatch, smoke signals, carrier pigeons, and any other visual and manual means of communication like the old Civil War flag code.

Of course the rumors went on without Billy knowing what was accurate, embellished, or legend. But SPARTAN was an exception; at least, one SPARTAN unit would be. Through their flexibility and creativity, Myre realized that the mind was similar to a radio receiver or transmitter. Thoughts and memories are electrical patterns in the brain. They noted that when a married couple has been together for a number of years those patterns become more alike, which allows them to finish each other's sentences or have the same idea at the same time. This would also help to explain the "psychic" connection between twins or a mother to her child. As the electrical patterns of thought or memory become more similar, the more thoughts can be shared between individuals. Telepathy wasn't science fiction or magic, it was science.

"Think of a radio," Myre was quoted as saying in his initial pitch. "When two radios are set to the same frequency, communication is achieved." They assumed that when two minds are "tuned in" or in freq ("freek" – short for frequency), then communication is achieved, although non-verbal. This telepathy communication is more in the form of thought or imaging rather than words.

It was also believed, although unproven, that certain dreams could be a stream of another person's consciousness. In sleep, the brain isn't as distracted (so less interference) and is better able to pick up on other streaming signals (thoughts), especially if they're very emotional in nature – which is why people sometimes dreamed of dying or being killed. Perhaps they were dreaming about actual events through the eyes of the person experiencing them – they wake up at the point of death, because that's when the signal is cut. It was an idea that fascinated Myre, but he was never able to prove the connection.

Further research into the ability they were calling "The Silent Voice," or "Sierra Victor," showed that this transfer of thoughts happened to some degree with practically everyone on a subconscious level. The Silent Voice was also called "the Mind," or even referred to simply as "the Ability." They believed and argued that a rational person could be subconsciously persuaded to do something irrational when in a large mob or crowd. They compared this phenomenon to adding tin foil to an antenna.

Many minds focusing on a single event transmits louder than a single one. And since this type of communication takes the form of thoughts and not words or letters it comes as natural to the individual as coming up with the idea themselves. In fact, that's exactly what happens – an individual thinks the idea is his own.

Another point with this group-mind persuasion, is that the more traumatic or emotional a thought from a mind, the easier it is to transmit. The stronger the transmission, the more likely it is to be received.

Myre and SPARTAN also realized that not all minds are created equal. Some were excellent transmitters but could not receive, or vice-versa. There were also those that could seemingly do little to nothing, while others (although few) could receive and transmit equally well. They did note that the more time subjects spent together the more their minds got in tune.

The company selected nine men that "were of strong mind and of reasonable physical ability" to train initially on basic infantry tactics and to focus on communications with "the Silent Voice" in lieu of the unit's radio. This experiment was coded "Flagstaff."

Even though these men had already displayed talents in psychic abilities and passed the evaluation process for the Silent Voice, they still struggled in the beginning. People are programmed to encode their thoughts into words from youth. It became evident that breaking old habits was tough. It was hard to leave a thought as a thought and send it intentionally and even more difficult to differentiate between which thoughts were being sent and which were being created.

The more time they spent together the easier it became within the group. Flagstaff eventually began to move more fluidly and with more precision and speed than any other combat unit compared to it. Flagstaff did not have to turn their heads or be in ear- or eyeshot of anyone giving commands, they simply knew what must be done and what their members were doing instantaneously. There was no delay in information and seemingly no barrier or range restrictions. They became one mind. Eventually this led to some concerns.

During the training and team isolation they began to lose self-identities and began to share one group identity. Thoughts were streaming between members at such a constant rate that they began to lose sight of who was sending or receiving, there were only ideas, thoughts. A member of the team became just one part, one limb or extension of the organism Flagstaff. This seemed to only enhance their combat effectiveness, but was still not predicted and therefore somewhat troubling to Myre and the SPARTAN Board. As a result, expansion of the program was "put on hold until further observation and research could be compiled." They also kept the members of Flagstaff away from everyone else because "they're just weird," according to the official report's terminology.

Myre was intrigued, however, to find that once Flagstaff had begun riding horses, due to the depletion of resources the wars had contributed to worldwide, that they could communicate by mind with their animals as well. The more they trained with their beasts the stronger the bond. Myre thought that the members of Flagstaff looked like centaurs, riding aggressively without the need for reigns, shooting freely and smoothly from horseback. In fact, Myre had renamed the unit "Centaurus," but the name never stuck and ended up going no further than the official, classified file. To Myre's disappointment, Flagstaff would forever be known as Flagstaff.

Despite Myre's disappointment with his experimental unit's name, it was Flagstaff that once again emerged on top when most armies were struggling with the adaptation of having lost the combustion engine, their communication devices, and especially with the loss of HELIOS. It was as if Flagstaff had been favored by HELIOS himself.

Billy wasn't sure about the beginning of the wars or exactly how Flagstaff was created, but he knew how he lost his leg. He knew enough to be afraid.

Chapter 8

War (Flashback)

Inside the safe zone, the street was now filled with smoldering debris and body parts under the spotlight of the warm sun. The Quick Reaction Force arrived with guns roaring, spitting brass and spewing smoke; sending their heavy suppressive fire over the head of one lone soldier they pulled up behind, who was also firing his rifle into the buildings in front of them.

The four trucks came to a stop among the smoking wreckage, carelessly and frantically firing round after round for several minutes while the QRF commander advanced on foot to the dismount who was still firing into the buildings as hot empty brass rained to the pavement.

"HEY!" the commander yelled, trying to be heard over the gunfire, as he grabbed the soldier's shoulder.

The soldier, whose uniform was coated with dirt, sweat, soot, and splotches of blood, shrugged the hand off of himself as he turned defensively, but was immediately relieved to see a friendly.

"HENDRICKS NEEDS A MEDIC!" he shouted with wide eyes.

The QRF commander looked at the soldier's uniform; his rank insignia was corporal, and his name tape read, "Pratt."

The gunfire ceased and dismounts were pouring out of the gun trucks forming a defensive perimeter as survivors were searched for, as medics rushed out to render aid to CPL Pratt's mate, Hendricks, and as a squad rushed to the entryway of the building they had destroyed with their gunfire.

"What happened?" the QRF commander finally asked, as Hendricks was being placed on a stretcher.

Jeremiah answered, "Ambush. I think it was SPARTAN. They ambushed our convoy."

"Where's your helmet?"

Jeremiah said, "Don't know," glancing upward, as if he was just now realizing he wasn't wearing it.

"Your HELIOS is damaged," the commander commented as he looked Jeremiah over. "We didn't have a reading of your vitals or position. We weren't sure we'd find survivors."

Jeremiah shrugged as they made their way to the gun trucks evac, "Uh, yeah... I guess it's broken."

The commander surveyed the scene as they reached the evac vehicle and saw several wrecked convoy vehicles in a broken and contorted line, now blocking the street: two gun trucks and one supply truck that were completely destroyed, and two other supply trucks that, despite bullet holes and superficial blast damage, were otherwise alright.

"You were in one of those supply trucks?"

"Gun truck," Jeremiah said, nodding to what was left of the lead gun truck, as he climbed in the truck next to Hendricks's stretcher.

The commander looked and saw the lead gun truck laying in two crumpled pieces, now engulfed in flames and black smoke. A bloody boot rested just outside the back half of the truck, and a burnt torso lay awkwardly next to the front half.

"You were in that?"

Jeremiah wiped his forehead, "Where's the air transports?" ignoring the commander. "Hendricks is in bad shape."

"We're rolling out now," the commander said, climbing in his vehicle as a whole platoon was arriving to clean up the scene and pursue what was left of the ambush party. "No air transports; we can't get anything bigger than a small drone in the air."

Jeremiah looked over at him in surprise, but said nothing.

"Enemy air defense and fuel rations," the commander added, "just can't get anything in the air." The commander turned in his seat to look at his cargo. "Your man Hendricks will be okay. We'll get back to Powell in plenty of time. He'll be okay."

Jeremiah removed his magazine, looked at it, and slapped it back in its well, then lay his head back for the ride home. He had three bullets left.

Body bags were being loaded in the other vehicles.

Nearing the gate of Fort Powell, Jeremiah no longer thought much about how it had changed since the conflict began. On his first day at the fort as a private, the entry had manicured lawns and flower gardens, well trimmed hedges, and a thick patch of pines that lined one entire side of the fort, east of the gate. Now, all the pines had been leveled to open up line of sight and were left in place as a field obstacle. The lawn and flowers were gone, mostly beneath the dirt mounds and barriers that had been erected for wartime protection.

Jeremiah didn't notice anymore. Today he was preoccupied with the losses his team had just sustained, and he dreaded the faces of the others once he returned to the company.

***

Everyone watched in silence as Jeremiah walked through the door. He looked just awful, and he walked in as if he hadn't noticed anyone was there. Still filthy and coated by the elements of battle, he walked silently to a table where he began removing his body armor and inoperable HELIOS.

Still, without any word, everyone returned their silent gaze to the screen on the wall which was silently playing a newsreel of drone footage from that morning's convoy ambush. They watched the entire event on the screen just after it had transpired. They watched more of their comrades slaughtered by rocket attacks and small arms fire. They watched SPARTAN's brazen daytime attack, and so far inside the safe zone. They watched Jeremiah on screen and now at his table.

Jeremiah removed his gear, placed his rifle on the table and sat. He didn't want to be there and didn't feel like doing anything, but he broke his rifle down and began cleaning it.

He tried ignoring the others, who had now begun whispering.

"No one in Pratt's team ever lives long..."

"How did he survive that?"

He glanced over his shoulder to the screen and saw the drone's view of the first rocket. Jeremiah turned back to his rifle, not wanting to watch. It was still replaying in his head. He had never seen the first rocket but had just felt the effect of it; the thunderous boom and the earthquake of the shockwave.

He noticed the others watching, but tried not to. *Tourists*, he thought to himself in self-righteous disgust. Subconsciously he knew they weren't wrong or bad for watching the battle replay on the screen, but in that moment, emotionally and physically fatigued, there is nothing they could have been doing that he wouldn't have thought ill of.

What could I have done differently? Jeremiah wondered as he brushed dust and carbon off of his rifle. After the first rocket had catastrophically disabled the second vehicle in the convoy, the vehicle which was directly behind his own, Jeremiah immediately yelled for his gunner to return fire when his truck was hit with another disorienting crash of thunder from a second rocket.

Staff Sergeant Parks walked over and placed a bottle of water on the table next to Jeremiah. "You okay?" she asked.

Jeremiah nodded without looking up. Parks left him alone.

Jeremiah noticed SFC Booth approaching him, but acted like he had not. Jeremiah remembered the deafening silence, followed by the ringing in his ears, as his vehicle was torn and tossed by the rocket blast. Carter's legs fell to the truck's deck while Jeremiah watched his torso fall from the gunner's nest outside. It all replayed in his mind again and again, just as it replayed for everyone on the screen now. He recalled reaching for the button on his helmet to bring up his heads-up display, and after feeling around his cheek for longer than it should have taken, he had finally realized that his helmet had been knocked off his head in the blast.

SFC Booth stood at the end of the table where Jeremiah sat cleaning his rifle.

Jeremiah pretended not to notice him standing there while the day's earlier events continued to unfold again in his mind; behind Carter's severed legs, where Weeks had been sitting, the vehicle was completely sheared off and pluming black smoke. Only now did it occur to Jeremiah that Weeks had to be dead; at the time all Jeremiah knew was they were under attack and that sitting was not a strategy. Jeremiah grabbed his driver, Hendricks, by the shoulder to see if he was okay, then yelled at him to get out of the truck.

"How's Hendricks?" SFC Booth finally asked.

Jeremiah Shrugged, "Not good, but I think he'll live." Jeremiah never looked up, not wanting to speak to the man at all, although he was relieved that Booth was not lecturing him, but only inquiring about a soldier.

Jeremiah didn't have to look at the screen; he remembered kicking his door open and nearly falling to the ground. He remembered the sight of damaged and twisted vehicles with black smoke billowing from frantic flames as body parts lay around them. He remembered the sound of small arms fire, first faintly, then building into a crescendo of rapid gunfire, the metallic sound of bullets striking the vehicle's bodies. He remembered seeing the black SPARTAN uniforms emerge from the surrounding building, firing their weapons into the convoy as they rushed to the cargo trucks.

They must not have expected any survivors from the gun trucks after the rocket attacks because Jeremiah had gone unnoticed by the SPARTAN ambush party until he began killing them.

"And..." SFC Booth prodded.

Jeremiah just looked up at him in confusion.

"I'm a little surprised that I have to go over this," SFC Booth said. "Your ACE report; why haven't you given it?'

Jeremiah looked around the room.

"I had to ask about Hendricks," SFC Booth said, looking grim. "What about the others? Your Ammo, Casualties, and Equipment, what about them?" SFC Booth was now standing rigid, looking like he was either ready to pounce or to defend an attack.

In response, Jeremiah turned to the screen playing the drone footage behind him, then turned his eyes and pointed them into Booth's.

SFC Booth reeled, took a step forward, pointing his finger at Jeremiah Pratt but was interrupted before any words could shoot from his open mouth.

"Sergeant Pratt," a familiar voice called out behind Booth. The owner of the voice was approaching them both and said, "Your orders," as he reached across the table, handing the paper to Jeremiah. "Guess they printed them out for you because your HELIOS was damaged."

Jeremiah, taken aback, slowly took the paper, saying, "Mick," in disbelief. He was now feeling even more disoriented. Jeremiah hadn't seen Mick since basic training, and Mick was enlisted with orders to Fort Drum at the time, but Mick was standing in front of him and was no longer wearing the insignia of an enlisted man.

"Lieutenant Towers," Mick said with a slight grin. "Field Commission."

"He's our new LT," SFC Booth said flatly. "I'll get Corporal Pratt squared away with a new HELIOS issue."

"It's Sergeant Pratt now," Mick said, nodding toward the orders. "Sergeant Pratt, I'm sorry about your losses today and wish there was more time to grieve and hold a memorial, but since we don't have that time, maybe it's some consolation that we've just been tasked with a mission to root out and eliminate the element responsible."

Jeremiah nodded, trying to hide any emotion. The abrupt promotion, after this day's events felt like poison almost; those with him had died and he not only gets away without injury, but gains a promotion. Something about it was sickening.

"There'll be a platoon brief in an hour," Mick continued. "SFC Booth, I need to go over a few things with you now," he added as he turned to leave.

Neither Booth nor Pratt exchanged any more words. SFC booth left with LT Mick Towers. Jeremiah sat back down and stared at his rifle. Jeremiah couldn't remember how many he killed or how many got away, he just recalled firing viciously at his attackers, throwing grenades, and moving, always moving and shooting.

Jeremiah stoically reassembled his rifle, stood and walked up to the arms room, "I need ammo."

***

After briefing his new platoon the mission plans, Mick checked their gear before they were to set off. SPARTAN was believed to have been after a specific item, the item being classified and too sensitive in nature to allow a platoon of grunts to know much about. As it turns out, had it not been for Jeremiah Pratt, SPARTAN would have been successful. And now First Platoon was just tasked to attack and eliminate the SPARTAN force responsible for the ambush.

Weapons were clean, HELIOS was up and running with the preprogrammed radio frequencies for the Platoon and Squads. Everyone's vitals were registering. Current maps were loaded with each soldier showing as a blue dot and each vehicle as a large blue rectangle.

"SPARTAN uses HELIOS too," SFC Booth said as he walked along the inspection with LT Towers, "That's why it's such a struggle."

"Huh?" Mick asked, no longer walking.

"Yeah," Booth affirmed, "that's why we're having such a hard time with 'em – it's the first time the US has faced an enemy that's also had a HELIOS System."

"SPARTAN uses HELIOS...," Mick said to no one as he looked back up at the screen which was still showing loops of that morning's ambush.

Mick started to say something but stopped himself. It looked like something was wrong with him, but no one commented on it. SFC Booth stared at him with a little grin, assuming Mick was green, inexperienced and confused, letting fear take root.

"These are all wrong," Mick said, suddenly looking confident again. "Remove your HELIOS and let the comm sergeant correct them."

For a second no one said or did anything.

"Let's go!" Mick shouted.

As the Platoon began switching off and removing their HELIOS for one last systems check, SFC Booth said, "Sir, this isn't necessary, we need to move out."

"Thank you Sergeant Booth, please remove your HELIOS."

There was whispering and murmuring, but once all HELIOS systems had been removed, Mick told the Platoon to place the devices in the gun trucks.

"In the trucks?" SFC Booth questioned. "I thought you said comm needed to run another check, sir?"

Mick knew they were confused, and before anyone else could protest, he pointed to the screen, "Look, SPARTAN is using our HELIOS. Look!"

The whispers continued as all eyes were watching the screen again.

The events were still fresh and replaying in Jeremiah's head. He looked up at the screen along with everyone else and saw an aerial view of the battle, now mixing in with his firsthand experiences; the feel of blood splatter on his neck, the way his rifle stock felt against his cheek, the wind chime sound of spent brass falling to the ground, and the smell of carbon and gunsmoke... His friends dying... But then he saw it.

"No, sir," SFC Booth said loudly, with no effort to conceal his frustrated contempt, "everybody, get your HELIOS and put it on."

"No, he's right," Jeremiah said, also pointing at the screen. "He's right. SPARTANs have been all over us this entire war, but here, *look*, they don't see me."

Jeremiah had wiped his face off, but hadn't had a chance to change uniforms, and he could tell the dirt and blood was a reminder to his new squad that the last men that went into battle with Pratt hadn't come back, but Jeremiah ignored it.

The grainy bird's eye view of the battle showed Jeremiah Pratt stumble out of his severely damaged gun truck, with no one paying him any attention at all, until he had shot several of them.

SFC Booth stood silent like everyone else, staring at the screen. "But..."

"Sergeant Pratt's HELIOS was damaged," Mick said while the entire platoon watched the drone footage. "Our own people didn't know he was alive or there."

"But sir," Booth said again, now as if he were trying to convince himself, "I mean, that doesn't really prove anything. And we're out of time, we have to go now."

"They've been on us ever since the start," Mick said, "because they can see our HELIOS. They know where we are and what we're doing." Mick paused. He looked around the platoon. "Since this war started, they've had the jump on us at every step," he continued, " pretty much with the only exception of today."

"We're blind without it, sir."

"They're blind without it," Mick said pointing to the looping newsreel. "Stack your HELIOS Systems in the back of your trucks. Make sure all mics are off."

"Sir, you should get permission from the TOC," Booth said, since the Tactical Operations Center was the nucleus of battlefield command.

Mick grinned, "We're out of time, Sergeant Booth; we have to go now."

***

The sun was setting into the horizon of a beautiful red sky. The convoy of gun trucks stopped long enough for everyone to dismount except for the drivers and gunners. When the last foot left the last vehicle, the convoy started off again, disappearing down the road.

The streets were deserted here, outside the safe zone. Intelligence had shown the remnants of the ambush party had retreated to a small unmarked outpost just outside the US safezone, which they believed housed a slightly larger, but hastily established forward operating force of SPARTAN.

The platoon followed Mick's lead and silently assembled into platoon formation and ventured off road through a patch of woods.

SSgt Parks rushed up alongside Jeremiah, "You think this new LT knows what he's doing, or's he gonna get us all killed?"

Jeremiah looked at her, "He knows what he's doing."

She looked back at him like he was an idiot and whispered, "We're losing this war, and he took away *the tool* that eliminated anyone from competing with the US in battle."

Now Jeremiah looked at her like she was the idiot.

SSgt Parks smiled, understanding the point.

Jeremiah whispered, "If SPARTAN is looking in on our HELIOS, they'll think we're in the trucks and won't be looking for us in the woods."

"If we get lost in the woods, it may not matter," SSgt Parks said and backed off, back to her squad.

Coming to the edge of the woods, Mick brought the platoon to a halt with a hand signal. With another gesture of his hand, the entire platoon took a knee, spread apart by three to five meters between each of them.

Mick knelt beside Jeremiah, and they both peered across the small field with tall, flowing grass and into the cluster of industrial buildings beyond it, which they believed to be temporarily housing the SPARTAN element.

"Think they're still there?" he asked.

Jeremiah, still surveying the location in front of him, responded, "Well, if they are there, maybe they really are looking at our HELIOS, and we can't see 'em, cause they're all on the side by the road."

Mick looked at his watch. "Well," he said, "guess there's only one way we'll find out."

He stood up and gave the signal to move forward.

The platoon moved quietly through the tall grass. A shiver went through Jeremiah; it was like playing war as a kid: no HELIOS, just dismounted Army men sneaking cautiously through a field.

The platoon had seen no one, nor any sign of anyone being there at all as they left the field and began crossing the concrete roadway and old loading lanes, until two men in dark uniforms walked casually out of one building and into view.

The two men stopped like deer in headlights, and their appearance actually caught First Platoon off guard, most of them assuming the intel was bad or old and that no one would be there.

Mick raised his rifle and shot the two men, ending the uncomfortable silence, kicking things off.

Dark uniforms started spilling out from around corners and out of buildings, clearly taken off guard, but firing wildly.

First Platoon returned fire and had the initiative. Jeremiah took his squad to flank the right side, securing one building at the corner of the compound and killing two SPARTAN occupants.

SFC Booth yelled for Jeremiah, "Split up your squad and stay here!"

Jeremiah nodded at first, but as he was about to obey, he didn't understand the order. He wasn't sure how he could adequately control two divided teams, one of which he would lose complete sight of, if he were to send them ahead without him. And with no reliable comms on this mission, splitting up like that just didn't seem to make sense, so he ignored it and went on ahead with his team intact. He was careful to look through windows or around sides of buildings to make sure he wasn't getting too far ahead or separated from the rest of the platoon – as they'd catch up, he'd lead his squad to another building or another area ahead.

The SPARTANS were resisting, but were also clearly out of sorts and disoriented; although, they were beginning to settle into a decent defensive perimeter.

Jeremiah felt like his team was making good progress. So far all were uninjured and had taken several lives along with the ground they had secured.

Watching from the flank, he could see the progress of most of the squads and teams: Mick firing away, yelling orders and moving ahead, looking natural in his role as an officer in charge; SFC Booth yelling in fury, which made Jeremiah grin, though he couldn't hear and didn't care what he was shouting.

SSgt Parks's squad was bounding ahead taking heavy fire, but still advancing.

The unprepared SPARTAN force had sustained heavy casualties with a remaining few being forced to fall back into one large concrete industrial building, firing furiously and lobbing grenades and rockets from it. One rocket trail led straight to Staff Sergeant Baker's squad, killing three and wounding four more.

SSgt Parks, whose squad had sustained two casualties, directed heavy suppressive fire into the building while they advanced forward, hoping to storm the building when the time came.

Jeremiah's team had secured nearly an entire half of the compound themselves and were staged at buildings across from the SPARTAN Alamo, looking to take shots where they could, but not advancing across the large roadway that had become a no-man's-land.

From there, Jeremiah could see the rest of the platoon pretty well.

Mick hunkered down behind a concrete wall and looked at his watch. He grabbed the flare gun out of his assault pack and fired, sending the flare into the air like a tiny red comet. SFC Booth took out a small, hand-carried spotlight, using it to light up one side of the SPARTAN's stronghold. A moment later, a torrent of heavy machine gun fire roared from the platoon's gun trucks that had been waiting a safe distance away for Mick's signal. The heavy metal being played from gun trucks' weapon turrets were turning the concrete fortress into swiss cheese.

After the onslaught, all guns stopped. The air was thick with the smell of carbon and silica, and aside from those rendering first aid on the wounded, all eyes and guns were focused on the now heavily damaged target building. There was no sound, and the only visible movement was smoke and dust floating out of the windows in the full moonlight of the early night.

SSgt Parks's squad was to clear the building, with Jeremiah's squad to remain where they were and provide oversight. SSgt Parks's squad stacked along the outside of the building, ready to breach as wounded were being carried to the gun trucks and LT Mick Towers was on the radio, trying to reach the TOC.

SFC Booth made his way next to Jeremiah for a better view of SSgt Parks's squad. Booth and Jeremiah watched silently as her squad shotgunned the door and stormed inside. Jeremiah held his rifle to his cheek, scanning the windows of the building through his scope, feeling tense anticipation. He lightly touched his trigger with his index finger, as if he were making sure it was still there in case he needed to pull it, and then placed his finder back on the magazine well. All was quiet.

"Somebody's got to be in there," SFC Booth whispered, but before he could complete the sentence an eruption of gunfire sounded off in a fury, looking like strobe lights or lightning through the building windows.

Everyone flinched backward, except Jeremiah, as he sprinted forward and into the building without the faintest hesitation. SFC Booth yelled, "PRATT!" but to no one that cared. Jeremiah was halfway to the building when his squad began taking fire from the second floor windows. Jeremiah disappeared inside the building as his squad took cover the best they could as they were returning fire. Mick held the heavy guns of the gun trucks off, so that they wouldn't kill any friendlies inside.

The gunfire in the building began to wane, and SFC Booth, cursing Pratt's reckless foolishness, was trying to organize Pratt's squad to enter the building next, until a man in a dark SPARTAN uniform screamed as he was being tossed out of a window, and two or three gunshots later, there was silence.

Private Brown stumbled out of the building's door, screaming, "FRIENDLY! FRIENDLY!" with another soldier crawling out behind him yelling for medics.

SFC Booth and Pratt's squad just stood there for a moment, taken aback, as Jeremiah exited the door, cradling SSgt Parks, whose arms were wrapped around his neck, her head buried in his chest.

In the dark, it was hard to see the blood leaking down her arm and soaking through her pants, but it was clear that she was hurt.

"There's more injured inside," Jeremiah said urgently, with clear concern in his voice, as he carried Parks to safety. "Building's clear…"

SFC Booth sent Pratt's squad inside to help with the wounded and to double check and ensure the building was indeed clear.

SPARTAN's dead were lined up, the number being close enough to intel reports, and the bodies and location was searched for additional intel. Not much was found since SPARTAN's standard operating procedure was to remotely disable their own HELIOS in the event of capture or kill, so it yielded nothing, which was unsurprising.

Later in the evening, Mick found Jeremiah keeping watch alone a short distance away from his squad. "See anything?" he asked.

Jeremiah shook his head, "Nothin'."

Mick took a seat next to him in the dark parapet shadow, cast by the full moon, "The medevac should be arriving back at Fort Powell anytime now."

Jeremiah nodded, "Yeah."

"Staff Sergeant Parks should be okay," Mick said, eyeing Jeremiah.

"Yeah," Jeremiah said, looking into the vastness of the clear night air, now unencumbered by light pollution, "She's tough. She'll be fine."

Mick just watched Jeremiah for a moment. "What was that back there?" he finally asked.

Jeremiah looked over at him.

"I mean, you're a natural leader, a great soldier," Mick said. "But charging in the building like that... what was that?"

Jeremiah, looking a little perplexed said, "I was going to help."

"What about your squad?"

"They should have followed me."

Mick shook his head, "Their squad leader left them without a word, with no direction." And looking into Jeremiah's eyes said, "You carelessly left your squad to charge into a blind firefight..." He paused a moment before continuing with, "You didn't know what you were running into, and you could have made a bad situation worse."

"What was I supposed to do, stand there and watch?"

"C'mon," Mick said with a half grin. "Organize your squad and raid the building."

Jeremiah sat silent.

"There's reasons why it took so long to allow women in combat roles," Mick said.

Jeremiah looked up, "You think I have some emotional need to protect women?"

"I think you have too much of an emotional connection to Sergeant Parks."

Jeremiah scoffed.

"No, no, we all saw you. Just... be careful."

Jeremiah didn't say a word or move his head, but he acknowledged with his eyes.

"You are the luckiest guy I've ever heard of," Mick said with genuine wonder.

Jeremiah laughed.

"Do you know what wisdom is, Sergeant Pratt?"

"Wisdom is the application of knowledge, Lieutenant Towers," Jeremiah said with a sarcastic tone.

Mick nodded, "Wisdom is the appreciation of reason, the careful wielding of knowledge, and the recognition that the best solutions come from careful consideration, as opposed to the whims of random emotions."

Jeremiah looked back up to the stars and moon.

"It's alright to have feelings, but you're an NCO, a leader of men, and must be governed by reason and not by feelings," Mick said, looking out into the sky himself.

"We gonna be here long?" Jeremiah asked.

"Probably not. Not after the report I sent back with the wounded." Mick added, "They'll want to bring us in and debrief us after they read what I had to say about HELIOS. And if it's right, everything's about to change."

"Think anyone's actually pulling guard?" Jeremiah asked softly.

"Nah," Mick answered in nearly a whisper, holding his gaze above, "the sky's too beautiful."

Chapter 9

LaMS to the Slaughter

After watching in disbelief the young fool with the large belt buckle kill his own friends and their horses before being dragged back into town by his own horse, Jeremiah took a bag and a rifle from the dead, leaving them where they lay, before descending Watchman's Hill for the tree line. On his back, he toted the bag he found and had the newly acquired carbine at the ready. He was certain that the gunfire would have attracted unwanted attention from anyone within a few miles.

Jeremiah entered the woods, walking a zigzagged course before coming to a rest once he had gotten deep enough into the brush. It was more than paranoia; it was years of habit ingrained forever from nearly a lifetime of war and efforts to stay alive. It was natural for him to forgo nighttime fires, which would ruin his night vision and pinpoint his location in the dark; just as it was second nature to make erratic changes in direction when trying to evade anyone – even if he wasn't sure there was anyone to evade.

Jeremiah Pratt stood still for a few moments and listened, looking grizzled with his beard and long hair tucked behind his ears. He unconsciously pulled a pair of old dog tags from his pocket, running them between his finger and thumb, as he strained his senses to listen for any sound and to scan the horizon. He heard the wind blowing the leaves, the chatter of squirrels and birds chirping, but nothing else. No heavy-footed movements. No talking. No distant whispers. When Pratt was confident that no one was near, he rested his new carbine at arm's reach against a tree, took the newly acquired bag off of his shoulders, and sat down. He opened the bag hoping to find some food, water, or maybe some supplies.

While he had been walking he could tell there was no water. Fluids feel a certain way when carried on foot, and his short trek off the hill was absent of that feeling. He had wanted water and soon would be needing it, but would not second guess his decision to grab that bag over the other. The temptation was always there to nag yourself into thinking that you "should have done it this way, or that way;" in this case, "should have grabbed the other bag, or taken more time to look for water…" But there was never any real use in that. Pratt knew that there are times when quick decisions had to be made, and you must make those decisions work. Jeremiah could still hear Mick's words: "Anybody can make a decision, although many times they don't, but the trick is in seeing those decisions through."

Pratt would not let himself get worked up over the water. He'd eventually find some; he always did. He knew that worrying wasn't going to make it rain, so he sat there and began rummaging through the bag to see what it did hold.

Pratt was a little dismayed to find no food, but he did find some paracord, which was always useful, a pair of socks, and some underwear. Pratt discarded the underpants, making note to wash his hands the first chance he got. In the bag he also found an old towel, some random papers (which he would keep for kindling); and an old key chain with several trinkets on it, which Pratt tossed to the side. It was worthless and had the chance of making noises, plus there was no sense in adding any weight without good reason. Years in the Army had taught Pratt to keep his gear as light as possible and to take care of his feet, if nothing else.

Pratt was happy, overall, at his score. He had some paracord, a bag to put food and water in when he eventually happened upon some, and the socks. Pratt was happy to have a fresh change of socks, and once changed out, he would be eager to leave Engine's Rest behind and be on his way.

Pratt began unlacing his boots when he happened to glance back at the keychain he had carelessly tossed aside. Amongst the assorted keys, trinkets, and mini-tools, something caught his eye. Pratt had one boot off and stopped moving as he brushed a long strand of gray hair out of his eye and squinted, as curiosity forced him to reach for the keychain for a closer look. He had thought his eyes were playing tricks on him, but once he grabbed the key chain and put his fingers on one particular item in the assortment, his heart skipped a beat. With the item in hand he sat back and held it in his hands, just staring at it in disbelief. Jeremiah could feel the rhythm of his heart picking up pace and the adrenaline welling up within him. *How?* he thought to himself. *How could these people have this?* He had to know, which meant that he had to go back and into Engine's Rest. His current plans would have to wait, and the dangers of those who pursued him would have to take a backseat to this; he'd let the world burn down now. He couldn't ignore what he'd found on the key chain.

Pratt neared the outskirts of Engine's Rest at dusk. He walked as quietly as a whitetail along the town's perimeter and knelt down, carbine at the ready, watching and listening. They were there, waiting on him. He didn't know how many there were, but saw two, and was sure there were more. He even saw some LaMS scurrying about, busy with security stuff, he guessed. He should've left, should have packed up and headed back toward his objective, but he couldn't.

They didn't seem to be on guard. Pratt suspected that by now they knew that he had passed through the town, so he surmised that they wouldn't be expecting him to turn back up there. Pratt hoped that the dark would be his ally as he cautiously crept into Engine's Rest. He'd have to find out where the Champ was; the idiot with the belt buckle.

***

Tyler woke up in a bed surrounded by the night. His head hurt, his mouth was dry, and he had no recollection of how he had gotten there. His clothes were off, and he could see them lying over the rail of the bed's footboard. He couldn't see much else, although the moon shone through the window in a bluish hue.

Tyler sat up in bed and grimaced as his head pounded from the sudden movement. He could tell that he had been bathed clean and just then noticed the bandage on his left elbow and the big one that wrapped around his chest and back.

He swung his legs around and lighted off the bed where he had to steady himself against the wall. The floor creaked loudly as he applied his weight onto the wood floor. "Sounds like my mom," he whispered, and grinned to himself. His head wasn't hurting quite as badly and had settled into a slight ache. He opened the window and peered out into the night. His bladder felt full, but he couldn't see a bedpan, not that he really looked; so he used the window. Tyler stood up straight, stretching while he passed water out of the second floor window of Engine's

Rest's only hotel. Chuckling briefly to himself, he whispered "Be gone with you!"

Once Tyler had certified that the flow had ceased, he turned for his pants. The floor moaned with every step. It occurred to Tyler that it was odd that he felt the need to whisper and to move slowly over a noisy floor when he was alone, but being loud in the dark silence was something that even Tyler subconsciously would not do. Tyler slid into his pants and began to fasten his belt buckle that read "Champ" on it. "Yes you are," Tyler whispered.

His clothes had been cleaned. There were some stains on them and nothing had been mended, but they had definitely been washed. Tyler had been feeling good as he picked up his shirt, but when he looked at the tears and holes in it as he put his arm through the sleeve, he remembered Ted and Jim. He paused for a moment as if he were undecided whether he should finish dressing or not, but only for a moment. Tyler Johnson was not the type to stay down. He slid on his shirt, grinning as he buttoned it up, and said without the whisper, "You're gonna pay for this." He was speaking as if to Jeremiah Pratt.

"Pay for what?" a voice in the dark room said back. Tyler's stomach sank to his knees. He was terrified out of his mind – too scared to breathe. "Do you need anything?" the voice said again, as a large figure appeared to rise out of the shadows on the room's floor. Tyler screamed and jumped backward, smacking his head on the wall with a thud. His footsteps were heavy and loud on the wood decking. Tyler's body ached all over, reminding him of his last horse ride.

"It's okay, it's okay," the voice soothed as an oil lamp was lit. Tyler saw a large man, and then two other people sitting up on the floor next to him.

"What's going on here?" Tyler asked, grabbing his head from the bump on the wall.

"You were beaten and robbed," the man said. He was not walking, but reaching out to Tyler with a look of concern.

"We took you in, cleaned you, dressed your wounds, and gave you water," one of the younger ones added.

Tyler's look of fear and confusion gave way to realization. "Oh, no. You're Preachers?" Tyler said, reaching for his boots.

The large man stood up tall, losing the look of concern, replacing it with annoyance and answered, "I'm Uriah, and this is Josiah and Jonas," motioning to the two young men. Josiah had expected thanks, or gratitude, something besides sarcasm and disdain. Josiah had even hoped that the good deed that they had done would lead to a conversion, even praying for such as he had bedded down several hours earlier.

"Nobody's robbin' me," Tyler was mumbling as he quickly put his boots on, clacking them loudly on the floor.

"You were pretty hurt," Uriah said flatly. He was getting irritated; no good deed goes unappreciated. "You can stay, and we'll leave," he said. And turning to Josiah and Jonas, he said, "Gather your things." When he turned back around, he saw that Tyler had paused, hunched over, hands still on his boots, just staring at the three Preachers with what looked like disgusted confusion.

"Weird," Tyler exhaled, finishing with his boots, and marched loudly to the door, swinging it open. The door slammed behind him.

Uriah, Josiah, and Jonas just stayed still, trying to make sense of things. No one said a word.

Tyler headed straight for the stairs at the end of the hall. He could only hear his own footsteps on the old wooden floor and the creaking of the floor boards. *This place is old*, he thought to himself and was appreciating the fact that he was not.

Tyler was about halfway to the stairs of the old building's hallway when a stern-looking, gray-bearded man carrying a rifle emerged quietly from the staircase. Tyler froze. It was Jeremiah Pratt, who had stopped and was looking right back at Tyler. Tyler inhaled in panic, turned on his heels, and raced back to the room he had just left.

Jonas was about to break the silence and suggest that he get the bed when Tyler reentered the room and braced himself against the door as he slammed it shut. The Preachers were startled, but before they could react, the door was kicked in as Tyler was starting to say something with wide eyes.

Tyler had been thrown back onto the bed by the force of it being kicked in, and the only thing that entered his mind was why his boots were so loud when Pratt's were so quiet. As soon as he hit the bed, the Preachers saw a very serious man glide quickly into the room, swinging his carbine to his back as he thrust his hand firmly around Tyler's collar, pinning him to the bed. Tyler's eyes were cinched shut, bracing himself for what he feared was death.

"Look at me," Pratt demanded, and he slapped Tyler hard across the face, knocking his eyes open. The Preachers watched, frozen in place. Uriah and Josiah watched in horror. Jonas watched intently as if the scene in front of him were on a scripted stage.

Pratt's grip tightened around Tyler's collar as Pratt reached in his pocket with his now free trigger hand. Tyler was holding his cheek with one hand, and the other was trying to loosen Pratt's grip, his feet kicking childishly as he was pressed onto the bed.

Pratt's hand came back out with a tiny metallic circle between his thumb and forefinger, which he waved in Tyler's face.

"Where did you get this?" Pratt demanded in a rough whisper. Tyler only grunted and struggled, not to break free, but as a reflex; still afraid of being beaten or killed. Pratt punched Tyler in the face with the hand that held the tiny object. "Where. Did. You. Get. This!" Pratt whispered grimly again as he presented the round piece of dark metal at Tyler's eye level.

Jonas was leaning forward, eager to see what would happen next, in complete awe of the older, hairier stranger that was dominating the scene.

Tyler focused his eyes on the thing in Pratt's hand. It was a small, dark, swirled, colored metal ring. Tyler glanced at Pratt's face. Tyler couldn't have expected questions about Ted's ring collection; instead, if anything, he'd have expected to be choked to death considering the previous day's events and in light of Pratt's current death grip. In his confusion and alarm, Tyler only blinked in response. Despite the violence of Pratt's actions, and gravity his stern face and tone commanded, Tyler couldn't help but wonder, *Didn't Ted keep those rings wrapped up in his old underwear...* which brought the slightest grin to his face.

Pratt head-butted Tyler in the nose, frustrated that his simple commands weren't being followed and aggravated at the amount of time this interrogation was taking.

Tyler screamed out in surprise as blood spewed from his nose. Pratt's hand was there in a hurry, striking Tyler's face again. "Shut up!" Pratt whispered directly into Tyler's ear.

Tyler began crying and sheepishly pleaded, "Sto-oopp hit-tt-ting me," spewing nose blood from his mouth, while tears began to stream from his eyes.

At the sight of such violence, Uriah stepped closer in an effort to quell anymore injury and was instantly struck in the chest by Pratt's boot, sending Uriah to the floor. Josiah was taken aback in fearful surprise and began praying silently for his father's safety, careful not to ask too much for his own, afraid of being selfish. Jonas's eyes widened in amusement at the show of violence.

"Stay seated," Pratt said to the Preachers over his shoulder, never taking his gaze off of Tyler. Jeremiah Pratt was getting very frustrated. This was taking too long; it was getting too messy and too noisy. He had known that Preachers had taken the Champ into the hotel to care for his injuries, but had not expected the Champ to be as mobile as he was now. He expected to enter the room silently, rouse the Champ, question him, and then be on his way. Pratt couldn't focus on anything else until he learned more about the ring. He wanted to know where and how they came to have it.

Now he wasn't sure what attention all the noise had drawn. Wasn't sure now what to do with the Champ or the Preachers, but he hoped that the Champ would answer up and he could leave the Preachers be.

Pratt was about to ask Tyler again about where they got the ring, when he heard a single gunshot followed by shouting outside. He covered Tyler's mouth with his hand and fell on top of him, trying to lower his silhouette below the hotel room's window.

He couldn't make out what the voices were saying, but there were several men shouting. The Preachers took Jeremiah's cue and sank lower, each trying to listen as well. Even Tyler had stopped struggling and seemed to be trying to hear what was going on outside when the gunfire erupted converting the words being shouted into unintelligible shouts of war – the speech that knows no language barrier.

"Old and stupid," Pratt said to himself as he pulled Tyler off the bed and onto the floor. There was a lot of gunfire and a lot of yelling, but only one or two bullets crashed through the walls or through a window pane. Pratt was angry with himself for acting rashly.

"They're not shooting at us," Uriah said as he was trying to cover over Josiah on the floor.

Pratt looked over at the Preacher and realized that he was right. There would be more bullet holes in the room, if all that gunfire were directed at them. But Pratt had been sure that it was Flagstaff members that he had seen earlier in town, and he couldn't fathom who else they'd be after, other than himself, given what had happened before he got anywhere near Engine's Rest. Whatever the case was now, at the very least he had another moment to get out of town, but he would not go anywhere without access to the Champ's information. He hoped that whatever was happening outside would divert Flagstaff long enough for him to get out with the Champ.

Pratt was looking around the room for an exit idea when the south wall of the hotel room exploded. The men in the room felt the shockwave in their chests as the force scattered splintered wood in all directions. The building creaked and moaned until the old wood floor gave way and crashed down to the first floor below them in a cloud of dust and debris, breaking the oil lamp and releasing the fire, freeing it to consume at will.

***

Earlier in the day, Billy and Randy Squire discreetly excused themselves from Jerry's Tavern. Randy was concerned by his brother's demeanor. "Who are those guys?" Randy asked about the strange men that had entered Jerry's, as they hurriedly walked toward the detachment's building.

"Get Jones on a horse and get him to QRF," Billy said, too busy planning things out to answer his little brother.

"Should we light the signal fire? What's going on?" Randy asked as he tried to keep up with his brother's pace. Billy was moving pretty quickly for a guy who had one metal leg; he was moving with purpose.

Billy shook his head as they walked on. "They would see the fire too," he said. "Get Jones on that horse and get back to HQ."

"It'll take longer," Randy said as he unconsciously slowed his pace, smiling as if his older brother was an imbecile until he was knocked off his feet by his brother's fist cracking into his jaw.

Randy looked up off the ground with astonishment. Billy stood there sternly. "A signal fire works both ways, Randy," Billy said through his teeth, trying his best to remain calm, resisting the panic he could feel creeping up. "It will alert these guys faster than it will alert the QRF."

"Who are these guys?" Randy asked from the ground.

"SPARTANs," Billy answered, offering a hand to Randy. "The SPARTANs that took my leg," he finished as he got back into pace toward the detachment's building. Randy jogged to catch up with him, suddenly afraid to be left alone. "Get Jones on that horse," Billy said again, not bothering to look at Randy, "and get back to HQ and get kitted up. I'll get the others their gear and get them positioned in town. I'll brief you of their locations when you get back."

Randy nodded and started to head off when Billy grabbed his arm, stopping him.

"Be discrete, and be careful," Billy said and then went on his way, leaving Randy alone. Randy watched him walk off, and he realized that his adrenaline had gone and left him with nothing but fear.

When Randy got back to the detachment HQ, Billy was the only one there. The detachment building, which was called the sheriff's office by the civilians, had one holding cell built out of cinder block walls and iron bars. The rest of the building was made of rough-cut timber and had a couple of rooms and an armory closet. The armory closet's door was open and most of its contents were missing. Billy was wearing his armored vest and placing magazines into the vest's ammo pouches.

"Where is everybody?" Randy asked as he entered the building, sure to close the door behind him.

Billy secured his last magazine, slung his rifle over his shoulder, and walked over to the town's map that was tacked to the wall, pointing out the locations of the other LaMS. "Day is at the north intersection of town, Williams at the south, Franklin at the east, and the twins are west near the hotel and Jerry's," Billy explained. "Figured I'd have two at the hotel and tavern since that's the most likely place they'll be," Billy added.

"The twins?" Randy questioned as he went for his vest and ammo in the armory closet. "Thomas is kind of spastic."

"He's with his brother," Billy reasoned. "Plus, Marcus is the best one we have, and I didn't trust Thomas alone."

"How many SPARTANs are there, and where are we going to be?" Randy asked, looking at the map.

"We saw two, and Day saw a few more. We could be looking at eight to ten," Billy said. "We're going to head over toward the Tavern; keep our distance and just watch from the linen shop across the street. Hopefully we can hold out until the QRF gets here."

Randy nodded, "So there's around eight or so of them and seven of us until Jones and the QRF get here." Randy looked back over to Billy. "I think we'd be fine without the QRF," Randy said as he slung his rifle over his shoulder and leaned against the office's desk.

Billy shifted his eyes over to Randy. "No. These guys'll kill us," Billy said without an ounce of hesitation or any hint of exaggeration. Billy eyed Randy intently. "That's why Franklin armed some of the guys from town," Billy added as he motioned toward the armory closet.

Randy swallowed uneasily, but remained as he was, trying not to look shaken. He hadn't noticed before just how many weapons were missing until now.

"I think these guys are Flagstaff," Billy said, waiting by the door with his hand on the knob. He wasn't opening the door; just standing by it, or trying to work up the nerve to open it and walk through it.

Randy shrugged unimpressed, as if to say, "Who?"

"SPARTAN's elite," Billy said. "I've only seen 'em once before. It was years ago," Billy said as he released the door knob and began to rub his metal leg. "It was when my leg was blown off. Only me and one other guy lived," Billy said and swallowed hard. His mouth was dry, so he left the door and walked over to the water keg. "Sergeant Wilks," Billy said. "He didn't lose any limbs, but he was shot up so bad that the blood loss crippled his mind."

"They wiped out your squad?" Randy asked; surprised to hear a part of the story that he had never heard before.

"They wiped out our company," Billy said, wiping a drip of water from his mouth as he walked back toward the door.

"Eight guys..." Randy said in a near whisper, "took out near a hundred?" unsure if he wanted to leave the desk now.

"There was only three, then," Billy said and walked out the door.

***

The LaMS waited in place until night fall, watching the townspeople come and go, keeping a watchful eye out for the strangers that had entered town. The strangers were... strange. They never appeared to actually speak one to another, but they seemed to know exactly what the other was thinking, as if everything they did had been rehearsed unto perfection.

"Who'd you say these guys were?" Randy asked.

Billy didn't answer, but kept watching through the window of the building across from Jerry's Tavern. "How long has Jones been gone?" Billy asked, trying to predict how much longer they'd have to wait until the QRF arrived.

The door opened behind Billy and Randy, and Randy quickly raised his weapon. "Whoa! Whoa!" Alex said, raising both arms up.

"What're you doin?" Billy snapped in a whisper.

"Been lookin' fur ya, Billy," Alex said, lowering his hands since Randy had lowered his weapon.

"How'd you know we were here?" Billy asked.

Randy was looking back out the window again. There were a few people moving around outside, even though it was pretty late.

"Franklin said you might be here," Alex answered back. He walked up beside Billy and began to peer through the window too.

Billy just sat back and stared at Alex, clearly annoyed that Alex was there. "What do you need?" Billy snapped, but before Alex could answer he added, "Franklin? You were all the way over on the end of town?"

"I said I've been lookin' for ya, Billy," Alex whined.

Billy rubbed his eyes, "Well?"

"Well, Jerry sent me to find you," Alex said, "Said that an old guy came in the back of the hotel and asked about the Champ."

"So?" Billy exclaimed. "Get out of here," Billy added, dismissing Alex with a wave of his hand.

"How old?" Randy asked.

"Who cares?!" Billy said sternly, silencing any further discussion on the matter. "Unless anyone has anything to do with these SPARTANs out here, then it can wait.

"SPARTANs?" Alex said, taken aback. "But I thought the treaty said..."

"Get out!" Billy said shoving Alex toward the door.

"Man, Billy!" Alex said, regaining his balance. He looked back over his shoulder at the LaMS and left mumbling, shutting the door softly behind him.

As soon as Alex had left the room, Randy thought he could hear a faint stream of water being poured onto a tin roof. He and Billy looked across the street at the second floor window of the hotel and saw a man urinating onto the tin eve below it. "Pretty vulgar," Randy said in disapproval, shaking his head.

Billy nudged Randy's arm, and motioned to a couple of men who walked into view just down the street. "I think this is them. Keep a lookout," Billy said.

From their dark room, Billy and Randy watched three more men walking toward Jerry's Tavern. As the men neared the Tavern, the two men that were in the tavern walked out and joined the other three seamlessly, and the five of them continued toward the hotel.

"Remember," Billy whispered, "we're just watching. We won't need to act until the QRF gets... here." His sentence trailed off as they watched Alex, from the window, walk slowly and conspicuously down the street. Billy and Randy thought that Alex was trying, quite obviously, to look like he wasn't looking at the strange men, at Flagstaff, as he headed back toward the tavern. "He acts as good as he plays guitar," Randy whispered in disbelief.

Billy and Randy just watched helplessly, fearing that Alex might have given everything away. "I hate that idiot," Billy said.

"Where's Marcus?" Randy asked.

"At the hotel..." Billy answered back, returning his gaze toward Flagstaff, through the window.

"Why isn't he watching Thomas?" This question managed to snare Billy's attention.

"What?!" Billy said as he broke away from the strangers gathering at the Tavern. He glanced over and saw Thomas shifting from the back corner of the hotel raising his rifle. He did look like a spaz, and he also looked like he was approaching Flagstaff.

Billy couldn't believe his eyes. He had been so careful to explain to his men that they were not to engage unless fired upon, and they were to wait for reinforcements. Between Alex's conspicuousness and Thomas's actions now, Billy could accurately predict the following events. The cause and effect of these actions, unfolding before his very eyes, would coalesce into an unfavorable eventuality. The pendulum had been set in motion and there was no stopping it now.

Billy and Randy looked from Thomas, to the men, to Flagstaff, standing at the tavern's entrance. Everything seemed as if it were in slow motion. One of the strange men looked up at Alex, and immediately, the rest of the men all looked up as well. Alert, each one scanned in separate directions, and one looked directly at Thomas who was emerging from behind the hotel with his weapon at the ready.

Without signal or conversation the strange men silently spread out a few meters while the one who first saw Thomas, and the only one who still appeared to be looking at him, fired a single shot into Thomas's chest. Thomas was knocked backward to the ground, gasping for air and staring wildly at nothing. He brought his rifle to his chest and held it tight with both hands. It would be a fearful, painful passing, but he was sure to pass. It wouldn't take too long. The lungs just don't work when they bring in more blood than air.

The gunshot was loud, and it violently broke the night's relative silence. "THOMAS!!" Marcus shouted, running from the hotel's front door to his brother's side on the ground. Marcus frantically tried to cover the wound in Thomas's chest, never quitting although he could see that it was futile. Flagstaff's shooter kept his weapon raised but did not shoot, while the rest of Flagstaff held their ground as they watched more LaMS and townspeople emerge from alleyways and buildings; all armed for conflict.

Back in their place of concealment, Randy had attempted to engage the strangers the minute he saw one of them prepare to shoot Thomas, but Billy stopped him. "They'll kill us all," Billy said, staying his brother and gripping his arm securely. Billy looked earnestly at Randy, adding, "Don't."

Randy was dumbfounded. Randy knew that he was not the veteran and that his older brother Billy was, but he couldn't stay. He couldn't watch his friend and comrade get gunned down and simply stand idly by, cowering down in a hiding place. He shrugged free of Billy's grasp and gave him a confused and disgusted look, but said nothing. Randy exited their room and went out into the street.

Randy walked out into the street, revealing himself to all that were there. He walked with his weapon raised and trained his sights on the man who had shot Thomas. Randy glanced over at Thomas whose legs were fidgeting uncomfortably. He was gurgling blood, straining for air. Randy looked back toward Flagstaff and then glanced back to Marcus who was hunched over his dying brother with tears pouring down his face. Randy could see a few of the other LaMS closing in with dozens of armed Engines Rest residents. He could see Flagstaff. None of the five men had moved. They were breathing and blinking, but none had said a word or looked past their respective fields of fire.

"PUT 'EM DOWN!" Randy demanded behind his rifle as he slowly and deliberately moved toward them. No one in Flagstaff moved. "YOU'RE IN VIOLATION OF THE TREATY," Randy shouted, "NOW PUT YOUR WEAPONS DOWN." Randy was feeling pretty good. He felt in control. And there they stood, scores of townspeople and a hand full of LaMS, all surrounding five SPARTANS.

"No," a bearded member of Flagstaff's crew answered back, never lowering his weapon and never turning to look at Randy.

Randy's mouth was instantly dry, and he swallowed hard. He was suddenly less confident now and wished that Billy had come out with him or that he had stayed inside and hidden away with Billy. "YOU WON'T SURVIVE THIS," Randy shouted trying to reassert his authority, ignoring the sweat that was beading on his brow. He was baffled by their insolence and scared of their apparent disregard for reason. They were clearly outnumbered, and it was unfathomable that any would survive if it came down to it. "PUT YOUR WEAPONS DOWN," Randy demanded again, finally coming to a stop and standing his ground.

"You can let us get Jeremiah Pratt and live, or you can all die," Flagstaff said. The five men still stood at the ready, never faltering their view, never relaxing their weapons; the bearded one staring a hole through Randy with fierce blues.

Randy didn't answer back and felt a small grin awake on his face. *Jeremiah Pratt?* Randy thought to himself. He just looked at them for a moment in bewilderment. *Do they really think that Jeremiah Pratt lives here?* he pondered. Randy shrugged, no longer caring what they thought, and removed his finger from the side of his weapon and placed it upon the trigger.

Randy's head cracked open like an egg shell from the bullet of an unseen sniper before he could pull his trigger, and his lifeless body fell gracelessly to the ground. Flagstaff immediately opened fire into the crowd and moved gracefully to the tavern's entrance and effortlessly took turns in a bounding retreat into Jerry's Tavern while providing cover fire.

Instantly, ten or so of the townspeople dropped dead, having their souls expelled by a rain of lead; and more would fall.

Ignoring the shouts and screams, and oblivious to the crisscrossing of lead, Marcus grabbed his fallen brother's rifle and was shot before he could turn it onto his brother's killers. Marcus fell to his side firing off the rifle's grenade launcher with a dull "THONK." The un-aimed grenade struck and exploded in the hotel's second floor, which towered over the now crowded street. Timbers caught fire instantly, raining flaming debris down upon the street as the old building rocked, moaning and creaking painfully.

Billy, watching through his dark window, saw that his brother had been shot in the back of the head by an unseen marksman. Billy's head was spinning, but he was in survival mode. He would mourn over his younger brother later, and the fact was, his brother's death let him know that there was at least one other Flagstaff member than the five he now watched massacre the town.

When the hotel had a fiery hole blown into it, Billy decided to use the confusion to make an escape. Apparently many of the other townspeople had the same idea, because when he left his building's back exit he could see families, women, children, and the men who had decided not to take a stand for their Laughton & Mills Territory, all leaving on foot, by horse, or by carriage. Many of them were getting shot along with those who tried to fight. The gunfire was unrelenting and coming from every direction; there were definitely more than just five of them. The deafening noise, the smell of smoke and gunpowder, and the sheer fear of dying that all the piling bodies invoked was panic-inducing.

Billy ran as fast as his prosthetic leg would take him as he crossed the street, trying to make his way to the backside of the hotel where he knew Jerry's horse and cart would be. Billy braved the hail of gunfire as he crossed the road, just down from where the dead twins now lay, and from where his brother's body rested, using the smoke from the hotel's ruins and the darkness of night to hide his escape.

As Billy rounded the hotel's corner out of breath, still carrying his rifle, he felt relief when he saw the horse and cart. He barely noticed that the backside of the hotel had caved in on itself, nor the dust and soot-covered people who were now crawling out of the rubble. Billy was only concerned with getting in that cart and getting out of Engine's Rest. He was beginning to actually imagine a clean getaway when he was hit hard in the chest, twice. Billy was off of his feet in an instant and fell onto his back, confused and befuddled. He would not ever figure out that he had been shot, nor would he remember that he had died.

Jonas and Josiah had both nearly lost bowel control when Jeremiah Pratt fired his weapon directly in between the two, mid-stride. The boys had been making their way out of the collapsed building and were following Uriah to the horse cart when the pair of loud pops, mingled with the metallic clinks of a rifle bolt slamming its next round into the chamber, sounded off without any warning from the crazy old man behind them. Jeremiah Pratt had been pushing the Champ with one hand, and fired his carbine with the other, from the shoulder, into a gunman in green fatigues who had run around the corner of the hotel.

Jonas and Josiah turned to watch the running LaMS get stopped dead in his tracks and fall quietly to the ground. They both instantly turned toward the shot and watched Jeremiah Pratt force the Champ into the cart as if he had killed that other man without any thought or effort.

Josiah grimaced in disapproval but followed after his father and climbed into the cart behind Jeremiah Pratt, amidst the still sounding gunfire, screams, and billowing smoke and flames. Uriah got the cart moving after he had unsecured the horse, and only after he saw that Josiah had climbed in. He never asked where he should be going; Uriah knew that they just couldn't stay where they were. Others could be seen fleeing in various directions, just trying to escape the new SPARTAN invasion; their fear wasn't too far from reality.

Jonas had to run to jump into the departing cart. He landed hard, but looked up smiling, waving the LaMS's carbine at Jeremiah Pratt, seeking his approval. Jeremiah was not paying the boy any attention and lay on his back, looking down his rifle sights at the town shrinking behind them, ready to shoot any pursuers. His legs were across the Champ's chest, holding him down. The Champ might have struggled had Jeremiah not buried his handgun into the underside of the Champ's jaw with his left hand. Things being as they were, the Champ just lay still and quiet, still bleeding from his nose, wishing that he had just stayed home.

Jonas looked back over at Josiah and winked. Jonas knew that Josiah wasn't impressed that he now had a gun; he could see that plainly on Josiah's pious face, but Jonas was pleased with himself and pointed his rifle toward the town, mimicking Jeremiah Pratt. They would ride without anyone speaking until morning.

By sunrise, Engine's Rest was quiet again, although the hotel was still smoldering and would never be the same. Some buildings were still burning, lifting their black smoke into the air as a giant smoke signal. Bodies littered the streets and bullet holes riddled every wall in view. There was no more resistance, and few people now lived in Engine's Rest.

Many had fled during the night, and most of those that had stayed were now dead. All eight men of Flagstaff not only controlled Engine's Rest, but now represented the majority of its population. Five had been dispersed through the town to keep watch until they decided to depart. Some were on rooftops to gain a better overwatch position while the others remained hidden, but always and diligently watchful.

The other three members of Flagstaff were in what remained of Jerry's Tavern, where they were questioning Day, the only surviving LaM Security member, and Jerry. Flagstaff had been tipped off during the night that Jeremiah Pratt had reentered Engine's Rest, which was why they had been making their way to the hotel before the gunfight broke out. After it was all over, Jerry told them that Pratt had been seen fleeing the hotel with Preachers. Day only confirmed the number of security personnel in Engine's Rest.

"Six of your LaMS were found; all dead," Flagstaff said to Day. "You're here... so where's the other one?"

Day was injured badly. He was in visible agony. Two of his fingers were missing. He had been shot at least once and had been riddled with shrapnel down his side and leg. "Jones?" Day replied.

"Tell us about Jones," Flagstaff said tenderly.

Day smiled; blood on his teeth. "He was sent for QRF," Day said. "They should be arriving soon," he finished, and looked up at Flagstaff like he had something on them.

"Ohh," Flagstaff said with pity in his voice as he knelt down by Day. "An army is coming; but it's not your QRF" he whispered softly to Day, who had stopped smiling. Day was breathing rapidly and moaned lightly in pain. "Ssshhhh," Flagstaff soothed and ran his hand through Day's hair. "It'll be over soon. Just close your eyes." Flagstaff frowned, and wiped his eyes. "You, your friends, your town, and your QRF are dead," Flagstaff said and stood, looking out the window. "Your QRF," he said again, "we eliminated them before we ever came into town."

They didn't quite know where Pratt was, but they knew who he was with and where they were from; the sun was shining outside; it was promising to be a fortuitous day.

Chapter 10

The Detail (Flashback)

"The northern front is collapsing. Raven is unraveling, so we're having to divert some of our resources to that front."

"How?" the general asked in frustration, "We don't have the resources to send if we don't currently have the resources to hold this front."

"We're losing. That's all there is to it."

The general sat back in his chair and looked out the window.

"We can't just give up, sir. The LaMS are being held; if we could only contain SPARTAN..."

"We can't," he said stoically, still looking out his window. "We can't win. We can't give up... does it matter anymore?"

"Sir?"

The general chuckled, "The world is falling apart, Jim."

The colonel just stood there.

"We were colonizing Mars, and now we can't even fly toy airplanes. Refineries, utilities, and airports bombed and destroyed..."

"HELIOS," the colonel added, but immediately regretted falling into this tangent.

"HELIOS," the general scoffed. "What a fiasco; can't wait to see our learning curve when we watch our troops adjust to horseback and foot-marches... if we're around that long..."

"Sir," the colonel said, trying to bring the conversation back to pressing matters, "without Raven holding the North, it creates a weakness to our flank that SPARTAN will exploit, unless we send reinforcements."

The general looked away from the window and down at the floor.

The colonel tried answering the general's concerns before he could voice them, directing the general's attention back to the map. "Sir, you're afraid we don't have the resources to move north, but if we pull our main forces back to this line, we could divert enough to the north."

"For now."

"Sir?"

"If we fall back, we'd have enough reinforcements to hold FOR NOW," the general said. "It's a bandaid; just a temporary fix – and we're always falling back, always giving up more ground to SPARTAN or L&M... Now Raven's falling apart..."

"It may give us time..."

"Time?" the general laughed. "Time for our counterattack?" the general continued with a mocking laugh. "Jim, our plan is a *hail mary*; just a shot in the dark." The general grimaced and cut his eyes to the colonel. "You know that's just a last ditch effort? We can't afford, *or want*, to do that now! By the time that could even begin to take place, we'll have one foot in the grave."

"Do we have a choice, sir? Are we supposed to just give up?"

"Of course not. We just don't have to be fools and believe our own rhetoric."

"If this offensive fails, we still have Phase Line Omega and the facility."

The general nodded, "The facility's really a shot from the grave, colonel.... And we don't know when it'll be completely up and running; especially with our supply shipments getting attacked. Let's pray it's ready when we need it; I'm afraid it's our best shot. As for our 'great offensive,' I'm afraid all it will do is slow the inevitable, and that's if we're lucky."

The colonel was a little disgusted that the general had such little faith, but tried to keep that to himself. "Would you like me to send word to the POTUS?"

"For what?" the general asked in annoyance. "And please don't say, 'POTUS.' There's nothin united anymore. He's just the president of a shrinking, dying, and corrupt shadow of a nation."

The disgust was plainly visible on the colonel's face now. The general grinned in amusement, "I'll inform the President, while you send two battalions to the North to support what's left of Peterson's Raven forces. Draw the rest of our forces back to Phase Line X-Ray, and have them dig in." And under his breath, the general muttered, "Tired of falling back…"

"Yes, sir," the colonel answered, sounding a little relieved.

"The facility," the general said, "What does Doctor Jackson need in order to have it complete? How much more time is needed?"

"They're waiting on one more shipment, which is of a sensitive nature, but the timeline to install and bring it to an operational level hasn't been given yet, sir."

"Are we able to guarantee a secure and discreet transport."

"No real guarantees, but it's agreed that the best way to keep the transport discrete is to make it look just like any other random supply run without deviating from standard protocols. The fear is that any difference would draw attention to it."

The general nodded.

"Dr Jackson specifically requested Jeremiah Pratt for the security detail."

The general looked up with a raised eyebrow, "The good doctor thinks that we have the luxury of fulfilling any frivolous request for the brainiacs, *chillin'* in their cushy, air conditioned facility while we fight and die in a losing war?"

"Well, sir, I don't think it was like that."

"Fine."

"Really?" the colonel said in disbelief. "I, I thought you'd shoot that down."

"What difference does it make?" the general asked. "They think they're getting some comic book hero, a handsome movie star, 'the Audie Murphy of our day...'" The general grinned. "I've met Sergeant Pratt. He's all soldier and no show; no personality. Send him. Give 'em what they think they want. Maybe it'll boost morale and get them working so they'll finish faster... and maybe they'll quit asking for stupid things for fear of actually getting it."

The general composed himself and sat back into his chair. "Sure," he continued calmly, "Sergeant Pratt can be on the security detail for the shipment. I want the shipment en route, now. Pratt and his detail can link back up with their unit at Phase Line X-Ray. Send the order."

"Yes, sir."

***

Parks loaded her ruck in the guntruck and pulled out her map to review the route one last time. "No wonder they call it 'Phase Line Omega,'" she said.

Jeremiah looked over at her from his guntruck, where he and his squad were also prepping their vehicles. "You know we're going to X-ray, right?"

"Yeah, now... but look, it's literally the last line." She held up the map as if Jeremiah could make out anything on it at that distance. "Omega is right at the foot of the capitol."

"Hey," Jeremiah said sarcastically as he continued to load his truck with gear and check its fluids. *"I'm* going to the capitol," he said, feigning surprise at the suggested coincidence.

"Marshall!" Staff Sergeant Parks yelled. "I told you to make sure the truck was filled up, why's it only at half a tank?"

"Rations, sergeant. That's all I could get with the shipment order we have."

Parks looked over at Jeremiah, "Yep," she said, "Still no batteries either."

Jeremiah was making sure the rucksacks were properly secured to his guntruck. "Yeah, well," he said without turning, "that's why we got iron sights."

"Ah, right, tough guy," she replied. "Easy to say, but when you've got the entire Army who's only ever fired from their reflexive fire optics (for how many years of war?), let's see how easy they go from those to iron sights..."

Jeremiah nodded as Parks just stood staring at him.

"In the middle of a gunfight..." she added.

"We ready to go?" Jeremiah asked, ignoring her last remark. "Convoy Commander?"

"Get in your truck," she said to Jeremiah, then shouted so that Jeremiah's truck and the supply trucks could hear her, "Get on your comms; we start up on my count."

Each driver sat beside their vehicle radios, which at this point had become as second nature as HELIOS once was, and started their vehicles in unison at the conclusion of SSgt Parks's countdown. The convoy rolled out with Sergeant Parks's truck running point, in front of two supply trucks, with Jeremiah's truck pulling rear security.

After fifteen minutes or so of driving, Sergeant Parks picked up her radio handset and asked, "How'd you get us on this cushy detail? Over."

"No idea, and I don't care," Jeremiah replied over the radio. "All I know is, I'm taking a real shower, sleeping in a real bed, and eating chow at a real table tonight. Over."

"I think some bigwig just wants an autograph from the 'Great Jeremiah Pratt,'" Parks said, her obvious sarcasm bringing grins to everyone in Jeremiah's truck.

"Well of course," Jeremiah said with a grin, "I mean... it's pretty obvious, I just didn't wanna say it," the guys in his truck snickering like a bunch of teenagers... most of them *were* still teenagers.

"Yeah," Parks replied, "that would've sounded vain."

The comment made Jeremiah smile, which was uncommon. The entire radio conversation, as brief as it was, brought a new aspect of Sergeant Pratt to the soldiers in the guntruck. They were used to a serious and stoic leader, a larger than life figure who'd become the most well known fighter of this war. By this time, everyone had heard the name of Jeremiah Pratt, but this moment of levity made him a little more human, and his soldiers now felt an even closer bond and tie with him, feeling included in a moment of his humanity that 'outsiders' hadn't seen and didn't know. They'd known his legend status, heard the stories, worked under him, seen his integrity, fairness, courage, and at times his ruthlessness; but now this small, brief moment, which would have otherwise seemed trivial and insignificant, was the moment that those three young men riding with him in the gun truck went from respecting him to loving him. He was like their father and protector, teacher and mentor.

**

The convoy ride had been smooth, and the farther away from the front line they were, the fewer damaged vehicles and buildings they saw. A lot of the population, whether to avoid conscription, or war, or because of actual faith, or a combination of all of the above, were running away from the war, the suburbs, and the cities to live in religious communes in the woods and mountains, but the closer the convoy got to the city, the more evidence of a working populace was visible.

The capitol city wasn't pristine. During the earlier years of the war, when aircraft and drones were still able to fly without immediately being shot down by smart air defense weapons, most places, and especially large cities, had been attacked, including this city. Most buildings were still standing, even the taller skyscrapers, but most also had scars of war: bullet holes and larger craters and holes from rockets and artillery rounds. Despite the increase in intensity of fighting on the frontlines, these places far behind those lines had been able to clean up and rebuild a little, except where war rations limited activities.

Sergeant Pratt, Sergeant Parks, and their soldiers, who'd been on the frontlines for so long, were in relative awe of the city, but more so for the lack of ever-present violence.

The convoy made several turns before entering a parking garage at the base of one of the taller buildings.

"Is this the right place?" Jeremiah's driver asked. No one replied, and the driver didn't seem to expect one, he simply continued behind the vehicles in front of him.

The convoy drove in a downward spiral inside the garage until they hit what looked like a dead end. Jeremiah watched two guards and a dog exit a small room and approach Sergeant Parks's guntruck. As the first guard spoke to Parks, the other escorted the dog around the convoy, the handler making eye contact with Jeremiah, but neither spoke.

The guard was saying something to Parks, and while Jeremiah couldn't make it out, he assumed it was instructions on where to go next. The guard moved away from the convoy, and the wall at the dead end opened up, revealing another downward path. Once the convoy drove through and the door closed behind them, the secret underground roadway lit up brightly, so that it no longer resembled the Batcave, but more of a sanitized spaceship from some old movie, with white shiny walls and a gray polished concrete ceiling and driveway.

The convoy drove slowly down the well-lit winding tunnel and were met by armed guards at what appeared to be the facility entrance, some four floors below the street entrance. The guards directed the guntrucks to parking spots and the supply trucks to some loading docks, where people in clean olive coveralls were waiting to unload the cargo.

A security car and two motorcycles were parked in the corner. "Electric," one of the privates said.

"How can you tell?" someone replied.

"They're plugged in," Sergeant Parks answered, with a tone that said, "If you're gonna say something stupid, don't say anything all."

Jeremiah smiled in amusement as he admired the three motorcycles attached by charging cables.

The guards' uniforms were spotless and perfect. Their weapons were clean and shiny, and Jeremiah wondered if they'd even been used at a gun range. Jeremiah couldn't help but view them with disdain, as if these clean and tidy guards were vagrants or lepers. There'd been an intense and devastating homeland civil war; young men and women were conscripted by both sides to fight and die, and these guards got a shower every night, routine laundry, daily shaves with clean and fresh razors, and now stood watch over Jeremiah and his ragged set of warriors that were with him. Jeremiah knew it wasn't fair, but couldn't help from thinking, *We keep you safe by fighting dirty in your war, but you clean and sparkly, toy soldiers can pretend to stand watch over us tonight.*

Jeremiah knew Parks and could tell that she was thinking the same thing. Neither Jeremiah nor Parks acknowledged the guards, and while their lower enlisted soldiers didn't speak, they gawked at the guards as if they were an exotic exhibit at a zoo; something that brought the slightest grin to Jeremiah's face. Jeremiah took a sense of pride that he and his were the workhorses, something he'd prefer over being a showhorse.

Before Jeremiah and his crew reached the entrance, the doors burst open and a small-framed, middle-aged man spilled out wearing a lightweight gray sweater underneath his white lab coat and exuded sincere excitement as he welcomed the soldiers, "Ah, Sergeant Pratt, it's a real pleasure to meet you," extending his pale, uncalloused, soft hand for a handshake – which Jeremiah took and shook.

The hand felt cold and weak. Usually such a trait in a man may ignite the feeling of contempt, but it seemed to fit this kind man.

"Nice to meet you, sir," Jeremiah replied, feeling immediately at ease by their greeter's pleasant disposition.

"Terry," the man said cheerfully, "please call me Terry." He then reached for SSgt Parks's hand and spoke before Parks could introduce herself, "Sergeant Parks, it's so very nice to meet you, ma'am. We are humbled and honored to have you with us. Please, follow me and I'll give you the tour and show you to your rooms for the night. I'm sure you'd like to rest and maybe shower before dinner tonight – our cafeteria has prepared a little feast for you all."

Jeremiah was feeling a little embarrassed at the red carpet treatment and thought it was a little silly, but kept that to himself.

As the door opened they felt the rush of cold air erupt around them. It was a temperature just below comfortable, especially for a group that had forgotten what air conditioning felt like. The facility was shiny and spotless with dark gray floors and white walls and ceilings. It was a secret underground facility that met every cliché and smelled like bleach.

"Of course," Parks said, commenting on the scene.

Jeremiah's grin returned.

"Can we eat off these?" one of Jeremiah's soldiers asked, referring to the sterile floors in a tone so dry and matter of fact one couldn't help but laugh.

Terry pointed out a few things, but most of the words he used were over everyone's head; technical terms that he was rattling off as if it were common knowledge, but the soldiers let him speak, nodding here and there, completely devoid of understanding. If Terry acted excited about anything he was sharing, several in the group would add in a "wow," or a "whoa," in an effort to be polite and to avoid any possible uncomfortable silence, except when Jeremiah's driver, specialist Munson, asked, "What's a computer?" making everyone, even labcoat Terry, laugh.

"Dr Jackson is eager to see you again," Terry said, still smiling his genuine and friendly smile as they approached a small group of several lab coat-clad individuals who were gathered around, discussing business and science, of course, until they became aware of the soldiers approaching.

"Did he say 'again'?" Parks whispered to Jeremiah.

"I'm sorry, have I met Dr. Jackson before?" Jeremiah asked, confused, as he squinted, trying to get a better look. "I don't recall ever meeting the guy before…"

"Jeremiah," one of the people in the group blurted out excitedly as she quickly walked over to meet them.

Jeremiah felt a jolt of shock and confusion; he *had* met her before. Jeremiah felt tingles on the back of his neck, and his heartbeat increased its pace. "Lilly," he said with a suddenly dry mouth, staring at her in utter confusion.

SSgt Parks looked uncomfortably at Jeremiah. His reaction was not one of jubilant elation at reuniting with an old friend, it was something else… something awkward.

Lilly smiled and hugged Jeremiah, "It's been such a long time. It's so good to see you."

Jeremiah, still in shock, stood still for just a moment before he could hug back. "Yeah," was all he could get out, reluctantly placing one arm around her in return.

Jeremiah thought Lilly was glowing as she smiled widely and stood back, still holding Jeremiah's arm. "I'm so glad you're well," she said. "We've all been watching the exploits of your valor on television."

SSgt Parks said, "It's not a movie," but no one seemed to listen.

Jeremiah, still looking confused, said, "Dr. Jackson?"

Lilly smiled, "Oh yeah," she said as she held her hand up, displaying her ring.

Jeremiah felt an unexpected sting at it being said out loud, and at the size of the ring; something he'd never have been able to afford. "You married," Jeremiah said, trying to sound happy for her, "and you're a doctor.... Well, congratulations," he said, trying his best to sound sincere, but suddenly wanting to be out of the situation. "I guess we better put our gear away and clean up…"

Lilly, losing her smile at Jeremiah's reaction, said, "Oh, of course." Now she appeared to be the one trying to act natural. "Terry will show you to your rooms, and I hope to see you at dinner?" she said with the last part landing as a question. "But I'm really looking forward to catching up later."

"That would be great," Jeremiah said as he tried to smile.

"It was nice meeting you all," she added, making sure to look at each of them, even though none had been introduced to her. When she looked at SSgt Parks, her eyes darted toward her shaven head.

Terry was either aloof or polite enough to act as if nothing awkward had just happened and escorted the soldiers to their rooms. The individual rooms were small, but more adequate than what the squads were accustomed to, and the shower room had large individual stalls with seats and coat hooks. The soldiers in Jeremiah's squad knew better than to ask any questions, but once Terry left them to clean up, Parks said, "You were sort of embarrassing us there," in a sarcastic tone. "What was that?"

Jeremiah laughed, but grimaced. "Sorry, I grew up with her… Just didn't expect to see her again..."

"Well, get yourself together," Parks said, annoyed.

Jeremiah nodded, "Roger, sergeant."

Parks punched his arm with a grin, "Prick." And then added, "Did you see her look at my head?"

As Jeremiah showered, he didn't quite understand the mixed emotions he was feeling and was embarrassed by them. As he showered he fought off flashbacks from high school, which made him feel stupid and pathetic, and realizing those thoughts in those terms only fueled his frustration and feelings of isolation. He felt like he was a teenager again, which he absolutely despised and would've liked if he could have kept that even from himself. He wanted to see Lilly, and he also never wanted to see her again. "You're an idiot," he said to himself as he shut the water off.

The dinner was fine, the food was good and hot, and there was more than enough. Jeremiah felt a little conspicuous, but he was genuinely happy that his young soldiers could experience celebrity status from the upscale, educated class, considering what they've endured, and because of the dark times that were still ahead.

Jeremiah was at a table with Terry and Lilly, who told a few old stories of Jeremiah, and SSgt Parks who told a few more recent ones, which were all embarrassing in a jovial way. The food and easy conversation did succeed in making Jeremiah feel less anxious and more relaxed. He caught SSgt Parks's eye a few times, which made him think back to the first time he arrived at Bravo company before the wars started. He even noticed SSgt Parks eyeing Lilly with contempt, but she remained polite. Jeremiah didn't pay it much attention – despite the meal, pleasant conversation, and other amenities, Jeremiah was somewhat preoccupied with the surprising feelings that suddenly resurfaced. The unexpected reunion had taken him completely off guard.

The look on Parks's scarred face under her shaved, infantry head didn't seem to approve when Lilly excused herself from the table and offered to take Jeremiah on a tour so that they could catch up, but she never uttered a word of protest, only, "We roll out at oh seven hundred to link up with Bravo at X-Ray."

Jeremiah nodded in agreement and added, "Later."

In an attempt to make casual conversation with Lilly in the tense quiet, Jeremiah said, "How are your parents?" as they left the cafeteria.

"They're great," she said smiling. "They were smart enough to get out early..." her smile faded as she realized what she had just implied.

"Jeremiah, I'm sorry about your parents..."

Jeremiah shrugged, "I'm glad yours are doing well."

"Have you kept up with anyone else from back home?" Lilly asked. "Anyone from high school?"

"No," Jeremiah said, shaking his head as they walked the empty halls. "You?"

"No," she said, "but I did hear that Trevor is an officer for SPARTAN. Can you believe that, with all that's gone on?"

Jeremiah was shocked at how much he still hated hearing her speak his name. He wasn't surprised to hear that Trevor would belong to SPARTAN, but what he had trouble believing was how jealous he still was of him. Nevertheless, he kept all of that to himself. And wanting to find a way off of the entire subject, he pointed ahead in surprise, "You guys have a movie theater?"

Lilly smiled and pointed to the sign in front of them, "We have a movie theater," she said.

"You sure do," Jeremiah said playfully. "Can we watch one?"

Lilly laughed. "I thought for sure that you'd think of it as much too frivolous with the state the world is in now," she said without any hint of sarcasm. Instead, she sounded embarrassed, as if she felt guilty for having such luxuries while the vast majority of the population were either engaged directly in the war, or struggling to provide the daily necessities.

"Hey," Jeremiah said, "if I could take a break and watch a movie I would..." Jeremiah was suddenly distracted by another sign across the hall, "You have a bowling alley?"

"We're not bowling, Jeremiah."

Jeremiah smiled, "Well, no... Who could watch a movie or play games, considering the state of current affairs?" He looked around the corridor, and with the same playful tone said, "So you live here, with all of this, huh?"

Lilly laughed, wrapping her arm around Jeremiah's as they walked down the corridor, past the theater. "No," she said laughing at him. "I have a home, Jeremiah. I work here, I don't live here."

"Oh," Jeremiah said.

"But I am staying here tonight," she added with a smile, leaning playfully into Jeremiah. "I have someone looking after things at home."

Jeremiah nodded, not knowing what to say.

"You haven't changed, Jeremiah. Except for all this gray," she said as she ran her fingers through the side of his salt and peppered hair.

The hairs on Jeremiah's neck bristled. Looking down at her, he was caught by her eyes, which were bright and kind. "You have," he said.

"Have what?"

"Changed," he said. "You're even prettier now."

Lilly smiled widely, but Jeremiah suddenly felt uncomfortable as the words left his mouth. He discreetly pulled free of her, taking a few steps ahead, "So what is this place? What do you do here?" he asked.

Lilly was still smiling, "That's classified, sergeant," she said playfully.

Jeremiah nodded as if she had explained it all.

"It's a multi-purpose facility," she added as they both continued walking the building, "one of, and maybe even the most important of our functions is plans development, and we're finalizing the last few phases for a large scale weapon."

"Ah," Jeremiah said, surprised that she offered so much, but also saw how vague the explanation was, or at least at how vague the description had been so far.

"Turn to the right, here," she said. "This leads to the command room where the weapon will be initiated."

Jeremiah just looked at her, but kept walking.

At a closed door in the middle of the corridor, Lilly placed her thumb on a glass plate, which opened the door. "Soon," she said, "we'll be replacing the locks for something more effective and up to date."

Walking through the door, the command room was visible, and through the glass walls they could see people manning the work stations inside. "This is it," she said with unmistakable pride.

Jeremiah didn't say anything, but he was impressed by all the hardware and monitors and clocks, each displaying something different. Along with the staff at the workstations, there were technicians working on networks, cabling, cable-trays and whatever else.

"This facility also has a sizable information bank, and we're backing up more data everyday, just so we're prepared," Lilly said, still guiding Jeremiah along the command center and beyond the door inside it.

"Prepared?" Jeremiah asked.

"The war's been devastating, and it's not over yet," Lilly said. "When it's finally over, we want to be sure that we don't lose all the things we've learned and gained."

"Makes sense," Jeremiah said, thinking their plight now felt worse after considering the implications.

"But here," she said nodding through the glass into the command center, "when we're done here, we'll have something that should provide us with an edge, or at least level the playing field. It's a huge weapon, one that will lead SPARTAN into the kill lane and will turn them into glass." The look in Lilly's eyes didn't look kind now, but gravely serious.

Jeremiah laughed, "That was stone cold, madam."

Lilly smiled a little embarrassedly and grabbed his arm again.

"So when's this weapon ready for deployment?" Jeremiah asked.

"We still have a few things to work out," she said, "a few hurdles to jump." Then added, "We needed a few of the components out of the shipment that you just brought us."

"So... weeks or months?" Jeremiah Prodded.

"More like months or years."

"That long?" Jeremiah commented with obvious disappointment.

"You're afraid SPARTAN will either have won or sacked this facility before then?" Lilly asked, but without waiting on a reply, added, "And while that is an unfortunate possibility, there's still a chance that this place could be used to finish them off anyways."

Jeremiah shrugged silently as they walked arm in arm around another corridor. Jeremiah opened his mouth to say something but was distracted by a large panel, whose door was left open, with a roller tray with assorted tools, tape, wire, and a dirty coffee mug on top of it; signs that it was still being worked on. "Main Command Center Panel," Jeremiah said, reading the panel's label.

Jeremiah smiled and said, "Clever tag," finding the name tag so perfectly and simply named that it seemed nearly absurd.

Lilly just said, "When you're troubleshooting a problem in a system of this significance, you want the newest guy, at any IQ, who's under a lot of pressure, to find the problem quickly."

"I guess so…" Looking ahead, Jeremiah asked, "So where are we headed?"

"The backdoor," Lilly said. "This is the tour no one ever gets, so this is the tour no one can know about, or I'd have to kill you."

Jeremiah smiled.

Lilly smiled too, "But really, you really don't have clearance for any of this, so I really expect you to keep it all to yourself."

"Of course," Jeremiah replied.

"The backdoor's more of an escape exit, but it has the best view," she said as they neared what looked more like a large hatch.

Jeremiah was expecting another thumbprint or retina reader to open the door, but Lilly simply flipped a toggle, which Jeremiah only assumed was the door's alarm, before she unclasped the hatch locks and rotated its lever opening the door into a rock tunnel.

The outside of the door hatch itself appeared to be rock. Jeremiah touched it as he walked by, and it was actual rock that had been fastened to the outside of the hatch.

"So, if anyone were to ever stumble into your escape route, they'd think they just reached the dead end of a cave," Jeremiah said, voicing his realization aloud.

"See, you *are* smart," Lilly said sarcastically.

"At least one of us is," Jeremiah quipped with a subtle grin; the first reply that came to mind.

"Jerk," Lilly said, smiling. "This just winds around the corner and opens up," she said, leading him through the cave with a small light. "You'll see."

The mouth of the cave opened onto dark soil covered with leaves, twigs, small ferns, rocks large and small, and moss. Lilly switched off her light, letting the stars and moon filter through the tall, thick, twisted oaks, dogwoods, and sweetgum trees that surrounded the opening. Jeremiah could tell that the area opened into a clearing just ahead.

"I did not expect this," Jeremiah said in genuine awe.

"Yeah," Lilly said quietly, trying not to disturb the quiet, sounding almost reverent. "So, the city's behind us; our facility branches out beneath a surprising portion of the city's footprint, and as you can see, empties out here, just beyond it."

Lilly pointed ahead into the moonlit clearing, "You can't see it, but the river's that way."

Jeremiah only looked at her in the faint moonlight; delicate and beautiful.

Lilly leaned back into Jeremiah. "I'm cold," she said, "put your arms around me." And reaching up, she kissed him.

Feeling his heart speed up, Jeremiah struggled internally. "Lilly," he said softly, placing his hands on her shoulders. "Lilly *Jackson*," he said again, pushing her away.

"Jeremiah…"

"What are you doing?" Jeremiah said, sounding hurt and confused.

"What…"

"Jackson," Jeremiah said again with frustration, lifting her left hand between them. "Why'd you get married? What're you doin' now?"

Lilly was clearly embarrassed and pulled away. "Tim's stationed down south, and we haven't seen each other in months," she said in defense. But then the embarrassment transitioned to anger, "And I really didn't expect you to judge me!"

Hearing her say her own husband's name stung. Jeremiah didn't understand why it hurt, but he certainly felt the sting of jealousy. "What?" Jeremiah questioned harshly, "You're married, and we just kissed."

"Pfft," Lilly scoffed, "It's just skin, Jeremiah."

"Just…" Jeremiah questioned in sincere astonishment. "Not to me… Neither of us have changed," he said heading back into the cave, back to the facility.

"Wait," Lilly said, following him inside. "Jeremiah…"

"Thank you for the hospitality," he said walking ahead, feeling like a teenage fool again. He wasn't running away from her, and couldn't have even if he wanted to, since he needed her to let him back through the secured access doors; he was just ready for the night to end.

She caught up to him, and they both walked silently. He was angry with himself for being stupid and felt frustrated and confused with her. He was partly elated that she was showing interest, partly angry that it was impossible to have something he felt was pure with her, angry that she got married, angry about the past and present, and also partly sick at the thought of possible infidelity, something that always seemed so anathema. He wanted to talk to her, but didn't know what to say. There just weren't any good answers anymore.

Lilly began to speak, but Jeremiah, anticipating an uncomfortable apology, cut her off before she could begin. "I am glad I got to see you again," he said, telling himself to not say anything more, forcing himself to keep all his thoughts to himself.

Lilly smiled a little and looked down, "It was good to see you too." Then, trying again, said, "and I'm…"

Jeremiah cut her off again, wagging his head, "Please. It's alright." There was more he wanted to say, and he stood there looking at her with all the words swirling around in his mind as he watched her open the door with her thumbprint. "I've got to head out early and get back to my unit."

"Yeah," Lilly said, nodding. Jeremiah couldn't tell whether she was feeling embarrassed, or guilty, or even maybe a little sincere longing, but he tried to make himself stop wondering.

Despite his efforts, his walk back to his room seemed impossibly far. With each lonely step, the emotional cocktail in his mind became more volatile and unstable. By the time he made it to his room he was becoming emotional. He could feel the tears welling in his eyes and his heart beating in his chest and throat. Noticing this, he suffered the added stress of fearing that his soldiers could see him like this, and feared that to allow that, would compromise their trust and faith in him. Jeremiah felt trapped and isolated; angry and confused. It wasn't just Lilly, Lilly was just more or less the final straw.

He skipped his room and went for the shower room, where he walked into the stall without bothering to disrobe and turned the water on and just stood there, alone with himself, all quiet except for the water from the shower head. He stood there feeling sorry for himself, feeling angry with himself, and just wanting to relax enough to get some sleep before they left in the morning.

He had only been in there a few minutes when he heard the door open, which startled him and made him dread having to explain why he was showering in his clothes. "Someone's in here," he said, hoping the individual would recognize their mistake and quickly leave. He never heard a response, but he did hear the door shut and feeling relieved, he turned back to the stall and rested his head on it as the water poured down upon him, soaking his uniform.

He felt someone grab his shoulders, which usually would have made him jerk in surprise, but these hands were touching softly and tenderly, as if to embrace. Jeremiah turned around slowly and was surprised to see Sergeant Parks in the shower with him.

She was in her undershirt and shorts and looked up at Jeremiah with surprisingly feminine eyes. He barely noticed the deep scars on her arm and leg anymore. He liked the one on her face. For no more than a second the two comrades looked at each other in silence as Parks ran her hands over Jeremiah's shoulders, neck, and face. She removed Jeremiah's camo blouse, down to his undershirt, before she kissed him under the flow of water.

Jeremiah was taken aback. He was shocked that this was happening, shocked that Parks could be so tough and then be so feminine in an instant. And at the moment, he wasn't thinking of the past, or of Lilly, but of Parks's soft lips and how she felt in his arms, under the cool water.

He turned the lever toward hot and held onto her, neither saying a word.

***

Jeremiah woke early the next morning to find Sergeant Parks staring at him. "Jeremiah," she whispered softly, "no one can know about this."

"I know," he said quietly, gently touching the scar on her cheek.

Parks rubbed her own shaven head. "I'm not pretty like she is."

"How do you do that?" Jeremiah asked, his eyes searching into Parks's.

"Do what?" she whispered.

"Make yourself look so delicate and feminine."

Parks kissed Jeremiah again.

"We need to pack. Get your soldiers up and get some chow," Parks said, saying soldier things, but still with her delicate voice. "We roll out in an hour."

"Roger that," Jeremiah said as Parks walked away, pulling her hand slowly out of Jeremiah's.

***

Having left the facility, Jeremiah rode silently, as his and Parks's squads headed to Phase Line X-Ray, where they'd link back up with their unit. Jeremiah had hoped that they had awoken early enough to leave without having to see Lilly again, but she was there to see them off. Her eyes looked tired, but Jeremiah couldn't tell if it was lack of sleep or from crying. She was kind, and both she and Jeremiah were trying to act like nothing awkward had happened the night before; and as far as that went, Jeremiah and Parks were doing the same for a different reason.

Lilly approached Jeremiah as his squad was loading their gear into their guntrucks and making sure their vehicle's comms were up and SSgt Parks and her squad were doing the same.

"Jeremiah," she said, looking tired, "I'm happy that I got to see you and that you're doing well."

Jeremiah nodded. "Yeah, and it was good to see you too," he replied as he set his ruck in the back of the vehicle.

"Be careful," she said, now looking more concerned than tired.

"I will."

"No, Jeremiah," she urged. "I'm not just saying that. Things are about to get really bad. Just please be safe. Don't be the hero – just do what it takes to stay alive."

Jeremiah looked at her a second or two as if trying to figure out if there was anything between the lines to read into or not, and finally just nodded, adding, "I will."

There was no embrace, no long goodbyes.

Chapter 11

The Interview

Several hours after Pratt, the Preachers and the Champ had last seen any other people deserting the massacre at Engine's Rest, the horse cart they'd escaped in came to rest as the sun's exuberant light was breaking in over the horizon. The morning was cool and still dimly lit as Pratt tossed his bag out and ushered everyone out of the cart and onto a two-trail buggy path that had a forest of leafless trees to one side and empty hill-laden fields to the other.

There's nuthin here," Tyler said, stumbling out of the cart along with Pratt and the Preachers. His nose was not bleeding anymore, although it was sore and swollen. Jeremiah Pratt ignored the comment, or simply didn't hear Tyler at all, and smacked the horse in the hind quarters, sending it on down the trail with an empty cart in tow.

Old Man Pratt felt his pocket. Once he reassured himself that he still had the ring, he shouldered his bag, placed his hand on the pistol grip of his rifle, and looked at the Champ after taking a quick glance at the Preachers. Pratt frowned and nudged Tyler toward the tree line, saying, "Let's get out of the open. Once we have some concealment, you can tell me how you got this ring."

Everyone was looking at Pratt, unsure of what they were supposed to do. Pratt didn't acknowledge any of them and nudged Tyler, pointing him toward the tree line, as his patience was leaving him.

Tyler had started to snap back with, "I ain't doin' nuthin, until…" Until Jeremiah's left fist struck Tyler into silence. Tyler didn't even look shocked by the blow, but merely closed his eyes, nodding in understanding, and started walking for the trees. "The old city," Tyler said, motioning with his hand childishly, not bothering to look up. "Just up the way, there."

The old city meant nothing to Jonas or Josiah, but Uriah knew exactly what city the Champ was referring to. He first assumed the Champ was lying, but Jeremiah Pratt seemed to believe him. Uriah wasn't too interested, however. He was happy to be alive, happier for his son to be alive, and would be happier still if he never experienced war again. It made him remember why he had escaped to the congregations years ago. He didn't like the idea of going into that old city again and just wanted to get Josiah back home and to be with their brethren.

Jonas fell in step behind the old war hero and the Champ, slinging the carbine he found over one shoulder, doing his best to carry it as Jeremiah Pratt was carrying his. "Jonas," Uriah said, halting the parade. Josiah was standing by his father, looking on. "We should go back home," Uriah concluded, standing right where he had exited the horse cart.

Jonas looked disappointed, which disappointed Uriah and Josiah both, but it was Pratt who spoke next. "Not a good idea," Pratt said, shaking his head. "This group will make every effort to find what they want and pursue any lead to get to it." Jeremiah Pratt nodded toward the trees and the direction he had been heading, "Let's get out of plain sight and we can talk about this then, but now isn't the time." Pratt shoved the Champ forward, and the two started walking again. Jonas turned to follow.

Uriah was getting aggravated, but tried to stay his frustrations. He swallowed hard and exhaled loudly through his nose. "Jonas. Stop. We're not going with them," Uriah said evenly, but sternly to Jonas. Jonas turned back to his uncle and cousin, visibly annoyed. "'My son, if sinners entice thee, consent thou not,'" Uriah said to Jonas, who in response looked down in frustration, and walked slowly back to Uriah.

"Leave the gun, Jonas," Uriah said as Jonas approached, defeated. Jonas stopped walking at Uriah's last command and looked up defiantly.

"It's not a sin to hold a gun!" Jonas said, looking directly into Uriah's eyes. The loud response caught the ears of Pratt and the Champ, both turning around, halting them in their tracks.

"Don't sass your pa, boy," Tyler called out. No one acknowledged him. Tyler put his head back down.

Josiah was surprised by Jonas's defiance, but didn't say a word and looked from Jonas to his father, Uriah. Josiah could see his father getting angry, but Uriah didn't raise his voice, and took a thoughtful moment to let things settle down before responding. Uriah didn't want to act out of anger.

Uriah was annoyed by Jonas because of Jonas, but he was especially annoyed now at Jonas's response. Uriah had made great efforts to teach Josiah, his son, that service to the Lord was more than blindly following the "do's and don'ts" of the scriptures, but rather it was a lifelong endeavor to gain understanding; a real attempt to become more like Christ and live in His example. Uriah knew that holding or even owning a firearm wasn't sinful, but Uriah could see where this was going. He could see that Jonas was doing more than holding an inanimate object. Uriah had held weapons before, and he could remember the feeling of power and control that it could give people. He recalled the type of person that let the power of a rifle lead them into peril; people like Jonas.

"Christ has the power, Jonas," Uriah said evenly, holding Jonas's gaze, "He's in control. But I'll leave it up to you as to whether you leave the weapon or keep it." It was a compromise that Uriah was willing to make, and even though he knew what the outcome would be, he was still disappointed when Jonas kept the gun. It was enough, however, to convince Jonas to follow him.

The Preachers took two steps in their congregation's direction when Pratt called out, "It won't be safe there, Preacher."

The Preachers stopped and looked back at the Great Jeremiah Pratt. It was hard not to be in awe of the man. One of the oldest men Uriah had seen in years that still had all of his limbs, but with a body that was not only whole, but also still very powerful. "If the SPARTANs find out that any Preachers were there in Engine's Rest, they may head to your home if they think they can get a lead there," Pratt concluded.

Uriah looked puzzled and called back, "If those were SPARTANs, and if they are headed to our congregation, then we have to go back!"

Jeremiah yelled back, "What are you going to do if they're there? Fight 'em?" as he started walking back toward Uriah. "No," Pratt answered, shaking his head, walking closer. "I know you people, Preacher. You'll go, and if SPARTAN's there you won't do a thing to save your friends or family. If you get there in time, you'll just die with 'em; turning your other cheek."

Josiah was getting angry at the old man and fearful at the thought of his congregation being destroyed like Engine's Rest.

"Save them?" Uriah said with genuine confusion. "Mr. Pratt, if our Lord's Kingdom were of this world, then would we fight. But this life isn't what we're after... it's the next. 'For his sake we are killed all the day long; we are counted as sheep for the slaughter.' Nothing shall separate us from the love of God, not peril, not persecution, and not the sword."

Uriah looked over at Josiah and Jonas, and then back at Jeremiah Pratt, who had stopped advancing, and who was being polite enough to let Uriah finish before walking away. "We have to go back, *especially* if things will be bad," Uriah said as he turned back to his course, determined to get home.

Josiah followed proudly behind his father, and was reminded of his father's namesake. Jonas followed happily behind them both, hoping to find an opportune excuse to use his gun.

Jeremiah Pratt frowned and looked up into the sky. The sun had completely risen now, and he became frustrated with the delay. He pointed Tyler, the Champ, back toward the woods once again and marched on. "Suit yourself," Jeremiah said quietly. Jeremiah was simultaneously impressed by their courage and annoyed at their foolishness. Uriah had reminded him of Mick: both in appearance and, to a degree, in mannerism. *Mick just wouldn't have been so stupid*, Pratt thought as he and Tyler entered the forest.

Most of the trees' leaves covered the forest's floor, making each footstep loud as they crunched the dried, brown, dead leaves. Jeremiah guided Tyler in a jagged direction before coming onto a shallow ravine. Jeremiah directed the Champ into it before climbing in himself.

Tyler was about to speak when Pratt silenced him with a gesture. Pratt was listening; listening for voices or footsteps. He heard nothing. While Pratt was listening and watching Tyler, he would occasionally glance away, scanning the surrounding horizon.

"Where did you get this ring?" Pratt asked just above a whisper as he took the unique metal circle out of his pocket. Pratt was still in complete awe to see it again.

Tyler looked up quickly, and in a desperate effort to avoid further physical abuse, asked, "Jed's ring? Uh, Ted's ring?" It was a stupid question with an obvious answer, but in his haste to respond it was the first thing that came to mind. Tyler nervously swallowed, wanting to look unconcerned.

Annoyed, Pratt opened his eyes wide as he brought the ring higher into view, as if to say, *this ring, you idiot*. Pratt didn't care about the name of the dead guy he had found it on; he wanted the circumstances and the location.

Tyler fearfully braced for another strike, but when he realized one wasn't coming, he said as much on the subject as he could remember. He told Pratt that he, Ted, and Jim had played in the old city as kids, rummaging through the old building ruins. From his ramblings it was clear that the ring had not been given by a relative, but that they had found it in an old building several years ago. "We weren't supposed to go into the city," Tyler said with a smirk, "but we weren't scared of the old places like the other kids." He hadn't been hit in awhile and was regaining his confidence. Pratt tried to listen to every vague detail, trying to get an idea of the exact area Tyler was referring to.

"How far from here?" Pratt asked.

"I don't know... up the way," Tyler said, motioning in a particular direction. He wanted to ask why the old man cared so much about it, but was afraid to question him.

"Can you take me there?" Pratt asked.

Tyler understood that he wasn't really being asked, but told. Tyler nodded, hoping that he could remember where the old building was in the old city of ruin. The old cities were larger than the ones most people lived in now. There had been so much carnage during the wars that the bombed out cities were virtually abandoned, leaving all the dead in place. By this time, the smell had gone, but people were scared of disease and plague and usually avoided the old ruined cities altogether, and the people who typically remained in those places were not well thought of.

Jeremiah Pratt would have been able to find the old city himself. But unlike the last time Jeremiah had seen it, the city was a ruin. Finding the specific building he needed on his own, much less the specific room, seemed impossible. Even with the Champ's help, Jeremiah wasn't sure what he would find, but something compelled him to go. Obsession, he guessed.

***

Uriah, Josiah, and Jonas neared their congregation as night began to fall. Jonas had not complained the entire way, but eagerly awaited what he might find there, hoping for a reason to pull the trigger. Josiah had actually managed to purge all worry from his own mind, believing whatever state they found their brethren in would be God's will. Josiah was content with that.

Uriah was nervous. He remembered the wars and all the dead bodies that went with it. He shuddered to think of finding his friends' and family's lifeless bodies, gray, without life; deformed and damaged beyond recognition. He desperately and fervently prayed within his head for their safekeeping as they marched back home. Uriah had not seen who or what had caused the gun fighting back at Engine's Rest, but Jeremiah Pratt had said it was the SPARTANs. Uriah hoped that was incorrect. If it were the SPARTANs, then they would be in violation of the treaty, which would likely mean that the wars were about to flare back up. He was fearful for Josiah, his son.

As they entered their congregation's land, everything was quiet like a blackhole and as peaceful as the dead; an uncomfortable description for one's home. The sun was down but the moon was full and high. The first several houses they came upon seemed vacant. Aquila and Priscilla Townsend weren't sitting on their porch or tending to their chickens. The Wilsons didn't appear to be home, and their sheep were left unattended and unsecured.

Jonas forgot all about his fantasies of gunplay and ran for his own home, now afraid and desperate to find his father. Uriah and Josiah said nothing as he ran off for his home. The father and son were looking around, dumbfounded.

There was no sign of any violence; at least that they could see so far. They both stopped in the silent and empty street and looked around. Both Uriah and Josiah felt incredibly uneasy and uncertain at what they were seeing.

They could see laundry flapping in the wind, hanging from their lines. No one left laundry out to dry at night. They could see the livestock and fields, but no people. It appeared as if everyone had vanished. Had it been Sunday, they would have thought to check their meeting house, but today wasn't Sunday.

"HELLO!" Josiah shouted.

Uriah turned to Josiah and shushed him quickly. Uriah didn't like noise, especially noise that broke uneasy silence. It was too much like a beacon that the unwanted might find.

A long way down the street from them, near their meeting hall, they did see the silhouette of a man lean out from behind a building, obviously looking for the source of Josiah's call. Uriah and Josiah squinted, trying to identify the man. Uriah waved, but stayed silent, as he tried to figure out who he was looking at.

The figure, who was too far away to identify in the moonlight, stood up straight and made his way to the center of the street, where he stopped, continuing to face them. Uriah nervously lowered his hand. Without taking his eyes off the man, he leaned over to Josiah and said, "Let's cut through here," and turned in between two houses. He wanted to head home and get out of the figure's line of sight. Whoever it was, his presence was just unsettling in the unnatural quiet.

As they made their evasive detour, they could hear running horses that were fast approaching. Uriah tried to stay calm and marveled at Josiah's stoicism. Although the two tried to walk on bravely, the horsemen were on them a few short seconds after they had first heard the horses' sprinting hoof strikes. The horses came to an abrupt halt, nearly running over the two Preachers. Uriah was taken aback, and Josiah was frozen with fear as they were surrounded by three uniformed horsemen towering over them. These men wore the uniform of SPARTAN cavalry.

The cavalrymen were armed with semi-automatic rifles, ammo/utility vests, and sidearms holstered to their hips. They wore wide-brimmed cowboy hats, which made it even harder for Uriah and Josiah to see much of their faces. The cavalrymen surrounded the father and son, trying to intimidate them with their large, muscular horses, which stamped and snorted about, unruly like. The parade brought a bit of glee and sadistic satisfaction to the SPARTANs, who felt a little bit bigger with the thought that their military arms and cavalry horses impressed the religious zealots to the point of fear.

And indeed, the weary father and son were intimidated, standing uneasily side by side as they could feel the warmth of the horses' breath as they stormed about them, until the horses suddenly stopped. Uriah and the cavalrymen were each a bit unsure of why the horses suddenly became still and at ease, with the cavalrymen ribbing their mounts, doing their best to get them started up again, but to no avail. Josiah and the horses, however, were content.

Giving up and getting to business, one of the men bearing the rank of sergeant dismounted his steed, handing the reins to his comrade, and swaggered up to the Preachers and said, "Identify yourself and state your business here." The cavalryman's hand was on his rifle's pistol grip, but he kept the weapon oriented at the ground. Despite what the dismounted SPARTAN was doing

163

with his rifle, Uriah could see that the other two cavalrymen had their weapons trained on them.

Uriah, with some alarm but without hesitation, answered the man. "Uriah, Uriah Morris… and we live here."

"Morris?" the SPARTAN asked, briefly looking over to his mounted comrades. "Who's this? Your boy?" the SPARTAN asked, nodding toward Josiah.

Uriah simply nodded in affirmation as he felt anxiety flood him. That nearly forgotten childhood feeling of being caught with your hand in the cookie jar, but unsure if the person who caught you was aware of what they caught you at. If Uriah had taken the time to ponder it, he wouldn't have been able to explain why he felt this way, whether it was because he'd been with Jeremiah Pratt at Engine's Rest, or simply because SPARTAN represented some authority that Uriah viewed as harsh and unfairly critical.

"Where is everyone?" Josiah asked, causing Uriah to hold his breath out of fear of what the unsolicited question might evoke from their SPARTAN interrogator.

"They're in your church, Preacher," the man said flatly. He casually pointed his carbine at the Preachers and motioned for them to walk on toward the congregation's meeting house. The sergeant ordered one of the riders to inform the general that Morris was found. As the cavalryman sprinted his horse for the general, the sergeant said, "The general is waiting to see you, Mr. Morris."

Josiah was as confused as Uriah, but probably less afraid. As Josiah was trying to make sense of things he couldn't help but think, *meeting house… It's a meeting house. The church is the group of Christians, not a building*, Josiah thought to himself. He was a stickler for accuracy.

Uriah was very tempted to ask what they wanted, but he kept silent, knowing that they would eventually get to their purpose. He also wrestled with his earlier decision to head home instead of staying with Jeremiah Pratt. *Would they have been safer there? Were they in danger now?* "The Lord is in control," he reminded himself under his breath. As the quiet words left his lips, the sergeant looked back at him, but said nothing.

As they were escorted down the dark main street of their congregation's town they could begin to hear the faint and muffled sounds of the congregation singing as they neared the meeting house. The sound of untrained *a cappella* voices were simultaneously nostalgic and alien. Uriah had heard that singing most of his life, and for Josiah, his whole life; but neither were accustomed to hearing it from outside the walls of their meeting house. Hearing it now, in this way, made Uriah sad.

Both Uriah and Josiah were expecting to be put in the meeting house with everyone else – for what, they weren't sure – so both were surprised when they were stopped short of the meeting house and ushered into one of the elder's houses.

It was a modest but clean and well organized home. Uriah and Josiah were led up the steps onto the small wooden porch. They had both been in this house many times, but this was the first time without Elder Thomas or his wife to welcome them. The dining room table had been made into a makeshift map table, with several uniformed SPARTANs surrounding it, studying and discussing plans or routes. Everyone paused briefly as Uriah and Josiah were moved inside, which made them both instantly feel very self-conscious. They were the only two not dressed alike. Odd, Josiah thought, that they now felt like strangers in their own congregation.

"Bring them in here," a voice called out from the den.

The sergeant escorted the Preachers through the dining room and into the den and snapped to attention, saluted the man sitting in one of the chairs between the fireplace and the coffee table, which had an old and tattered folder on it, and said, "Presenting Uriah Morris, as ordered, sir."

The general casually returned a half-hearted salute and dismissed the sergeant. The general kept a neat and clean uniform appearance and looked to be in his early fifties. On the opposite side of the fireplace from the general was another chair – sitting in it was a rough and dirty-looking man who wore no uniform and had a large scar mingled in his beard. In front of those two chairs, and on the other side of the coffee table was a couch. The general stood, extending a friendly hand to Uriah, and introduced himself. "General Simmons," he said as he gestured for the Preachers to take seats on the couch. He did not introduce the man sitting at his side in plain clothes, nor did the man rise or make any pretense of pleasantries.

Uriah, not knowing what else to do, reached out and shook the hand extended before him, "Uriah Morris." He swallowed uneasily and nodded toward his son, "Josiah, my son." The Preachers sat, noticing the armed guards in the corners of the room who were nervously eyeing the other man in the chair.

The general sat back into his chair, crossing his legs, "Would any of you like some tea?"

Uriah blinked and Josiah just sat blankly. They were a little taken off guard by the question. Neither was sure what they had expected, but it certainly wasn't refreshments. "Excuse me, general, but is everything alright?" Uriah asked.

The general smiled politely. "You have no need to be concerned, Mr. Morris," he said reassuringly. "I can tell that you're nervous, and I don't blame you," he added as he uncrossed his legs and leaned forward, toward the Preachers. The general donned a sympathetic face and said, "I know there'll be some questions about why SPARTAN is here, and we'll get to that, but right now you can be assured that SPARTAN is not your enemy and that your congregants are fine." He motioned out the window toward the meeting house, "The singing. I love it. It's beautiful in its simplicity." The general sat back in his chair and crossed his legs again. "Making music with the instruments God has made instead of with the instruments made by the corruptible hands of man."

Josiah was impressed and even nearly excited at the general's comments on their music. He had never thought to phrase it in such a way, but he found those words to adequately express his own thoughts on it.

The bearded man in the chair simply sat, seemingly unimpressed by the harmony that caught the ears of the others. He sat stoically, looking intently at Josiah with the coldest blue eyes.

"What's the title of this song?" the general asked as he visibly turned his ear back to the window and to the muffled sounds of singing.

"Um, 'Be With Me Lord,'" Josiah answered.

The general raised an eyebrow and said, "Indeed," as he nodded reverently.

The general's comments, as charming to Josiah as they may have been, seemed like pandering to Uriah. He couldn't tell how much he could trust the general. He had never had any trust for SPARTAN in the past and had always previously viewed them as dangerous and the greatest instigator of the wars. And he was definitely uneasy about the man sitting in the chair that the general seemed perfectly content to ignore.

"Oh, please, have some tea." The general gestured to one of his guards, "We'll all have some, thank you." The guard left the room, closing the door behind him. Addressing Uriah again, "Your friends and family will be getting some food as well. Placing them in your meeting house was for their safety."

Uriah nodded and was feeling some better.

"Mr. Morris... may I call you Uriah?" The general asked.

"Please," Uriah replied.

"Uriah," the general continued, "you had previously worked with the United States government."

Uriah was unsure if it was a question or a statement but felt his stomach fall to his knees. He was surprised at how much he was tempted to lie. He saw Josiah staring at him out of the corner of his eye. Uriah nodded in affirmation, nervously.

"Uriah, please," the general said at seeing the apprehension on Uriah's face, "this is not an interrogation, and you are not in any trouble. We just…"

The general was interrupted by the guard returning with a tray of hot tea. The tray had four coffee cups, a pitcher of hot tea, and a sugar dish.

"Ah, tea," the general said with delight. The general grabbed the pitcher and began to fill the coffee mugs as he said, "I know most people enjoy coffee around here, and that's why I have to bring my own tea wherever I go."

Uriah noticed for the first time that the general was missing two fingers on his left hand. *This man has seen combat,* Uriah thought to himself. It was a habit that most men old enough to have fought in the wars did... sizing other men up by their battle scars. Uriah didn't dwell on it and made an effort to not look like he looked. He was still uneasy and certainly didn't want to come off as rude. He cut his eyes to the man in the chair only to see the quiet man staring back at him. Uriah just glanced back away and took the tea, "Thank you."

Having poured the tea, the general set the kettle down and gave himself two scoops of sugar before offering the sugar to the Preachers. "Even here in this house," the general said, looking around the room, "plenty of coffee and no tea. Where do you get your coffee?" the general asked. "I thought you Preachers grew everything yourselves; I mean, I can see that this is your cane sugar here," he said with what seemed like genuine interest.

Uriah was intrigued by this entire encounter. Feeling eased by the general's charisma and charm, he answered, "We trade for the coffee."

"*Trade,* of course," the general said, satisfied. He began handing the cups of tea to Uriah, then Josiah and the man to his left, who took it with a nod but offered not a word. "You Preachers remind me of SPARTAN – self reliant and resourceful. You can't grow good coffee at this altitude, but take what you can do to gain what you want, and by extension you help the coffee growers who can't grow or raise what you have."

Uriah and Josiah sat quietly, holding their tea.

The general went on, "Coffee is too heavy for me. Don't get me wrong, I'll have a cup every now and then, but if there's tea, why, I'll have that." He took a sip of tea and sounded his satisfaction as it went down. "Antioxidants, light, and satisfying," the general said.

"Now, you have no reason to be alarmed," the general said again trying to reassure the Preachers who were sipping on their tea and still trying to figure out exactly what was going on. "Uriah, we know that you worked for the Old Government, but that fact is not what interests us. What does, is what you did while working for the Old Government, or rather what you were trained in and what you had access to."

Uriah was stunned and nearly choked on his tea. Josiah's interest was piqued; his father had never talked to him about his life before the congregation.

Uriah stopped coughing and said, "That was so long ago..."

"Uriah," the general interrupted, "we know how long ago it was, and before you begin to ruin our friendly conversation with excuses, at least hear the question." With a friendly face, the general waited on Uriah to acknowledge.

Uriah nodded and glanced over to Josiah, who was quietly fascinated now and keenly interested to learn more about his father.

The general continued, "You worked in a facility, yes?"

Uriah, confused by the apparent staleness of the question, answered, "Yes, but..."

"Uriah," the general said with playful scolding, "you're doing it again," wagging his finger at Uriah. "Let's back up a bit, Uriah. I want you to understand me perfectly. Is that alright with you?" the general asked politely and looked to Uriah with wide eyes, waiting on a response.

"Yes, sir," Uriah answered back, unsure of where this was going. Although the general was being polite, Uriah was beginning to regain his anxiety as his eyes went back and forth between the general and the other man. Josiah knew enough to stay quiet, besides he was in some degree of shock and disbelief that SPARTAN was taking such an interest in his father.

The general closed his eyes and nodded in recognition of Uriah's answer and said, "You probably remember the Old Government, the United States, and how fouled up everything was, how they were poor stewards of the people's goods, property and finances. SPARTAN had to liberate the people..."

General Simmons was distracted by the skeptical look on Uriah's face. "...It's true. It's true," the general insisted. The Old Government, regardless of how noble their beginning was, had become so corrupted, so ineffective, that something had to be done." The general looked over to Josiah and gestured toward him, "Can you spend money you don't have?"

Josiah shook his head.

"Is it fair, or just, to take bread from a hardworking man only to give it to a lazy man who wouldn't work to earn the bread for himself?"

Josiah shook his head again.

The general smiled and nodded in agreement, "No. No, that doesn't work so well." He turned for the first time to the bearded man on his left and looked at him as if to silently express how smart the young lad was. He then looked back toward Uriah, "Even your own book says that 'if a man doesn't work, then neither should he eat.'"

Uriah said nothing.

"That's why SPARTAN likes you congregationals," the general said. "You have the same dedication to work, to principles, and to community – each one diligently doing their part. A horse cart needs a driver, a horse, a frame, wheels, reigns, et cetera. Just like a horse cart needs all of its components to work, a productive community and society need all of its people to do their part. They need someone to grow coffee and tea," holding his own tea cup aloft, "and someone to raise cattle and someone to grow sugarcane..."

"And someone to fight and kill..." Uriah added without intending to. He instantly regretted saying it, but the general didn't seem angry. In fact he smiled.

"Yes, there's a time to kill, Uriah," the general said, "and a time to heal."

Uriah was relieved that his uncharacteristic interjection hadn't foiled the friendliness of their conversation, and he was also impressed by the general's apparent knowledge of the scriptures, and his ability to reference them so readily. He had not met many people outside the congregations with any real ability to quote scripture other than the "don't judge" parts.

The general sat back and angled his ear toward the window. "Ah," he said with feigned disappointment. "They must've gotten their food. They've stopped singing," he added, leveling downtrodden eyes on the Preachers.

"SPARTAN is actually organized in a way very similar to your congregation," the general stated, getting back on point. "SPARTAN has... *HAD*, I should say, a triumvirate of sorts to lead and a well organized system. The Old Government had too many drivers, and as a result, the horse was always confused where the cart should go. They failed and have fallen away," the general said looking at the Preachers, giving it time to sink in.

"Look at the world now, Uriah," the general said. "Your current territory is also falling away. Laughton & Mills lacks structure and organization and will soon spin out of control into chaos and anarchy like the northern territory."

The northern territory had been established as Raven International's lands through the treaty that ended the wars. Raven International had been a Security Contractor like L&M and SPARTAN, although the weaker and smaller of the three. SPARTAN had been surprised that Raven had outlasted the United States (if one could count its fractured state as "lasting"), but could tell that its weakened infrastructure and leadership would crumble soon after the treaty had been made. SPARTAN decided that it could patiently wait for their demise from within instead of wasting more men and resources in further conflict.

"Raven International, to our astonishment," the general continued, "not only fell into anarchy, but fell into madness." He sat back in his chair. "Their leadership just spontaneously evaporated. Those people up there in the North are every bit as backward and ignorant as those in the dark ages," the general said enthusiastically, waving his arm across his body. "And L&M isn't far away from that doom."

Uriah and Josiah were both listening. If the general didn't have their attention before, he did now.

"Since the wars have ended, L&M has struggled to survive and rebuild itself," the general went on. "Since the wars decimated all of the old world's resources, only SPARTAN's territory has been able to re-establish any form of public utility services, but even ours is limited. The Old Government was too shortsighted, allowing most of its knowledge to be stored electronically and failing to protect its libraries of written material during the wars. As a result, most of our knowledge was lost, and we see what that eventually leads to in Raven to the North."

"Are you saying that SPARTAN wants to rebuild the government?" Uriah asked with skepticism.

"What I'm saying is that SPARTAN wants to reestablish order in a world of chaos," the general answered. "The world is slipping. We had sent people to Mars and to the farthest reaches of our solar system before the wars, now people are dying of diseases that used to be cured by soap!" the general concluded in passionate frustration.

That last point sunk in hard for Josiah. His mother had died some years back due to fever. Josiah looked to his father and saw the faintest tear develop in his eye, but Uriah held it back.

"What I'm saying is that SPARTAN wishes to circumvent that fate," the general said, lowering his tone again, opening welcoming arms. "That's what brings us to you and to your former place of Old Government work."

"But I don't know if it's still there, or if I could even help you with anything there," Uriah said.

The general placed his hand on top of the old, water-stained folder and said, "It's there, and we have very good reason to believe it is still operational, although very likely abandoned."

The general lifted the folder from the coffee table and faced it toward Uriah. "We also know how to get inside. You."

Uriah didn't know what to say. He had tried to leave that part of his life, tried to cast it off and into the fire, so to speak. "I don't know if I'm still able," Uriah said, looking down. Uriah was embarrassed by his past, but the colonel misread Uriah's embarrassment as feigned humility.

"It'll come back to you," the general said, looking back toward his quiet, un-uniformed colleague. "SPARTAN is actually good at that particular ability." The general frowned for the first time, placed the folder back down on the coffee table and tapped it with his index finger. "You were only trained to use your ability as a key, weren't you?" the general asked with what sounded like pity. The quiet man with the scarred beard and blue eyes was staring intently as if he was analyzing everything Uriah said.

Uriah looked quizzically at the folder under the general's finger and then back to the general, unsure of what he was getting at. Uriah had been screened and then selected for "advanced concentration training" back when he was first drafted for service.

Josiah was completely lost and devoid of any hint of understanding. The conversation had left his understanding a while back. All he could do was sit silently and pretend to actively listen.

"Forgive me, Uriah," the general said, "it's just that this is so fascinating to me. I don't have your particular ability, but there are those in SPARTAN who do."

The quiet, bearded man was grinning.

The general was delighted to see that surprise Uriah. "Oh, you didn't know that we knew of those abilities?" the general asked, amused. "Well, SPARTAN would have put your talents to better use, but to be fair, we never thought to use the mind as a key."

The quiet man was looking back toward Josiah again.

The general noticed Josiah's bewilderment. "You didn't know, did you?" the general asked, looking back and forth between father and son. "Your father has a special ability and is one of only a few…" the general paused in thought before continuing, "… perhaps the only one left with this ability that has been trained to unlock a Gordian Security Lock." The general looked back at Uriah with intrigue, "A special lock that can only be unlocked with a particular gift of the mind."

Uriah was visibly uncomfortable. In his old life he had been trained to rely on his own abilities, but since then he had tried, quite successfully, to leave that behind and put all of his reliance in his God.

The general, cognizant of Uriah's current disposition, added, "We simply want the information stored within that facility's data banks," with concern on his face. "We know there is engineering data, *medical data*," the general added with emphasis, "and astronomical data; all of which can help us rebuild and prevent us from slipping into another period of Dark Ages."

Uriah's recollection was that there was more to the facility than academic information, but he wanted to trust the general. He wanted to believe the general's noble presentation. Uriah could also tell that he wasn't really being given an option.

The uniquely scarred, bearded man shifted uncomfortably in his chair.

"Oh," the general said looking back at the un-uniformed man with the beard and blue eyes. "There is one more question we have for you," the general said as he turned back toward Uriah. "Jeremiah Pratt," he said evenly, "we understand you had contact with him in Engine's Rest."

Uriah couldn't hide the shock he felt. He felt like a child caught with his hand in the cookie jar again.

"Where did he go?" the general asked.

"He's a Blacksmith, isn't he?" Josiah asked, almost without thinking. He certainly hadn't thought it through beyond feeling like he may have something to contribute to an adult conversation, but as soon as the words left his mouth, he regretted it – mostly from the instant look of disapproval from General Simmons.

"No!" the general exclaimed with disgust. "No, I do not like that term! I will not use the term '*Blacksmith*,' in such a way and certainly not for such a man as Sergeant Jeremiah Pratt!"

Josiah's remark must have struck a nerve in General Simmons, because his rant continued without any pause.

"What's it even mean?" General Simmons sneered rhetorically. "It's stupid and moronic! If anything, if anyone should be called a 'Blacksmith,' aside from an *actual* and *literal blacksmith*, would be this fellow here," motioning to the bearded man with the blues eyes seated at his left, "or perhaps even your father! They've mastered their skill; they manipulate and expertly fashion these basic elements, which are naturally buried deep within the soil of their brains!"

Uriah sat quietly for the tirade, as did Josiah; Josiah feeling scolded for stupidity.

"Elements that are just as available to the rest of us," the general continued, "but we're, for whatever reason, unable or too unskilled to make any use of them! Instead, we rely on these expertly skilled men, these '*Blacksmiths*,' to work these elements for us; so NO! I refuse to refer to Mr. Pratt as anything but 'Criminal,' or 'Murderer;' certainly not 'Blacksmith!'"

General Simmons sat back in his chair and composed himself. Then he said, "He's a very dangerous criminal," and wiped his mouth. "Where is he?"

Uriah was surprised at how tempted he was to lie again, but answered anyway, feeling guilty for even having been tempted. Uriah swallowed uncomfortably and said with a shrug, "Said he was going to 'the old city.'" He now felt guilty for sharing.

The general sat back in his chair and said, "Hmm," in consideration as he looked again to the man at his left, "It's what we expected."

The bearded man, with the cold blue eyes, nodded silently.

Chapter 12

Falling Towers (Flashback)

The enemies of the US were steadily gaining ground. Five years after retreating to Phase Line X-Ray, the US forces had to fall back two other times, giving up ground to SPARTAN and L&M alike. This last retreat was to Phase Line Omega, which represented the last defensible line before the capitol was exposed.

As Bravo Company rolled into their designated location at Omega, First Sergeant Parks slapped Sergeant First Class Pratt on the rear as he climbed out of his vehicle. Jeremiah smiled, careful not to draw too much attention to their playing. They had successfully kept their relationship a secret, or they at least believed that they had. Every so often, in their private time, she'd make some comment about Lilly – of course, she'd brought her up much less often over the past few years, but initially, she'd even make jabs, disguised as jokes, regarding Sergeant Pratt's married girlfriend who worked at the facility in the capitol.

Jeremiah would laugh it off, but it annoyed him. He had been troubled by Lilly, and Parks's comments bothered him probably because they touched on a bit of reality. Jeremiah had made real efforts to forget about Lilly and had made real progress.

Jeremiah pushed it all out of his head and endeavored to focus on the task at hand, preparing his platoon and getting ready to do their part in the upcoming assault.

As the US forces staged their units and prepared for what may be their last major operational effort, the stringent rations were beginning to become painfully evident. New uniforms for the recruits were sparse, leaving many wearing a hodge-podge of different uniforms; desert mixed with woodland, or even simple olive drab, etc. Parts and fuel for vehicles were limited and there simply weren't enough for all the needs of every unit.

There was plenty of ammunition, however. The top brass had been quoted as saying, "We have enough ammo to fight five world wars," to which the mass reply was typically a grand Army "Hooah!" as if it were something to celebrate. But despite the prodigious stock of rounds and weapons, rifle scopes and hologram sights, which the Army had used exclusively for decades, were harder to replace and repair, and the batteries that powered them were now no longer available.

In preparation for the rapidly approaching operation, each unit was to have its soldiers acquaint themselves with iron sights. Once upon a time, firing a weapon from iron sights was a basic soldier skill, but those days had long passed in favor of the electronic optics that allowed for faster and more effortless aiming, range finding, and even magnification in several instances. The current situation highlighted an obvious problem; despite the benefits, no matter how helpful a technology is or can be, the dependence on such a thing can be crippling when or if you suddenly find yourself without it. The military had gotten lazy over time, due to the luxury and excess of a cushy golden age, assuming the luxuries and technologies would always be available. It was hubris that lulled them into neglecting skills that should be considered basic, like the familiarization with the primitive and consistently reliable iron sights.

The shortage forced the troops to return to the range and re-qualify with their weapons, but with the archaic iron sights and without the high speed optics they had been accustomed to. Soldiers were spending longer than expected at the gun range trying to zero in their iron sights and get used to them. Time was short, so tensions were high, which made the learning curve a little greater. This is not to say that all soldiers had a difficult time with it; many zeroed their sights in quickly, even if most of those had to take longer for follow-up shots than they would have with the superior optics. Others, however, like Jeremiah

177

Pratt, seemed to take to them naturally, showing little to no reduction in ability by switching to iron sights, or "irons" as they were calling them.

Jeremiah Pratt had already been a bit of a celebrity, much to the disapproval of his old platoon sergeant, Sergeant Booth, who was now the battalion sergeant major. And to Booth's annoyance, after Jeremiah's performance on the gun range with iron sights, the range sergeant exclaimed with excitement to all present at the range, "Sergeant Pratt is a magician! He *is* a wizard with *his* weapon! He makes a living with his iron sights… with his *irons*, like some sorta… *Blacksmith*!"

Everyone laughed, but "Blacksmith" stuck, becoming a label, first for the soldiers who were proficient with their irons, and then after the wars, coming to mean any highly skilled marksman; typically only a few of the older veterans were honored with the unofficial title by that time.

Sergeant Major Booth grimaced at yet another standout moment for their celebrity, but kept it to himself. He hated Jeremiah Pratt, and the two always seemed to be at odds. After Jeremiah had rescued SSgt Parks, carrying her out of the SPARTAN Alamo, Booth had just steered clear of SGT Pratt, thinking that with enough time and enough and rope, Pratt would hang himself… but patience was difficult and Pratt's noose never seemed to pull tight.

Sergeant Major Booth was reminded of the other reason why he avoided Pratt now, as he watched Sergeant Pratt approach Captain Towers at an observation platform near the gun range.

"What's up, Sergeant Blacksmith?" Mick said wryly when he noticed Jeremiah join him.

Jeremiah grinned, "I don't like labels."

Mick laughed silently. Mick looked preoccupied and in deep thought, which wasn't unusual, but he didn't ignore anyone and seldom ignored any comment, no matter how seemingly trivial. Once, someone had criticized Mick for focusing on trivial things, to which Mick replied, "Jason Lee said that 'there are no trivial actions, only trivial thoughts.'" Jeremiah didn't know who Jason

Lee was, but was always impressed with the amount of knowledge (no matter how trivial) Mick seemed to store and was able to recall at the right moments.

"Labels," Mick pondered, "yeah I don't like 'em much either. But here, with this, it's valuable." He nodded to the guys on the firing line, still trying to get a hold of their irons, "Something as small as a goofy label can mean a lot in circumstances like these; they can give these guys something to aspire to and also offer a small reprieve from the stress and anxiety of knowing that they're preparing to launch themselves into a major battle against a superior force... and all that implies..."

Jeremiah wasn't ignoring him but didn't comment on Mick's bleak commentary either. "What are you doing?" is all he asked.

Mick nodded to the nearside of the firing range where the brand new recruits were, "Watching these guys. Thinking."

"Oh," Jeremiah said, directing his gaze toward the new guys.

"How's Lieutenant Jones?" Mick asked.

"Young," Jeremiah said, "but smart, and I think he's got courage."

"Can't shoot," Mick said, nodding toward the firing line, and both Mick and Jeremiah laughed at the remark, while the new lieutenant struggled to hit his targets using his irons.

"I'll watch after him," Jeremiah said, still grinning.

The two of them watched the new soldiers firing into their paper targets.

"Listen to em," Mick said with a bit of disappointment, commenting on the young soldiers' obnoxious boastings. "Already singing their own songs of glory...,".

"Maybe it's the way these young guys cope and chase off the fear of the upcoming fight," Jeremiah offered.

Mick nodded, "Maybe," he said. "But maybe it highlights one of our biggest vices." Mick paused a moment, and Jeremiah stood quietly with him, leaning against the rail, watching the young guys talk big and struggle with their iron sights.

Mick was looking frustrated as he said, "Section thirty-one of the Tao Te Ching reads, 'Weapons are the tools of violence; all decent men detest them. Weapons are the tools of fear; a decent man will avoid them except in the direst necessity and, if compelled, will use them only with the utmost restraint. Peace is the highest value. If the peace has been shattered, how can he be content? His enemies are not demons, but human beings like himself. He doesn't wish them personal harm. Nor does he rejoice in victory. How could he rejoice in victory and delight in the slaughter of men? He enters a battle gravely, with sorrow and great compassion, as if he were attending a funeral.'"

Jeremiah paused a moment, maybe for feeling a bit small for having never contemplated similar thoughts himself. Unsurprised by Mick's typical, profound commentary, he replied, "Maybe you're expecting too much out of a few stupid teenagers..."

"Or maybe our low expectations for society and our culture's overall lack of compassion is the ultimate cause of these wars and all this death," Mick countered.

"You're sounding like those 'Preacher' religious extremists," Jeremiah countered, simultaneously trying to lighten the mood and still make a point.

"My father was a Preacher," Mick said. "He believed the sins of society would lead to such a fate, but I disagree with him on the solution. He thought that by running away, living in secluded communes and congregations, that they could avoid conflict and condemnation; but they're hiding their heads in the sand, like the unfaithful servant who buried his one talent."

"Sir..." Jeremiah said, but not knowing what else to add to it.

"The Lord decides when we leave this world," Mick said, still watching the young soldiers, "so as long as we're here, I think we have work to do – and hiding seems the opposite of work."

"I don't know if the Lord has anything to do with it," Jeremiah said, both annoyed with the direction the discussion had taken and also envious of his captain's conviction and discipline. "And I don't believe in fate or destiny. I believe in our company and my platoon. I believe in you, sir; and will follow you anywhere. I believe in you and your abilities because of your character. You're followed by all of your soldiers, not because of the rank on your collar or because we're told to follow you by written orders; we follow you and respect you because of the character you've demonstrated time and again; we respect and follow you because we can't help it."

Mick smiled. A tear welled in his eye as he shook his head. "You're wrong, Jeremiah," Mick said, looking down, "You of all people should know that. You've survived this long, without a scratch, despite all the firsthand action, and you'd suggest it's all just random chance? You don't think providence or fate play a part?"

Jeremiah thought about all the others who'd died and those who'd been killed under his watch, but said nothing.

Mick shook his head again, "We'll never figure it all out, but it's not our job to. We just have to move forward with all that we have. Whether or not there's such a thing as fate, moving forward is the only viable option anyways."

Jeremiah still couldn't find any words to share, but somberly and quietly mulled everything over.

"Well," Mick said, "even if fate has nothing in store for you, you've finally made it to 'Blacksmith' status, and no one can take that away from you."

Jeremiah smiled.

"But there is fate," Mick said with a grin, "and destiny has a plan in store for you." Looking back at the new guys on the firing line, Mick added, "And it's looking brighter than it is for them."

After a brief pause, and with the opposite of enthusiasm, Mick added, "Whether these guys are ready or not, it'll be time to go soon."

Jeremiah nodded. "Did I hear we're moving out on foot?"

"Mmhmm, not enough fuel to go around."

"The odds appear to be stacked against us," Jeremiah said, and with a grin added, "We'll see what fate and destiny think about that."

Mick smiled, "Yeah, we fall our forces back to here, hoping to draw SPARTAN and the LaMS in with a feigned retreat, so that we can launch a counter attack once they've crossed into the open, where we have a slight advantage – it's the only chance we got."

Both Mick and Jeremiah were taken aback and suddenly distracted by the sight of a courier sprinting into their battalion area on horseback.

"Did, did I just see that?" Jeremiah asked rhetorically. "Are we doing so badly that we're fighting from horseback?" Even though they were well aware of fuel shortages, they had not expected to see soldiers on horseback. To see the regression from aerial transport, back to horses for mobilization, was astonishing to behold, and something that had not been commonplace since the first World War.

"Worse," Mick said in a sarcastic quip, "We'll be on foot."

A whistle blew shortly after the horseman arrived, signaling everyone to report to their battalion areas. The messenger brought word that SPARTAN forces were advancing as expected, and once the battalion commander briefed everyone and offered a few last words of encouragement, the companies dispersed. Now the commanding officer of Bravo Company, Mick would have the radio man with him, since at this dire point, there was only one radio per company due to battery shortages. First Sergeant Parks ensured the company troops had their ammo and water before marching out.

Jeremiah had been in many battles, but the path to this one seemed as surreal as his first one. The new guys were wide-eyed and silent, the veterans were making a few jokes and clever one-liners, while double-checking their ammo, weapons, and the snaps on their gear. Something felt different or even monumental about this to Jeremiah, and he wondered if it felt that way to the others, but never inquired.

He tightened his fingers around the pistol grip of his rifle. He looked over at Parks and winked at her. He found her looking back at him. She smiled and mouthed the word, "blacksmith," in a playfully mocking way, sticking her tongue out at Jeremiah, which made him smile in sincere amusement.

Despite the obvious reasons to feel grave, sober, and even fearful, Jeremiah felt energized and excited. Parks's playful exchange added to it, letting him feel confident and light on his feet.

The company navigated on foot through an abandoned town and positioned themselves behind abandoned cars, on rooftops, or inside vacant houses and buildings right where the town crested high ground as it overlooked a depressed lowland area of fields and a few farmhouses that separated Bravo's position from a denser city where the SPARTAN forces would approach from.

The soldiers of Bravo company set up crew-served machine gun positions and mortars, and then of course the hasty fighting position for the rest of the riflemen. Once established and rooted in, they waited for the first signs of the encroaching SPARTANS.

Jeremiah began double checking his platoon's weapons and ammo, making sure they had water and range cards to prepare, as a supply vehicle drove around delivering crates of loaded magazines and MREs.

The soldiers dug in and waited. Each soldier watched the horizon intently, expecting to see a large SPARTAN force approach at any moment, each with their cheek on the butt stocks and their eyes lining up their iron sights as best as they knew how. Hands were firmly grasping their rifles, with their index fingers lightly feeling for the trigger and their thumbs nudging the safety switch, ready to fire indiscriminately at their enemy when they appeared. After a few hours had passed, their alertness began to waver.

Once the ever-exuberant presence of day began to unravel, ushering in twilight and pursuing darkness, the soldiers again began to tense up in anticipation of a nighttime attack, feeling that the gunfire would open up at any moment. Again, after a few hours of waiting, they relaxed until dawn was approaching. But at daylight, no attack; no sign of SPARTAN.

Jeremiah's platoon was tired and stiff from hours of being in a sitting or prone position, muscles tensed, as they waited for targets that never seemed to arrive. "Well this feels just stupid," one of his privates said in aggravation, making Jeremiah and the rest of the platoon laugh. But before anyone else could say anything, Captain Mick Towers approached them with Private Miter attached to his side, who was carrying the company radio.

"Sergeant Pratt, Lieutenant Jones," Mick said, "round up your platoon. Gather extra magazines, water, and MREs."

Jeremiah's platoon gladly got up and began gathering their things. LT Jones never said much, but got to work alongside his soldiers. Jeremiah asked, "What's going on?" as he did the same.

"Intel was bad, and the plan was busted. Third Battalion was hit hard up at Post Whiskey and was overrun. Our company's been tasked to go and meet the SPARTAN force just south of there, before it's too late to close them off."

Mick then went off to round up his other platoons. Evidently the US plan was to fall back to Phase Line Omega, as if in retreat (which it actually was) in an attempt to draw SPARTAN into a tempting lane of pursuit. The US placed the bulk of its forces in that lane, believing that SPARTAN would not take the other routes, like the one through Post Whiskey, since the terrain was much more rugged and difficult to maneuver large forces through. SPARTAN, however, attacked the lane the US least expected and easily overpowered the small contingency force placed there to defend those outposts. It was brilliant really; SPARTAN didn't take the US bait and used the US's plan against them. With the bulk of the US forces waiting on the enemy at the front door, SPARTAN walked right through the side door as if they owned the place.

Now the US was scrambling to mobilize whatever units they could to try and keep them from getting too far, though they would find that they were too late. A Quick Reaction Force, mostly comprised of long range recon, took the available vehicles as the rest of the forces were left to make it on foot. Bravo Company left behind their rucks, taking only the essentials of water, ammunition, and a bit of food. Traveling light, they double-timed it north to cut SPARTAN off. It was too late to reach Whiskey, but the hope was to reinforce the surviving elements of Third Battalion that had been able to retreat to a small town and install proper defences there.

After a klick and a half or so, Bravo arrived to find a large town, nestled in the foothills and divided by a large creek. It was already encased in a fog of smoke, and the streets were littered with debris, burnt and broken vehicles, and battle-marred buildings. Gunfire could be heard, but mostly just a few single shots here and there. Two recon scouts met Captain Towers to fill him in, but it was fairly obvious; Bravo Company was reaching the town the same time SPARTAN was, so there was no time to plan adequate defenses. Instead, Bravo had to split into platoon formations and join the remnants of Third Battalion in the fight.

"There's always a line," Mick said under his breath to Jeremiah as they crouched, finally reaching the town's limits. They could hear plenty of gunfire, but so far they saw none and no one.

Jeremiah looked over at First Sergeant Parks, who was falling in alongside one of her platoons behind an adjacent building.

The platoons paused for one final moment, as their company commander, Captain Mick Towers, stayed on the radio trying to pinpoint friendly positions.

Without any radio response, Mick looked at Jeremiah and frowned, saying, "What if SPARTAN attacked Post Whisky up the way there, just to draw our forces away from the main attack? What if we don't get the reinforcements because SPARTAN is attacking there, back where we came from, now that we've come here?"

Jeremiah's stomach sank. "Well why'd you say that?" Jeremiah asked, trying his best to make it sound like a joke, even though he was indeed quite serious.

"That's what I'd do," Mick said.

The thought of it did make Jeremiah feel sick. And what irony, to devise a plan to suck the enemy into one particular avenue of approach so that they could be ambushed, but then to suddenly abandon that plan because the enemy telegraphs a punch from the opposite side, drawing your defenses that way, just so they can make their real attack where you initially planned that they would... The thought was nauseating, but he laughed.

"What're you laughing at?" Mick asked, almost annoyed.

Jeremiah shrugged and said, "Gotta die sometime; let's see how many of 'em we can take with us." But as the words left his mouth, a bit of the bravado left him as well. He looked back over at Parks.

Mick, without offering a response, shifted his rifle in his hands and glanced at his iron sights, as if making sure they were still there. He didn't feel good about this situation, and for the first time he thought death was coming today. He wasn't scared really, or nervous, but sad. He wondered how long it would be before his mother and half-brother learned of his death. He thought about the children he'd never have. He thought about the children and the families of his soldiers that would also likely die along with him today. It wasn't fear, it was sobering sadness, it was mourning as if he were attending the funeral of a friend. In that moment Mick thought that if he were going to die, he just wanted to die well, with honor and integrity, not failing his soldiers; to die with his boots on.

"'I will not fear the terror of night, nor the arrow that flies by day, nor the plague that destroys at midday. I will not fear though tens of thousands assail me on every side,'" Mick uttered quietly to himself.

Jeremiah heard his friend and could see the disposition of his face and brow, but said nothing, letting Mick have a moment alone.

Mick noticed Jeremiah watching him. "Something my mother would say to me," he said. Then added, "whenever I was scared as a kid, she'd say it to reassure me."

Jeremiah nodded, having nothing to add to such a memory, and found it fitting in their current circumstance.

Jeremiah peered around the corner and saw their enemy approaching, silhouettes just becoming visible in the haze of the smoke. "Roger that," Jeremiah said, lining his iron sights up on the first silhouette he saw and squeezed the trigger, putting things into motion before the Commander could get to it.

The quiet erupted into thunderous roars of gunfire, grenades, and rockets. The flicker of muzzle flashes, grenade explosions, and tracer rounds cast frantic shadows against every surface, as empty brass fell to the ground amongst the shouts and screams of war; a chorus of terror and catastrophe; a symphony of righteous destruction; and there's no place Jeremiah would rather have been. This odd, counterintuitive truth was shared by others, even the pragmatic and wise Captain Mick Towers.

Jeremiah would have had a difficult time putting it into words, but it wasn't bloodlust, or warmongering; Mick may have said it was because war was one of the most real settings one could experience, where nothing petty or frivolous existed, no worries regarding fashion or aesthetics, no thoughts or concerns dealing with what celebrity tweeted or said about this or that; instead it was a test of oneself, in valor, in courage, in strength of will and in grit; it was an intimate dependence upon comrades and those next to you, a kinship built upon the direst necessity, and a closeness that could only be built under the grave stress and immense gravity that comes from the intense conflict of war.

The volley of return fire was thick, knocking chunks out of the walls and making craters and dust plumes in the ground. Dust and silica from the peppered construction was mixing with the gun smoke and smoke from the various fires that littered the battlefield. Jeremiah fired relentlessly, magazine after magazine, while never losing awareness of his soldiers there with him, or Mick. As they fired, Jeremiah wasn't thinking about the rest of the company, his mind was focused on the enemy, his platoon, and the new, young lieutenant's commands as they advanced into the violent abyss.

First Sergeant Parks took two squads and rounded the corner out of sight, engaging the enemy and preventing a flanking maneuver. Sergeant Wilken's squad did the same on the other side, and all three squads of First Platoon advanced, slaughtering SPARTANS, matching round for round, trying to gain ground, trying to repel SPARTAN.

Mick was trying to call in targets for mortars while he and his radio man hunkered down as his platoon fired relentlessly into the enemy line who were delivering generous amounts of lead themselves. He wasn't having much luck on the radio and eventually handed the mic back to his radioman, then shouted at Jeremiah. "WE CAN'T STAY HERE! WE DON'T HAVE ANY MORTARS!" Mick paused as the cracks of near-missed bullets popped off around him, pulling his radioman behind some cover, before continuing with, "GET SOME GUYS IN THOSE WINDOWS! I'LL BE RIGHT BACK," as he scrambled up to peek around the corner and check on First Sergeant Parks and the two squads she had rounded the corner with.

Jeremiah was slowly moving forward with LT Jones and his platoon and finally sent one of their teams into a building to provide overwatch from the second floor windows. Amongst the gunfire, a rocket came spiraling in, leaving a long smoke trail suspended in air behind it, striking the ground in front of Jeremiah's team. In the dust, dirt, smoke, and debris of the explosion's concussion, Jeremiah was thrust back into the wall of the building behind him. It took a split moment before the dull ringing crescendoed into the unintelligible shouts and screams of alarm, fear, and pain. One of his soldiers had taken the brunt of the blast, shielding the others, and his mangled remains coated Jeremiah and the other three soldiers there with him. Without the luxury of time to weep or mourn, they couldn't try to pick up any pieces, Jeremiah couldn't take the time he'd like to ensure his other soldiers were completely uninjured, instead he shouted for them to return fire as he threw a grenade into the direction of the rocket's origin.

Jeremiah glanced upward when he heard gunfire and breaking glass, and seeing that his second team was in place and firing away, he began scanning forward for a better position to bound towards, while he continued firing at any target he lined up with his iron sights.

Mick ran back around the corner from Parks's direction, yelling, "PRATT, ALRIGHT… WE'RE GONNA…" but was instantly cut off from finishing his sentence by a bullet to his helmet, throwing him backward to the ground behind a wall.

At hearing his name, Jeremiah turned in time to see Mick get hit and felt like his heart had stopped.

Mick rolled over on his back with wide eyes while Jeremiah held his breath with surprise. Mick reached up with quick, unsteady hands and felt the indention in his helmet. Relieved that the helmet worked better than he ever would have guessed, he looked over at Jeremiah and calmly said, "Make sure you stay low," before noticing the gruesome casualty of Jeremiah's squad.

Mick re-focused, managed to climb to a kneeling position and made eye contact with Jeremiah, "STAY PUT! I'VE GOT TO LINE WILKENS OUT," he shouted. And pointing to a place across the street in front of them added, "WHEN I GET BACK, WE'RE GONNA MOVE FOR A BETTER POSITION," and was off again to Wilkens's position.

Jeremiah eyed the place that Mick had pointed out and quickly reviewed the ground there and where he currently was, selecting lines of approach and advancement, making himself ready for the order to go.

In an instant, Mick was back behind Jeremiah again. "ALRIGHT! LET'S GO," he shouted as he fired a grenade from the launcher under the barrel of his rifle, signaling it was time to move.

Without hesitation, Jeremiah moved forward with his platoon while his other team fired from their place in the building above. They charged forward, firing on the run, while the two other squads emerged from their alleyways firing bullets and grenades as they advanced in unison.

The platoon made it to the side of the street and dug in. Sergeant Wilkens's platoon lost five men, but didn't appear to have any other casualties.

Jeremiah's platoon made it, but with some difficulty, losing several soldiers, with a few others getting injured in the rush. One of his men had just realized that he had sustained minor shrapnel wounds from the earlier rocket blast.

First Sergeant Parks made it safely, but was trying to deliver aid to one of the squads which had two injured during their advance; one was shot in the thigh and had to be dragged the rest of the way, and the second injury was when the guy dragging the first man was shot in the arm and both were getting bandaged up. The arm casualty was bandaged quickly and he immediately took up a fighting position and began shooting along with the others. The thigh injury had lost a lot of blood and the squad had to apply a tourniquet and a dose of morphine.

Mick was back on the radio calling for medics, requesting artillery or mortar fire and relaying his new position to anyone who'd listen. It sounded like there was finally a reply, but Jeremiah couldn't hear it over the gunfire.

Seeing that the situation was what it was, Parks yelled toward Jeremiah, Mick, and the others, "WE'RE GONNA MOVE UP THERE," pointing to a large office building that could provide overlook and a little more cover. "GIVE US COVER," she added as she departed with the remains of her platoon.

Jeremiah's and Sergeant Wilkens's platoons delivered volleys of suppressive fire. Mick leaned up to Jeremiah's ear while they all fired, and yelling over the gunfire said, "There's an infantry platoon holed in a few blocks to the north! They're gonna try and take one block to the south, while we take one block to the north and meet them in the middle. We'll need to bound Wilkens's platoon ahead next!" And all the while, Jeremiah kept one eye on Parks, making sure she got to the building safely.

After Parks and her soldiers disappeared into the building, Sergeant Wilkens's platoon prepared to bound ahead, but were abruptly stopped by an onslaught of lead from a SPARTAN advance. The company was now taking more casualties, and the fury of the attack made it difficult to patch wounds.

As everyone was trying to fire back from behind cover, Jeremiah yelled for Wilkens and said, "You can take your platoon around that way," pointing to an alternate route, which he hoped could flank the current assault. He was adding, "We'll fire a few grenades to get you going, then offer suppressive fire," when a large round struck the building that Parks and Third Platoon had been firing from.

The eruption of dust and smoke, along with the deafening blast, turned all Bravo Company's heads that direction. "Was that a tank?!" Mick exclaimed.

Jeremiah's stomach sank to his knees. He looked over to see pieces of the building fall to the streets below and what looked like SPARTAN troops advancing toward the gaping hole it left.

Wilkens and his platoon fired a few grenades among their gunfire. Mick picked up the radio, "This is Bravo-Six, over! Enemy Tango 100 meters out, need artillery, over!"

Jeremiah's head felt fuzzy with desperation, and his vision narrowed into a hazy tunnel. The gunfire, the radio static, the shouts of his platoon, and encroaching SPARTAN enemies were an overwhelming crescendo, which should have zeroed Jeremiah's focus to his platoon – except they all drew his mind to Parks. Jeremiah rose, firing a grenade into the crowd of SPARTANS who were trying to storm Parks's building, then began firing from the hip as he sprinted toward the building entrance.

"PRATT!! WAIT!" Mick and LT Jones yelled after him in vain, as their company's position was being advanced upon.

Jeremiah heard Mick's call somewhere in his subconscious, but it did not register; not over the urgency he felt. Jeremiah sprinted, deftly leaping and dodging obstacles, debris and rubble, all the while firing bullets from his rifle like it were an extension of his own body. And SPARTANS were falling.

Jeremiah reached the building and kicked the door in, rushing in alone and without hesitation. He fired a burst of rounds through the hole left by the tank round, then loaded another grenade, firing it into the chest of an approaching SPARTAN, turning his life into a pink vapor and killing a few others around him.

Seeing the staircase in the dark, dusty building, Jeremiah sprinted up to the second floor where Parks and Third Platoon had been. At first all he saw were several KIA of Third Platoon, but was relieved that Parks was not among them. In addition to those bodies, he saw SPARTANS who were entering the second floor on the opposite end, so he crouched to a knee, bringing his rifle to his cheek, and squeezing his trigger whenever his front sight post touched on a SPARTAN. He shot four and emptied what was left of his magazine as he rose to his feet and moved forward, making sure they wouldn't get back up.

While dropping his empty magazine, Jeremiah was knocked to the floor by another huge blast, engulfing him in a tsunami of dust and pebbles. He scrambled to his feet, wiping the dust from his eyes, and heard people storming up the stairs. He frantically clawed for a new magazine to slap into his rifle, as he saw a grenade being tossed into the corridor from the stairwell.

Jeremiah dove into the first room he saw just as the grenade exploded, again sending plumes of dust through the second floor and shaking the walls and ceiling. Jeremiah quickly reached for that magazine and finally slapped it into his rifle's magazine well, then immediately rounded the doorway back into the corridor just in time for the rifle of his muzzle to bump into the chest of a SPARTAN infantryman who was coming for him. The two men were both taken aback, and for a split second stood there with wide eyes, just looking at one another in surprise before Jeremiah shot him, ending their awkward silence.

Bullets were being fired at him in the dark hallway, and he didn't notice them, or that they struck around him. He fired and fired and fired. Through all the battles and action he'd seen before, he'd never been so close to the enemy in a gunfight. The first few were close enough to touch, and many of them were struck by his muzzle before they were struck by his bullets, and ironically, this close proximity is what may have saved him – the SPARTANS toward the back of the corridor shot frantically into the dark, often hitting their own men in the process, while Jeremiah kept low, shooting them, while becoming disoriented in the relentless onslaught until he had killed the SPARTANS in that hallway. Coated in a thick layer of dust, and covered in other people's blood, Jeremiah was scared, but just for Parks. Without seeing her, the fear of not finding her alive grew – until he heard the gunfire on the floor above him.

Without another thought, Jeremiah rushed upstairs to the other floor to find Private Meeks, from Third Platoon, shooting at SPARTANS at the far end of the corridor, with Specialist Oliver lying lifelessly on the floor next to him. Jeremiah rushed up beside him, firing away and asking, "Where's Parks?!"

Private Meeks nodded to the room next to them, saying "THERE," as he continued to shoot down the hall. Jeremiah grabbed Oliver by the collar and dragged him into the room with Parks. Once in the room, Jeremiah dropped Oliver without another look and hurried over to Parks, who was injured, though alert and bandaging her own forearm. He hadn't noticed any others of Third Platoon, but didn't care enough in that moment to inquire about them.

"Jeremiah!" she exclaimed in relief, through teary eyes. She wasn't crying, or at least she wasn't sobbing. Jeremiah wasn't sure if the tears were because of the pain, or the situation in general, or at seeing him, but they brought on an unexpected and uncontrollable surge of emotions for him. Tears welled in his eyes, but through an even tone asked, "You okay?"

Parks nodded and finished her dressing. She said, "Me and Meeks are it," as she scrambled to her feet, looking at Oliver's body; "We need to get out of here."

"Stack on Meeks," Jeremiah said, "I'll toss a grenade, and we'll head back down the stairs."

Parks was looking pale, but she wouldn't have admitted any weakness, plus, it wouldn't have done any good – they had to move or they were going to die. Jeremiah still felt frantic, being overly worried for Parks, but choked it back and threw his grenade.

The blast silenced the gunfire long enough for them to enter the hallway, where Jeremiah situated Parks to be the first to enter the stairwell, while he and Meeks took turns shooting and falling back.

Jeremiah made it to stairs next and hurried down after Parks, arriving in time to see her shot in the thigh. Her scream sounded feminine. He watched her fall to the ground, where she immediately fired back, killing the SPARTAN who shot her. Hit with a sting of fear and alarm, Jeremiah rushed down after her, firing on the run, hitting the infantryman behind the one Parks killed, and without slowing his pace, rushed to a third SPARTAN, breaking his jaw with the butt of his rifle, sending him to the ground in a painful thud. Jeremiah stuck his muzzle in his man's sternum and fired three rounds until the life departed the eyes looking back up at him.

He turned to find Meeks trying to aid Parks. "HOW IS SHE?" he shouted.

"I'm shot," Parks retorted in aggravation, as if it were stupid to ask such an obvious thing.

Jeremiah grabbed her, and threw her over his shoulder, desperate to get her out of the building, urgently trying to get her down one more flight of stairs as their building was being overrun with the enemy. "MEEKS, GO!"

They were suddenly stopped again by the sound of mortar blasts. Though outside, the building shook, dropping bits of plaster, gypsum board, and more dust. After half a dozen or so rapid mortar drops, there was an audible explosion outside, a small distance away. Relieved, Jeremiah took it to be friendly mortar rounds, with the last explosion striking the tank. "Atta boy, Mick!" Jeremiah uttered before turning back to Meeks. "Go!"

Meeks ran point down to the first floor, firing here and there as needed, until reaching the ground level, where a squad-sized element of SPARTANS were entering through the gaping hole left by the initial tank round. Meeks yelled in alarm and sprayed lead from his automatic battle rifle into the squad before him.

Coming down the stairs, Jeremiah nearly fell down at the sight, but managed to keep to his feet. The SPARTAN squad had begun firing back, striking Meeks in the calf, causing him to fall to the floor. Jeremiah returned fire with one arm, while he held Parks over his shoulder with the other.

Parks screamed out in pain, and Jeremiah realized she'd been shot again, the force of it knocking him down. Meeks was shooting again now, but unable to get to his feet. Jeremiah had no choice but to release Parks as he rolled over, lifting his rifle with both hands, firing into the incoming troops. Alongside Meeks, he fired from the floor and continued firing as he climbed back to his feet. Jeremiah advanced on the squad, and the few remaining men of that squad advanced on them.

When his rifle ran out of ammo, he deftly transitioned to his pistol, killing them with it, until he was face to face with the last two. The first died with a point blank gunshot from Jeremiah's forty-five, as the other grabbed the muzzle of Jeremiah's pistol with one hand, while shoving his own muzzle toward Jeremiah with his other.

Jeremiah split the man's nose with his forehead, let go of his own pistol, and began pummeling the soldier with his bare hands in furious and terrifying violence. The two fell to the floor, where Jeremiah continued to land punch after punch, altering blows, left and right, till the man ceased struggling. Jeremiah rolled off the man exhausted, found his pistol, then shot the man twice, although he was probably already dead...

Jeremiah stopped for another breath, then crawled back over to Parks. Parks was ghost white, with closed eyes, but breathing lightly. Her pants were soaked in blood. Jeremiah cut away her pants with his knife and tried applying pressure to the wounds in her legs, as he called softly to her, "Parks. Parks," trying to wake her.

Meeks hobbled over, his leg bleeding at the calf, but not badly. It must've been little more than a flesh wound. "Sergeant Pratt," he said, "We can't stay here."

Jeremiah ignored him, hunched over First Sergeant Parks. "Sarah," he said again, applying pressure to her bleeding legs, "wake up, please."

Her eyes opened slowly, as if from a deep sleep, but there was no peace in her eyes, no moment of clarity or tender comfort. She didn't feel cold, and she would not experience the sudden calm that someone in her circumstance was often portrayed to have in some film; she winced from pain, but lacked the strength to cry out. "Jeremiah," was all she said, feebly.

Jeremiah felt helpless. He felt foolish and felt like her wounds were somehow his fault. "We're gonna get out of here," he said as he tried to pick her up. She screamed in horrible pain, "STOP! STOP," she begged with what was left of her might. Jeremiah fell back down with her, tears rolling down his dirty face.

She winced and groaned in pain, tears streaming down her cheeks, between painfully clinched eyes. Just as Jeremiah was about to pick her up again, she opened her eyes widely and reached her hands, gray and powdery with dirt, up to Jeremiah's face. She had a look of complete fear in her dust and tear-stained eyes; panic.

Jeremiah just looked at her and held onto her. He placed his hand on one of hers while she held his face. He wanted to say something, but either couldn't think of the words, or couldn't speak with the lump in his throat.

Meeks stood nervously but silently in the doorway hoping Sergeant Pratt would hurry and join him before more SPARTANS arrived.

Parks opened her mouth as if to speak, but nothing came out but air. Her eyes went dim, and the feeling of life left her fingers. Jeremiah lifted her body to his chest as he stood, as tears streamed down his dirty face. Her body felt different, lifeless. Jeremiah felt nauseous, clinging to Parks's soulless mass, which felt less like a person and more like a liquid filled sack of stuff.

Jeremiah followed Meeks out the door, half in a daze, squeezing Parks's body tight against his. The outside was quiet. Not completely quiet, there were noises of war, but they were now at a short distance away, somewhere north of their position, beyond their sight, like the storm had just passed.

Meeks suddenly took off running, and with the recent events and who he was carrying, it took Jeremiah a moment to get angry over it. He started to shout at Meeks, when his eyes focused on the mess.

His stomach turned, and he stumbled, nearly falling, nearly dropping Parks's body. Managing to keep his feet, he rushed over to Meeks, who was now bending over, looking for something. It was his First Platoon.

Jeremiah's head was spinning. Confused, not believing what he was seeing, he turned toward the enemy tank and saw it smoldering, plainly destroyed. He looked back to the mass in front of him and almost vomited. He fell to his knees, laying Parks down, and looked for Mick and the rest of the company.

The carnage was ugly; bodies torn to pieces, pieces of legs and arms strewn about – clearly a direct hit from a mortar barrage. The young lieutenant's body was charred, tattered, and grossly disfigured, but intact. Jeremiah's sorrow and despair were gradually turning into fury, as he finally found his friend. Mick was dead; body torn asunder; imprinted into the surrounding scorched earth.

Mick Towers was a tremendous, larger than life figure. Perfect example of military leadership, wisdom, compassion, and understanding. He shouldn't have died like this. Jeremiah was no fool, he had known full well that war was a dangerous game, and that each of them would likely die in it; but with Mick he had thought there'd be some last words, a profound final exchange... Instead, Mick Towers was ripped apart in an instant due to a targeting error by a friendly mortar team. Jeremiah took Mick's tags and stuffed them in an empty grenade pouch on his chest rig.

"Sergeant Pratt," Meeks said quietly, but with clear alarm in his voice, "They're coming."

Jeremiah looked up and saw trucks arriving in the distance with more SPARTAN troops. He couldn't see any more of Bravo around, and didn't know whether they had moved positions or been killed too. Jeremiah became angry that SPARTAN had fuel, while they did not, but he pushed that brief thought to the side.

Jeremiah realized that he was completely unarmed. He had left his rifle and pistol back inside the building, thinking of nothing else at the time but Sarah Parks. He grabbed Mick's pistol out of its holster and slid it into his own. The hand grips were pockmarked and scarred from the shrapnel, but the weapon appeared otherwise undamaged from the mortars. There was a little blood on it, a detail that Jeremiah noticed without comment, though it made him feel like it was now more of a part of his friend.

Jeremiah then knelt and lifted Parks's body back upon his shoulder and headed off with Meeks, deciding that there was nothing else that they could do to keep SPARTAN from having what was left of the town.

"What about Third Brigade?" Meeks asked.

"I don't care," Jeremiah said grimly, exhausted from the fight, distraught from the losses, and tired of life, as they wandered off. He hugged Parks's body as they walked away as if it gave him strength to go on.

Meeks and Jeremiah eventually decided to move into the woods. They weren't sure where to go. They had no idea whether they should go to another front, or just try to make it back to friendly territory – wherever that was now. Jeremiah had no idea how far SPARTAN had advanced. He wasn't really sure if there was a friendly position to make it back to, so they just headed back toward Phase Line Omega at the threshold of the Capitol.

From sheer fatigue, Jeremiah and Meeks had to stop and rest. Jeremiah couldn't go on carrying Parks's body, but couldn't bring himself to just abandon her. Meeks had probably considered asking Jeremiah to leave it, he may have even considered leaving Jeremiah and going off on his own, but he didn't. Meeks and Jeremiah made a stretcher out of paracord and small trees after they'd rested awhile, and carried her together the rest of the way.

Neither had kept track of how far they had gone or for how long they'd been walking when they heard a nearby vehicle. Jeremiah told Meeks to set the stretcher down and to stay with it while he went to have a look. Jeremiah drew Mick's pistol and moved quietly through the brush toward the street. As he drew closer he began to hear voices and marching. He slowed his pace so that he could move even more quietly, and finally came to a point where he could see.

Relieved, he didn't bother going back for Meeks; he left the woods and called out, "Hey," crossing the street.

The soldiers were startled by this figure emerging from the woods, colored like the forest over every inch of himself. They flinched, and a few raised their rifles in response.

"Whoa! Whoa!" Jeremiah exclaimed, raising his hands in the air, never dropping his weapon. "It's Sergeant Pratt," he reassured them. "I've got wounded. I've got wounded."

Jeremiah, Meeks, and Parks were gathered and taken to a makeshift base just inside Phase Line Omega. Meeks was taken to a medic office so that his leg could be disinfected, cleaned, and bandaged. Parks's body was placed among the other dead that had made it back that far, which weren't many.

Jeremiah sat outside the temporary mortuary and wiped his face. He sipped water, but not for thirst, just to find something to do, something or anything to mask his emotions and the loss he felt. For the first time, he felt like he'd lost everything, and he no longer felt a connection to anything.

And then he saw Sergeant Major Booth. Booth had seen him first and was approaching him with purpose. At first Jeremiah was confused. Jeremiah, at first, couldn't make sense of seeing his former platoon sergeant. Jeremiah had thought all of his company had been killed back at Post Whiskey, along with Mick and Parks, where they tried to aid Third Battalion. As CSM Booth neared, Jeremiah's confusion turned more into frustration. Jeremiah could see the smug and pretentious look on the man's face and predicted the forthcoming scolding or lecture.

Jeremiah lowered his water bottle to his lap and sat stoically, watching this man march toward him. "Sergeant Pratt," CSM Booth called out, accusingly.

Jeremiah just sat, still wondering what this man was doing.

CSM Booth walked right to Jeremiah and started in on him, saying, "Sergeant First Class Pratt! Where have you been! And what the…" until he was cut off.

Jeremiah decided that he didn't want to hear any more. He sat outwardly expressionless as Sergeant Major Booth began talking, but he was boiling on the inside. He wasn't even listening to the man's words, he just kept staring at his clean uniform. Parks lay behind him, inside the little room, dead. Mick and First Platoon had been torn to pieces back at some nameless town near Whiskey, the rest of Bravo and the battalion were likely dead, and Jeremiah sat there, still wearing Parks's blood, and the blood of SPARTANS from close quarters combat, and he still had Mick's dog tags in his pouch. But Sergeant Major Booth's uniform was clean. Jeremiah stood in an instant, launching a violent and furious uppercut into Booth's chin, instantly silencing the man.

Those nearby watched in awe as Booth rose off of his feet, with blood leaking between shattered teeth, as he fell backward, either unconscious or dead, before he hit the ground with a hollow thump.

The onlookers watched Jeremiah stand there for a moment, looking down at Sergeant Major Booth. No one said a word. They watched as Jeremiah walked away. No one was really sure what had happened, why Sergeant Pratt struck a higher ranking NCO like that, but nothing came of it. Of course, there may not have been time or opportunity for anything regarding it to materialize.

.

Chapter 13

SPARTAN Invasion

General Simmons climbed upon his horse and watched his army begin to move forward. The last of the supply wagons and trailers were still being loaded. A few troops of the cavalry were sent ahead, with the foot soldiers already marching behind.

The general watched their newest recruit, Jonas the Preacher, or 'Former-Preacher,' he corrected in his own head, march past Uriah and Josiah, who had been placed in a wagon for the movement forward.

"He's a good lad," the general said to Uriah as they watched him march on, carrying his rifle.

Uriah didn't say anything. He didn't think that Jonas was "a good lad," and he strongly suspected that General Simmons knew the Congregationals' view on weapons and war, so he sat quietly.

General Simmons smiled in amusement. "Don't worry, Uriah," the general said, "He's on the right side of history, as are you and your son."

The general gently kicked his heels into his horse's gut, goading it forward. As his horse slowly began to move past Uriah's and Josiah's wagon he added, "Without your part, Uriah, none of this would be possible."

Uriah was feeling very uneasy about all of it, and while no direct threats had been made, he certainly felt like, had he not agreed to go, that the people of his congregation would suffer for it. As it was, they were now allowed to go back to their houses and lives.

Uriah had tried his best to assure the general that he'd go and do whatever they wanted as long as Josiah was allowed to stay home with the congregation and as long as Jonas would not be allowed to join the SPARTAN Army. The general wouldn't allow it, or even hear Uriah out. It was clear that Josiah was there to further ensure that Uriah played along and that Jonas was deliberately being paraded in front of him as a SPARTAN soldier to reinforce the idea that General Simmons, that SPARTAN, was in control.

As the general rode ahead, he was joined by two un-uniformed men who rode their horses carelessly and without any reins. The general nodded at them and said, "You're off to gather Sergeant Pratt, yes?"

The man with the beard and blue eyes nodded and said, "The boy," nodding back toward Josiah, "you shouldn't bring him."

The general looked at the men quizzically, raising an eyebrow. "Does he make you nervous?"

"He does."

The general laughed. "I didn't realize Flagstaff was so skittish," he said. "Don't worry about the boy. Besides, all he's going to do is make sure his father walks the line. All you need to do is fetch Jeremiah Pratt."

The man with the blue eyes nodded.

"And it's important to take him alive, please," the general added.

"You know that's up to him," Flagstaff said. Flagstaff was about to move along, but the blue-eyed man with the beard paused a moment and looked back over at the general, while the other rode on ahead. "Why are we going to all this trouble for that old man?"

The general looked at Flagstaff, "It should be obvious."

"Which part?"

The general looked annoyed at the look on Flagstaff's face. "Sergeant Jeremiah Pratt is some war hero, never mind that he's an imbecile, or that he's only famous because he's *alive* and was lucky in combat a few times, but because the ignorant and idiotic masses hold him in some high esteem."

Flagstaff's face said that they still hadn't heard a good response.

General Simmons huffed. "We tried getting him on our side. That didn't work. So now we need to make him a bad guy, and simultaneously make us a good guy in the minds of the people. That will require a trial and an execution – and we can't very well do that with a corpse. In fact, just killing him may do the opposite of what we want."

The general glared at Flagstaff, annoyed he'd had to take the time to explain things. "So read my mind if it helps it sink in," the general said. "Get him, and take him alive."

Flagstaff only nodded before riding away effortlessly to join his others in their pursuit.

***

The city was in complete ruin. Tall grass, thorn bushes, other shrubs and small trees were growing in the streets and crevices in the concrete sidewalks. Wrecked cars, gun trucks, and tanks littered the streets, hindering line of sight and providing easy concealment for anyone or anything. No building seemed to have escaped the war unscathed, with each having at least pockmarks of bullets and shrapnel, and at worst having been completely razed.

Pratt and Tyler entered the city's threshold cautiously. A pack of feral dogs could be seen running across the street several blocks away.

"I haven't been here in a long time," Tyler said.

"I haven't been here since the city was being invaded," Jeremiah said, not commenting on the Champ's uncharacteristically nervous tone. "Do you remember where you found it?"

Tyler swallowed hard, "I... I think so."

Pratt didn't believe in being "overly cautious," or "too stealthy," not since the fall of everything. He guided Tyler slowly through the streets, sticking closely to shadows and concealment, being as cautious and as stealthy as possible.

Neither spoke much. Both of them scanned down streets as they passed and listened for anything. Jeremiah wasn't sure what the idiot with the big "Champ" belt buckle was thinking, he was just glad the fool was actually quiet. Pratt knew some people had to be there somewhere, and in places like this, without grazing pastures or fields to till, people in a city like this were likely very desperate and therefore very dangerous.

The city was an eerie place; large and seemingly abandoned; a carcass-like ghost of its former self. The wind could be heard rushing between the derelict builds and through the vacant streets, but the wind and their own footsteps weren't the only sounds. Dogs and rats scurrying about could be heard along with the occasional movement of something else; a brief rustle here or there, or the occasional sound of an empty bottle rolling over pavement, but Jeremiah wasn't sure whether it was just stray dogs and racoons or if it was *someone*.

"Uh, what's that?" the Champ asked as he gawked down a side road.

Pratt looked and saw the silhouette of someone standing and staring back at them, about 200 meters away. "Just keep moving."

"He just stood up and… and just started staring," the Champ said.

"Be quiet," Pratt retorted as if scolding a child. "How much farther is it?"

Tyler "the Champ" Johnson pointed ahead and off to the right, "Just up there a bit, I think. Another turn ur two."

Most of the buildings were several stories high. There were a few towering buildings up ahead as well. All the buildings had signs of damage. Some were badly damaged, either caving in on themselves, or spilling rubble and debris onto the street like the petrified entrails of a titan's eviscerated carcass.

As they walked onward, Jeremiah noticed other people here and there; vagrants scattered in different streets, alleyways and rooftops; all of which stopped and looked at them as if they were trespassers. Jeremiah glanced behind him and saw the first figure tailing some distance back. "Pick up the pace a bit," he ordered Tyler quietly.

"Hey!" a dirty, hooded woman yelled as she appeared in front of them from around a building's corner. It wasn't a friendly greeting, but sounded more like it was being used as, "Halt."

"Hi," Pratt said as he ushered Tyler right past her without the slightest delay.

To the great war hero, Jeremiah Pratt, these people were a nuisance, not a real threat. He could see where this was leading. It was easy to see that they wanted something, and that they planned on taking it from whomever stumbled into *their* city. He could imagine these people feeling like their greater numbers equalled greater strength; he was sure that they expected an easy victory, that they'd intimidate their prey to the extent that people would just give in and give up anything without resistance... The mere thought of it only bred resentment in Pratt's old mind.

By now, others were in the street and even more began spilling out from buildings or alleyways as the woman shouted another "HEY!" after them. Pratt and Tyler eventually did stop as five men out of the larger gathering encroached upon them, entering the street from a concealed place, blocking their path.

Each of them was armed; four had carbines, each weapon layered in dirt, which they held in a way that suggested they were mimicking a poster. One had a pistol and was holding it carelessly down by his side.

They were now surrounded. A girl caught Tyler's eye when she turned to say something to the person behind her. The girl was in her early twenties, with dirty cheeks, blonde hair in pigtails, and wearing a black jacket that read "Player" across the back. *Nice jacket*, he thought with sincere admiration.

"Hi," Tyler said, but she didn't seem to notice.

Pratt grabbed Tyler's collar firmly with his left hand, securing his property, and thumbed his rifle's safety, readying himself.

"This is a toll road," the filthy old woman said, as she and several others caught up to them from behind. "And it's our road."

"Oh, a toll... Well," Tyler said with a sly look, "You don't have to pay me. Although, I may charge this fellow twice," nodding his head back toward Pratt.

The woman looked confused. Of course, she looked dirty and used too. Her knuckles and forearms were scarred and weathered with age. Her face and neck were leathery, and she was missing a few teeth. She had a double barrel shotgun slung around her back, but the others with her, an assortment of men and women of various ages, although none as old as Pratt, carried their weapons at the ready. Each weapon, whether pistol or rifle, were as filthy as the people carrying them; negligence which bothered Pratt more than the hold up.

It was like a pack of terriers trying to scare a cage-fighting pitbull.

"Naw, you're both gonna pay double," the woman replied dryly.

Pratt didn't say a word, just eyed the woman, measuring her up, but Tyler couldn't help himself. "We're not together," he said, again speaking of Pratt. "But I'll pay 'Player' there twice…" he added with a wink, "… in love."

The old woman frowned, "What good would four seconds do anybody?" It was hard to tell if she were being sarcastic or making a serious remark. "Naw, yur just gonna give whate'er we want."

Pratt, holding Tyler tightly, heard a subtle approach from behind him just as he saw the group behind the woman stepping forward. With only his right arm, Pratt raised his rifle at the hip and shot the woman in the face. She dropped instantly, with the bullet exiting the back of her head, striking the man behind her in the neck.

He fell clutching his throat, with eyes open so wide that they seemed like they were screaming, as Tyler jerked in surprise, letting out an animated, "WHOA!"

The rest of the group flinched backward, not a one raising their weapons or returning fire, but each appearing in shock. Their reaction angered Pratt. It wasn't that he wanted to be shot or that he even wanted a fight, but that he loathed the entire scenario; people ganging up on a perceived weaker force and trying to intimidate them with physical harm, but when the first punch comes their way, they break down, scared and frightened. These people looked as though they merely played tough, relying solely on intimidation to gather their "tolls."

Easy to be brave from a fortress, Pratt thought.

And many of these people now looked completely and utterly shocked at the violence they saw. No one was making any effort to check on their woman or to help the terrified man who lay gurgling on his own blood.

The Champ had his hands in the air, as he was held in place by Pratt's firm grip. It was all he could do to try and keep from being the next one shot. "You're crazy!" he exclaimed.

***

The SPARTAN army arrived at what was left of Engine's Rest. Uriah and Josiah were taken aback at the destruction. While fleeing in the dark they could only see so much, but now returning to the scene in daylight, they found it surreal. It looked like most people had fled, and the main drag had two entire buildings that had been completely consumed by fire and all the others were riddled with bullet holes or even bigger craters.

"Flagstaff," General Simmons muttered to himself, both annoyed at the mess and state of ruin and impressed with the battlefield effectiveness. "Captain, we'll leave a few supplies here for the townspeople, but keep the main element moving. We won't be delayed here long."

"Roger that, sir," the captain answered back, before parroting the order and sprinting his horse ahead to the lead element of the march, leaving a trail of dust, rising like off-white smoke, behind him.

As SPARTAN troops were dropping off some provisions to the few people who were left in the damaged town, General Simmons took advantage of the opportunity to spread propaganda. "Men and women," he called as the goods were being unloaded, "What you have all suffered here, the unspeakable carnage and terror that were inflicted upon you cannot be taken away."

The general paused a moment for a breath and then shouted, "BUT THERE CAN BE JUSTICE!"

He went on, "SPARTAN cannot sit by any longer while these crimes are allowed to happen without any response from the governing body! SPARTAN cannot simply sit idly by and watch its neighbors be tormented and slaughtered. Where's L&M leadership? Where's the LaMS' relief efforts?"

The general made eye contact with the people who were present to hear him. "Jeremiah Pratt is a terrorist and murderer, and while I cannot erase his crimes or bring back the lives he stole, or replace the buildings he's destroyed, I can bring him to justice! SPARTAN will restore law and order, *AND PEACE*, to our broken nation!"

While the supply wagons finished unloading and set off to rejoin the rest of the army, General Simmons looked upon the crowd with an expression of knowing sympathy before he went further.

He continued with, "Jeremiah Pratt will stand trial for this. I know it's not much, but I'm afraid all we can offer you now is *justice* and these morsels of food and water, until order can be reinstated."

The general looked over at Uriah and Josiah, whose wagon had just departed and who were looking on as they moved ahead, and said "God bless you all," bidding the people of Engine's Rest adieu.

Alex the guitar player was there. He was just Alex now, since his guitar had recently been destroyed in the little war the town had recently endured. He had run to hide at first, but slowly gathered the courage to approach the show. He didn't have a guitar anymore, but he had food and water, thanks to SPARTAN; and Alex liked food and water. Despite witnessing the massacre and destruction, and having a front row view of the men who initiated the violence, at hearing the general's monologue, Alex might have even been convinced that Jeremiah Pratt was a jerk, the ruthless villain and destroyer of cities. By the gift of free food and a charismatic speech, even Alex, who'd witnessed the first shots in Engine's Rest, may have been charmed into forgetting what he had witnessed and coaxed into believing old man Pratt was the aggressor. "That old man killed Tim n' Jed," Alex shouted in solidarity.

As the general approached the wagon that Uriah and Josiah rode in, Uriah said, "None of that was true," flatly. Uriah didn't like being taken against his will, he did not like his son being used as leverage, and he detested liars and loathed those who would use God to pander or invoke approval from the masses.

General Simmons smiled and slowed his gait to match the speed of Uriah's wagon. "Why, Uriah Morris, what's 'true' will be what's written in the history books. And it just so happens that we're on our way to make history," he said with a wink as he rode on ahead.

"It will all work together for good," Josiah said, trying to reassure his father.

Uriah nodded without expression and looked out into the horizon, afraid for his son and also proud of his son's faith. Uriah fought back the frog in his throat and the tears welling in his eyes, resisting the combined emotions of fear and love. "Yeah," he finally said as the tops of the city's buildings were just coming into view, "It'll all be okay."

"Wow," Josiah marveled, never having seen anything like it in size before. "Like the Tower of Babel."

Uriah nodded, "But instead of dispersing the people by confusing their languages, this time God has dispersed us all with the confusion of violence and war."

Josiah said nothing and just stared at the tall structures coming into sight as they approached.

Uriah began to dread their arrival, afraid of what they may find or of what might happen once SPARTAN got into the facility. He feared what General Simmons may do if he couldn't remember how to unlock the door.

"Are you really afraid that you can't do it?" Josiah asked, still staring into the cityscape.

"Huh?" Uriah asked.

Josiah looked at him. "Oh, sorry," he said, "I thought you said something."

Uriah shook his head in confusion. "I didn't," he said softly, looking at his son in wonder.

***

The gang of shocked city people were nervously taking in the scene; an old man with a hostage and a rifle that worked, a dead woman, and a dying man. If it were simply a numbers game, the gang of people knew that they had the advantage over the old man, yet they were scared and he was still and quiet, with intense, dangerous eyes, watching them all like he was a predator and they were prey.

It was unnerving and a little confusing, and none of them quite knew what to do next.

But the old man spoke. "Unless anyone else wants to die, he and I are gonna go," he said as he backed slowly away, still holding Tyler.

The group of people clearly didn't like that idea, and nearly all of them shifted uneasily, but also slowly, keeping a diligent eye on the muzzle of his rifle.

A younger female, likely in her early twenties said, "You can't just come in here and kill people!"

"I'll keep that in mind for next time," Pratt said as he continued his snail-paced retreat, weapon still at the ready.

Maybe if he had not given any reply it would've turned out differently, but the tart remark was apparently the straw that broke the dirty camel's back, since the man next to the girl changed from alarm to anger. Pratt watched his shoulder move, his head rise in anger, as he lifted the rifle in his hands.

Pratt released the Champ, quickly securing his rifle with both hands as he raised it to his cheek and fired into the crowd, quickly dropping the man, the girl, and three other men beside them. The pig-tailed beauty in the Player jacket ran, along with several others. A few tried to fire back, with at least one's weapon failing to fire (due to the filth, Pratt suspected), one firing accidentally at the ground, and the other firing wildly into nothing before Pratt killed them.

Jeremiah Pratt continued firing a furious hail of bullets as the few ran away and most others dropped dead or dying.

Tyler Johnson stood, shaking with his arms still up, otherwise frozen and silent with fear and horror as the old man dispatched the group that had only a moment earlier had them surrounded. Tyler looked on, too scared to move, afraid that his heavy breathing would somehow make him a target, as the firing stopped. Four people had managed to flee, and eight others lay in pools of blood, either dead or wishing they were dead.

Tyler, still in shock, began lowering his hands slowly, until old man Pratt walked over to a downed man who was moaning and fired two more rounds into his chest. Tyler gasped and shot his hands back up into the air.

Pratt walked back over to Tyler. "C'mon, let's go," he said, grabbing Tyler by the arm and dragging him on.

They navigated down one street, then turned down another. Neither Tyler or Pratt spoke unless to give or ask for an immediate direction. They found themselves on a residential street, crammed with what used to be upper-class townhouses, but the decorative sidewalk trees that were once protected by elaborate wrought iron cages had either been cut down for firewood or for some other purpose, or had overgrown, giving the walk an eerie vibe. The sidewalks were riddled with weeds sprouting up from the cracks and control joints or had centipede grass spreading across them like kudzu.

Most of the streetlight poles were damaged, and of course, none worked anymore. None of the townhouses had any visible glass left in the windows or doors, many being boarded up or simply left open. There were wrecked and abandoned cars strewn about, all of which had been robbed of rubber, and in the few cars that still had seats, the upholstery was gone.

"The real estate market in this area has really taken a nosedive," Pratt quipped in uncharacteristic wit.

Tyler looked at the old man in quiet surprise.

"Is this the street?" Pratt asked through his bearded, stern face, taking in the dismal scene.

Tyler nervously answered with, "I think so. I think this may be the house up here."

***

SPARTAN crossed a field of tall grass and approached a cluster of trees that surrounded a rocky foothill at the boundary of the city. The buildings here at the outskirts weren't tiny or insignificant by any means, but they were still dwarfed by the high rises at the city center.

Uriah and Josiah's wagon pulled up in front of a halted army. Near the front of the line, they saw Jonas standing there with his rifle, holding it with a grin that said, *See what I got.*

Uriah looked away like he had not seen the boy, not wanting to give him the pleasure of any reaction.

Their wagon soon came to a stop where they were made to unload in front of General Simmons, who'd already dismounted and was waiting on them with a warm smile. "Mr. Morris," he said with sincere elation, "how does it feel to be back?"

Josiah looked around, confused. He had thought that they were going into the city and didn't understand why they were stopping here at a tree line just outside of the city in an undeveloped field. It looked like a flood plane with its proximity to the river. He wanted to ask what was going on, but didn't. He stayed quiet, although he was growing more and more nervous watching his father in this position.

"Come on," the general beckoned both of them, pointing them to a path, lined by a row of SPARTAN soldiers.

Uriah looked behind him to find another squad following. He reached for his son's arm and guided him along as he followed the general.

The general spoke the entire way, like an excited child. "I cannot articulate how excited I am to finally see this place," the general said gleefully. "I am not sure how much of the facility you got to see with your clearance..."

"Well I know there's a backdoor, but I've never been through it. We always entered from the main front entrance."

"Ah, sure," the general said. "Well, we're not going through the front. We haven't been able to verify if the tunnel through the parking garage is still intact, and we'd prefer to avoid the hassle of the local riffraff."

"General," Uriah said meekly, "I just mean that I'm not sure that I can open the backdoor... If I could even remember how to open the front door... I mean, I think these locks work off of a power source..."

The general smiled arrogantly. "There's power. And the lock will work," he said. The general pointed his eyes toward Josiah, "It would be unpleasant if we brought you both all this way for nothing."

Uriah looked ahead, trying to remain calm.

Patting Uriah on the shoulder the general added, "I feel certain it'll come back to you."

The group entered the mouth of the cave to find its path lit by torches and lined by more SPARTAN soldiers, leading to what looked like the end of the cave.

"Is this it?" the general asked one of the SPARTAN soldiers nearest the end wall of the cave.

"It is, yes sir."

"Well, here you are, Mr. Morris," the general said with an excited smile adorning his face.

Josiah thought the man looked evil, there in the darkness with the torchlight flickering on the general's features, the shadows dancing upon his face in eerie animation.

Uriah approached apprehensively and bewildered. "Here?" he asked, looking around quizzically.

The general at first seemed confused by Uriah's confusion, but then looked behind him at the barren cave wall. "Ah, stupid me, of course," he said with amusement. "The wall… It's a hidden door. But it *is* a door." The general patted it with his hand, "Yes, it seems the ole US was just starting to get clever at the point of their demise." With a smile and wide eyes, he added, "Had they been this clever all along they may still be around."

The general stepped behind Uriah and gently pushed him toward the cave wall. "So Uriah, here you are," he said, placing an arm around Josiah's shoulder, for Uriah's benefit.

Uriah nodded and turned to the wall. He tried to clear his head and focus. He tried to remember his former training, which he had spent the last twenty years trying to forget.

The general leaned over to Josiah and whispered in his ear, "Do you know what on earth he's doing?"

Josiah shook his head.

"The Gordian Lock is a special lock that is basically set to a certain frequency," the general whispered. "You probably don't know what 'frequency' means, do you, since Preachers don't do school." It wasn't a question.

Josiah said nothing.

The general added, "Your father's a gifted man, who's been trained to match that frequency with his mind. Only a handful of men have the Ability, the ole 'Silent Voice,' and he may be the only one left who's been trained to open this one."

Josiah watched his father intently. He pondered the significance of what the general had said. There was so much he didn't know about his own father.

Uriah looked as if he were having stage fright, placing a hand above him on the cave wall, with his head down and eyes closed, trying his best to focus.

"I'm not spending the night in this cave, Uriah," the general said, getting annoyed. "Hurry up, please."

Uriah was trying. He was beginning to sweat from a combination of effort and panic. He just couldn't remember. He couldn't seem to grab it. "I, I can't," he said.

"You can," the general insisted matter-of-factly.

Uriah shook his head, but kept searching, continued trying.

Josiah looked on, worried for his father and fascinated by the idea of the lock and the important function his father once served to the old government.

"Uriah," the general said evenly, clearly losing his patience, "Open the door."

Uriah felt defeated. He felt like he was letting his son down. With panic in his mind, he didn't want to admit that he just couldn't do it. It had been too long. He just couldn't find it.

"Well," the general said, releasing Josiah and taking one frustrated step forward.

Uriah slowly backed off the wall and turned around with his head down.

The general's brow furrowed in anticipation.

Still looking down, too afraid to face anyone now, Uriah opened his mouth and began to speak, but was cut off at, "I...," by the sound of the door unlatching, and the door opening.

Uriah popped his head up in astonishment.

The general exclaimed, "HAHA! I Knew you'd do it," clapping his hands together in approval as he walked forward.

Uriah looked behind him at the opening door in bewilderment and then back at Josiah who was standing there quietly, staring back at him. Uriah didn't say a word and didn't have to. He knew what had happened, and he was not going to share that with anyone – certainly not SPARTAN. Uriah shushed silently at his son, directing him to refrain from mentioning it either.

The general bounded toward the door, feeling the cold air rush around him. "Wooo!" he exclaimed giddily. "Air conditioning!"

"Get the tech guys up here," the general shouted. "You," he called to a soldier, "have them bring the boxes in here." And pointing to the Preachers, "Bring them in here, and we'll find a place for them."

"General," Uriah said, "If it's alright, now that you have access, we'd like to go back home now."

The general straightened and looked back at the Preachers with what looked like authentic sympathy. "I know," he said without any hint of sarcasm, "I know you do. But you're still needed here. I promise we'll let you return home soon."

The general looked back at the soldier, "Bring them inside, please."

Chapter 14

At Last (Flashback)

Jeremiah was still covered in dust and blood as he walked away from the place where CSM Booth now lay. Jeremiah didn't know whether the man was conscious or not, and didn't care. He wouldn't have cared if the man were dead. He did care about Parks. He cared about Mick and the rest of Bravo Company.

He wouldn't give CSM Booth another thought. He walked away with no destination in mind and his only plan was to find a solitary, quiet place where he could collapse and reset; where he could let down his guard. He was still reeling from the decimation of Bravo Company. He could still see Parks's eyes staring into his, pleading soul to soul as she released her last breath.

Jeremiah left everyone and went off alone into the woods. He walked aimlessly for a while, and it wasn't just due to the loss of Parks or Mick. It was everything. It was all the losses, from his parents, to his comrades, to the end. And it was the end. There was no saving the nation now. It was just a matter of time, and the two people he cared about the most went down with the ship, leaving Jeremiah alone, again, without hope.

Feeling sorry for himself, mourning the loss of his loved ones, he found a tiny clearing beneath a cluster of small trees and lay down. Jeremiah covered his face with his hands and cried. He lost all sense of time, but after combating both the deepest despair and the most furious anger, he fell asleep beneath the trees, accompanied only by the dark.

When Jeremiah woke, the sun had been up for a while. He sat up slowly, still sad and still angry, but with a sense of purpose. SPARTAN wasn't done. They didn't attack that far only to stop. Jeremiah picked himself up, reached down at his side and felt Mick's pistol, holstered to his thigh, reassuring himself that it was there, and made his way back to what was left of the US Army.

The FOB (Forward Operating Base) was busy with activity; soldiers in and out of uniform were scurrying about, rounding up supplies and ammo, or trying to direct civilians to different routes out of the city. SPARTAN was coming.

If Jeremiah had felt any fear before, it was gone now; after the previous night, he was resolved to a fate of battlefield death. He walked back in among the camp as easily as he'd left it the previous night. He spoke to no one. He had no unit to report to anymore. He had not paid any attention to the expressions of disgust and shock from those who happened upon him as he walked toward the shower room, but looking at himself in the mirror, once there, he was reminded of how badly he needed a shower and clean clothes.

To many, it may seem odd, considering the recent events and current situation, that he'd take the time to wash and put on fresh clothes, but to Jeremiah, it was preparation for what was coming. And after his shower, he'd shave and put on a fresh uniform. He'd even have himself a last meal, or at least have a plate to stare at – he doubted he'd be able to eat anything.

Jeremiah donned his chest rig and placed new magazines and grenades in the pouches. He slapped a new mag in the grip and holstered Mick's forty-five to his leg. Jeremiah picked up his freshly cleaned carbine that he had just acquired – he didn't have the time to zero the sights in, so he clicked his windage and front sight post the same number of times, in the same direction, as he had on his old rifle. He pulled the charging handle back and let it slam forward, driving a round into the chamber, and he flicked the selector switch to "safe."

Slinging the rifle over his shoulder and around his back, he went to find Alpha Company, hoping that any other survivors from Bravo would also go there first. The area was in chaos, the very last of the fuel was being used to move the remaining tanks behind berms at the outer edge of the FOB and Phase Line Omega, just so their cannons could be used as field artillery against the pending attack.

Companies, platoons, and squad-sized elements were moving into position. Even onesies and twosies, like Jeremiah, weren't uncommon at all, as the civilians continued to flee on foot or by wagon – really, any means available. Children were scared and crying.

And then the sirens began just moments before artillery and mortars began falling within the perimeter. The explosions and resulting plumes of smoke and dust gave more life to the scene, providing an immediate and grave sense of urgency. People were now frantically scrambling about as the US artillery and tanks began firing back, the shockwave of their recoils spewing dust in symmetrical waves around the weapons.

Jeremiah wasn't at the perimeter and couldn't see if the SPARTAN forces were in view yet or not, but he assumed they'd let the artillery rounds do as much damage as possible before sending in an assault, so he didn't feel the urgency to rush to the wire just so he could aim at targets that weren't yet there. Plus, with the heavy artillery onslaught, everyone was falling back farther and farther. He ran back with them, looking for Alpha Company, or Private Meeks, or someone he'd recognize.

People were everywhere, and panic had set in. This was the end; soldiers were deserting along with the civilians, and even to Jeremiah, those that were resolved to stand their ground began looking more and more foolish. There was no stopping SPARTAN, and Jeremiah didn't even know about the L&M forces to the south, nor would he have cared, not with the current climate. The artillery rounds were striking everywhere, even deeper into the city. SPARTAN evidently didn't intend to take over the city, but level it.

Amongst the chaos of the artillery rounds being volleyed back and forth, and the screams and the crying or the frequent shouts here and there, Jeremiah was suddenly distracted by the frantic sobs and screams of one particular person. The noise caught him like a snare and pulled him from his current course. He turned and looked, and after dodging a few people saw a woman falling to the ground, in blatant, consuming despair.

Jeremiah rushed over and helped the woman up, surprised at who it was. "Lilly," he said both in disbelief and out of sincere concern as she wildly threw her arms around him, clinging to him tightly like a life preserver. At that moment, Jeremiah wasn't even sure that she recognized him.

"Lilly," Jeremiah said, trying to get her attention. "LILLY," he pleaded, just holding her tight, hoping it made her feel somewhat secure.

"Gone, gone, gone," she sobbed uncontrollably, clutching Jeremiah like a vice.

Confused and becoming upset himself, Jeremiah began trying to walk with her while holding her close. "Why didn't you stay in your bunker?" he asked, not expecting any reply. "Why are you out here?"

"HE'S DEAD!" she screamed in horror. "TIM'S DEAD!" she cried miserably.

"Okay, okay," Jeremiah said soothingly. "We have to go. We have to leave here," he said trying to get her to release her hold on him so that they could walk through the tumult.

"Don't leave me! Don't leave me!" she pleaded with frantic eyes, still trying to pull him closer.

"I'm here," Jeremiah reassured her. "I won't leave you," he concluded, pulling her along. "We have to go."

He led her through the city, leaving the military forces and trying to distance them from the artillery and the invading enemy that would follow it. The farther they went, the fewer people they saw, but at first, there were lots of scrambling people, civilians and soldiers alike, all running, trying to get away.

By the time they found their way out of the actual city, blasts and small arms fire could be heard in the near distance behind them. Neither Jeremiah nor Lilly had spoken the entire way. Lilly was still crying, but wasn't sobbing anymore. She looked despondent and drained. Jeremiah worried about her, but had no words to offer, and only held her hand as he guided her away from danger.

Out of the city, Jeremiah steered off of the road and toward a patch of trees. The faint, rapid pops and burps of automatic small arms fire was still chorusing behind them, augmented with the occasional thunderous boom of something exploding. No one was close by them, but in the distance around them they could see others still fleeing; all too far away to hear, though they could be seen.

"Where are we going?" Lilly said, sounding utterly exhausted. She was looking at nothing, as if in a fog. There were bags under her red, swollen eyes.

"We won't go much farther," Jeremiah answered softly. "We'll find someplace up here out of the way and get some rest." Jeremiah looked over his shoulder and squinted at the setting sun. "We'll figure the rest out in the morning."

They walked into the tree line, Jeremiah wanting to avoid the streets and stay as concealed as possible. Under the tree canopy, the fading light was even fainter. The dead leaves and pine straw crunched beneath their feet with each step, a sound that usually annoyed Jeremiah a great deal. He'd typically chastise himself within his own mind for being too clumsy, while wondering how deer could move through thick brush so stealthily, but now his mind wasn't centered on his footsteps. Instead, it was divided between Lilly and his sense of duty.

As much as he fought it, and as much and for as long as he'd denied it to himself, he was drawn to Lilly, pulled by some gravity that he was unable to completely resist or even understand. He had an internal need to help her, he wanted to do whatever he could for her, he always had, and he always would – even if she couldn't return it.

But he had a conflict of wants. He wanted to be there for Lilly, but he also wanted to fight his enemies; he wanted to adhere to his sense of duty and loyalty. His closest friends had just died in battle, but here he was running away? There was no winning. No good answers: be there for Lilly and trample on the memories of his comrades and oath of service, or stay and fight, likely die, and neglect the opportunity to render much needed aid to someone he loved…

Jeremiah began to wrestle with this dilemma as he led Lilly to a patch of straw at the base of a tree. He instructed her to stay put while he gathered a few sticks and branches.

As she sat, she began to whine like a child who was falling asleep. "Don't go," she said. "Please stay with me."

"I'm not leaving you," Jeremiah said tenderly. "I'll be right here. Just close your eyes."

She may have been asleep before he finished speaking. Jeremiah would've looked silly climbing the small dogwood next to Lilly's tree, but she was asleep and no one else was around to point and laugh. It began to bend under his weight as he reached the top of the scrawny tree. Reaching the point where he didn't want to climb any higher, he gripped the trunk above him like a vise and flung his legs and body away from the tree, bending it to the ground, lowering Jeremiah as though it had been designed to.

The dogwood bends easily, but it's springy. Jeremiah wanted it to break, not raise back upright, so while the top was bent to the ground, he applied all of his weight to it, jarring it up and down until it cracked. He didn't want to break the tree in two, and doubted that he'd be able to without an axe or hatchet, but wanted the tree to bend between three and five feet off the ground, with the top leaning at an angle onto the ground. He then placed sticks on either side of the angled trunk like a ribcage. He wasn't planning on staying long, so he didn't bother trying to tie any of them in place. Once it was framed out, he packed it with leaves and straw until it was mostly covered. It wouldn't stop a hard rain, but he didn't think rain was coming; he did think it would be a shelter that held in some heat while also offering a bit of concealment as they rested.

It was dark when he finished. He roused Lilly enough to move her and cram her inside. She began sobbing again, and occasionally between breaths and sobbing gasps, she'd say, "I can't believe he's gone... he's gone..."

Jeremiah crawled in his hasty dogwood and stick shelter and held Lilly close. The flimsy shelter actually provided an incredible sense of security. He nestled up against Lilly, shushing her softly, pulling her against him, wrapping her in his arms until she fell back asleep. She slept restlessly. Jeremiah didn't sleep at all. He thought about her, about Parks, and everyone and everything else. He hurt for her, but was also jealous, even still, of her husband. He also thought of a compromise to his dilemma.

In the morning, he'd get Lilly to some other civilians who were holed up in a rural area, or fleeing to safety somewhere, and he'd then return to the capitol to fulfil his duty to his country and for his friends who'd never shirked theirs. It was the best he could do under the circumstances.

Lilly woke up slowly. The sun was shining and Jeremiah was sitting against the tree next to their shelter, watching her. She still looked tired and heavy-hearted as she lay there without moving. With expressionless eyes, she looked up to Jeremiah and meekly said, "Thank you."

"We should go," Jeremiah said quietly.

He led them a few more miles through the woods, careful to stay out of the open, wanting to avoid any enemy patrols that he was sure were out and about. They heard horses passing on the roads just beyond the trees that they were concealed by, but otherwise had an uneventful walk.

They had veered away from any main roads and tried to find more remote areas. After crossing a dirt road, Jeremiah felt like he was getting the distance he had hoped for, and within another mile or two, they stumbled upon a clearing where they found a mobile home with a homemade shed behind it.

Jeremiah knelt down behind some bushes, still inside the treeline, and surveyed the dwelling. There was a rope hanging from a tree that looked like it was used to hang deer from. There were boots and shoes on the wooden deck of the mobile home, a few pairs for adults and a few others for children. And there was a modest garden in the backyard and an empty clothesline. This place was clearly occupied.

Jeremiah now mulled over the best approach. People were understandably skittish these days and especially wary of anyone in any military. The US, the companies, they all were conscripting people into service, so those who weren't associated with any army didn't want to be and made every effort to stay out of it. Desperate people do desperate things, so if they were desperate to remain anonymous and free, well then...

But as Jeremiah thought it all over and began to formulate his plan, the backdoor opened in a screech, with a young girl and boy spilling out. The door slapped shut behind them, bouncing with reverberation in the door jamb from the closer spring.

"Excuse me," Jeremiah said, walking out of the woods toward them.

Jeremiah's rifle was slung to his back with one hand raised high and the other guiding Lilly by the hand. He spoke loudly, hoping the parents or adults would hear him from inside.

"Sorry," he said trying to look and sound friendly, "Can you help us? My friend needs a place to rest."

The startled children turned to face them but said nothing. Looking confused, they glanced between the pair who had emerged from the woods and their backdoor. They looked to be somewhere between the ages of eight and ten. The girl's hair was long and free, and she was carrying a basket. The boy's hair was cut short, but messy. He was wearing boots with his pant legs sloppily tucked in, and all he was carrying was a stick.

"Your mom and dad home?" Jeremiah asked, stopping a very safe and unthreatening distance away.

The boy stared at them blankly, and the girl turned her head to their home and yelled, "Daddy... Somebody's here..."

Jeremiah had an urge to grab his weapon just in case an angry and armed father stormed out, but he resisted, instead holding Lilly's hand and keeping the other one raised lazily to just below shoulder height.

An average-sized man walked out. His disposition was hard for Jeremiah to read initially. The man had a darkly tanned neck and face. He was wearing overalls with just a t-shirt underneath. His arms were also tanned, with big forearms and calloused hands. He looked to be in his mid to late thirties, with dark but thinning hair.

The man looked at them a moment, in a brief, but uncomfortable silence. "She alright?" the man asked, looking at Lilly. But before Jeremiah or Lilly could answer, the man looked at his little girl and said, "Abigail, run on in and grab some water, baby."

"Yessir," she said and darted off.

"Thank you," Lilly and Jeremiah both answered.

"If y'all ur here for some shade 'n water and fur somethin t'eat," the man said, "yur welcome to all we got, but I can't let ya have my wife 'n kids. Not ma' gun neither, sorry."

Jeremiah laughed until he realized it wasn't a joke. "Oh," he said, realizing his mistake, but also still confused at how it wasn't a jest. "No sir," he said, "We won't take anything without your consent, but we would very much appreciate any hospitality."

The man nodded, "Aw'right. Y'all can sit over there in the shade," he said as he pointed to a large oak. "Thomas," the man called to his son who was still standing, and still seeming unimpressed. "Go grab 'em some chairs, son."

"Yes, Daddy," the boy said and sprinted off to the shed, wanting the new people to see how fast he was.

"Abigail's gonna bring y'all some water in a bit," the man said, extending his hand to Jeremiah. "Peter," he said.

Jeremiah shook his hand, "Jeremiah. And this is Lilly."

"Well that's a pretty name, miss," Peter said.

"My wife's name is…" Peter began to say, until their attention was diverted by the sound of their backdoor opening again. "Aw, well, there she is. Y'all, this is Martha; Martha, this's Jeremiah and Lilly."

Martha was carrying two glasses of water with her. "Good to meet ya," she said with a genuine smile. She was wearing plain pants and a button-up shirt. She had long dark hair that was pulled back in a ponytail.

"Where's Abigail?" Peter asked.

"Sent her off for those eggs."

"Ah," Peter said in agreement. "If y'all want some eggs 'n grits, we'll have some ready here n'a'bit."

"Thank you," Jeremiah and Lilly both said in response to the breakfast and the water.

"Did y'all come from all that racket yesterday?" Peter asked, looking over in the direction of the city.

Jeremiah nodded. "I was hoping that you could watch after Lilly. I need to go back."

"What?" Lilly said, coming to life, as Peter and Martha looked uncomfortable at the request. "You can't leave me here," she said, beginning to get upset again.

"I have to go back. I can't just run away."

"Yes you can," she pleaded. "Why would you go back?
There's nothing left – don't die for nothing!"

Jeremiah just stood there.

Lilly reached out for him and held onto him, beginning to cry
again.

"Sir," Peter said, trying to inject some reason, "You don't
want to go back there. L an' M have the whole place. They took
the capitol before sunset yesterdee. No one knows if the
President's alive 'r not."

"You mean SPARTAN took the capitol," Jeremiah said,
confused.

Peter shook his head. "Paul, the fella with the chickens,"
Peter said, pointing down the road where Abigail could be seen
returning from. "He said L an' M come up from the south and
sacked it. Said it's over."

Jeremiah looked shocked. "How did he hear this?"

"He's got a lot of chickens," Peter said.

"An' beef," Martha added.

Peter nodded, "N' beef too."

Jeremiah just looked at them. Even Lilly had stood back up,
and would have gawked at them too, had she not been busy
wiping her tears.

"Well," Peter explained, "he's got a lot, like I said, and he's
been sellin 'em all over. He'd come up here yesterdee afternoon,
n' said he'd gotten outta there just 'n time. But he was sure it
was L an' M."

Jeremiah didn't say a word, but felt dejected. He realized
that the significance of L&M being the ones to sack the city was
that it meant the entire southern front must have collapsed, which
also meant that it was a very good probability that all US-held

territory was now compromised. The thought gave Jeremiah a helpless sense of urgency, but he just sat back down in his chair.

Seeing Jeremiah's poor disposition, and considering Lilly had just been crying, Peter said, "Well, at least we'll have grits 'n eggs ready in a bit." After offering something to be happy about, Peter raised his head and yelled, "THOMAS! Get these folks some more water!" He then headed back to his house and muttered, "Where is that boy," to himself.

"You can't go back," Lilly insisted once they were alone again.

Before Jeremiah could say anything, she said, "There's nothing left. We can go. I need you to go with me. Take care of me."

Jeremiah was trying to tell himself to not listen to her, nor to read too much into her words, and maybe he would have done all of that had she not said, "I need you…" It pulled him much harder than his outer shell suggested. Trying his best to remain stoic and appear reasonable, he asked, "Where would we go?" He was genuinely looking for an excuse to leave her and go back to the capitol, trying his best to ignore his old attraction for her, his deep and sincere affection. Then, surveying their surroundings he said, "I'm not staying here."

"We should go north," Lilly said.

"North?" Jeremiah questioned, not expecting that answer. "There with Raven?"

"Raven's fractured," she said. And she would know, with her clearance and position in the government, she'd have had access to all the intel. "A lot of their forces have separated and are just living alone, without attachment to anyone. Even though Raven still has a central government and some remaining forces, they've essentially all but withdrawn from the fight, keeping to themselves. Even SPARTAN has mostly left them alone."

"Why?" Jeremiah asked. It was the first time he'd heard much about anyone or any group other than what he had been directly involved with firsthand. "Why would SPARTAN just leave them alone? I thought Raven was our ally."

"Because SPARTAN doesn't see Raven posing a threat."

Jeremiah sat back in his seat, pondering.

"We can go there and be away from it all," Lilly pleaded.

Jeremiah looked at her. Her eyes were beautiful, and he just looked into them and nodded.

After breakfast, they thanked Peter and Martha again and departed after they said their goodbyes and once Peter prayed with them. "If you're intendin' to find peace, then Godspeed," Peter said.

Lilly and Jeremiah departed.

They walked cautiously and kept to the woods and the shadows when they could. They'd scavenge for food, rummaging through abandoned cars, military vehicles, buildings and houses along their way. Jeremiah had been able to find civilian clothes to wear instead of his battle dress uniform, though he still kept his weapons, of course.

They did their best to avoid people, and on a few occasions, had to hide as an L&M patrol would pass by the area they happened to be in. Every so often, in the weeks and months that they traveled, they would happen upon other people that they couldn't avoid. Some were the religious Congregationals, like Peter and Martha, and others were just random travelers like themselves, trying to leave fallen places or avoid the fighting between L&M and SPARTAN.

In the weeks and months that they traveled, every once in a while, they'd share a fire or meal with someone they'd see along their way. They'd tell and listen to stories. They'd laugh. They'd feel all alone, and they'd feel hospitality and humanity in brief encounters. They'd see the carnage of war and the loving compassion of strangers, they'd see catastrophic ruin, and they'd see breathtaking sunrises and sunsets. They'd hear rivers and creeks rushing over boulders and rocks, and in the distance, they'd hear gunfire or voices of fear and pain.

When they were alone, which was most of the time, they'd talk about when they were younger. Jeremiah would talk about training or the people he had met. Sometimes Lilly would ask about a battle or bring up what the media reported about him; he'd usually ignore those questions or change the subject.

Lilly would talk about her college experience and how she came to work with the government and how she'd acquired a top secret clearance; she even shared some of those secrets with Jeremiah, thinking that there wasn't any point in keeping them to herself anymore. She had told him they'd abandoned the facility because the weapon was never completed. She had said that they'd had another idea for it, but abandoned that idea at the last minute as well.

During one of Lilly's stories, Jeremiah laughed after being told some of the "grander" US secrets.

"Why is that funny?" Lilly asked, beginning to chuckle herself.

"It's not," Jeremiah said. "It's just crazy," he said, still smiling in frustration. "Crazy that they'd think up all that elaborate stuff, such intricate plans, but they couldn't get us proper intel on where the enemy would be… they couldn't drop mortars on the enemy without dumping a few on us…"

Lilly didn't know what to say. She had stopped smiling.

"No wonder we lost," Jeremiah said in aggravation.

Most nights Lilly would cry. It pained Jeremiah to see her despair, and it annoyed him that he was jealous over a dead man. But more and more, Lilly began to seem like the person she once was. A light could be seen shining in her again, even if dimly. Jeremiah loved her; he always had.

They walked for 130 days before they saw Raven soldiers, and even then there were only three or four. The North was different; people there gave off a greater sense of normalcy and no one was being conscripted; no one was being attacked. To Jeremiah, it looked as though they were trying to rebuild, and at a time when the other two groups were still fighting farther south.

The Raven troops wore dark gray, almost charcoal-colored fatigues, with black, subdued rank insignia on the sleeves (or shoulder tops for officers). When Lilly and Jeremiah neared the town, they had only seen a handful of Raven soldiers. By and large, the vast majority of people there seemed to be civilians, so no one seemed to care much about Lilly and Jeremiah, who looked like just two other, random people – it seemed odd to the both of them because of where they had come from, but they went with it.

It was a larger town and appeared to be mostly unscathed from the war that everywhere else southward had endured. Both Lilly and Jeremiah were a little envious. There were no skyscrapers, but there was a nice little downtown, and the town appeared to be spread over a wide swath of the area – a big-small town that lay at the edge of a Great Lake. The sign at the threshold of town read, "Entering South Harbor."

"How much farther are we going?" Lilly asked.

"Let's stop here for the night," Jeremiah said. "I think they actually have an inn where we could get real beds – maybe even a real bath."

"I mean how much farther until we stop for good?" Lilly asked, clarifying her previous question.

Jeremiah smiled at his misunderstanding. "Oh," he said. " I don't know, maybe another day or two… or three, northwest-like – I'd prefer to be farther away from any armed forces."

Lilly agreed and also liked the idea of a real bed again. "Maybe some freshly cooked food, too," she added.

They had found some old hotels and motels, but the first two they saw were closed. They had thought about kicking in a door and squatting for a night, but decided to try a little longer before joining the other squatters who had taken up residence.

They entered a little cafe that was operating out of the first floor of an old three story building in the downtown area and ordered a meal and some coffee. The server eyed Jeremiah, and more specifically the rifle slung to his back and the pistol at his thigh, but they said nothing – everyone carried weapons, it looked like.

They ate their warm meal, both eating too much, and also learned that the cafe also rented rooms in the floors above it. When it looked like Jeremiah was about to request two separate rooms, Lilly stopped him.

"One room," she said.

"One room," Jeremiah said to the woman, while still looking at Lilly.

"I don't want to be by myself here," Lilly said.

The woman looked like she wasn't happy about taking the currency that Jeremiah had, but she took it anyway, even if reluctantly. "There's runnin' water, but you'll have to light the lamps," the woman said.

They entered the third floor room to find it clean and tidy, with its own bathroom. The sun was beginning to go down, but it still lit the room through the window well enough for them to see everything easily. Jeremiah lit the oil lamp while Lilly turned on the shower faucet.

"Whoa!" she shrieked, "It's freezing." Despite the cold temperature, she was delighted to have a shower, and the fact that there was running water in an indoor room brightened her mood. "I won't be long," she said, closing the door before disrobing.

Jeremiah placed his rifle on the nightstand and took off his boots. He sat in the room's only chair, a wooden, armless chair, careful not to touch the clean bedsheet in his present filthy condition. He sat there while Lilly showered, unsure of how he was supposed to feel. It felt alien and foreign to be there, with her, away from the fight. He felt guilty for being there, with a full stomach and waiting to shower while Parks and Mick and the rest of them had been killed, standing their ground, fighting valiantly for their nation, while he had run away and fled to safety.

He smiled kindly at Lilly when she opened the door, wrapped in a towel, happily saying, "Your turn."

Jeremiah shrugged off his clothes before he climbed in the shower underneath running water that was so cold it took his breath away. Despite the uncomfortably cold water, he forced himself to stay under it. He began to break down under the frigid water, alone. He scrubbed himself roughly with soap. He hated himself for fleeing and for surviving. He was angry with himself for being upset over it.

By the time he was done, he was shivering… and clean, of course. He dried off, wrapped himself in a towel, and exited the bathroom.

Lilly looked alarmed at seeing him. "Are you okay?" she said rushing over to him. She touched his arm and exclaimed, "You're freezing," mistaking the effect of his internal burden for that of the frigid water.

Jeremiah tried to still himself and said, "I'm alright. Just need to get my other clothes," and he headed for their bag and its contents that had been scavenged along the way.

"No," Lilly said as she pulled the blankets back from the bed, "lay down here. I'll cover you up and get you some soup and coffee from downstairs."

Jeremiah didn't argue and climbed in without a word.

When Lilly got back to their room and opened the door, Jeremiah roused abruptly. "Were you asleep?" Lilly asked.

"I guess so," Jeremiah said, rubbing his eyes as he sat up.

Lilly handed him a bowl of soup and placed his coffee on the table. The sun could no longer be seen outside, just the faint glow of it fleeing behind the horizon. Street lights were being lit by torches, which surprised them both, although neither commented on it.

The happiness in Lilly's eyes were fading. Jeremiah could see it slipping away as she stared silently out the window, as if the retreating sun were running off her contentment, or turning the lights off to her joy. Jeremiah didn't say anything, but suddenly didn't want any more soup and set it down.

Lilly lay back in the bed, turning to the wall, as Jeremiah just sat there watching her silently. After a moment, Lilly's sorrow spread in the room like a contagion, and Jeremiah lay back and stared blankly at the ceiling.

"Please hold me," Lilly said softly.

Jeremiah looked over at her. She was still lying on her side, facing the wall, away from him. Jeremiah wanted to be strong and wanted to be there for her. He wanted to hold her and make her feel safe and secure, but while he'd never say it, he needed to hold her. He needed comfort from her. He'd never admit it, and wouldn't even say it to himself, but he hurt – he felt lost. He grabbed her and held her tight, closing his eyes and relishing the moment.

His heart hurt when she started to cry again. "I'm sorry about your husband," he whispered, but as soon he spoke the words he regretted saying anything.

Lilly sniffled as she turned to face Jeremiah. "No," was all she said in a tender whisper before kissing him. It reminded Jeremiah of high school. Her lips felt just the same. He ran his fingers through her hair and along her cheek as they kissed.

For Jeremiah, it was an intrinsic act of love and the eventuality of a yearning that he'd never been able to articulate. Somewhere deep down, he had the smallest fear that for Lilly, it was more of a temporary relief to her pain than it was a deep-rooted or profound affection for him, but his subconscious tried to conceal that fear.

Jeremiah awoke several hours later to a noise. He sat up, alert and listening, unsure of whether he'd dreamed the sound or was awakened by it. Then a few gunshots rang out, now waking Lilly.

Jeremiah was already scrambling out of bed and peered out the window, into the darkness. Torch-lit streetlights were still burning.

"What's happening?" Lilly asked with clear concern.

Jeremiah couldn't see the source of the shooting from the window, but he heard a few more random shots, some shouting, and saw two people sprinting away from the noises, down the dark streets.

"I don't know," Jeremiah said as he put on his clothes. "But we need to go," he added as he reached for his boots.

Lilly jumped out of bed and began throwing on her clothes as well. Neither bothered packing anything, only Jeremiah grabbed his weapons, and they ran out the door. Other residents had come to the same conclusion and were hastily spilling into the inn's corridor, alarmed that the shouts and gunfire were growing louder and more frequent.

The uncertainty of it all was disorienting; the crescendo of approaching gunfire and the shouts of frightened and fleeing people were scary enough by themselves, but not knowing what it all was over made it worse. Was it SPARTAN, was it highwaymen, was it drunk Northmen having a typical evening?

Jeremiah ignored everyone else, leading Lilly down the stairwell from their third floor hallway. He ran down the stairs with his weapon at the ready, making sure to not get too far ahead of Lilly, who was fast behind him. When he was halfway down the second flight of stairs he saw the wide eyes of utter surprise in three armed men who were ascending the stairs, each in dark gray uniforms. He immediately thought back to the building in the town near Post Whiskey, and the incident in the stairwell with Parks, and an instant fear shot through him, a terror that Lilly would succumb to the same fate as Parks. In that fraction of a second, Jeremiah instinctively squeezed his trigger, killing the three men in the dark gray uniforms; Lilly screamed in surprise.

When Jeremiah realized that he had just killed Raven soldiers, he nearly panicked. In all the battles and close quarter fights he'd been in, he'd never been a part to friendly fire. Despite the sick feeling in his stomach over the mistake, he couldn't afford to sit around and dwell on it; the earlier distant gunfire had turned into an immediate onslaught outside. Jeremiah and Lilly climbed down the remaining steps onto the first floor.

Outside, people were being shot, windows were being broken, and buildings were being set on fire. Jeremiah and Lilly were shocked to see Raven soldiers killing civilians. Raven was raiding its own town. The lunacy of it, the senselessness of the massacre, enraged Jeremiah. The entire world had gone mad. The Ravens he had accidentally killed in the stairwell weren't coming to help, they were coming to kill whomever was in the building.

In the following days, Jeremiah would learn that these soldiers would post signs and flyers with the Raven sigil at each entrance of town that read, "Submit to Raven rule or be counted as an enemy." The meaning was clear enough to Jeremiah – the Raven leadership believed that the Northerners had become too self-reliant and too self-centered. With the wars still raging in the south, Raven decided that that if the people of the North didn't realign to Raven rule, and completely submit to their authority, then Raven would count them as enemies and cut them off. Evidently, Raven attacked their own people, not just because they refused to be conscripted, but also because many had refused to contribute to Raven's war effort with food and supplies.

Jeremiah turned on his heels and pulled Lilly toward the back entrance and away from the Ravens and violence. They sprinted out the backdoor and through a narrow alley, before barging through a door into the neighboring building. Running through the rooms and corridors of that building, they ran past other people who had been hiding in dark corners or beneath whatever furniture that they could fit under. Although neither Lilly nor Jeremiah understood why Raven was attacking, neither thought that finding a place to hide was a good option. Jeremiah and Lilly ran room to room, building to building, trying to avoid the open streets that seemed crowded with panic and chaos, and trying to stay ahead of the approaching Raven soldiers enough to make an escape out of town.

Gunfire could be heard right outside all the while; automatic bursts and single shots alike. Screams of terror and alarm mingled with the gunfire and shouts of battle, created the harmony of war. Lilly was tired of that old song, and Jeremiah would say the same if asked, and he may have even tried to convince himself that it was true.

Jeremiah had shot two other Raven Soldiers in one alleyway, killing at least one of them, but saw no others. Jeremiah kicked through the door of the last building mid-sprint and barged outside into the street with Lilly on his heels.

They joined a crowd of other civilians who were fleeing. Some appeared to be running into the woods or down other streets, while others were headed to the great lake to board ferries and boats, trying to escape by water. Jeremiah and Lilly ran that direction, with their flickering shadows pointing the way, cast by the fires that Raven troops had set to the town. More gunfire and hollering felt close behind them as they ran, like the boogeyman that chases youngsters down dark and empty hallways of old houses.

One might have expected frantic maniacs at the docks, or people fighting over spots on the ferries or boats, but it wasn't that way. There wasn't a lot of time, of course, but the passengers and boat crew members were actively trying to help others aboard.

Jeremiah and Lilly arrived with the last group that was able to board. They were able to jump on deck just as the boat was pulling away, just as the random gunfire began to cease being random. The passengers screamed as a volley of rounds were sent directly at them, but despite Raven's assault, the ferries pulled away, out of range, headed for safer shores.

The screams in the ferry didn't stop, however. Several were dead and others were injured. Jeremiah had returned fire, almost comforted by the familiar sound of the bolt rocketing back and forth and the feel of the stock against his cheek, while hugging the rifle tightly into his shoulder. He was not alone; among the passengers on the ferry, most were armed and many returned fire to the shore.

But as the boat was reaching safer distances, the hair on Jeremiah's neck stood up as he lowered his carbine. He had an awful premonition and began to turn pale before he ever turned around. Amidst the screams and panic of the wounded and those trying to render aid, he found Lilly.

She was pale and hemorrhaging blood. Jeremiah was sick as he fell by her side, scrambling frantically to find and plug the wounds. Nothing else in the world existed for Jeremiah; it was only he and Lilly, stuck in the nightmare of terrible horrors. She was struggling and screaming in agony. Her eyes were wild and wide, but looked almost vacant and unfocused, as she moaned and screamed. Jeremiah began to cry with fear and frustration;

nothing he was doing was working – his every effort only appearing to cause more excruciating pain.

He tried saying her name, shouting it, but no words left his mouth, only the incoherent sounds of pain. But Lilly was screaming his name, as she writhed beneath him on the deck of that ferry. Jeremiah was sobbing now, as he worked futilely and desperately to fix her. It was mercy for them both when she finally died.

They had to subdue Jeremiah; several men took his weapons away from him as they held him down.

When the vessel landed, Jeremiah didn't know where he was, just that they were no longer in South Harbor. He hadn't listened to anyone; he was still in his nightmare, still alone with Lilly. He carried her body away from the shore until he couldn't anymore. Then he fashioned a stretcher that he could drag behind him. He placed her body carefully on it and covered her with a blanket he had acquired from the ferry. He couldn't bear to look at her any more; the dead do not look asleep, they just look dead. He didn't want to see her that way any longer.

He pulled the stretcher behind him for two days as he ventured deeper into the wilderness. He thought about all of the losses, but predominantly her. He thought about their last few months together; the way the firelight would reflect in her eyes, the way her forehead would wrinkle when she smiled, the way her hair would fall to her face, the sound of her voice, the touch of her hands. He thought about their last night together, and he thought about lying down and crying, asking why, pleading to God for comfort and answers – but more than anything else, Jeremiah was a man of action, not self pity. More and more Jeremiah thought about Raven.

When Jeremiah had reached a place of tall trees on a hill that overlooked a full creek with picturesque rapids, rolling over boulders and stones, he buried her body in the earth; having finally delivered her to a safe place in the North.

Jeremiah lay over the grave that night. The following morning he set out. He headed for Raven's capital.

Chapter 15

The Old City

The house was dark and musty. Beams of sunlight shone through cracks in the windows with floating dust particles filling the rays of light. Dust covered everything. There were holes and cracks in the walls and ceiling. And although it was evident that looters had been in and out over the years, there were still pieces of furniture, which were all bearing stains, or ruined with water, or had become nests to mice or some other vermin.

Jeremiah had entered the house with reverence and now walked through it slowly, looking carefully at everything. There were pictures, some on the floor or knocked over on a hutch or shelf, but some still hung on the wall. Jeremiah inspected only a few, carefully wiping the dust away. He was still struck by how pretty he thought Lilly was. He felt pangs of jealousy when he saw a picture of her husband. "Tim," he said in a whisper, with both envy and hatred in it, not bothering to look at any other pictures.

Tyler had not spoken a word. Jeremiah hadn't even noticed the uncharacteristic silence of the fool with the obnoxious belt buckle, being too preoccupied with the old house. Perhaps it was a combination of the mass murder he had witness just a few blocks down the road, or maybe it was because he now saw the seriousness of the old man who had dispatched those murders, whatever the case, Tyler tread lightly and silently on the heels of that old man.

Old man Pratt wiped his eyes and tried masking it by brushing his hair behind his ear. "Which room?" he said, almost in a reverential whisper.

Tyler pointed to the stairs and said, "Up there."

Jeremiah motioned for Tyler to lead the way with a little nod of the head.

As the pair reached the top of the stairs, Jeremiah's eyes were caught by the first bedroom they came to, while Tyler kept walking forward, toward what had been the master bedroom. Jeremiah paused at the door and felt his heart fail, as his stomach sank to his knees. Tears welled in his eyes as he surveyed the room.

Tyler had turned at the entrance of the master bedroom and quietly watched the old man.

Pratt just stood motionless at the doorway. Like the rest of the house, the room was dark and in ruin. Dust and debris were everywhere, and it was obvious that some things had been removed or lay broken. A few photographs still hung from the walls, and one or two others were lying awkwardly on the top of a chest of drawers, but Pratt wasn't looking at those. He was looking at the old toys that were now covered with layers of dust, strewn about the room. He read the name that had been stenciled in a childlike font along the far wall, above the child-sized bed; it read, "Timothy."

Jeremiah turned back toward Tyler with red eyes. "In there?" he asked, walking toward Tyler.

Tyler only nodded, not understanding what had just occurred, but certainly feeling the gravity of it. He stepped aside, averting his eyes, allowing Pratt to pass. Tyler was surprised to see the old man lay the rifle against the doorway, right next to him. Tyler pointed to a closet door, "I think he found it in there."

Without breaking stride, Pratt walked right up to the closet door where he stood motionless, staring blankly into the dark closet.

Still at the doorway of the room, Tyler looked down beside him at the weapon and then back over to Pratt, who was standing like a statue, peering into the old closet. Tyler reached for the rifle which Pratt had set down and picked it up with care. He looked at the weapon for a moment and then back at Pratt again, as Tyler moved his fingers around the pistol grip and touched the trigger as though to make sure it was still there.

Tyler's mouth was suddenly dry, while the rifle became more and more comfortable in his hands. He tried swallowing as he now stared at the old man.

"Get outta here," Pratt said without warning, still staring motionlessly at the closet floor.

Tyler abruptly jerked at the remark, now feeling silly with the rife in his hands.

The old man, without looking at Tyler, withdrew his sidearm and with a cold tone said, "If you don't leave now, I'll make sure you never do."

Tyler swallowed again. He gripped his rifle, which now felt out of place in his arms, and wondered if he should say anything. Deciding not to press his luck, he left Pratt alone in the house and departed.

Jeremiah knelt down in the closet as soon as Tyler turned his back to leave, resting his pistol on the floor next to him. He thought about that child's bedroom as he rummaged through garbage and miscellaneous clothes and shoes on the floor of the closet.

He felt angry, but at no one in particular. He also felt sad. "Why didn't you tell me you had a son?" Pratt finally said out loud. He almost felt betrayed. He had thought that they'd shared everything in those last months that Lilly had been alive. He'd thought that they'd shared a rapport and some deeper connection, and now, as he rummaged through her old possessions in the abandoned closet, he realized that he'd only convinced himself of those things.

"Tim," Pratt said aloud again, now without any envy or malice, but with a knowing sorrow. It wasn't her husband she was sad about, if he were even dead, but her son. His heart hurt as the pieces fell together.

He found a small cardboard shoebox underneath all the other crap. He opened the lid and found several keepsake items, some old letters and other trinkets. He felt sure the ring had been in there as well, and his hand subconsciously went to the ring in his pocket as he thought about it all. Unable to eschew his curiosity, he looked through the letters. He was delighted to find that she had kept some of the letters that he sent her while he was in basic. But then he found letters signed by Trevor, and wounded again, he cast them all aside, not wanting to see any more.

He looked old and nearly defeated as he clumsily climbed off of the floor and out of the closet. He looked up to see several pairs of eyes looking back at him.

Three men were standing in the doorway. Their silhouettes were hazy through the rising dust of the derelict room. "Sergeant Pratt," one of them said, "the general still wants to meet you."

Despite the poor lighting conditions, which practically concealed the men's identities, Jeremiah Pratt had seen these men before. They were Flagstaff, but at the moment, he just didn't care.

***

The facility was once again bustling with activity, except now the operators were wearing SPARTAN uniforms instead of the lab coats and business attire that the majority of workers and technicians had worn when under US control.

For Uriah, things were essentially the same as they were the last time he'd been there, except that the smell of bleach was missing and there was just a tiny bit of dust on the computer screens and desktops. Otherwise, the janitorial drones had been left operational and had kept the floors spotless and free of dust.

The hardware had never been completely shut down, instead it had been left dormant, as if it were expected that someone would return. The thought of this made General Simmons gush with pride, that he'd outsmarted the old USA and was taking possession of the weapon they had built to defeat SPARTAN, but was now using it to further the SPARTAN cause.

Most of the SPARTAN Army had set up camp and guard posts outside the back gate where they had initially arrived, but many others had now moved inside and were exploring the installation, moving things in, performing clerical duties, or acting as the technicians and operators trying to bring the weapon system online, as well as performing systems checks on the entire facility.

The general was in the command room, overseeing the efforts of the techies. The tech guys were older men and women, as they'd have been the only people with experience. The general knew that given the amount of time the world had been without power, his personnel would be a little rusty. But while set-up may take longer than they'd all prefer, he expected that it should still be fairly straight forward.

The only others who were inside the command room were the newest recruits, who had been volunteered for the detail of moving miscellaneous supplies, equipment, and furniture, or fetching drinks and snacks for the computer guys or the good general. Jonas was among them.

Jonas's eyes were wide with wonder and awe. Uriah and Josiah might have even been impressed with him under different circumstances. His new position in the SPARTAN Army may be bad for the Judgement, but it had seemed to improve his manners and work ethic – he seemed eager to please and hadn't complained since being enlisted. He was amazed by the technology and air conditioning, as well as the overall appearance with the entire place. The technicians were busy connecting wires and cables, or opening panels and fiddling with a jumbled network of circuits and wire, and Jonas was immediately impressed by it.

The general's eyes lit up as he saw Flagstaff through the glass wall of the command room, escorting the old and bearded Jeremiah Pratt down the corridor. Most of the work had ceased in the command room, with all eyes fixed on the old war hero.

"Back to work, everyone," the general said, as he left the confines of the command room to pursue Flagstaff and their prisoner.

As Pratt was led into a small, empty room, the general caught up and walked in right behind Flagstaff and Pratt, closing the door behind him. He first looked at Flagstaff and asked, "Where's the rest of you?"

Only three men of Flagstaff were present, and the man with the blue eyes, with the scar hidden behind his beard, said, "With the horses; they feel better with company."

The general said, "Ah," with raised eyebrows, and then turned his attention to the old man in the room. "The Great Jeremiah Pratt," he said as he looked at the old man with disdain while Pratt sat quietly in his chair. The general thought he looked defeated and almost feeble, as Pratt avoided eye contact and gazed at the floor.

"Pathetic," the general said in feigned pity. "You killed your old friend, under his hospitality, and then rushed all the way here only to fail... just as your Army did in the war." The general studied the old man as he waited for a response or some reaction, while three of Flagstaff watched on, standing quietly in the back. When he didn't get either he goaded the old man with, "Is this the 'way of man,' Mr. Pratt? To plan poorly and fail miserably?"

The general smiled at himself, while Pratt neglected to react. "You're a fool. You survived this long by luck, or chance, and you somehow mistook dumb luck for something more; you somehow convinced yourself that you're intelligent or a grand strategist... except you aren't. You're an overly publicized grunt, who survived by shielding himself behind his comrades; and I have defeated you, because you're a feeble-minded, self-promoting, delusional fool. I am intelligent. I am smarter than you, which is why you'll always lose to me," the general said, standing tall and looking down his nose at Pratt, who still seemed dejected and unresponsive.

"You look so... defeated and beaten," General Simmons said. "You know," he continued, "I'm glad it went this way. Really. Your trial and prosecution will help us more than having you as a spokesman and ally, and assassinating your old friend not only made that easier to pull off, but also provided me with more control," he added with a smirk.

The general was beginning to get a little annoyed at the lack of response, and he had certainly become bored with it. He concluded by saying, "Soon this weapon will be under my control, and once I make a show of SPARTAN power with it, I'll make a show of SPARTAN justice and resolve by trying you and hanging your guilty and pathetic neck from a rope."

The general turned to Flagstaff and said, "Put him with the Preachers and go play with your horses."

***

Tyler nervously walked the city streets alone. His trepidation heightened when he noticed circling buzzards overhead, realizing that he was stumbling upon the intersection where Pratt had slaughtered the gang of city people. He held his rifle close, with his trigger finger at the ready, fearful of running into more city dwellers, and simultaneously cursed himself for being too cowardly to finally kill Jeremiah Pratt when he had the chance.

He cautiously navigated the streets, thinking of missed opportunities, his late friends, Jim and Ted, and all of his boasting, as well as the expectations of grand success that his other friends had. He didn't want to let them down or face them again with failure. The Champ was feeling all the regret in the world for letting the old man go. "If I see him again," the Champ whispered to himself, "I'll blow 'im away."

No sooner was that thought out of his mouth than he heard a noise, or maybe it was movement, around a street corner. Alarmed, and desperately wanting to avoid any contact, Tyler disappeared into an abandoned building and peered out of the window, hoping no one could see him.

Through the dark window, Tyler saw some of the same city people return to the scene of the earlier slaughter, but they were also accompanied by others, by *more*. Tyler hid, breathing as softly as he could, hoping and praying that he hadn't drawn any attention to himself, planning on hiding out until they went away.

***

The Preachers had been huddled together in their chairs, with heads bowed as they muttered something; it was assumed they were praying, but both looked up when the door opened and Jeremiah Pratt was shoved inside. The door was shut behind him with an audible latch. His long hair was down in his face as he went to a chair in the corner, slumping into it, ignoring them both.

The Preachers looked at him, surprised to see him, and unsure as to whether they should feel in danger at being locked up with a violent criminal, or whether they should feel some kinship, being imprisoned together; although, they doubted Sergeant Pratt would like to sing hymns with them. Each had pondered greeting him or asking him how he was, but both decided not to disturb him, as he looked like he wanted to be by himself.

And indeed, Jeremiah wanted nothing to do with anyone. He kept thinking about Lilly, with every conceivable emotion surrounding the thoughts of her. But those thoughts, in addition to General Simmons's comments, had also stirred up thoughts and guilt regarding Mick and Parks, the rest of his company, and even the nation he eventually walked away from. He deserved to die, he thought.

Even though they had decided to leave Jeremiah Pratt alone, the interruption in prayer shifted the gears in Josiah's mind. "Were we wrong in coming here with SPARTAN?" he asked his father. Josiah wasn't asking if they were wrong in the sense of being unwise, but asking his father if they had sinned.

Uriah sat upright, thinking. "We didn't have a choice," he replied, regretting his answer as soon as he spoke it. They always had a choice, even if death was to be it. Physical death wasn't as harsh as spiritual death. "'Be thou faithful unto death,'" Uriah muttered, so quietly that even Josiah couldn't hear it. Uriah was scared to be there, and that fear was almost completely because his son was there.

Josiah likely had the identical thought as his father, but didn't comment on it.

Uriah wondered if his own past sins had led to him endangering his own son now, somehow. He also feared for his son regarding that lock; Uriah was shocked that Josiah had opened it, especially since he could no longer seem to do it himself after being so long out of practice, and he hoped that SPARTAN never found out, fearing they'd exploit it somehow, and fearing that the Ability may even be witchcraft of some type. He hadn't mentioned anything about it to his son, but he prayed silently that his son would always trust in the Lord, never relying on tricks of "science" or witchcraft, whichever that ability of the mind happened to fall under.

"What if God led us here?" Josiah asked innocently.

Uriah frowned, unsure of what to say, not wanting to take a firm position on the Lord's intentions. "I don't know," he said softly. Then he added, "'As it is written, For thy sake we are killed all the day long; we are accounted as sheep for the slaughter.'"

"'Nay,'" Josiah said with a grin, "'in all these things we are more than conquerors through him that loved us.'"

Uriah smiled at the exchange. "It could be," Uriah added, "'and who knoweth whether thou art come to (this place) for such a time as this?'"

Josiah smiled at the reference; he had always liked Esther. "Like fate," he said wistfully. "Destiny." To the Preachers, fate and destiny were synonymous with God's Providence.

Jeremiah sat silently, listening as he stared at the floor and reflected.

"Maybe," Josiah said, "maybe we are here for some purpose..." Realizing that he didn't know the will of the Lord, and recalling that many of the saints died in service to God, Josiah's smile faded as he added, "Of course, we should walk faithfully, even to death."

Uriah nodded gravely, soberly.

The majority of Uriah's fear revolved around the most pressing urgency, and that was their captivity and the danger that he and his son were potentially facing. Trying to reassure himself, he whispered, "'I will not fear the terror of night, nor the arrow that flies by day, nor the plague that destroys at midday. I will not fear though tens of thousands assail me on every side.'"

"What was that?" The old, bearded Pratt spontaneously asked, to the surprise of the Preachers.

"I'm sorry," Uriah said, uncertain of what Jeremiah Pratt had been referring to.

"Wha'd you say?" Jeremiah asked again, staring at both of them. "Somethin' from Psalms..."

Josiah perked up anytime a lost soul showed knowledge or interest in the scriptures.

Uriah nodded, "Yes, it's Psalms ninety-one and Chapter three."

"Why'd you say it like that?" Pratt asked as if it were an interrogation.

Feeling like he was being made fun of or criticized, Uriah responded, "We're people of faith, so we turn toward God's Word in times of trial."

"No," Pratt said, "I mean, why that order?"

"I don't understand," Uriah said, looking completely confused.

"You quoted a section of Chapter ninety-one before quoting the part from Chapter three," Pratt insisted, "Why?"

Josiah was again impressed that Jeremiah Pratt knew the scripture at all. Uriah, unsure of what the big deal was, only shrugged, unsure of what else to say, or why he was being pressed on it.

"Is there some reason it's said that way, or did you hear it from anyone?" Jeremiah pressed. He wasn't tearing up at the eyes, but there was definite emotion behind the prodding.

"My mother would say it," Uriah said. "Whenever I was scared about something, she'd reassure me with it."

Josiah said nothing, but thought back to his own younger years, remembering when his father, Uriah, would recite the same to him.

Jeremiah looked at Uriah, more reminded of Mick than ever, and couldn't help but wonder. He couldn't help but think of the "what ifs," associated with it all, *what if Uriah was Mick's half brother, the product of Mick's mother remarrying after Mick's evangelist father had passed?* but he wouldn't comment on any of that. He wouldn't expose himself, but he felt the feelings of self-loathing subside, and he could feel the sense of hopelessness give way to the thought that he could still contribute a verse and try to live up to Mick's expectations, having failed them so completely before.

Pratt stood up and moved his chair against the wall of the adjacent room and stood upon it. He reached above him, pushed a ceiling tile open, and slid it out of the way before turning to look at the Preachers again, who were both completely quiet and still with perfect confusion.

"When I tell you," Pratt said to them, "and only when I tell you, knock on the door and tell the guard you need to use the restroom."

Uriah started to say something and ask what Pratt was doing, or why they'd need to take a restroom break, but Pratt silenced him before he could get a word out.

"Do as I say if you want your son to live," Jeremiah commanded, looking directly into Uriah's eyes. "I'm getting you out of here," he said just before climbing into the ceiling.

The two Preachers stared blankly at the ceiling as sounds of thuds and whops, banged above them and then down the wall, presumably on the other side. If they had been morally troubled about asking to use the restroom when in fact they did not need to, they were saved from the test when the door to the room opened suddenly, with the guard pouring in.

The Preachers turned abruptly toward the guard, with looks of guilt all over their faces. The guard was about to ask what the noise had been, but all he got out was a, "Wha-?" before he was silenced with the realization that Jeremiah Pratt was not present and the Preachers were standing sheepishly beneath a hole in the ceiling.

As the guard frantically turned to shout for help and sound the alarm, he was greeted by Jeremiah Pratt, whose welcoming hands clenched tightly around his throat as he was forced to the floor. The old man's forearms flexed and rippled with the strain, and the Preachers looked on in petrified horror as Pratt squeezed the life out of the guard's neck. After a moment of intense struggle, the guard's wild and terrified eyes glazed over, and his face faded to a sickly white as soon as Pratt released the dead man's neck.

Neither of the Preachers knew what to say or do, but it was alright; Jeremiah Pratt was making decisions for them. Breathing heavily from the struggle, he grabbed the guard's rifle and turned to the Preachers with haste and said, "This way," as he pulled them out of the room into the abandoned and sterile hallway.

Pratt was surprised with himself at how well he could still recall some of the directions to take, and when needed, he made use of the hallway's signage. It didn't take long until he was able to get them to an exit. "Head straight out this tunnel," Pratt said, ushering them out the door into the darkness. "There aren't any turns, just head straight out and by the time you see light, you'll be able to figure the rest out."

"Aren't you coming with us?" Josiah asked, uneasy about the entire thing.

Jeremiah Pratt shook his head, "I've got somethin' to do." He nodded down the tunnel with his head and said, "This dumps you into the city. The old capitol. Just keep going, but avoid people and move and move and move. Don't stop for anything," he finished, closing the door, shutting them out into the darkness of the tunnel.

Jeremiah rushed stealthily through the corridors, occasionally having to duck behind a corner to avoid being spotted by a SPARTAN soldier or techie. When he reached his destination, deep within the installation, he opened the big metal panel door that read, "MAIN COMMAND CENTER PANEL," and peering inside at the tangle of conductors and cable and the galaxy of circuits, he reached inside.

***

The general was relieved; everything was connected and everyone seemed to be logged into the system. The large flat screen on the wall was displaying the monitor view of the command prompt.

"Make contact with the satellite," the general commanded, watching the commands being typed onto the screen with a response that indicated "PROCESSING." The general held his breath in anticipation. The whole plan hinged on access to these orbiting satellites, as the satellites comprised the weapon. As soon as they could connect with the nearest one, they'd position it over L&M's capitol headquarters and obliterate the entire city, demonstrating that SPARTAN was now controlling the continent.

"PAIRING SUCCESSFUL," was now on the screen, with a highlighted cursor flashing after it.

"Plug in the coordinates," the general ordered with a grin and a bit of relief, as a SPARTAN soldier barged into the command room.

"What is it?" the general asked in a scolding tone.

"Bailey," the soldier said, with urgency, "he's dead."

"What?" the general asked as he felt the hairs stand up on his neck. "The Preachers…"

"Gone, sir," the soldier answered before the general could complete his question, "Sergeant Pratt's gone too."

The general clinched his teeth in fury and roared, "FIND THEM!!"

"PLUG IN THE COORDINATES!" he shouted, refocusing the command room from the distraction.

The general's agitation subsided some when the coordinates were locked in and the satellite began to relocate itself to a position that allowed deployment. Everyone watched the screen intently as a computer rendering of Earth's terrain zoomed into view, with the buildings, roadways, and other terrain features traversing in front of them as the satellite moved into place. The screen began a countdown for how much longer it would be before the weapon was in line of sight and ready to be fired.

***

Jeremiah was frantically digging through wires, trying to find the right ones, when he heard the facility intercom buzz to life. The sound of static coming from the speakers made him feel even more rushed, but with the announcement of, "Security Code Alpha. Security Code Alpha. Prisoners are mobile, shoot on sight," Pratt felt like he was again presented with an impossible and unwinnable decision. Always before, he'd seemed to screw up by abandoning his mission to help an individual, so he reached back inside the panel and rummaged through the thick coil of cables, trying to ignore his thoughts about the Preachers, telling himself that he was stupid and foolish for comparing those strangers to his old and gone friends.

But as he searched around the contents of the command panel, and as the intercom sounded the same message again and again, he found himself more and more distracted. He found himself more and more concerned with the two Preachers; if anyone in this world needed to be protected, or deserved to live long lives in peace, it was those people, he thought.

Frustrated with his fruitless search, and feeling like all time was up, he gave up and departed, intending to reach the Preachers and see them to safety. Pratt encountered only one SPARTAN on his way out and cracked him in the forehead with a violent swing with the butt of his rifle, sending the man either unconscious or dead to the floor. He had tried to silence the man without the noise of gunfire, but the crack on the head was loud enough that others were alerted.

Reaching the same exit he had pushed the Preachers through, he quickly shut the door behind him, hoping to make it up the tunnel before the pursuing SPARTANS could catch him. He was struck by how dark the tunnel was and felt the tiniest bit of guilt for tossing the Preachers into it. "Man, it's dark in here," he said out loud, but then he noticed a small green glow on something in the corner of the tunnel and couldn't hide a smile at the discovery.

Jeremiah slung his newly-stolen rifle across his back and rushed over to the dark mass in the corner, drawn to it by the faint green light. He climbed on and flipped a switch to find the instrument panels light up, and the motor quietly emitted its subtle electric pur. He reached down and yanked the cable out of it and rolled away in near silence, as the pursuing squad of SPARTANS spilled out into the tunnel after him. The young SPARTAN troops were taken aback at the sight of him speeding off on the old electric security motorcycle, headlight showing the way forward.

The initial surprise had delayed their reactions, but a few began to shoot as he disappeared up the tunnel ramp. One of the others lept on one of the remaining motorcycles, and having managed to turn it on, peeled out maniacally and slammed unintentionally into a tunnel wall, having never ridden anything with a motor before.

***

Tyler awoke to the sound of buzzards flapping away from the dead in the street. Even Tyler was bewildered that the other city people hadn't buried the dead or tried to move them. And now, he was wondering where the other city folks had gone, ill with himself for falling asleep and not keeping better watch.

Peering out the window in the other direction, he saw what had stirred the buzzards and dogs away from their meal, as two people were approaching. He almost thought they looked like the Preachers he'd seen in Engine's Rest, but decided the distance was playing tricks on him. He feared that they might still be more city dwellers, and even if not, their presence may draw the city dwellers. Tyler ducked back away from his first floor window and ran to the second floor for a better look and a place with more concealment in case he had to spend the night in order to avoid the undesirable city people.

Coming off the stairs onto the second floor, Tyler could see that the place was in major disrepair; badly damaged from the old war. There was a gaping hole in the street-facing side of one of the walls and a bunch of debris and toppled furniture, laden with layers of dust and mice droppings. Tyler moved with deliberate caution to the nearest window for a better view. It wasn't the best position, but he didn't want to risk exposing himself by going near the mammoth hole in the wall, just a few feet away.

***

In complete silence, all eyes watched the last few seconds tick away on the corner of the screen as the computer image of the satellite feed positioned itself at the center of L&M's capital and command hub.

The general stood tall and triumphant at his kiosk and pointed across the room. "Major Hernandez," he said as he placed a key in his control panel, "Turn on my count."

The major inserted his key into his control panel on the other side of the room. With one hand on the key, he watched the general raise his hand as he counted down from five, ready to turn his key in synchronization with the general.

"Five. Four. Three. Two. One," the general counted before the final, "Now," dropping his arm.

Both of them turned their keys and the screen read, "ARMED."

The general looked at the firing station and gave the order, "Fire!" in exclamation, as he could feel the surge of adrenaline from the perception of being endued with power.

The large screen blinked once, but nothing else seemed to happen.

Confused, the general looked between the large screen and the work stations, and then asked, "Did it work?"

The personnel in the command room began looking down at their screens and kiosks, wondering the very same thing. The young soldiers in the room, who'd been used as remedial labor and errand boys, stood meekly in the back, even more confused than everyone else.

"Try it again," the general said. "Initiate the weapon. Fire," but this time the general said it without the sound of confidence or exultation in his voice, as he watched the screen intently.

Again, nothing. Again, the tech personnel looked down, either looking for the problem or pretending to.

"It's not working, sir," the technician at the command desk said.

The general just glared at him in response until he felt the light bulb of epiphany click on. With the look of recognition, the general said, "Pratt," in accusing annoyance. Without looking at anyone, he barked, "Search the facility and look for any signs of sabotage," which sent Jonas and the other SPARTAN privates scrambling throughout the installation. The general shouted after them, "We'll leave the intercom on, so if you see something, shout it out so we'll know what and where. NOW GO!"

The general then turned to his command room, and before the grunts could exit the door, ordered, "Begin a diagnostic of all systems. Check the root code and make sure no one left a computer turned off…"

***

Jonas began by following the other soldiers as they ran out of the command room and scrambled to find something or anything that might be a sign of malicious tampering. Jonas was soon bored with following his peers. Jonas thought of them as peers, but they didn't see him that way. To them, Jonas was the new guy, as well as the oddball Preacher. Regardless of how Jonas and the other lower ranking SPARTAN enlisted saw each other, Jonas grew annoyed at following them and separated himself, taking other corridors alone.

Jogging down the halls, Jonas looked high and low and in any nook and corner for any sign of anything that may be the slightest bit out of place. Oddly, Jonas never seemed to second guess himself or question his own qualifications for this task, despite having never seen a place like this and knowing nothing at all about the technology related to the weapon SPARTAN was trying to use. Jonas searched his self-determined route with an unwarranted confidence that could be viewed with admiration if it weren't so misplaced.

Jonas stopped at the sight of a large metal panel door that was just barely cracked open. "Main Command Center Panel," Jonas said quietly, reading the label. He was tempted to shout out for all to hear through the active intercom and inform everyone that he found something, but he waited. Proud of his patience and wisdom, he opened the panel, thinking it was better to know more about what he had found before offering an incomplete report.

Chapter 16

Reunion (Flashback)

Jeremiah walked out of the woods with a small, wild pig on his shoulders and with his sidearm holstered to his hip. His old face looked stern and unfriendly through his thick beard as sweat beaded on his forehead.

Morgan followed behind him, carrying Jeremiah's muzzle loader as well as her own. Morgan was about seventeen years old, with her shoulder-length dark hair pulled back in a ponytail. She was lean, and her exposed, muscular forearms revealed experience with manual labor, while the subtle scars spoke of an active childhood. Other than the two muskets, she carried a tomahawk in her belt. She was about half a foot shorter than Jeremiah, but kept pace with the old man well.

Morgan nearly walked right into Jeremiah when he stopped so abruptly upon walking out from beneath the tall hardwoods and onto the open pasture near his cabin. The clearwater creek could be heard babbling nearby.

She first looked at him and then, following his gaze, looked toward the cabin to find a man reclining on a porch chair near the front door.

"Who's that?" she asked.

Jeremiah shrugged, "Not sure who'ee is," he said, then turned his head to look down the road and added, "or them."

Morgan looked eighty to a hundred meters down the road and saw several men on horseback, all sitting still and quiet on their still and quiet horses. "You gonna kill 'em?"

Jeremiah didn't recognize them, but he had an idea as to why they were there; they all tended to come for the same reason. He shifted the pig on his shoulders and set off again toward his cabin and the man waiting on them there. "C'mon," he said to Morgan, ignoring her and leading the way. No sense in stealth now – they'd already seen him, and none seemed to fall into any ready or tactical posture.

"Jeremiah Pratt," the man said, greeting Jeremiah at his own cabin. The man had clear blue eyes and a thick beard of his own. He wore no uniform, which wasn't out of the norm there in the North – no one wore them there anymore. The blue-eyed man was sitting in a chair with a book in his lap.

Jeremiah eyed the book and said, "Who are you?" as he dropped the pig on the ground at the foot of his porch.

"A diplomat," the man said, without any sarcasm.

"Morgan," Jeremiah said, looking over his shoulder at the girl, "go ahead and clean 'im up," referring to the pig, not the man. "I'll be there in a bit."

Morgan set the muskets on the porch, leaning them against the wall, and dragged the pig's carcass around back.

"A diplomat?" Jeremiah asked, returning to the man.

"For SPARTAN," the man said, to which he could see Jeremiah bristle. "The war's over, Sergeant Pratt," the blue-eyed man added before Jeremiah could say a thing. "We'd like to seek your support and partnership in rebuilding."

Jeremiah looked at the book resting on the man's lap, "What's that?"

"*The Way of Man*," the man answered, grabbing it in his hand and extending it toward Pratt.

"You always go through people's things when they're not around?" Jeremiah asked in annoyance as he took his own book from the man's extended hand.

"It is the best time to go through someone's things..." the man retorted.

Jeremiah didn't seem amused.

"But no, the book was here," he said as he placed his hand on an oak log that was serving as a coffee table on the porch. "Did you write that yourself?"

"What is it that you want?" Jeremiah asked as he discreetly tucked the book under his armpit while he talked with his intrusive diplomat.

"The SPARTAN leadership would like to meet with you and discuss plans on how to rebuild," the man said from his chair.

"Meet here?"

"Oh," the man said, almost laughing. "No, not here. You're to come back with us."

Jeremiah looked down the road at the other horsemen again.

"You're wondering if I'm asking ya, or telling ya," the man said. "Both. It's both, but you have nothing to fear. The war's over, and you're not our enemy."

Jeremiah looked like he was thinking it over.

"It'll be fine. Plus," the man added, "you'll get to reconnect with an old friend."

Jeremiah looked at the man quizzically.

The man stood up, raising his hands with a shrug. "I was instructed to tell you no more. But if we're going, it needs to be now. Please tell your friend goodbye and grab whatever you need."

Jeremiah really didn't like being told what to do, and despite the politeness with how he was being told, he was still being told. And while he didn't like SPARTAN, he hated Raven and had managed to live in the North all these years, so maybe he could get over the past with SPARTAN, especially if peace and rebuilding was really their agenda.

He looked back over at the horsemen. *What would happen if I said no?* he thought. He looked through his front window, through the cabin, and out his back window, where Morgan had already strung the pig up and was pulling its insides out, and he didn't want to risk anything happening to her or his neighbors over something like this.

"Alright," Jeremiah said to the blue-eyed, bearded stranger. "Give me a bit."

***

Jeremiah felt odd, not only at being surrounded by SPARTANS, but walking through the corridors of their headquarters and command center – an old, multi-story concrete building that had once been an early 20th century luxury hotel. Some other building may have made more sense; that is, one would have made more sense had they not all been destroyed during the war. SPARTAN, even though they came out on top, had still endured their share of casualties and destruction, even deep within their territory.

The current SPARTAN capitol appeared to be doing well. The towns under their control and occupation were doing well, considering electricity was scant and medicine was still scarce. SPARTAN seemed to have organized their communities perfectly for the state the world was now in, and unlike L&M, SPARTAN forces were very present in each region and regulated nearly everything, from farming, to livestock, to judiciaries who heard everything from petty disputes to egregious violent crimes. SPARTAN took their resources seriously and invested a lot of them into educating and providing for their people (what they considered their greatest resource), from whom they expected and demanded much. SPARTAN ran a tight ship.

Jeremiah's escorts, Flagstaff, who ushered him down from what had become his home in the North, dropped him off at the headquarters building, leaving him with a SPARTAN lieutenant. Jeremiah was pleasantly surprised that he had been allowed to keep his sidearm, though they required him to clear the chamber before entering the compound.

Lieutenant Williams was a stout, twenty-something guy who looked robust, fit, and self-confident. Jeremiah noticed the young LT sizing him up, but Jeremiah ignored it. The LT led Jeremiah to the room he'd be staying in for a shower and fresh clothes before leading him up a few flights of stairs to the colonel's office. The office had obviously been a luxury suite once upon a time, with tall, double entry doors, intricately designed. The room had fine crown moulding, with tall ceilings and wainscot between the floor-to-ceiling windows. The room's focal point drew the eye to the colonel's antique desk, which was set just in front of incredible French doors that opened up to a balcony, overlooking the street below.

The colonel was standing at his desk, discussing something with a young woman, whom Jeremiah assumed was a secretary or assistant. The colonel's hair was white, thick, and appeared to be a source of pride for the old SPARTAN officer. The colonel looked to be in his early sixties, like Jeremiah. The flowy white hair rustled gracefully as the colonel looked up from what he and his assistant had been discussing and smiled widely.

Jeremiah was genuinely shocked to recognize that winning smile. "Trevor?" he asked with squinted eyes as he left the escort of the young lieutenant to greet Colonel Trevor face to face.

Trevor's smile grew even wider at the reaction, "HAHA!" Trevor laughed with pure delight, "Jeremiah Pratt! It's great to see you," he said, meeting Jeremiah with a warm embrace.

"Whoa!" Trevor exclaimed as he hugged his old friend, "You've kept fit, old man! If it weren't for your long hair and crazy-guy beard, I'd swear you were just the same!"

Jeremiah genuinely had no words at the unexpected reunion and awkward embrace of his old high school acquaintance. "Well," he said in response, "we both have more wrinkles and a few more grays."

Trevor laughed heartily, "You have gray, I have white."

Jeremiah smiled.

"And scars," Trevor continued, "We've certainly got more scars," he concluded, pulling the leg of his pants up, exposing his prosthetic limb.

"But we're alive," Jeremiah said, trying to sound happy about it.

Trevor nodded, and through his winning smile added, "Now, I heard that you don't have any scars." Trevor stared at Jeremiah curiously, "Is that rumor true?"

The young assistant and bulky lieutenant stood quietly, like pieces of the peripheral scenery and listened intently, each also very curious.

Jeremiah shrugged, looking suddenly uncomfortable.

Trevor's smile faded into what looked like sincere pitiful compassion. "To live this long, through that much... I guess no one makes it through without scars... Some just aren't visible on the outside..."

Jeremiah didn't reply.

Trevor donned his smile again, eager to move on, and keen on leaving the sudden, uncomfortable moment behind them. "Kelly," he said, "once you've filed that report, do you think you could bring us some drinks while we catch up?"

"Yes sir."

As Kelly shut the door behind her, Trevor motioned for Jeremiah and the young lieutenant to sit.

Jeremiah politely declined, "I sat on that horse the whole way here; I need to stand and stretch out a bit."

Jeremiah looked back at Trevor's desk, placed a hand lightly upon a grenade body that appeared to be there for decoration, and said, "So what's all this?"

The big wooden desk of elaborate craftsmanship was covered in all sorts of paperwork. There were several file folders sitting on top of an open map. Though much of it was covered, Jeremiah could see that the map had the old government's capital with surrounding cities and towns on it, plus the aforementioned grenade.

Trevor's eyes lit up, "Oh that?" Trevor picked up the heavy grenade. "It was a gift from the lads," he said, handing it over to Jeremiah. "A similar grenade had taken my leg in the wars," Trevor continued with a smile, "and they gave me this as a gift. This one's inert, of course, completely harmless; but it reminds me that life is precious... and that I'm just too wily to die." Trevor added the last part with a hearty laugh.

LT Williams laughed.

Jeremiah smiled. "Bet it hurt though," Jeremiah said, feeling the shot-put-like weight of it in his hand, then placing it back on the desk. Jeremiah said, "And what about the rest of this?" referring to the files and the map.

"Oh that," Trevor said, smiling like the cheshire. "We'll get to it." Through his smile, and with a glance to his young lieutenant, he added, "But first, tell us about the North."

"It gets cold," Jeremiah offered.

Jeremiah's retort caught Trevor off guard, causing him to laugh audibly. "Did Raven offer to promote you to captain if you changed your name to 'Obvious'?" Trevor said, still chuckling. "But for real, we've heard some rumors…" Trevor persisted as his laugh evolved into a sly grin.

Jeremiah raised an eyebrow. "Well you don't go around believing rumors, now do ya, Trevor?"

Trevor smiled widely. "Not always, no," he said in amusement, "But these involve you and Raven brass… It seems if these rumors are wrong it's quite a coincidence that Raven leadership started disappearing or turning up dead shortly after you were said to have arrived in the North…"

Jeremiah grimaced a bit and shrugged. "You also believe wild conspiracy theories?" Jeremiah asked rhetorically, dismissing the entire implication.

Trevor laughed again with excitement. "YOU *DID*!" Trevor said jovially, throwing a pretend jab at old man Pratt. "Raven was an ally of the US, granted not a useful one, but still… an ally…"

Jeremiah looked at him uncomfortably.

"What did they do to call down the wrath of the *Great Jeremiah Pratt*?" Trevor asked, giggling in friendly sarcasm.

Jeremiah shrugged off the question, annoyed at the turn of the conversation.

"C'mon, Jeremiah," Trevor goaded with a smile. "It had to be something?"

Jeremiah didn't want to answer, but he realized that no answer was just making it worse, so he decided it was better to offer something, even if small, than trying to insist on nothing. "They took something from me," he said in a tone and with an expression that indicated it was time to move on.

Trevor's smile faded slightly, mingling with sincere sympathy. "You never were one to share, I guess," Trevor added in response. Though the remark was sarcastic, it wasn't rude, and the tone with which it was delivered made it clear that the remark was an effort to lighten the now serious tone of the room.

"What's *The Way of Man*?" the young lieutenant asked, smiling.

Jeremiah couldn't tell if the lieutenant's smile was mockery, nerves, or lingering amusement from some earlier punchline, but he decided to give the lad the benefit of the doubt. "It's a code."

"You wrote it," Trevor said. "Isn't that correct?"

Jeremiah shrugged, then nodded modestly. "I did."

"Many people knocking down the door to join?" the lieutenant asked again, with the slyest of grins.

"It's not a church," Jeremiah replied flatly, eyeing the boy.

Trevor laughed as if everyone were laughing together.

"Is that *code* illustrated?" The lieutenant spouted out, barely holding back his laughter, "Can't be many Northerners who know how to read."

"No one's coerced into following anything," Jeremiah replied evenly, " People are free to do, or not do, as they like up there. The code's not for everyone." Jeremiah nodded toward the lieutenant, "I don't think you'd get much out of it; it tends to appeal to a mature and thoughtful mind and resonate with people who've seen combat or who've lived in conflict, but seek a higher calling or purpose."

Trevor laughed enthusiastically.

The lieutenant tried to mask his anger and embarrassment with a smile as best he could.

Jeremiah remained stoic and held the young lieutenant's gaze until the butterbar looked away.

"So what are we doing here?" Trevor said, raising his arms up beside him, changing the subject and getting to the overall crux of the meeting. Trevor may have been laughing, but he wasn't aloof, he wanted to get away from the tension without drawing attention to it. "SPARTAN wants to reunite the continent."

"Hmm," Jeremiah said. "Why?"

The young lieutenant smiled as if he'd just heard an amusing bit of silliness from a child.

Trevor laughed, "Yeah, indeed... Several reasons: resources, peace..."

"Things are peaceful now," Jeremiah offered, "with the treaty between SPARTAN and L&M... And the North is just the North, right?"

"Well *now*," Trevor answered, "but L&M and even the North are in disarray, and we want to mitigate the potential for future chaos by offering more security and oversight now."

Jeremiah didn't say anything else.

"And we may be getting too far ahead right now since the generals haven't joined us yet," Trevor added. "General Simmons and Monroe are actually en route, but still another day or two out," Trevor said. "I hope that's not too much of an inconvenience for you – you actually arrived a few days earlier than we initially expected."

Jeremiah's shrug said, "No worries."

Trevor smiled at his old friend and said, "But the thought was that since we feel this moral obligation to help our brothers and sisters who are dispersed among other territories, that having something like an icon at the forefront of it would be like the sugar coating on medicine."

"An icon?" Jeremiah asked, suddenly realizing what he meant.

"Yeah," Trevor insisted. "Everyone knows you. You're the only living *famous person*," he added with a chuckle. "'Jeremiah Pratt, the old United States War hero, and SPARTAN are reuniting the broken continent and mending a shattered nation'... and all that," he said, offering a tagline and slogan.

"Hmm," Jeremiah said again, putting a downer on the jovial mood. "Will L&M just give up their territory? Will the North simply give up their freedom to be told what to do by someone else?"

"Sure," Trevor said, looking serious now and cutting an eye at the lieutenant, who was still sitting comfortably in his chair. "We have something that will help us argue our case."

"I just don't know, Trevor," Jeremiah said, sounding as skeptical as the remark would suggest.

Trevor smiled wide again as he placed his hand on the file folders that were stacked on his desk. "We are getting a little ahead of ourselves," he said without any hint of real reluctance, "but we have recently located a facility, an *old US facility,* that is hidden in the old US capitol, just across the territorial treaty line."

Jeremiah perked up at hearing this.

"L&M won't protest," Trevor said, grinning from ear to ear, "Because we're going to take that facility by force, and L&M isn't prepared to mount enough forces right now to stop us."

"But when they gather enough people to counterattack, you'll have just started the wars back off," Jeremiah suggested.

"I wasn't finished," Trevor said, grinning like he held an ace. "We're moving in force to ensure nothing stops us from reaching the facility. Once we reach the facility, we won't have to worry about any counterattack, because the facility is a weapon!"

"Trevor," Jeremiah said with reluctance.

"It's all right here," Trevor said, holding the files under his pointed index finger. "The US built this weapon, but were completing it just as L&M sacked that city all those years back. We believe it's been sitting dormant all this time, yet still functional with its own devoted reactor. We have found the location of this facility and have found out where they've hidden the keys; with it, we'll destroy L&M's command post and their entire capitol with the push of a button... with them gone, who'll resist us? Who'd fight back against SPARTAN with a city-destroying weapon, especially when we're going to reunite the continent, making it better and more prosperous than before?"

Jeremiah shook his head while donning a small grin of his own, "Trevor... it's a trap."

"We've been planning this for some time now," Trevor went on, seemingly oblivious to Jeremiah's comment, "and once we display the dominating power of this weapon, we won't have any trouble getting everyone on board."

The young lieutenant was looking confused, quietly shifting his gaze between Jeremiah and the colonel, trying to decide if he had missed something or if someone else had.

Trevor could see the confusion on LT William's face, but before the colonel could comment on it, Jeremiah spoke again.

"The facility is a trap," Jeremiah said again, "not a weapon..."

The smile fell off of Trevor's face like wind falling out of a sail. "What do you mean?"

"... At least not a weapon for you to use," Jeremiah added.

"What do you mean?" Trevor pressed again with frustrated confusion.

"It was built to trap you," Jeremiah said. "They marketed it and advertised it as a weapon, using misinformation, hoping to lure SPARTAN there, while it was built as a giant landmine."

"No..." Trevor resisted, pointing back to the files on his desk, "it's all right here... It's a weapon..."

"...That the old government built, but never used?" Jeremiah asked rhetorically, eyeing Trevor as if the mere suggestion should give it away.

Trevor was opening the files now, not sure what to say, but flipping through the paperwork and documentation.

Jeremiah continued, "They knew they were losing... They knew that the only way to make a significant dent in SPARTAN was to make you believe it was a weapon so powerful... that SPARTAN leadership couldn't risk NOT sending a large force with high ranking leadership..."

The young lieutenant was listening with a gaping mouth, and Trevor had looked up from his files with a look that could've suggested he'd just sat in a puddle of diarrhea.

Jeremiah went on, "They thought that such a weapon would make SPARTAN too paranoid to send a lower ranking officer with only a small force to occupy. They wanted SPARTAN leadership to fear that such a weapon couldn't be trusted to anyone but themselves."

Trevor, still not wanting to believe the words coming out of Jeremiah's mouth, asked, "How would you know this?"

"I've been there," Jeremiah answered. "It was a few years before L&M sacked the capitol. And then I saw the director of the facility as L&M was invading."

"Doctor L. M. Jackson," Trevor said, looking back at his files.

Jeremiah nodded, somehow relieved that Trevor didn't know Dr. Jackson was Lilly, feeling like he therefore had something with Lilly that Trevor did not, and was content enough with that to continue keeping it to himself. "I led the doctor north," Jeremiah said, "and we talked a lot during that time."

"And he told you that?" Trevor asked with skepticism. "That the facility is a trap?"

Jeremiah nodded.

Trevor sat in his desk chair and leaned back in thought.

"What, is the door booby trapped or somethin'?" LT Williams asked.

Jeremiah shook his head, saying, "No. The system was set up to look like a weapon, displaying a satellite image of a target location, but when the trigger was hit, it would actually initiate a self destruct, completely destroying the facility and nearby surrounding area."

LT Williams looked to the colonel for a reaction or a response. Trevor leaned forward in his desk chair, flipping through the files again, not knowing what to say, no longer wearing his big smile.

"They didn't have the time or resources to actually construct a weapon of this type and magnitude," Jeremiah said. "So they programmed the system to look one way, but planted a ton of explosives, actually wanting it to work another."

"But the old government wouldn't risk that much collateral damage," Trevor said meekly, hoping something, anything, would discredit what Jeremiah was saying.

Jeremiah shrugged, "You push a fox into a trap and he'll do anything to get out of it, even chew off his own leg…"

Trevor looked down, trying to think things over, wondering how Generals Simmons and Monroe would take the news.

"But," Jeremiah said, rekindling a small ray of hope for Trevor, "ultimately you're right. Last minute, after everything was installed and in place, they bailed on the idea."

Trevor looked up at Jeremiah curiously.

"They did it hastily, though," Jeremiah said, adding, "There wasn't time to completely dismantle the demolitions or crash the system. When L&M invaded, there were still too many civilians around, and they didn't want to risk the facility being compromised and the potential collateral damage resulting from L&M finding it – so they just disconnected the mainline of the detonator as they rushed out the door."

Trevor was in complete shock, rocking back in his chair again as he ran his fingers through his flowing white hair, trying to decide what to do next. He started laughing as he rubbed his eyes, his winning smile reappearing on his face. "Clever. Clever," he said in pure amusement. "I am actually impressed."

The stocky lieutenant wasn't laughing, but still watching the colonel, trying to figure out what was going on.

"We can still use the facility," Trevor said, still smiling, "but this changes things of course." Trevor slapped his hand down on his desk and added with excitement, "I knew it was worth it, bringing you on."

Jeremiah smiled a little, "Well I don't know about that. There isn't anything I can do for you, really."

"I still can't believe it," Trevor said, beginning to laugh again. "I had no idea they had it in 'em." With a jovial look to Jeremiah he added, "If you guys had been that clever from the start, the war may have turned out differently," and started laughing again.

Jeremiah felt a slight sting at the comment, not able to help but think of his fallen friends and casualties of the war and institutions like SPARTAN, but he tried to ignore it and view it all in a larger context. The war was over now. Now Trevor and SPARTAN weren't the enemy, just another government. And despite his own personal losses, Trevor was right; had the leadership of the old government been a little more clever, things may have turned out differently.

Trevor, still laughing and seemingly no longer annoyed or put off that their master plan was shown to be no good, looked at Lieutenant Williams. "Hey, Williams," he said, full of energy, "learn from that. Tricks do work and can win battles and wars if you're clever enough."

The lieutenant smiled and nodded, beginning to come out from under his dark cloud of disenchantment and join the colonel's jubilation.

"One time," Trevor began to say to Jeremiah and LT Williams, until his assistant reentered the room with a tray of drinks. "Oh thank you, Kelly," he said.

"One time," he said again, before looking at Jeremiah with a pointed finger and sly grin. "Oh, we were clever, weren't we, Jeremiah?" Trevor laughed again, "You have to admit it, SPARTAN was clever."

Trevor picked up a glass, looking at no one, as he restarted his story. "One time," he said with a wide, wide grin, "we sent a small force up North." He eyed everyone in the room, making sure they were still paying attention. "This was right after the US completely fell," he said, "But we were afraid of Raven rejoining the fight, right?"

Jeremiah, thinking back, couldn't remember hearing about SPARTAN invading the North during that time, but said nothing. He just leaned against the big desk and listened to Trevor gloat.

"We were starting to fear that Raven may begin to reunify and attack us on our flank, since the arena changed," Trevor said, with pride beaming out of his smile, "Since the US had fallen and we were still busy fighting L&M..."

Jeremiah started feeling the hairs on his neck stand up, beginning to get a sense of anxiety rush over him as he listened to Trevor.

With his grand smile and animated arm motions, Trevor continued, "So we sent this small force up there, with the intention of hitting them once, in a way that would take them out of the fight for good."

Jeremiah felt like the walls were closing in.

"We had to drive a permanent wedge between Raven and the Northern civilians, okay?" Trevor continued. "So we dressed our small force in Raven uniforms and attacked one of their towns up there." Trevor was laughing. "Yeah, we burned it down and shot up the whole place."

Jeremiah couldn't believe his ears and was dumbfounded with utter surprise. He felt dizzy, almost.

The young lieutenant leaned forward, clearly enthralled. "So the people, the civilians, thought that they were being attacked by Raven?"

"Right!" Trevor exclaimed with pride. "We even posted signs, saying something like, '*if you don't join Raven we'll kill you*,' or somethin…" Trevor was clearly amused at their own cleverness. "It was kind of poetic, really," he added, "I mean, we prevented Raven from ever regaining real control of the North, or securing a real fighting force, by pretending to be Raven while killing Northerners…" Trevor was laughing again.

"South Harbor," Jeremiah uttered, as he felt adrenaline flood him in a rush to the head. He thought about that night, so many years ago. He thought about Lilly. He thought about how she died. He heard her screaming his name. He remembered burying her. He remembered the things he did to Raven leadership in the months following the event. Jeremiah was sick with rage.

Jeremiah couldn't hear much over his own heartbeat, but faintly heard Trevor say, "Yeah, South Harbor," through his wide smile; with glee and self promotion, as Jeremiah moved toward him. Before Jeremiah even knew what he was doing, his hands were fast upon Trevor, suddenly startling the jovial white haired colonel.

Reacting quickly, the strapping young lieutenant was on Jeremiah, securing a firm grip just as fast, in the colonel's defense.

Jeremiah's arm flashed like lightning, striking the strong lieutenant square in the nose in a sickening crack. The lieutenant fell hard to the floor with the initial sharp pain fading into numbness, which would soon give way into a dull ache. Disoriented by the severity of the unexpected attack, as well as the embarrassment of such a strong guy like himself being so humiliated by an old man, he struggled to get up, though every ounce of his pride was telling him to.

Though the lieutenant suffered a quick and violent response to his action, his act on Jeremiah distracted the old man enough to momentarily release the colonel, but due to Trevor's age, his prosthetic leg, and the sheer astonishment at Jeremiah's attack, Trevor only fell to the floor in bewilderment.

The assistant looked on in horror, frozen with fear, unsure of what was happening or what had prompted the brutality that she was witnessing.

It was pure hubris, young pride, that made the young lieutenant scramble to his feet. He could hardly see through his watering eyes, and his mind was rushing mere fractions of thoughts, and all he could really take hold of was the idea that he was young and strong and that Jeremiah Pratt was old and weak. So Lieutenant Williams stood for the last time, unwilling to yield to this old man.

Jeremiah, bitter with the world, lamenting his lost loved ones, and again despising SPARTAN with the purest hatred, the source of all of his loss and pain, grabbed the inert and harmless grenade from Trevor's desk, and with the whole of his arm, slung it down on the wobbly lieutenant's head in a wet smack. He fell lifeless to the floor.

The terrified assistant threw up at the grisly sight, never to sleep well again. Later, the only words she'd be able to share on this gruesome event would be, "...Such barbarism...," uttered hesitantly with clinched, teary eyes.

Jeremiah turned to Trevor, who was sprawled across the floor with a gaping mouth and wide eyes.

"WHY?!" Trevor shouted frantically. "YOU'RE INSANE! WHAT ARE YOU DOIN'?!!"

Walking toward Trevor, Jeremiah might have thought about giving a speech, lecturing Trevor, getting it all off of his chest.

At that moment he was certainly haunted by the ghostly images of Lilly, and of Mick and Parks, as well as the scores of others who had met their demise due to SPARTAN. All of the past revolving around Trevor and Lilly, festering to eruption, swelled within Jeremiah like a wild, burning fever, inflamed by the careless nature with which Trevor spoke of South Harbor; the place Jeremiah was last robbed of Lilly in permanent fashion.

Jeremiah might have been tempted to bring Trevor up to speed, eliminating all the confusion that intertwined with the desperate panic that Trevor felt grow with each step that Jeremiah took closer to him, but Jeremiah wasn't a talker. Jeremiah didn't always fold to temptations of that sort, and he felt no concern with whether Trevor understood or not. He wanted Trevor to be afraid. He wanted Trevor to be sent to the darkness in permanent fashion. There was only static in his ears; all he saw was red.

Pratt unholstered his sidearm, pulled back the slide, letting it slam forward, as it chambered a round in Mick's old forty-five, and unceremoniously squeezed the trigger, putting a slug into Trevor's forehead, ruining the floor.

Trevor's assistant passed out. Such barbarism.

Jeremiah looked around the room, unsure of what to do next. He half thought about sitting down and waiting for other SPARTANS to barge in, letting them kill him, either immediately or in some later execution. But that half thought only lasted a half moment before he realized he had a shot, no matter how long, of trying to beat SPARTAN forces to that facility and resetting the trap, getting his revenge in a more complete and more grandiose manner.

He took a quick survey of the map and headed out of the top floor office, shutting the grand doors behind him, leaving the way he came in. He received a few odd looks from people here and there, but no one stopped him. Evidently, the gunshot either wasn't heard, or people dismissed it as something other than what it was. But he knew that they'd realize what had happened soon enough, so he would hurry.

He had somewhere to be.

Chapter 17

Sierra Victor

As Uriah and Josiah Morris fled what was behind them, their anxiety of what lay ahead began to build as they noticed more and more feral-looking city people appear from behind street corners or abandoned and wrecked vehicles. The buzzards circling overhead gave the scene an eerie overtone, and Josiah wasn't sure whether the scavengers were there for them or for some other, out of sight kill.

The Preachers walked on, albeit at a slower pace. It wasn't necessarily courage, although they did indeed muster their own, and it wasn't due to foolish ignorance; rather they continued ahead because they knew what was behind them, leaving the only decision in direction to be the lesser of two evils. The Preachers, therefore, hoped the city people weren't as dangerous or as wild as they feared and felt little choice but to press on, placing their fate in the care of their Eternal Lord.

Tyler looked on from his place in hiding as several dozen city people converged on the two Preachers, carrying weapons and holding pit bulls on leashes. They were evidently erring on the side of caution, increasing the number of their toll collecting gang, after the earlier incident with Jeremiah Pratt.

"This is a toll road," a man with a balding head and bad teeth said as he approached the Preachers. His gang staged themselves in a rough semicircle, stretching around him like wings, whose tips began to approach the Preachers. Barking and growling at

288

the Preachers, the dogs looked vicious, barely being kept at bay by their handler's leashes.

Uriah and Josiah stood still, fearful, and nervous at the scene before them. The group of thirty or so people were armed with pipes, knives, and guns. All of the people were dirty, and they ranged in age from the lower teens to their forties or fifties. Many appeared to be malnourished, with most, if not all, looking less than reasonable.

Uriah shook his head subtly with concern and with the calmest and most sincere and sympathetic voice he could manage said, "I, I'm sorry, but we don't have any money."

The bald man, and those surrounding him, looked irritated by the response. "Food then..." he said, motioning to the men holding the dogs.

The dog handlers moved closer, trying to terrify the two with the fierce dogs, as the gang began to cheer and yell at the sport of it. But as the dogs got closer, they also got calmer. The gang quit cheering when Josiah reached out and petted the dogs, who had quit barking furiously and started licking his fingers.

Annoyed and embarrassed, the balding gang leader yelled, "GET THEM DOGS BACK!!" When the Preachers only had blank, worried stares in response, the bald man, wanting to get back on topic, hastily listed other options besides food and money, "Water, tools, weapons…"

Nothing.

"Then you'll have to pay with your shoes and clothes."

Uriah looked around at the scene before him. "Sir, please," he began to plead.

"Or the boy!" the bald man exclaimed in anger, approaching the two. Touching Josiah's head, he said, "Maybe we'll take 'im anyways; an extra fee fur yur extra hassle."

Before Uriah could act out of alarm and defense, the Preachers and motley city gang were distracted by the sudden and fast approach of eight horsemen. None of the men were holding reins as they galloped closer and closer, but holding carbines.

The sight was oddly unsettling, causing the rabble to break their ranks, taking several steps in caution backward. In an effort to defend his turf, his toll road, source of income, and in an effort to maintain face with his people, the dirty bald man, pointed his revolver at the approaching horsemen and through rotten teeth yelled, "THIS IS MY ROAD! AN' TO RIDE IT, YOU PAY THE TOLL!"

The father and son Preachers felt their stomachs sink to their knees, caught between a rock and now a harder, faster approaching rock. There was nothing to say. There was nothing to do. The pair stood frozen in fear as they could feel the gravity of the inevitable press upon them more and more.

The yuck-mouth, balding man's display of valor and show of strength emboldened his gang, gifting them the courage to stand their ground and aim their weapons at the horsemen. After the earlier events that tragically reduced their numbers, they had resolved to never be taken off guard, or to be beaten on their home field again. They stood, ready to fight, until Flagstaff engulfed them like a flood.

Flagstaff maneuvered deftly on horseback, firing expertly in mid-stride. Their formation shifted and advanced gracefully and fluidly, like a master-choreographed ballet. Some of the Flagstaff members dismounted their horses in an equally impressive and seamless manner, hitting the ground on the run, firing away as their riderless horses rammed and trampled city people, while the rest of Flagstaff contributed to the massacre by way of their guns.

The gang fired away frantically, with some of their weapons misfiring. Gang members with weapons that did fire, ended up shooting their own or simply missing any living target, firing wildly with fear. In addition to those on their own side, they did manage to shoot a few of the horses, but couldn't seem to slow the assault. They weren't soldiers, they weren't disciplined, and many of them weren't alive anymore.

Uriah led Josiah out of the gunfight as they were both bumping into others who were either busy fighting or fleeing. Uriah was frantically terrified for his son, not thinking of anything other than removing Josiah from harm.

Tyler, from above in his second floor hiding place, tried to sink lower in the shadows as he watched with wide eyes, unable to peel himself away from the grisly circus below. As several Flagstaff members apprehended the Preachers, and as the other Flagstaff members butchered crazy, toll-taking city people, Tyler could see something else approaching from the far end of the street.

Despite the events below, he squinted beyond the chaos and focused on what now approached. It neared with speed and appeared to be an individual on a machine, an old world motorcycle. Tyler strained his eyes, still careful to remain hidden from view by the violent crazies beneath him, and focused his full attention on the approaching biker. Astonished, and not knowing whether to be afraid or to see this as a new opportunity, he realized it was the old Blacksmith Pratt, on his way to join the tussle below.

Down in the street, below Tyler's place in the shadows, two of Flagstaff were wrestling the Preachers to the ground, while the others were finishing off what remained of the city gang or pursuing those who were fleeing down old, damaged side streets, cluttered with garbage and debris.

Without a word, the member of Flagstaff with the cold, blue eyes and thick beard had kicked Uriah in the back as he and Josiah tried to get away. Uriah had grunted in pain, and he fell hard to the sidewalk and against a building wall. Josiah screamed in alarm and concern as he tried to rush to his father for aid. Before Josiah could much more than turn around and face his father, the other member of Flagstaff was on him, subduing his arms behind his back.

Uriah winced in pain as he attempted to slowly roll over and pick himself up, but was kicked down again by the blue-eyed telepath, who scolded, "STAY DOWN!" Slinging his rifle to his back, he mounted Uriah, securing his hands behind his back with flex cuffs, as he lay painfully on the hard ground.

"Why'd you run?" Flagstaff complained. "You were treated well," he said, pulling Uriah up in a seated position against the wall. "We'd have let you go."

Josiah was terrified, being held down as his father was abused and lectured. Josiah pleaded to God in his mind, but looking skyward, all he saw were the vultures, still circling overhead. Josiah began to cry as he struggled to maintain his faith and courage. He began to fear that he and his father might be killed.

"You could've slept in a warm bed," Flagstaff continued, holding Uriah by the collar. "You could've had a hot meal and enjoyed the perks that come with being national heroes." Flagstaff pulled his sidearm out of its holster and said, "But you had to run away." Looking at Josiah and then back to the father, he said, "But we know. The general may not, but we do. He's the one who opened the door, not you. Maybe we can use him; maybe we don't need you."

Uriah felt sick and couldn't hide the fear in his eyes as they looked directly into the cold blue of the bearded Flagstaff that stood over him. Flagstaff grimaced, evidently unmoved. He looked over to the boy, but instead of the expected fear, saw bewilderment, as the boy looked at something behind them.

The blue-eyed Flagstaff quickly turned, raising his pistol, in time to see Jeremiah Pratt shoot two of the Flagstaff members who'd still been tangling with the city dwellers. Unaccustomed to being approached unawares, Flagstaff nearly screamed in surprise, but instead groaned at the agony of feeling the loss of two Flagstaff members. It was unexpected and disorienting, but before Pratt could shoot the two other Flagstaff men who were with the Preachers, Flagstaff dove behind the Preachers, using them as shields.

Tyler began to sweat as he watched, making himself as small as possible, angry with himself for being terrified. He was both in awe of the old man's tenacity and grit, and spitefully envious that he wasn't like him.

Jeremiah stood in the street, surrounded by bodies, with his rifle stock at his cheek, tight against his shoulder, as he stared down his iron sights at the blue-eyed, bearded devil, hiding behind the Preacher. Jeremiah said nothing, not planning on taking any prisoners of his own, but held his fire, not having a clear shot.

"We're gonna kill you," the blue-eyed Flagstaff said through a painfully angered laugh.

"Do it," Jeremiah replied evenly, steadily maintaining his aim.

Flagstaff laughed. The men of Flagstaff had fallen for cover behind the Preachers so carelessly that it left them in the precarious situation where if they raised their weapons, they'd likely expose themselves to Pratt. They knew their other four brothers were creeping up. And while they waited for their comrades, the two watched as Pratt kept his aim, carefully making subtle adjustments, trying to find a good angle of fire.

Something in Tyler perked up at the dialogue. He looked back up and managed to see a few of the other horsemen creeping back down the side streets that they had chased city people down, now trying to flank Pratt. Tyler felt an adrenaline surge and his heart rate increase. He chastised himself for failing back on Watchmen's Hill at Engine's Rest and for lacking the courage to even try back in the old house when Pratt had dismissed him. He remembered the rifle he held in his hand and suddenly thought that he might have a chance at redemption.

"We will," Flagstaff said from behind Uriah. "Your little girl's already dead."

Jeremiah ignored them, dismayed by what they were saying, unsure as to whether it could be trusted, realizing that there was no point in discussing it with them now.

"Yeah," Flagstaff said again, clearly annoyed. "When you fled the colonel's murder scene, no one was sure where you went. So the general sent a company up north in case you went home... and sent us toward the facility, betting you came here..."

Flagstaff laughed again, "Whether you were at your cabin or not, they were gonna wipe out whoever they found there." Flagstaff was grinning as he hid behind the Preachers.

The Champ slowly slid himself to a better position. He was more exposed, but he knew it was worth the risk. He raised his rifle, pulling the butt of his carbine firmly into his shoulder, resting his cheek on the stock, and supporting his forward elbow on his knee. He could feel the sweat beading on his forehead, and he tried to calm himself and slow his heartbeat. He carefully placed his index finger on the trigger and exhaled as he set his front sight post on Jeremiah Pratt's head. He could kill Pratt and be rewarded by the un-uniformed SPARTANS below him. The Champ knew a win/win when he saw one. "Your time has passed, old man," he whispered to himself.

***

Jonas peered inside the large panel box, overwhelmed by the sight. The network of circuitry and bundle of tangled wire, cables, and connectors looked alien to him and were unlike anything he'd ever seen before. But unlike problems back at the Congregation that would arise with the livestock, farms, or barn raisings, which would frustrate and bore him, this seemed more important somehow – there seemed to be more glory in this.

He looked once more and thought back to the technicians he had watched assemble, connect, and reboot the hardware, equipment, and systems in the command room. Looking again into the panel with those observations in mind, he began to pay more attention to the cables, many of them having couplings or plug-in connection ends. He narrowed his focus from the forest to just a few select trees and began to see which cables were connected where, until he saw a few cables that weren't connected to anything.

He looked closer and reached inside to find that the unconnected cables could easily be reconnected. "HEY!" he yelled out to the intercom, unsure if he should reconnect them himself or not. "HEY! I think I found something!"

It took General Simmons a moment to realize that someone was calling over the intercom. He and his technicians had been slowly making their way through the system's root code and had just found some programming that looked promising.

"You can't beat me, old man," General Simmons said to himself with a grin when they found the lines of code.

At finally hearing Jonas's calls, the general said to his command team, "Pull that up, find the problem, and let's get this show back on the road," before turning to the intercom.

"Yes," the general called out through the intercom, "what did you find?"

"An open panel," Jonas called back. "Looks like someone unhooked some wires or somethin'." Jonas kept staring at the cables. The longer he looked at them, the easier and more obvious the solution appeared. Jonas felt proud of himself. He felt like he was doing very well there with SPARTAN.

The general's eyes widened with approving surprise. "Good work," he said, before he was distracted by the technician at the command kiosk.

"Sir," the technician said. From his tone it was difficult to tell whether it was confusion or alarm. "Look at this."

The general looked up at the main screen, and as he read the program, his look of triumph faded into confusion. He shook his head and said, "Wait..." his mouth was suddenly dry. He cleared his throat and said, "Wait," again, but still struggled to get the words out. Reading the code a second time, certain he had initially seen it wrong, he realized what the weapon really was.

Jonas, unaware and unconcerned with code or programs, was smiling with pride at the general's "Good work," comment.

Jonas, eager to be the savior, and ready to demonstrate his intelligence and skills from his earlier observations, reached inside the panel and grabbed the ends of the cables and smugly said, "'Thou sayest,'" as he connected them.

***

The Champ began to feel powerful in his unnoticed position of overwatch. He pointed his sights on Jeremiah Pratt, placed the tip of his finger on his trigger and slowly expelled the breath from his lungs.

As the other four Flagstaff operatives were just emerging behind Pratt, and as the Champ was slowly beginning to squeeze his trigger, the atmosphere tore in thunderous fury as the facility exploded with enough force that every structure within a mile radius of the installation was razed, in what felt like the worst combination of earthquake and hurricane.

The shockwave and ensuing winds of heat knocked everyone to the ground, Tyler firing his shot as he fell from his second floor perch onto one of the Flagstaff and Uriah, below. The immense and unexpected blast threw the Champ's aim, sending his bullet square between the eyes of one of the approaching Flagstaff operatives and out the back of his head and into the heart of another.

As plumes of smoke rose into the air and dust settled upon them like a heavy fog, the disoriented men scrambled slowly to their feet with dull ringing ears, at first unsure of what had happened.

When Flagstaff realized that it was the facility that had exploded and that two more of their men had just been killed, they wanted nothing but revenge and sought to regain their composure and re-identify their targets through the thick haze of dust and smoke.

Tyler rolled painfully on the ground, without the attention or concern of anyone.

Pratt was scrambling to his feet, holding his rifle by his side at the pistol grip as he tried to wipe the dust from his eyes. He was coughing and trying to ignore the high pitched tone that filled his ears.

The blue-eyed man roared in furious aggravation, and fighting his disorientation, raised his pistol, pointing it at Josiah, to Uriah's horror.

Despite his own confusion from the blast, Uriah impulsively rushed to shield his son, placing his head in line with the barrel of Flagstaff's gun as the trigger was pulled. The pop of the gunshot was dulled, seemingly unimpressive, in the wake of the recent blast, as debris rained down upon them, and thick dust continued to roll in like a possessed fog.

Josiah screamed in horror and disbelief as his father's head popped backward, thick silt shaking free in the violent vibration, exploding brain and skull fragments onto the old and dusty wall. It wasn't a conscious decision, but a visceral reaction that propelled young Josiah into attacking the blue-eyed man in response.

It was almost like Josiah was slowly waking from a dream, his senses seemed dulled, and he felt like he was watching himself from somewhere above as he punched the bearded man wildly and relentlessly, knocking him to the ground. Gradually, the vision shifted from above to closer and closer until he was seeing through his own eyes. He wasn't sure if he was being hit back, but he couldn't seem to stop himself from unleashing everything he had into Flagstaff.

Something made Tyler open his eyes, which had been clenched in pain. It couldn't have been a sound, because he couldn't hear anything through the dull ringing in his ears. But whether through some premonition or something else, he opened his eyes to realize that he was now down on the street and no longer in his hiding spot. He stopped wincing as he tried to make sense of what else he was seeing. He blinked a few confusing times as he watched a silent scene of vultures and dogs attack what was left of Flagstaff.

He slowly turned his head to see what else was surrounding him. The sight was so unexpected that he watched on calmly as if he were dreaming. He saw a bewildered and dusty Jeremiah Pratt standing with a gaping mouth. To himself, Tyler smiled and said, "Heh, me and the Blacksmith are having the same dream."

Jeremiah regained his composure and focused at the sound of the gunshot, making him look up in time to see the Preacher slump backward, lifelessly. Jeremiah reflexively raised his rifle, unaware of or unconcerned with the two Flagstaff men behind him, pointing it at the Flagstaff men near the Preachers as young Josiah launched himself into the bearded man.

Unable to shoot the blue-eyed man due to Josiah's aggression, Jeremiah fired two rounds into the Flagstaff operative who had been behind Josiah. He was angry with the lad for getting in the way of his shot, but simultaneously impressed with his tenacity. Suddenly sensing something behind him, Old Man Pratt spun on his heels, raising his rifle as he saw a muzzle being brought down in line with his head.

In that fraction of a half second, Jeremiah had the feeling of his life flashing before his eyes. He felt a lot of regret and a tremendous amount of guilt, but no fear at the prospect of death, just the feeling that this made sense. Even so, his nature was to fight and press on, so while he knew he couldn't swing his rifle around in time to beat the bullet of this assailing Flagstaff operative, he tried his best, wanting to go down with his boots on.

In that fraction of a half second, before the final shot came for Jeremiah Pratt, a large dark object shot down in front of him and onto Flagstaff. Startled by the unexpected event, Pratt stumbled backward, barely able to keep himself from falling.

Regaining his footing, he staggered back to an upright position and watched in bewilderment and awe as vultures and a gang of dogs were attacking Flagstaff, knocking them to the ground, furiously pecking eyes and flesh, while the dogs viciously bit and tore chunks of meat from their bodies. Jeremiah felt real and nearly-consuming fear for the first time as he watched the unnatural attack, too frozen with fear and too overcome with confusion to run or hide.

He slowly turned his head back to the boy, who was still swinging with rapid fury into the man beneath him, while two pit bulls tore into that blue-eyed man's torso and legs. As he watched on, and as little sense as it seemed to make, something in Jeremiah's mind told him that it was the boy. That the dogs and buzzards were acting on his behalf, fighting with the same furious fervor as Josiah.

The vultures and the dogs were like additional arms and fists, harkening to Josiah's will with effortless thought, or even involuntarily through some reflex or adrenaline-induced fight or flight. In truth, Josiah didn't even realize it at the time, or at least at the start – he just attacked, unable to resist or sit back. So he attacked with all of his purpose and with the entirety of his might. And somewhere inside, his silent voice called to them, and at that moment of dire gravity, Josiah and the beasts were of a single mind, Josiah's, and the beasts' were striving for a single purpose in perfect harmony. At that moment, they were one.

With the bewildered confusion of a nightmare, the old man said, "Josiah," as small tears from the heavy dust, confusion, and even sympathy, began to well in his eyes. "Josiah," he called again, with a few cautious steps forward.

Josiah sobbed as he began to slow his assault from frantic violence to a fatigued futility. As his swings gradually subsided, the buzzards and dogs also relented, acting more like animals than possessed beasts. Josiah eventually stopped hitting the dead, blue-eyed man and crawled over to his father's body, clinging to it as he wept.

Jeremiah had stopped his approach, no longer feeling fear, only sympathy and urgency, always urgency. He watched the boy, unsure of what to do or say, uncertain of what had just happened. While he felt a certain amount of relief that the facility was destroyed and General Simmons along with it, he also felt compassion for the boy who cried over his dead father, and he also felt a pressing concern for the people he lived with up north. He feared that Flagstaff hadn't been bluffing in regard to the SPARTAN company that was sent north for him and the people he lived among, because that tactic made sense. Not knowing what to do with Josiah, he decided to do nothing and turned to leave.

"Wait!" Josiah cried, running up behind Pratt.

Jeremiah turned to face him.

"Please don't leave me here," Josiah said, eyes swollen, caked in dust and red from grief.

Jeremiah hesitated before responding. "I'm sorry about your father, but I have to go north."

"I'll go," Josiah said.

The old man shook his head. "You should go home."

"No," the boy said. "I don't know how to get back." He started to cry again and looked over his shoulder at his father's body, then added, "... or if I could make it back. You saved us... saved me."

"You saved yourself."

Josiah looked down, embarrassed and uncertain of what he had done or what had actually even happened.

Jeremiah didn't know what else to say, and he felt like now may not be the time for talk anyway. He stood silent for a bit, then said, "I'm going north."

Though Josiah remained silent, it was clear that he intended to follow.

Jeremiah nodded.

"Okay," the boy said, trying to stop his tears, not sure of what else he could say or where else he could go.

Jeremiah looked over at Uriah's body, adding, "We'll go after we take care of him."

The distraught boy wiped the tears from his dirty cheeks and made a concerted effort to get control of himself.

As they departed with Uriah's body through the thick fog of dust and smoke, one of the pit bulls followed, now Josiah's confederate. Jeremiah covered the damaged head, so that Josiah wouldn't have to suffer the sight of the grisly wound. Old Man Jeremiah Pratt carried the body with care and reverence, mindful of the young man and fully aware of what such a heavy loss felt like.

By this time, Tyler had realized that he had not been asleep. He was sore and still not completely sure how he'd ended up on the street, but he seemed otherwise unhurt. Seeing Pratt depart, he remembered firing at the old man, but nothing else. He frantically looked for his rifle, intent on finishing the old man off once and for all. He didn't find his rifle, but he did find another weapon, some pistol laying in the street. Unsure if it had belonged to a city dweller or a Flagstaff, he picked it up, rising to find someone standing in front of him.

The young girl with the dirty cheeks, blonde pigtails, and "Player" jacket, stood, gazing curiously at him.

The Champ was caught off guard by her presence and shuddered in surprise.

"You a Blacksmith?" she asked with apparent awe.

"Huh?" the Champ said, confused, just before he coughed, gagging at the thick smoke and dust, still engulfing them. He wasn't just confused at the question, but at her seemingly utter lack of recognition that there had just been an enormous explosion that was still raining down tiny bits of debris as it encased everything in a thick layer of dust.

"I bet you are. I saw you," she said with a playful grin and seductive eyes. "From the first time I saw yur belt, I knew you was a champion."

"Well yeah," Tyler said, thinking of the earlier event, now trying to brush the dust off of his belt buckle as nonchalantly as he could manage. Still unsure of the purpose or reason behind this interaction, he looked around the girl, trying not to lose sight of Pratt, making sure the old man was still walking beside the boy, but also not wanting to be rude to the lady.

"It was incredible," she marveled, "you jumped outta that buildin', shootin' them two guys there," and she pointed to the dusty Flagstaff bodies that were being picked at by buzzards. "And then jumped on that one there," nodding to the blue-eyed corpse. "I've never seen nuthin' like it," she said, clearly impressed. "You saved that old man," she said, referring to the departing Pratt.

Tyler made a practice of never questioning nor refuting any praise that was being directed at him, but he was confused. He looked at the bodies, then up at the second floor perch, and back to the blonde, pigtailed girl. "I didn't know anybody was lookin'," he said, hoping the line worked.

"I was hiding in there," she said, nodding to the building behind her on the opposite side of the street. "I saw the whole thing," she said, smiling. "I'm gonna tell everybody..." Biting her lip in excitement, she added, "I bet they're gonna write songs about you."

Tyler nodded, and looking into her eyes, he tenderly said, "They will."

With her, he suddenly didn't feel the need to kill the old man, and now the suggestion that he was impressive, selfless, and brave for saving Jeremiah Pratt seemed even better than if he'd killed him. "Yes," Tyler thought, "they will write songs..."

Tyler looked back over to the fading silhouette of the old man as he and the boy disappeared into the thick haze of dust that enveloped the scene.

"So," she said. "Don't you have a toll you owe me?"

Tyler grinned arrogantly. "A Blacksmith always pays his dues," he said, taking her by the hand.

Epilogue

Angel of Death

The silence of the still night was shattered by a heavy boot kicking in the front door, followed by a team of SPARTANs storming the small main room of the remote cabin surrounded by large coniferous trees. This wasn't these SPARTAN scouts' land, but the night was their time.

At the same time General Simmons ordered Flagstaff toward the old government's forgotten and abandoned facility, the general also sent this unit of scouts northward, to Pratt's homestead, in case he fled back to his home. Their orders were to capture the old man, if possible, and to eliminate anyone with him, using any means necessary.

It was unknown as to whether the old man was actually in his cabin, but someone was inside. Their brief reconnaissance of the property showed that at least one female was present and that at least three other people were located in the other two properties. All three properties were to be raided simultaneously under the concealment of darkness.

The only noise in Pratt's cabin were the footsteps of four SPARTAN soldiers on hardwood flooring, who were making their way inside. Without using words, as if planned and rehearsed, the two lead men continued to the single bedroom, while the last man stayed at the door, keeping watch, with the team leader (third man in the stack) moving to the window in the main room of the cabin that overlooked the other properties.

As the two lead SPARTANs entered the dark bedroom, neither the team leader nor the SPARTAN at the front door had noticed the bedroom door shut silently behind them until the unexpected loud bangs of two gunshots sounded from behind it; followed immediately by the sound of breaking glass and the horrid scream of a frantic and terrified woman.

The team leader and front door guard bolted to the bedroom, furiously kicking in the door. The two were shocked to find both of their teammates laying on the floor. One was motionless and the other appeared to have a severe wound to the neck; he was lying awkwardly against the wall, clutching his throat as blood streamed between his fingers. His eyes screamed of fear, as his mouth could not.

The team leader followed the wide, terrified eyes of his injured soldier across the room, where the girl was curled up on the floor, shaking and still crying. Through the faint moonlight that shone through the broken window, it looked like the girl was covered in blood. Her dishevelled hair was down in her face and she looked almost childish and vulnerable in the long white nightgown, now ruined with blood stains. Before the team leader could question the girl, she spoke.

"That way! He went that way…" she managed to say, in between frantic sobs, as she pointed to the window with shaking hands.

The team leader's eyes widened in grim realization. "Pratt."

The team leader rushed toward the broken window as he ordered the other soldier to stay with the wounded. The young private urgently replied, "Wait... what about her?"

In his rush, the team leader only responded, "It's just a girl," before jumping out of the window in pursuit.

The private returned to the wounded, cursing the situation and now cursing the dark, until the eyes of his dying comrade seemed to plead for him to look out behind him. Feeling the hairs stand up on his neck, the private turned quickly, raising his carbine, in time to see the girl, who now looked like an apparition in her blood covered nightgown, standing behind him as she swung her tomahawk into his head.

The girl released the grip of her little battle axe, which was now stuck fast into her third victim. The handle bore the inscription, "RAMSAP." As the SPARTAN fell to the floor, Morgan grabbed the carbine out of his hands and rushed to the broken window where she saw the back of the crouching SPARTAN outside in the cold darkness. As if by intuition, the SPARTAN turned back to the cabin.

The look on his face was one of regret; there in the cold night air, looking up into the window at the girl standing inside it, looking back at him. She wasn't crying. She wasn't frantic or scared. She was no longer shaking. She was standing sure. The white of her nightgown almost glowed in the moonlight, starkly contrasting with the huge bloodstains that were now covering much of it.

Pratt had never been here. She broke the window. In the half second it took for him to realize his grave mistake, he knew that the girl was no angel even if she looked like a spirit. His eyes were drawn to the military carbine in her hands; *angel of death maybe*. He also knew there was nothing to do as he fell to the earth after seeing two muzzle flashes. It wouldn't hurt for long.

Afterword

Originally, I had not intended to do many flashbacks, nor had I intended on any love interest like Lilly, and had certainly not planned on writing any aspect of high school love or heartbreak. It just just felt too cheesy.

I started writing this story in the summer of 2006 immediately after being medically retired from the Army and it took me over a decade to complete. Going back to college, working, and being a husband and a father took up too much of my time and I just wasn't able to write full time – but the other reason it took so long was writer's block. I had several moving pieces in place and had a hard time connecting them the way I wanted... until Lilly came to mind.

Lilly's character is based on an idea and not any person. I felt like most people could relate to some unrequited love, or adolescent romantic interest or crush, and Lilly was the product of that. She's intentionally not described in appearance with the hopes that she would be more relatable to others, where the reader filled in the blanks with their own knowledge, experience or imagination of such a person.

For the Blacksmith, she was necessary.

It's not all revealed in sequential order, but after reading through to the end, we now know that we first meet old man Pratt in Chapter 1 soon after his flight from SPARTAN HQ after having killed Trevor. We also know that he was on his way to reset the facility's trap so that the SPARTANs would fall into it. He had killed Trevor because Trevor represented SPARTAN, which was responsible for permanently robbing him of Lilly when fate finally had them together.

It was in Chapter 1 where Pratt first met the Champ whose friend had the very metal ring that Jeremiah had given to Lilly when they were young. It was only Lilly that could have distracted him from avenging Lilly. At finding the ring, he felt compelled to chase that rabbit.

By chance, Pratt's sudden obsession with the ring led him to the same old city where the facility was located, which would make sense since we find out that Lilly worked at the facility back during the wars. It was there in Lilly's long abandoned home that Pratt realized it wasn't the death of Lilly's husband that had her frantic when the old city was falling, but the death of a son, whom she never told Pratt about. That discovery was just another stab to the heart from Lilly's grave. Whatever Jeremiah thought he shared with Lilly, he now realized that it was mostly imagined, or else she would have shared something about a child.

It was that realization that made Pratt give up hope, and what allowed him to be taken alive by Flagstaff and hauled into the facility where he was imprisoned with the Preachers. And it was there, listening to the Preachers that Jeremiah was reminded of his friend and officer, Mick Towers. It was that correlation that woke Pratt out of his despair, giving him the new purpose of saving these Preachers who reminded him so much of Mick.

I liked the idea of a character, like Jeremiah Pratt, who seemed almost blessed or touched for surviving so much of war without ever suffering even a scratch from it, but was tormented and scarred in every other way; even if those scars weren't visible on the outside. I also like the idea of whatever destiny that led and followed Pratt through life was not for his own benefit, but for the benefit of someone else.

In the Blacksmith, destiny used Pratt to save Josiah while also delivering a severe blow to SPARTAN. Jeremiah Pratt is the central character, but Josiah Morris is the main character.

***

For Flagstaff and the Silent Voice, I just liked the idea of something that's usually viewed as being associated with the supernatural and explaining it as something more natural and physical.

In Chapter 3 I left a subtle hint at Josiah's ability of the mind. In the third paragraph of that chapter it is mentioned that Josiah had not slept well due to a bad dream the previous night. We're told that in Josiah's dream, he's an older man and is murdered by a friend who had just bludgeoned another person to death. Josiah awoke from the bad dream when the friend shot him in the head. In the Flagstaff Chapter, it is mentioned that the Silent Voice can manifest in dreams, and that often when someone dreams that they die, they're actually picking up on the highly charged emotional broadcast of another person's actual experience– in Josiah's case, his dream was through the real perspective of Trevor at the moment of his death.

In Chapter 11, where General Simmons goes on a bit of a tirade after Josiah referred to Jeremiah Pratt as a Blacksmith, he speaks of people possessing the Silent Voice or those with similar abilities as having "...mastered their skill; they manipulate and expertly fashion these basic elements, which are naturally buried deep within the soil of their brains! Elements that are just as available to the rest of us, but we're, for whatever reason, unable or too unskilled to make any use of them!

Instead, we rely on these expertly skilled men, these '*Blacksmiths,*' to work these elements for us."

For General Simmons, the true Blacksmith would have been Josiah. Naturally gifted in the mind, Josiah opened the Gordian Lock when his father could not, and he defeated Flagstaff by using their own gifts better than they did – Pratt helped of course, but Pratt's main purpose was to aid Josiah to that realization.

The greatest tool and weapon a person will ever have is their mind.

Made in the USA
Coppell, TX
18 December 2020

45670863R00184